Fluff

Fluff

RavensDagger

Podium

To my dear mom,
without whose love and attention,
I would have finished this book in half the time

Fluff

Anxiety

Emily endured her mother's hug, then squeezed her eyes shut as her cheeks were pecked. When, finally, she was released, she took a step back and crossed her arms to ward off the September chill.

"So, ah, this is it?" she asked.

Emily looked over at her parents. Her mom, short and kind of frumpy, was wearing the sort of dress that had gone out of fashion sometime in the late sixties. Her dad, tall and wide-shouldered, could have been one of the hockey players on campus if it weren't for the premature balding of his dirty-blond hair.

"You know our number," her mom said.

Emily nodded. "It's never changed."

Her mom sighed, then pulled her into another hug. "It never will. You call, okay? Day or night. Even if it's just to talk. Mom will be there for you if you have any problems with your schoolwork or—" She tittered. "Or problems picking the cutest boy."

Emily could hear her father's knuckles popping and held back the tiniest smile. Teasing her dad had been something of a hobby when she was young. She knew that he dreamed of giving some boy the shovel talk, but high school came and went without it ever happening.

"I . . ." She swallowed. "I love you."

Her dad smiled just a little, his stoic face cracking for a moment.

And then Emily had to endure more hugging.

She closed her eyes and prayed to whoever would listen that no one had seen her. Having her dad trade dorky jokes with some of the boys while helping her carry her things had been mortifying enough to keep her hiding in her blankets for a week.

When the hugging was over—and her dad had patted her head as his own little way of showing that he cared—the family pickup revved up and drove off. Emily found herself standing alone.

Alone for the first time since . . . since forever.

She looked around her, taking in the ancient stone buildings of the old campus, some of them next to modern steel and glass buildings. All of them were surrounded by winding cobbled paths that made room for tough old trees. She eyed the shadows, the few people walking around, and the open blue sky; then she shivered.

Emily had heard stories about girls on campuses like this one getting harassed and hurt. She had tried not to hear, had tried not to feed her anxiety, but the little snippets she overheard were preying on her now.

She tugged her long, pleated skirt down a little so that it dipped lower and closer to her ankles, then pulled down the hem of her sweater.

Turning, she faced the direction of her dorm and started moving. Her Mary Janes clicked across the pavement with a nervous pitter-patter that mimicked the hummingbird beat of her heart. She didn't like being out in the open, not if she could avoid it. She didn't like being indoors all that much either. Emily found just a few places comforting, none of which were anywhere near here. She tamped down the temptation to pull out her cell and call her mother and put the whole thing off.

It was too late for that. Her parents had sacrificed too much to get her into the school, and her future depended on her at the very least trying to pass all her courses.

Emily walked with a hand over her stomach, as if that could hold all the butterflies in place.

A few blocks and a parking lot later, she was at her dorm. The large brass plaque at the base of the building declared it to be the Quantum Mothman House. *An auspicious name for a dorm,* Emily thought. It was one of the newer buildings, built with money donated from some of the older local Heroes to promote higher education.

It was a bit pricey, but her father had insisted that she have the best they could afford. The fact that she didn't need to stay with a roommate reassured both her and her dad.

The front door unlocked with a swipe of her phone over a panel jutting out next to it, and she slid into the lobby only to freeze up the moment she was inside.

The lobby was divided into two sections. On the one side were some public restrooms and a small kitchenette that had a little fridge and some microwaves. On the other was a lounge with a big-screen TV, some couches, and a couple of square tables surrounded by benches. She'd seen people playing cards or looking at their phones while the TV blasted the evening news the first time she visited.

It was louder than she liked, but people had been minding their own business then. Now there were banners strung across the square ceiling tiles, and a few balloons added a bit of a festive air to the otherwise plain room.

Emily had the impression that everyone and their friends were there. Thirty people, all packed into a small room, some of them carrying red cups, others glass bottles. There was a sickly sweet scent to the air, a mixture of store-bought pastries, alcohol, and sweat that made her stomach twist.

"Hey!"

She turned to find a tall Black girl walking her way with a gleaming smile. "You're in five-oh-one, right?"

Emily's mind blanked. "Five . . . oh, my room number. Um. Yes?"

The girl's smile grew. She gestured to a table near the back that had soda bottles and a cooler sitting on it. "Grab something to drink! We're having a bit of a meet and greet slash Power Day bash."

"Power Day," Emily repeated. She shook her head. Of course, it was the fifteenth of September. She knew that. "Right."

The girl switched her cup from one hand to another and extended her hand. "I'm Sam."

Emily looked at the hand. She didn't want to take it, but not taking it would have been rude. The pressure grew in her chest until her hand snapped out and she took Sam's hand and shook it up and down. "Emily. I'm Emily. I, uh, need to go to my room."

"Come back down if you want," Sam said. "I can introduce you to everyone. Some of the boys are kinda cute." She wiggled her eyebrows, then looked Emily up and down in a way that made her skin crawl. "Some of the girls are cute too," she added with a wink.

"Right, right. Thank you." Emily skittered away as if she were being chased by some monster in one of those horror movies she'd made the mistake of watching once.

She reached the elevator at the back and stepped in at the same time as a young man who tapped the IV button on the panel. "Which floor?" he asked.

Emily had to take a couple of deep breaths before she could reply. "F-five."

He nodded, tapped the V for her floor, and much to her relief, pulled a phone out and began to stare at its screen. She caught a glimpse of some new article about Power Day and how the local police chief was going to be on the lookout for new Villains, but she averted her eyes as soon as the boy looked her way.

"So, you new here?" he asked.

Emily worked her jaw to answer, but nothing came out. By the time she had worked through the complex mathematics of social dynamics to say yes, the door dinged open and the boy left with a huff.

She swallowed again, huddled herself smaller now that no one was looking, and waited until she got to her floor.

The corridor to her room passed in a flash as she all but ran to her door, unlocked it with another swipe of her phone, and slipped into her room.

It wasn't her room yet, not in the sense that she felt at home inside it, but it would be one day, she hoped.

Emily had convinced her dad to move up a pair of bookshelves and her favorite chair from back home, a big plush thing made of faux leather that was far too large for someone of her size. She could curl up on it, legs bent under her, and still have room to spare.

The bed off in the corner was a twin that had been left open. It was so much bigger than her bed back home that she knew she'd feel lost in it.

She surveyed the desk, the charging laptop in one corner, then looked over at her little bathroom. It was a bit cramped, but she didn't need much more than the shower and amenities it had. The room, with its view out into an alley behind the Quantum Mothman building, was more than enough for her.

The sigh that escaped her left with all her worries and pulled a weight off her back. She locked the door, then trudged over to the bed and allowed herself to crash into it.

After a minute of recharging her social batteries from empty to near-empty—which was as full as they would go for her—Emily rolled over and pulled her phone out of her pocket. A scan of WriteIt showed that all the popular threads were about Power Day. People were placing bets and waiting for the new Heroic faces to appear.

She skimmed over a few "If It Happens to You" threads and found a web page filled with images of cute animals doing cute things.

If people were her kryptonite, then pictures of kittens, foxes, and dogs were . . . whatever the opposite of kryptonite was.

Her mind, the part not looping through a series of "aww"s at every picture she scrolled down to, was still working through a few things. She was alone now. No mother to call on, no huge stoic dad to fix every big problem. Just Emily.

Her classes would start in the morning. She didn't know how to describe what she felt about that but decided to settle on terrified.

When the ball of stress in her stomach grew too large, she set down her phone and jumped off the bed. GIFs of kittens being spooked by tinfoil weren't doing it for her.

With a long-suffering sigh, Emily undressed, realized she didn't have a hamper to put her clothes in, and settled for refolding them next to her bed; then she slid on some walrus-print pj's and settled in. She knew that she wouldn't fall asleep anytime soon, and that was okay. The internet was a never-ending font of cuddly things to look at.

Eventually, despite the early evening sun still bright outside her window, Emily blinked a final time and slid into a restless slumber.

CHAPTER ONE

Wake Up

Emily's dreams were all hazy nightmares.

She woke with a bit of a jerk, a sense of *wrong* racing through her that only faded when she heard the distant honk of a car and the sound of a toilet flushing somewhere. The feeling that she wasn't home was quickly followed by the realization that she was in her new dorm.

That much she had kind of expected. She had never spent that many nights away from home, but on the rare occasion her family went on vacation, she always had that sense of being misplaced on waking up.

Emily looked at her clock, realized that she hadn't actually set it up yet, then pulled her phone from the crack between the mattress and bedframe. Raising her head, she gave it a tap and read 6:34 on the top of the display.

Her head fell back onto her pillow. She had her first classes at ten. Sleeping a bit more was possible, but she wasn't tired, just lethargic and more than a little nervous.

With a heavy sigh, Emily climbed out of bed, picked out her toiletries from a still-packed box, then slumped her way toward the bathroom.

She set her pj's aside first. They were clean enough to be worn one more time, she figured, and she still didn't know too much about the laundry situation. The shower wasn't as warm or as strong as back home, but she didn't mind. Her blond hair took some scrubbing to look nice and neat, then she was out of the shower and wrapping a pair of thick towels around her waist and her hair.

Her last stop was the mirror, where she brushed her teeth.

The brush fell into her sink, dropped when her hands went slack.

Eyes that were still misty locked onto the reflection in the mirror. Not of her own freckly, still-pudgy face, but on the words hovering above her head.

Emily Wright
???, Level 0

She took in a deep breath, then another. "No," she said.

Her denial didn't do anything to the words hovering there. A shivering hand wiped the smog off the glass. All it did was make the hovering words shift along with her.

She wondered if it was a projection, some fancy hologram, but the words had to be written backward for her to read them in the right order when reflected.

Emily's eyes screwed shut. She went over the facts like her counselor had once taught her. It had been an exercise to keep the stress down.

Fact one: There were words above her. The kind of words that appeared above the heads of Heroes and Villains when they wanted them to.

Fact two: It had been Power Day when she went to bed the night before.

Fact three . . .

Emily grabbed the edge of the sink, then noticed her toothbrush. Carefully, she pulled it out of the sink's hole, wiped it clean, then spat into the sink. A simple gesture, one she'd done a thousand times before. It felt wrong to do something so normal while her life was falling apart.

"No, no, it's . . ."

She swallowed and ignored the minty freshness of it. Another exercise came to mind. The old three-tens trick. How would this impact her in ten minutes? In ten days? In ten months?

In ten minutes, she'd be . . . screwed. In ten days, likewise, and in ten months, her life would probably be ruined.

Emily felt tears stinging the corners of her eyes. None of the answers were good. The exercise had made it worse.

She wanted to rush to her phone and look up a guide. Some sort of "I woke up with powers, now what?" but she knew that half the responses there would be excited cheers from idiots, and the other half strongly worded suggestions from the government to join up right away . . . or else.

Her mom . . . couldn't fix this. Her dad wouldn't know where to begin.

She stumbled into her bedroom and got dressed with manic energy, clothes pulled from every box she could find until she was in a long skirt and a nice blouse with a warm cardigan to go over it. The outfit didn't expose any skin beyond the nape of her neck, and it was all in somber colors that would blend in.

And then she was dressed for a class she might not be able to attend, not if there were literal words hovering above her head.

Sure, there were some open Masks out there, people with powers who didn't care if people knew who they were out of costume. She didn't want people to notice her at the best of times.

Emily went over what she knew, which wasn't all that much. One thing she did know, though, was the magic word, the one that could give away a Mask with only two syllables.

"Status," she whispered.

A screen appeared before her.

Her eyes glazed over, and she stumbled back until her rear found its way onto her bed. Only then did she actually read the screen before her.

Name: Emily Wright		
Alignment: Undetermined		
Alias: None		
Level: 0		
Powers		
None		
Points		
Power Slots: 1	Skill Upgrades: 0	Skill Slots: 0

"Oh god," she said.

Fate accepted!

Rolling for alignment.

The screen warped into a simple bar. To the left, the word *Alignment*; to the right, a mass of words spinning too fast to read, which would determine just how ruined her life would be.

The spinning words wound down, ticking by at a pace that was slow enough for her to make them out. There were a few that were more common. *Hero. Martyr. Savior. Vigilante*... and then the words clicked to a stop.

Congratulations! Your ideal morality is . . . Villain! A life of crime and destruction awaits you!

Emily brought her hands to her face in time to smudge some of the tears welling out of her eyes. "No, no, no," she said.

It wasn't the end of the world. Just because the system said one thing didn't mean that she had to follow what it said. She didn't need to play its game. Plenty of people received powers and went on with their lives as if nothing had happened.

She shut her eyes as hard as she could, but it did nothing to stop the telltale impression that something was waiting for her.

When she opened them again, another prompt was waiting for her.

You have one Power Slot waiting for unlock. Unlock your first Power now?

She shook her head.

The prompt didn't go away.

Emily wanted to shove it all aside. To go back to bed and wake up as just another normal girl with perhaps a few minor disorders that could be treated with some therapy and a bit of experience.

She had dreamed of being a Mask, of course, of shrouding herself in an identity that didn't have any of her problems, but as she'd grown up, she discovered that that wasn't for her, that she . . .

Power Slot point spent! Unlocking new Power!

"What?" she squeaked. She hadn't agreed to that!

Congratulations! You are now Level 1. Power unlocked!

Emily stared around her room, expecting at any moment for something awful to happen. She swallowed, then poked at her bed. Nothing. Then she poked her thigh. Also nothing. The world didn't feel any stranger than it already had. Was it all a stress hallucination? She knew it wasn't but . . . "Status?"

Name: Emily Wright		
Alignment: Villain		
Alias: None		
Level: 1		
Powers		
Sister Summoning		
Create Sister	Rank 1	
Points		
Power Slots: 0	Skill Upgrades: 0	Skill Slots: 0

She blinked. That . . . didn't seem all that bad. She didn't know what kind of power Sister Summoning was, but it sounded . . . nice? It wasn't Demon Summoning, or anything that sounded outright evil. Did it let her teleport people?

The one skill on the list, Create Sister, didn't seem to indicate as much. And, just on thinking about it, a new screen opened.

Create Sister
Sister Summoning
Rank 1
Allows you to summon a sister, a being with power, who will aid and assist you on your path to Villainy. A sister has her own powers and skills that you may improve. Can be resummoned.
Activation: Voice command
Cooldown: None
Max Summons: One

"Oh," Emily said.

She considered—actually considered—using her new power. But as soon as the thought crossed her mind, she crushed it. There was no time for that. She had classes in . . . in less than three hours, and she would need to cross half the campus to get there.

Maybe she could find a counselor? Were they obligated to report to the police?

A distant rumble had her looking around. She wondered if it had been an explosion. She was still wondering when her phone buzzed.

To All: Please stay indoors. The HRF is on-site. All current classes are suspended until 9 a.m. All classes after this time are to resume normally.

There went her plans to get to class early to maybe build up the courage to say hello to her professor.

Emily fidgeted on the spot. Another boom rocked the dormitory windows.

New Quest!
Fighting Good
Join the battle against the forces of good.

Reward: +3 Skill Upgrade points per Hero incapacitated or killed. Villain +4 per kill!

Accept? Refuse?

"Refuse!" she squeaked. "I-I can't fight Heroes. I don't even know what Create Sister does," she whined to the box.

And then, as the words escaped her lips and an inward rush of wind filled the room, she realized her mistake.

For better or worse, a sister was coming.

CHAPTER TWO

Don't Panic

Emily decided, quite sensibly, not to panic.

The breeze shifting around her room settled, and Emily shivered as the air stilled. She sat on the edge of her bed, her hands folded on her lap and her breath coming in deep gulps.

Skill: Create Sister successful!

Emily stared at the woman, no, the girl, standing before her where no one had been a minute ago.

She was on the shorter side, with a squat figure and big chubby cheeks framed by brown hair that was cut off at neck length. Emily would have placed her at thirteen or fourteen, with some growing left to do. She had a simple beige T-shirt with the word *Bear* on it in big letters over a pair of green cargo shorts.

She looked, at least to Emily, like any other teenage girl. That is, if the girl hadn't had a pair of rounded ears poking through her hair and a few words floating about her head.

??? Wright

WereBear, Level 1

Emily looked away from the hovering words. The girl yawned. "What do you want me to do, Boss?"

"What?" Emily asked. She didn't know why she was surprised by the girl talking. She should have expected it, really. "Wh-who are you?"

The girl blinked slowly. "I dunno. You haven't named me yet." She reached under her T-shirt and scratched at her tummy. "So, we're gonna do that?"

"Name you?" Emily asked.

It kind of made sense. She'd never been one for games and such, but she knew that naming pets was normal. But this was a girl, an actual human . . . maybe. People didn't name other people, not unless they were naming a baby, and that was a comparison that Emily was really, really not ready to make.

The girl nodded. "Yeah. I mean, unless you've got something else that needs doing?" She looked around the empty room as if to confirm that there really wasn't anything to do.

"I . . . how?" Emily asked. She shook her head. That was moving ahead too quickly. She had to figure things out. "Can I . . . unsummon you?"

"Nah," the girl said.

Emily's heart sank. "Oh. Okay. Um."

"You okay, sis?" the girl asked.

"I'm fine," Emily said faintly. It was her favorite lie, one that came easily to her lips.

"All right, well, whatever." The girl stepped up and Emily flinched, but she wasn't attacked or hurt. The girl just climbed up onto the bed, shuffled around, and flopped onto her side in the middle of the bed.

"W-what are you doing?" Emily asked.

"Did you want me to scoot over?" the girl asked. She tapped the free space left on the bed. "There's room. You're not fat."

"N-no, I mean. That's my bed."

"Got another bed?"

"No?" Emily said.

The girl shrugged one shoulder, pulled the pillow down lower, and smushed her face into it. "Wake me up when stuff's happening."

Emily's hands danced uncertain gestures through the air. "O-okay?" she tried.

In the end, she did succeed in calming down. The girl on the bed next to her didn't feel like a threat or like someone dangerous. She was just a normal teenager who had appeared out of thin air and slid onto Emily's bed.

She was pretty sure there weren't guides for this kind of situation online, at least, none that wouldn't get her added to a watch list.

"Okay," she whispered to herself.

She needed a list. A nice checklist, with things to do and tasks that she could tackle in a reasonable and logical order.

Rushing over to her desk, Emily found a notebook in one of the drawers and placed it on the surface. Then she dug around for a pen that worked and got to making her list. It wasn't a terribly long one, but she didn't need a long list, she needed a functional one.

1. Learn about power
2. Turn off sign above head
3. Learn about bear girl. Name her?
4. Find a place to hide bear girl
5. Go to classes on time
6. *Call Mom*

Emily set her pen down, reread her list, then chewed on her lower lip a bit. It . . . was a list. She could do those things. Turning, she found the bear girl snoring on her bed, low rumbles that faded into the background as soon as Emily didn't pay attention. She could've almost pretended there wasn't a person in her room if it weren't for the words floating above her bed.

Step one was first. "Status?"

Name: Emily Wright		
Alignment: Villain		
Alias: None		
Level: 1		
Powers		
Sister Summoning		
Create Sister	Rank 1	
Points		
Power Slots: 0	Skill Upgrades: 0	Skill Slots: 0

That seemed normal. No, not normal. None of it was normal. But it hadn't changed from the last time she'd looked. "Um. Sister . . . page?" she tried. "Ah, maybe . . . bear . . . sister page?"

Name: ??? Wright		
Alignment: Villain, Little Sister		
Alias: None		
Level: 1		
Powers		
WereBear		
Rip and Bear	Rank 1	
Points		
Power Slots: 0	Skill Upgrades: 0	Skill Slots: 0

Emily took in the page. She . . . had no idea what that skill was supposed to do. Still, the fact that the girl had a status page that Emily could see meant something. She really was a product of Emily's power. Not that that helped all that much, but it was a lead. Emily could Oogle that kind of thing.

She had learned something, so she tentatively crossed that off her list. She had a lot more to learn, but for now, other things were more important. "Um. Miss? Excuse me?" Emily asked. She reached out and shook the girl's . . . the werebear's . . . shoulder.

Bleary brown eyes opened and looked up to Emily. "Yeah?" she asked, before a yawn revealed large canines.

"Um. I have some questions."

The girl sat up with a long-suffering sigh. "Okay."

Emily licked her lips, then nodded. She could do this. A glance at her list to keep her mind on track helped. "Okay. So. First. Do you know how to hide . . . that?" She pointed above her head.

The bear girl looked up and, presumably, at the name hovering over Emily's head. "Yeah. Just turn it off. Why?"

"Uh. I-I can't afford to let people know. They would . . . take me, and make me do things, and maybe they'd want me as a Hero or something, and that's a lot, and all I want is to go to school and maybe make one friend, or maybe two, and one day meet a nice quiet man and have a job I can do really well on my own, but being a Mask wouldn't allow me to do any of that and—"

Emily cut herself off midsentence as a pair of arms wrapped around her waist and a head pushed itself against her ribs. "You talk too much."

Emily didn't know what to do. The girl was lying all crooked across the bed and was hugging her with surprisingly strong arms that she doubted she could dislodge.

And then the girl let go and flopped back onto the bed. "There. Now you're better."

Emily wanted to protest, but hugs were sort of nice. She'd never had any friends, or close friends at least, but her mother was the hugging sort and Emily knew that they helped sometimes. "Thanks?" she said.

"Yeah, sure," the girl said.

Emily fidgeted. "Um. What about . . . Teddy?"

The girl blinked. "Teddy?"

"For a name? It could be short for, um, Theodora?"

The newly christened Teddy hummed, then nodded. "Yeah, okay."

Emily reached for the girl, then thought better of it. The words above her head twitched, then changed.

Teddy

WereBear, Level 1

She felt something nice in her stomach, like when she finally arrived at home from school. It soon faded though as she looked at her list again. The words were, presumably, still hovering above her. "Menu?" she tried. "Um . . . disguise? Hide?"

Do you wish to hide your identity?

"Yes!"

A run back to the bathroom had her shoulders slumping as a whole heap of stress oozed off her back. The words above her head were gone. She could go on living a totally normal life. That was, if Teddy cooperated.

Emily would need to find something to do with the girl, but classes were coming up and the roiling discomfort of being late was twisting in her gut already.

"Okay. Okay. Teddy?"

"Hmm?" came the response from the not-yet-snoring girl on the bed.

"I'm going to class. You, ah, behave?"

"Hmm."

As Emily collected her things and tried hard not to think too hard, she had the impression that she was walking along the edge of a sharp precipice. For a girl who knew that she had problems with sudden changes, all the things happening to her in one day were just too much.

But she couldn't see a way out of her situation, not one that didn't pose all sorts of risks.

So, determined to make the most of her day and to pretend that her life wasn't now a nightmare, Emily picked up her backpack full of books and headed for the door.

The moment her hand touched the handle, a screen popped up before her.

You have . . . 2 pending Quests!

CHAPTER THREE

The Smallest Barbearian

The door clicked shut, and just like that, the Boss was gone.

Teddy settled into the pillow, enjoying its warmth and its smell. Something about it felt nice and warm and safe, like a cave away from a harsh storm.

She pulled her blankets closer, wrapping them over her shoulders and tucking in tight, forming as small a ball as she could make herself. It was a bit chillier in the room than she would have liked.

Teddy didn't have many memories to rely on, just a few minutes spent with the Boss while the Boss flailed around and acted as if the world were ending. But those memories were nice ones. Especially the few little touches, and the hug she'd given to the older girl.

The Boss was warm.

Teddy liked that.

Her eyes, already heavy, started to droop down while the warm embrace of slumber crawled over her. She slid into the hazy world of deep hibernation, time moving along at a slow crawl only marked by the occasional thump of feet in the corridor or the rumble of passing trucks.

Something banged. A door, she guessed. It was enough to have her open one eye to peek around.

And then, much to her annoyance, something popped up in her vision.

New Quest!

Savage Ravage

Ravage an innocent!

Reward: +1 Skill Upgrade point per person incapacitated. +2 Skill Upgrade points per person killed. Villain +2 per success!

Accept? Refuse?

Teddy shifted in her bed. That sounded like a lot of work, and the Boss hadn't told her to go out and eat anyone.

Quest refused!

New Quest!

A Muggy Afternoon

Mug a stranger.

Reward: +1 Skill Upgrade point per person successfully robbed. Scoundrel +1 per item!

Accept? Refuse?

Teddy *could* use something to eat. The Boss hadn't left anything that Teddy noticed in the room, and she was getting to be a bit peckish.

Quest accepted!

And now her sleep was spoiled.

Sighing, Teddy flung the blankets off and rolled out of bed. She was still in her shorts and T-shirt, because they were comfy enough for sleeping in, but she had taken off her hiking boots before climbing onto the bed.

On the boots went, with only some frowning and pouting and a bit of grumbling as she tried to remember the rhyme for tying shoelaces, a rhyme that she sorta knew even if she didn't have memories to go with it.

Her boots all knotted up, Teddy went to the door and almost opened it when she remembered the Boss working hard to hide her identity.

A bit of focusing later and the words above Teddy's head faded away, and she slid out into a big corridor.

Another girl, way older, like the Boss, stood in the hallway. She stared at Teddy and waved.

Teddy wondered if she should mug her, but the girl didn't have any food on her so she just waved back and walked on past.

She had a choice between taking the elevator or walking down the steps, so she enjoyed the old pop music as she rode on down to the first floor. A few dozen more steps and she was outside.

The sun beamed down atop her head, warming her ears and making her feel all sweaty and lethargic.

Teddy turned around to go back to bed—she could mug people later—but the door was locked. She tugged at it some more to no avail.

Teddy frowned at it.

She could just activate her power and break it down. She knew she could. But that would just make her more tired, and hungry besides.

With a soulful sigh, Teddy turned back around and took in her surroundings. There were a lot of buildings around. She figured that if she wanted to find someone to mug, it would be best to just head out in the direction that looked the richest and wait to find someone alone.

Trudging along, Teddy kept to the sidewalks and let her head rotate around to follow all the posters and advertisements stuck to telephone poles and mounted on the side of passing buses.

A lot of the images were of people in tight costumes, standing tall and proud with their foot on the necks of ugly people. They looked like kings and queens, especially in the images where crowds of people were cheering them on.

The posters on the telephone poles weren't as colorful, and their art was a lot less interesting. Stuff like "Call 011 at the first sign of VILLAINY!" or ads with addresses to websites where people could give anonymous tips.

Teddy still preferred all those over the ads with food on them. Those made her tummy ache.

She was a long ways from home when she saw a reedy older guy, maybe a year or two older than her Boss, slip into an alleyway with a box under one arm and a suitcase in the other.

Teddy grinned. She'd struck honey!

Walking a bit faster, Teddy rounded the corner into the alleyway and found the man grumbling to himself as he faced a pair of crooked dumpsters. They were blocking his path.

She felt her grin sharpening as she stepped into the shadowy path. "Hey, old guy," she said.

The man jumped and turned around, revealing a reedy young man and a face covered by a big bushy mustache. "Yes?'

"Give me everything you've got," Teddy said.

The man blinked, and then he was smiling too. "You came for my rally?" he asked. Before she could ask him what he was on about, he knelt down and dropped the box he was holding. It was just a wooden crate with a step built into the side. Then he opened his briefcase and rummaged through it before pausing. "Ah, well, uh, this isn't the most auspicious place for this kind of thing, is it, comrade?"

"What?"

"Ah, and here I was hoping today I would be able to inspire the masses into joining in the glorious revolution against the Heroes and their fat capitalist pig leaders. But one girl is better than none. Sometimes it's the smallest ear that counts, right?"

Teddy reached out and touched her ears. They weren't that small. His were smaller than hers, probably. Definitely smaller if she counted the fuzzy fur around them. "I don't get it," she said. "I just want food."

"Don't we all! But the capitalists in their ivory towers won't allow it, not without breaking your back first!"

Teddy took a small step back. Someone wanted to break her back? She growled deep in her throat and stepped forward. "I won't let them. I'm too strong."

"Oh, I can see the fires of the proletariat burning in you already, comrade. Look, I'm sorry that the rally was canceled because of that nasty business with the Villain, but . . . here, take this. It taught me a lot, but I have other copies."

He pulled a book out from his suitcase, then stuffed it in his armpit to hold it in place as he closed the case. The man shoved the book into her hand, then rubbed the top of her head.

"Good luck, little comrade!" he said before stepping past.

Teddy blinked down at the little red book in her hands. She was confused. Who were the capitalists, and why did they want to break her back and not give her food? Would . . . the book tell her?

Quest Complete!

A Muggy Afternoon

Reward: +1 Skill Upgrade point per person successfully robbed. Scoundrel +1 per item!

Teddy grinned. A reward! And then her smile faltered as her tummy rumbled.

Sighing, she slipped her new book into one of her shorts pockets and went on to find someone else to mug. Maybe this time they'd have some food. She walked a little slower, still heading toward the richest sections. She was keeping an eye out for capitalists, though, just in case.

She didn't know what they looked like yet, but she figured she'd know one when she saw it. The man had said they were fat and piglike.

A loud gong sounded. Teddy tensed, expecting trouble, but it turned out that it only meant that a lot of people started leaving a bunch of buildings all at once. They all looked like normal people, though some were pretty fat (but not piglike, so they were probably not capitalists).

Teddy moved over to the side of one building where the entrance jutted out a bit and stood in the partial shadows there. A few of the people moving by looked her way, but they dismissed her as soon as they saw her.

Teddy waited until the crowds thinned out, a lot of them heading to some parking lots or toward a bus stop just down the street, others milling about and chatting animatedly.

What she was looking for was a loner she could mug.

And then a single girl stepped out. Her back hunched, her eyes downcast, her hands fretting over the strap of her bag. The perfect target.

That was, if she wasn't also blond and wearing the same clothes as her Boss.

Teddy sighed and gave up on the mugging idea. She could just ask Boss for food. She'd pay her for her work, right?

"Heya, Boss," Teddy said.

Her Boss jumped an impressive height and spun around so fast she almost knocked Teddy out with her swinging bag. "W-what are you doing here?!" she said before slapping her hand over her mouth.

A few people were looking their way now, but Teddy paid them no mind. She was too busy staring as the Boss took her hand and started pulling her along.

Had she done anything wrong?

She had left the house to mug people, but the Boss hadn't told her not to.

Teddy figured the Boss was just being cautious.

"We, we need to talk. Right now . . . as soon as we get back to the dorms."

"But, Boss," Teddy said, "I'm hungry."

The Boss made a weird noise. "Then . . . then food first."

Teddy's grin was enough to set a feral wolf running. The Boss was proving to be great. Teddy couldn't wait to tell her of all the work she'd done so far.

CHAPTER FOUR

When in Doubt, Look It Up

Emily's first class, an introduction to Literature 101, had gone . . . well. She'd only gotten to class with fifteen minutes to spare, but there were still plenty of seats left at the very back of the room. She set her bag down, placed her laptop onto the little desk mounted on one of the armrests of her seat, and hoped that the screen could serve as a sort of barrier between her and the rest of the world.

The professor was talking to a young man she assumed to be a teacher's assistant. Soon, that young man called out to her and asked for her name. It was all she could do to stutter through "Emily Wright." He didn't comment other than noting it down before moving to the door to take people's names as they entered.

She hoped that that was as much talking as she would need to do in that class.

Opening a word processor to take notes was easy enough, which left her with some free time.

Somehow she ended up on the front page of WriteIt and, instead of gravitating to pictures of nice animals doing nice animal things, she was staring at a thread that had been bumped to the very top.

You're a Mask, Now What?

Biting her lower lip, she clicked on the link. There was no harm in looking. The thread had thousands of comments already and it wasn't like her poking at it would be too strange. She wasn't being suspicious at all. At least, she hoped.

Most of the post was about contacting the government for help and such, but that sounded a little suspicious to her. There was some good advice though.

Your power will make choices for you. You don't know what you'll get, and generally, it will be very weak at first. It will also push you toward a certain kind of morality. You might not be a Hero when you first get your power. There are a lot more levels of morality than you might think. Most people don't start at the extremes, but somewhere near the middle of the scale. By doing good quests, you can improve your station.

The list goes something like:

Savior

Super Hero

Hero

Do-Gooder

Anti-Hero

Gray

Emily bit her lip. The rest of the information wasn't all that helpful, but it seemed to point her toward something she could actually do.

Good deeds would help her move away from Villain and toward . . . Gray and so on. She could do that. She had never committed a crime in her entire life. Never cheated, never jaywalked—she even felt guilty when she couldn't donate a dollar to charity when buying things at the grocery store. Doing perfectly natural things in the privacy of her own room even made her feel bad.

Her mother, a lifelong volunteer at every soup kitchen in the community and a big advocate for helping people, had always taught her to look out for others, so Emily figured it would be . . . doable, to not be a Villain. She just had to be a bit proactive about it.

Before she knew it, class was in session and she blissfully let herself forget about her Villainous woes.

Most of the lesson was more about credits, having books, when and how to hand in essays and homework, and other orientation things. The professor did give a nice speech, though, and Emily couldn't say that she didn't enjoy it.

There were going to be some modules later in the year where people would be working in small groups, but she figured she could handle that. She had made it through group projects in high school, and now her partners would be adults, which made everything a bit better. She hoped.

And then the bell rang, and class was over.

Emily waited until the big rush was out of the class before packing up her laptop and things into her bag. If this was how every class went, then she thought she might enjoy her time here. Maybe she would even make a friend.

Or maybe she was getting ahead of herself.

The building where Literature 101 was held was an old thing, one of the original stone edifices that had withstood the test of time. It was near the center of the campus along with most of the other stately houses of learning. For all that they were old, they had a sort of timeless elegance to them. Emily could imagine gentlemen with top hats walking down the same hallowed halls as her.

Stepping out into the bright late-afternoon sun was nice. There were a lot of people around, but they were all busy with their own things. Emily kept her head down, didn't meet anyone's eyes, and just enjoyed the fresh air and sunshine as she started to make her way back home.

"Heya, Boss."

Emily startled, then turned around to see the person who had addressed her.

Part of her knew who it was even before she locked onto the short chubby form of Teddy, standing in the middle of the path in her shorts and T-shirt and with poorly tied boots on as if she had every right to be there.

"W-what are you doing here?" Emily said. She slapped a hand over her mouth. Had anyone heard her?

She felt herself sinking as a few looks turned her way. She had to get out of the entryway, or off campus entirely. What if someone noticed Teddy's ears? They didn't stick out that much, and they might be confused for some sort of toy, but Emily couldn't afford the risk.

She grabbed the girl's hand and started to pull her along while stifling the blush that burned itself onto her cheeks. She felt like a mother pulling her kid along, or maybe a big sister. She hoped people thought it was the latter.

"We-we need to talk. Right now . . . as soon as we get back to the dorms."

"But, Boss," Teddy said, "I'm hungry."

Emily swallowed. Had . . . had she been neglecting a child? Forget the Villain quests she'd been rejecting all morning—that truly made her a bad person. "Then . . . then food first."

Teddy's grin had Emily's stomach twisting up. It reminded her a bit of the rare times her dad would smile at her for doing something he approved of, but with much bigger canines.

She held on to the girl and led her toward the end of the campus. A little Im Orton's there was run by a school club. She'd stopped there with her mom when they visited the place for the first time.

Everything had been far more expensive than it should have been, but she could splurge a little bit once in a while. And she really needed a coffee.

"S-so, um . . ." Emily began, then ended up not adding much to that. She didn't know where to start.

One of the things she'd read earlier about powers was that, generally, powers were helpful to their owner, regardless of their alignment. Someone who could control fire wouldn't be burned by their own flames, and minion creators wouldn't be harmed by their minions, at least not purposefully.

Was Teddy a minion? She looked . . . normal.

"What is it, Boss?" Teddy asked.

"You shouldn't call me that," Emily said.

"Can't call you Emily," Teddy said. "What if we're robbing a bank and someone hears your name?"

Emily felt a little faint. "No, no robbing banks, please. We . . . we don't do bad things, okay?"

Teddy frowned. "What about getting points and doing quests?"

"Only good quests, quests that don't hurt people," Emily said.

"Does mugging hurt people?" Teddy asked.

Emily had a bad feeling. "Yes, Teddy, mugging hurts people a lot."

"Oh. Shouldn't have mugged that guy, then."

Emily stopped. A quick look around revealed a nice little alleyway between two buildings, which she was easily able to tug Teddy into. "W-what did you do?" she asked.

Teddy was smiling, but a bit of confusion marred her eyes. "Got a quest to hurt people, but I was hungry, so I didn't take it. So I got a quest to mug people. Only got to the one, though. Made one point." She nodded proudly.

Emily shook.

"You want me to spend my point?"

"No!" Emily said. "No, Teddy, that's . . . no."

"Did I do bad?" Teddy asked.

Emily nodded. "Mugging is, it's bad, Teddy, really bad."

"Should have just taken the first quest, then," Teddy muttered.

Emily felt as if someone had just turned off gravity, and maybe dialed down common sense while they were at it. "Oh, Teddy," she said.

She wanted to be angry, but that wasn't in her nature. Worse, Teddy looked like she'd been proud, the same look Emily wore when she had "helped" her mother with the laundry and had turned all her dad's shirts pink.

"It's . . . okay?" Emily said. "No, wait, it's not okay, but, but it's not your fault. I . . . Let's grab something to eat at the dorm, and then I can explain things, okay?"

"All right, Boss," Teddy said.

At least her mood seemed easy to lift with the promise of food.

CHAPTER FIVE

Honey-Glazed Blackmail

Emily eyed Teddy, then looked up to the older woman behind the counter. She hated ordering in lines. She never knew what she wanted, and the pressure kept mounting until she was at the very front where she was expected to make a choice before the people behind her got angry.

It was incredibly stressful, and she'd always found herself envious of those who could just casually walk up to a counter and rattle off an order.

Did they know what they wanted that well? Did they not care that a wrong choice could cost more than they wanted or might not taste the best?

She cleared her throat as the woman stared at her, one eyebrow raising as if to ask if she intended to order before the sun went down. "R-right. I'll have a medium coffee, black, and a chicken . . . two chicken wraps. And, uh, half a dozen doughnuts. She'll pick." She pointed to Teddy.

Emily pretended not to feel guilty about putting the girl on the spot.

"Cool," Teddy said. "Half a dozen is six, right?" Emily nodded. "I'll take six honey glazed."

The woman blinked, entered the order in her machine, and let Emily tap her phone to the card reader. "Please stand to the side, your order will be coming soon."

"Thanks," Emily said. It was only when she was near the end of the counter that she realized she hadn't ordered anything for Teddy to drink. "Um. I'm sorry. Did you want something to drink?" she asked.

"Nah."

That . . . made her life easy.

Five minutes or so later, Emily and Teddy were heading back down toward their home. Emily's home. Was it also Teddy's? she wondered. How did people handle summons? Was Teddy a citizen or not?

"S-so, uh," Emily asked. "Do you remember things from before the summoning?"

"Nope." Teddy was bouncing along next to her, box of still-warm doughnuts held close to her chest.

That simplified things a little. Teddy wasn't someone her power had kidnapped. That would have been terrible. Emily would have had to run to the Heroes and explain everything and hope that they didn't punish her too much for what her power did.

Or was Teddy someone who was kidnapped and then memory-wiped? Or was she some sort of automaton? An alien? A clone?

Emily kept an eye on the girl bouncing next to her. Teddy's ears were twitching excitedly with every step, and she had a happy little smile on for the whole world to see.

The girl looked nice enough. Emily was willing to give a relationship a try. It certainly felt easier than trying to talk to a normal person. Teddy was beholden to her a little, like . . . like a pet.

Emily shook her head. No, that was wrong. People, even people made with powers, were not pets.

A sister. That's what the power called itself. Sister Summoning.

It wasn't superspeed, or flight, or something wonderful like healing, but it was what Emily had. She didn't know if she wanted the power. Sure, people dreamed of it, dreamed of being Heroes. Even Emily had had a few dreams like that. It was hard to watch Hero-sponsored cartoons as a kid and *not* want to be the one running from roof to roof in tights.

Maybe not tights.

She tried to focus again. Her mind was increasingly flighty as she tried to juggle all the possibilities going on all at once.

"Hey, Boss?" Teddy asked.

Emily looked down at the girl. "Yes?"

"Are we doing any quests today?"

"No, Teddy, I don't think we are," she replied. All her quests had been . . . less than good.

"All right," Teddy said. "What're we gonna do then?"

Emily really wished she knew. "I . . . we'll figure it out?"

Teddy looked up at her, innocent face completely bare of any of the doubt that Emily was feeling. "Okay. So after we eat, can I take a nap?"

She nodded. "Sure."

They arrived at the dorm and shuffled off into the elevator as quickly as they could. Emily didn't want people wondering what Teddy was doing, not if she could help it. There were some pretty clear rules about not having people overnight, but she suspected that some of the others weren't respecting those.

A swipe of her phone, and they were in the safety of her little room.

Teddy rushed over to her desk and placed the box of doughnuts on it. She started to tear the top off when Emily intervened. "No. Not yet. We'll eat first and save those for dessert."

Teddy turned big wet eyes toward Emily.

"J-just one?"

The girl's grin did something to Emily's heart, something that turned to horror as Teddy picked a squashed doughnut out of the box and rammed it into her mouth. She was chewing with her mouth open, and her hands were covered in honey glaze.

Emily didn't know what to do, but cold logic kicked in, and she found herself running to the bathroom, picking a cloth towelette from her supplies, and running it under cold water. A moment later she was next to Teddy and scrubbing the girl's face clean.

"Boss! What're you doing?" Teddy protested.

"Just keeping you clean?" Emily said. "Can-can you go wash your hands, please?"

Teddy grumbled as she stomped off to wash up. Emily ignored her and set the wraps on the desk, then she pulled her laptop out and set it up. She had a lot of things to look up.

Teddy returned, and soon they were both eating with only the occasional clack of the laptop's keyboard to break the silence.

Emily had a lot of things to learn. So many that she decided that a second list was in order.

Pulling out her notebook, she found the list she'd made that morning and "tsked" to herself as only half the things on it were complete.

Her new list was a bit different:

1. Find out what happens to people with powers
2. Learn how to get rid of Villain status
3. Find a way to take care of Teddy
4. *Call Mom*

That was a good list, she figured.

Nodding, she set the notepad to the side and pulled her laptop closer.

"Is that a dog?" Teddy asked as she looked at Emily's background photo. It was, in fact, a big smiling puppy.

"It is," she said.

"You should get a bear. They're better."

Emily nodded. She didn't think that bears were cuter, but she also didn't want to hurt Teddy's feelings. Her first step was opening her Ire-Wolf browser, and then ignoring the eighteen tabs set to cute animal sites.

She started to Oogle a few things, weeding out the searches that led back to government-owned sites, and then focusing on those from older forums where normal people asked questions.

It was surprisingly hard to get straight answers. Most of the people were talking about hypotheticals, and the few who claimed to have powers themselves were supersketchy, or, if they had any sort of verified account, all they did was redirect people to the same government sites that basically just told people to contact some official channel.

"Done!"

Emily looked to the side to find a nearly empty box of doughnuts next to the torn remains of a chicken wrap's wrapper. There was half a dough-nut left in the box. More like a third and a bit.

"I left you a piece, Boss," Teddy said with another honey-covered smile.

"That's . . . thank you?" Emily said.

"Cool. I'm going to bed now."

The girl started to make her way toward Emily's bed, but Emily was faster and managed to place a hand atop her head. "Sh-shower. You need to shower first."

Teddy slumped. "But I don't want to get wet," she said.

"I'll give you a big T-shirt and, um, some underthings, and you can get cleaned. And then you can go to bed. Okay?" Emily asked.

She would need to find a mattress for the girl soon, but for now, they would just have to make do.

Teddy grumbled a bit, but she didn't disobey as Emily ran around and looked for clothes the girl could wear postshower.

When the bathroom door was shut and Emily heard the water running, she returned to her search only to notice the icon of her email flashing.

She clicked, expecting a message from her school, or maybe her mom, or at worst an ad that got past her spam filter.

From: MysteriousStranger@spooky.com
To: E.Wright@email.an
Subject: How Very Naughty
Hello Emily,
Did you know that poking around while being so loud has the tendency to set off a few flags? Well, now you know.
Tomorrow at 4 pm, the Dark Cup on 4th and Instein.
Be there, and you'll have all your cute little questions answered.
Don't, and maybe those flags I burned will reappear.
With love,
A Stranger

CHAPTER SIX

Being Blankets

Teddy was a pile of blankets. She had become one with the warmth. The covers and her were the same entity.

From deep within the shadows cast by the blankets over her head, two brown eyes that were half closed with sleepiness were following the nervous movements of a girl who should have gone to bed a long time ago.

The sun had gone down already. It was past seven!

Teddy closed her book—she couldn't understand most of it anyway—and mumbled into her blankets, shifting just a little bit. She wanted to sleep, but Emily's stomping was keeping her awake. The Boss was worried about something that she'd seen, and it was making Teddy worried too.

Not too worried, but a little worried.

She wasn't sure what to do herself. Her job was easy; at least, she thought it was at first. Teddy would do what the Boss told her. If that meant eating people or beating people up, then that was no problem. She could even help by protecting the Boss from no-good capitalists and Heroes.

Now she wasn't too sure. The Boss wanted to do "Hero things" and that didn't exactly fit into what Teddy understood. It was probably part of a big ploy that the Boss wasn't telling her about yet. Teddy knew that the Boss was really clever. She went to school and everything.

Teddy's job was to hurt things for the Boss, but maybe the Boss didn't need that right then and there. Which meant that Teddy was free to eat and sleep all day.

Except she wasn't sleeping or eating, she was watching the Boss be worried.

It was all very confusing and Teddy didn't like it.

"Hey, Boss?" Teddy asked.

Emily paused in her pacing. "Oh, um, yes?"

Teddy tugged the blanket above her head back a bit so that she could see the Boss's face. "What's wrong?"

She watched the Boss's hands wiggle through the air like salmon leaping out of a river. "Everything," Emily finally said.

Teddy nodded. She had a solution for that. Raising the end of her blankets up with one hand, she tapped the bed with the other. "Come sleep."

Sleeping fixed everything.

"I can't," Emily said. "Just . . . so many things have gone wrong."

Teddy grumbled. If sleeping wouldn't fix it . . . "Did you try eating something?"

"I'm not hungry."

"Do you need to poop?" Teddy tried next. "Sometimes you need to push hard for it to come out."

"T-Teddy!" Emily squeaked. "Don't say that kind of thing."

That was probably a no. "Well, I don't know what's wrong then," Teddy said.

Emily crossed her arms over her tummy, like a sort of self-hug. Teddy shook her head. If it was hugs she wanted, then she could just slip into the blankets and Teddy would give her plenty. She was an expert at bear hugs.

"I . . . I got powers," Emily said at last.

"Yeah," Teddy agreed.

"And now I'm a Villain."

"Yeah."

"And now my life is ruined."

Teddy blinked. "Yeah, I don't follow."

Emily sniffled. "If I go to the police, they'll arrest me; put me, put us behind bars."

"Well, yeah, we're Villains," Teddy said. Hiding from the police was pretty much half the job of being a Villain.

Emily unhugged herself and started with the arm-waving again. "I don't want to be a Villain."

Teddy didn't get it. "But being a Villain is great," she said. "We can do whatever we want. Eat whatever, and go to sleep whenever. I mean, sure, we need to fight Heroes and capitalists, but that's all."

"I don't want to fight Heroes or . . . capitalists?"

Teddy blinked slowly. "Well, then don't, I guess. If being a Villain means doing whatever, and there's a thing you don't want to do, then don't do it."

Emily paused. "I know that," she said. "I won't fight the Heroes."

"Okay," Teddy said. It was probably for the best. For all that the Boss was clever and such, she was still pretty normal strengthwise. Not like Teddy, who was strong.

"Okay," the Boss agreed. "Right. And . . . and I'm going to work hard to make us become . . . not Villains."

"All right," Teddy said. Maybe the Boss wanted to be a Rogue instead? That was all right too.

"And then, uh, we'll talk to the administration, and we'll tell them about you, and we'll sort things out."

"Okay."

"And we can find a school for you, and . . . it'll be like, like being a teen mom. Which, uh, oh, that will complicate things. But I can do it."

"Okay?" Teddy said. She wasn't too sure about that school thing. She was very not sure, but it sounded like it was a ways off.

Emily started pacing again. Teddy had thought she was done with that. "And tomorrow, we're going to go see that Stranger person, and we'll show them that we're not a-afraid."

Were they going to go see another Villain? That could be dangerous. Villains could be territorial. "Well, okay," Teddy said. "I'll be there to keep you safe either way."

The pacing stopped again. This time, Emily balled her fists around the front of her pajama pants. "Thank you," she said. "Um. I don't . . . just— Thank you."

"Sure thing, Boss," Teddy said. "Now come on, you're keeping me awake." She raised the blankets again.

Emily's face scrunched up bizarrely. "I could get another blanket. I . . . ah, actually, I don't know if I have another."

Teddy wiggled her arm.

"I'm not, um, comfortable sleeping in the same bed as someone else," Emily said.

Teddy tilted her head so that one of her ears poked out of the blankets. "That's weird, but okay." The things she would do for her Boss. Teddy really was the best henchbear. With a grunt of effort, she slid off the side of the bed, blankets and all, and rolled herself up into a bear burrito.

A bearito.

"Now you can sleep on the bed," she said.

"Um. Are you comfortable on the floor?" Emily asked.

"Yeah, sure," Teddy said.

"Oh, well, thank you. I guess . . . we'll buy a mattress tomorrow. And more blankets."

"Yeah, okay," Teddy agreed. She snaked a hand up onto the bed, tapped around, and found her book. She set it next to her in case she wanted to read on waking up the next day's afternoon. "Turn off the lights, Boss."

The Boss searched through some of her boxes until she found a small blanket. Soon, the lights were off and the Boss was crawling onto her bed. "Good night, Teddy."

"G'night, Boss," Teddy said. At last, sleep.

"Why do you call me Boss?"

Teddy opened her eyes again. The room wasn't entirely dark, not with the occasional shifting light from the cars outside. "'Cause you're the Boss," she said.

"I don't feel like a Boss," Emily said.

"That's okay," Teddy said. "I'm sure you'll grow into a big strong Boss in time. Just got to eat lots and sleep lots and, uh . . ." Teddy knew there was more to being a good Boss. "And you need to put the needs of the proletariat before your own."

That sounded good.

"R-right. I . . . I know I'm not cut out to be a Mask, so I hope you're not sad that I'm your summoner."

"Why would I be sad?" Teddy asked. She got a warm place to sleep, some nice blankets, and honey-glazed doughnuts.

She heard the bed shift. "Because you could have been part of someone else's power, I guess. Someone better than me."

"Yeah, but I'm not. So you'll just have to be good enough."

Emily snorted. "That's . . . nice . . . I guess. I don't think I've ever been good at anything before. It'll be different."

"You'll figure it out," Teddy said. "Now stop talking; it's late."

"All right. Good night, Teddy."

CHAPTER SEVEN

Long-Distance Comforts

"Mom?"

The line was a tiny bit crackly, not owing to any sort of bad connection or anything like that. The entire city's phone service had been built by Optimaze years ago; it was hard to find any place where a phone couldn't connect, or where the internet wasn't decently fast.

It had been that way since she was twelve or thirteen. She hadn't really paid all that much attention at the time, but Emily still remembered the superpowered inventor going to court with Ell Telecom because he robbed them of a bunch of customers. His defense had been that their service wasn't very good to begin with.

No, the reason their line crackled was because Emily's dad had a thing against buying new stuff when their old stuff still worked fine. They still had a cathode-ray-tube television in the garage that he refused to toss, and the home phone was an old, corded thing that spat and crackled if it wasn't held just right.

"Sweetie!" Her mother's voice came over the line. "Oh, I was so worried when you didn't call yesterday. Why didn't you call yesterday?"

"Oh, uh, I kind of forgot," she said. It even had the benefit of being the truth. So many things had happened all at once the day before that Emily was having a hard time keeping track of all of them.

"You're already having so much fun that you forgot all about your dear old mom?"

Emily smiled and pulled her cell closer to the side of her head as if she could hug the voice coming from within it. "No, Mom," she said. "It was just a long day."

"An enjoyably long one? How were your classes? Did you make any friends yet?"

She wondered how she should answer that. "I guess it was okay," she said. "Um, classes were all right yesterday. Just a lot of explaining and stuff. You know, about homework and tests and credits. It's nothing I didn't know. But my professor seems nice."

"Nice or *nice*?"

"Mom!" Emily said. "He's an old man."

"Your dad is eight years older than me," her mom rebutted with a sing-song lilt to her voice.

Emily felt herself flushing. "Don't be silly, Mom," she said. "Um. I guess I made a friend too."

The line crackled and popped.

"Mom?"

"What sort of friend did you make, sweetie?" her mother asked.

Emily couldn't pin the tone. Definitely curious, but also wary, maybe. "It's a girl. Her name's Teddy. She's . . . a bit younger than me. She likes bears."

"That sounds wonderful! How did you meet?"

"Uh, it was in my dorm. She just kind of showed up and, um . . ." Emily thought fast. "She ate my doughnuts?"

There was a snort on the other end of the line. "That's certainly one way to make a friend. I hope she's good for you."

"Yeah. A-anyway, I have a thing I need to do," Emily said. "I just wanted to talk a bit before that."

"Busy already? I understand. You be careful, okay, sweetie? I know you're not the sort of girl to get herself into any kind of trouble, but try to be careful anyway."

"Yes, Mom. I love you."

"I love you too" was the quick reply. "Should I tell your dad that you love him, too, or did I finally win the best parent award?"

Emily giggled; she couldn't help herself. In just a minute or two, her mom had soothed the worst of her fears away. "Tell Dad that I love him too," she said.

"I will. You stay safe. If you need anything, I'm always there, okay?"

"Thanks. Bye, Mom."

"Bye, sweetie."

Emily clicked the call end button and let her arm drop onto her desk. Her room was quiet except for faint background noises, the kinds of things that were easy to ignore, like the thumping of someone's feet padding across the floor above her or the faint whistly snores coming from her bed.

She looked at the time on her phone and winced. It was nearly three already. She had to move.

The day had been a hazy mess—classes passing without notice, her attention drifting from the moment she'd woken up.

"Teddy," Emily said as she drifted over to her . . . summon, sister, henchgirl? She wasn't sure what terminology to use just yet. "Teddy, wake up, please."

The little bear girl blinked awake and pulled her head off Emily's pillow, though she did stay connected to it via a nice line of drool. "Huh? Boss?"

Emily nodded. "We need to head out soon," she said.

"Now?" Teddy asked.

"It's nearly three p.m. You're still in your pj's, so that means you must have slept since . . . seven last night. Do you really want to stay in bed ever more?"

"I got up," Teddy said. "I had to pee."

Emily figured that that explained how she got from the floor to Emily's bed. "Well, I might need your help today," Emily said.

Going to visit a mysterious person who sent her vaguely threatening emails was . . . probably not the smartest thing Emily had ever done. In fact, it was quite the opposite. It was the biggest thing making her rest the night before troubled, and what had been at the center of her mind the entire time she was in class.

Teddy yawned and rolled off the bed. "Why didn't you just start with that?" she said.

Emily turned away as Teddy got undressed and started to put on her shorts and bear-print T-shirt. She only turned back when she heard Teddy having a hard time tying her shoes.

She was putting all her hopes on the back of a girl who didn't know how to keep her shoes on. That was not terribly reassuring.

"C'mon," Emily said when everything was done and Teddy's shoes had acquired a nice pair of bows. "The faster we get there, the faster this will all be over."

"Cool. Can we grab a bite to eat, Boss?" Teddy asked as her hand slipped into Emily's.

Emily nodded. "Certainly. On the way back."

The walk out of the dorm was done in silence. Emily stepped out into a cloudy afternoon where the weather had taken a distinct turn toward the chilly. Not so cold that it was uncomfortable, but the sort of cold that reminded everyone that winter was right around the corner.

She had to pull her phone out to Oogle the address of the Dark Cup. It was supposed to be about four blocks away from the campus. Close enough that calling a taxi would feel like an indulgence, but far enough that she was afraid that she might work up a sweat on the way there.

Emily slid her phone into her purse. "Okay," she said.

New Quest!

The Mark of a Villain

Impress upon the people of the Dark Cup that you are a Villain to be feared.

Reward: +1 Skill Upgrade point per person terrified. Villain +1 per success!

Accept? Refuse?

New Quest!

A Rogue Delight

Make an offer they cannot refuse.

Reward: +1 Skill Upgrade point per person intimidated. Scoundrel +1 per success!

Accept? Refuse?

Emily read the two quests. They seemed pretty similar to her at first glance, though one was definitely less evil than the other.

She shut them off and both were removed from her line of sight. She didn't want to play the system's game of Villains and Rogues. She wanted . . . she didn't know what she wanted, but she knew what she didn't want.

"Come on, Teddy," she said.

"All right, Boss," Teddy agreed.

Emily wasn't out of shape, but she wasn't exactly an athlete. The only sport she really played was a bit of badminton with her mom and a few older women at an indoor court every week, and sometimes she would use her dad's little gym setup at home to burn off some excess anxiety. It kept her slim. That, and the way she lost all appetite when stressed, which was always.

Still, by the time they had made it three blocks over, Emily was regretting wearing a sweater and a thick skirt. She would need a shower the moment she returned home, or the sweatiness would bother her to no end.

What if someone noticed and thought she was a slob? What if the mysterious person in the Dark Cup noticed?

Emily's worries grew into a grand crescendo that reached their climax when she stood before a little coffee shop and bistro set between a tanning house and a store that sold clothes for construction workers.

The old label at the front looked like it belonged in the seventies. Big mom-and-pop-style lettering that read THE DARK CUP across a little awning over the front door.

She could barely see within, but the vague shapes through the frosted glass hinted at chairs and tables and people moving within.

Emily swallowed a gulp of air. "Here goes," she said.

CHAPTER EIGHT

Shady Dealings

The Dark Cup smelled like a coffee shop. Emily wasn't sure why that surprised her so much. It wasn't advertising itself as a den of moral dubiousness or anything like that. The signs, the decor, it all said "family-owned shop" without needing to spell it out.

But Emily had grown up watching cartoons about her favorite Heroes, and she'd seen the movies with the occasional Mask acting—poorly—as themselves. In those, the bad guys always hid in warehouses and places that were dark and dingy and that looked the way the Villains acted.

The Dark Cup didn't match any of that, and for some reason that set Emily on edge more than if she'd walked in to find posters endorsing the punting of puppies and the stealing of candy from babies.

"Can I help you, love?" the woman behind the counter asked. She was a midtwenties girl with her hair caught up in a net and an apron over otherwise ordinary clothes.

"Um," Emily opened her conversation as she did all others. "I-I, uh. Yes."

The waitress looked up from her notepad, one eyebrow rising. "You can sit anywhere," she said.

Emily shook her head and took a small step closer, tugging Teddy after her as she did. "No. I'm . . . looking for someone. A, uh . . . they call themselves a Mysterious Stranger?"

Confusion, then understanding flashed in the waitress's eyes. She looked Emily up and down, then did the same to Teddy. "Right. Okay. Follow me."

Emily tightened her grip on Teddy's hand until the girl returned the pressure. It made Emily feel a little better knowing she wasn't alone. Not that much better. Her only help was a girl who looked five years younger than her with powers that . . . that Emily had never really looked into. For all she knew, Teddy's power was the ability to sleep for more than fourteen hours straight.

They were led to the back. The restaurant was shaped like a large L, so that the seats at the back were around a corner with access to the washrooms and where the patrons at the front couldn't see them slip into an employees-only room.

"Next time, just come in from the back," the waitress said as she took them past a little janitor's closet and to a corridor with a door that presumably led out back and an old wooden staircase leading to another door at its bottom. "Down there. Good luck."

"Th-thank you," Emily said.

The waitress waved them goodbye and stepped past them and back out into the coffee shop. The door clicked shut behind them. Emily took a deep breath; the air smelled like dish soap and soggy mops. "Okay," she said.

"You all right, Boss?" Teddy asked. "You look like you haven't eaten anything in a bit."

"I'm okay," Emily lied. She wondered if it was too late to go back to her dorm. Or back home. She was sure her mom would accept Teddy, and her dad would like her, too, after a bit. Coming here, she decided, was a terrible idea.

Emily pulled her phone out of her purse and looked at the time. She had ten minutes before she was late.

The first step creaked underfoot. The door loomed above her, a thick old thing covered in hammered tin with a big handle that looked well-worn. Her knuckles tapped on the door with a quick, nervous one-two-three beat.

Emily was preparing to turn around and leave when the handle wiggled, something clunked on the other side, and the door creaked open.

The first thing that hit her was the faint odor of cigarette smoke, the kind of smell that clung to clothes and meant she'd need to take a shower on arriving back at the dorm. The second thing Emily took in was the size of the area before her.

She had expected a tight corridor, maybe some terrifying basement, but instead the room before her had more in common with a bar or a small pub. It didn't have any windows, and there were steel posts rising out of the floor every few feet holding up the ceiling, but the room had tables and sofas against the walls. A bar sat at the far end with a TV above it turned to an all-day news channel.

"Welcome."

Emily snapped around and found herself looking at the back of a young man as he walked toward one of the tables near the middle of the room. There was a pair of laptops set on it and some notebooks stacked up next to them. He even had a pair of empty mugs next to that, as if he'd been at work for a while.

The man turned around as he slid onto the couch on one side of the table and positioned himself behind the computers. He was younger than she expected, with thick square-rimmed glasses and a bit of a beard.

"Sit," he said with a gesture to the seat across from him.

Emily looked around, searching for anyone else in the strange bar, but they were alone.

"Um, do I have the . . ."

"You're at the right place," he said, not unkindly. "I'm Handshake. This is where I work most of the time. And I'm revealing myself because nothing I do is illegal. This is a neutral place. Do you know what that means?"

Emily shook her head.

"It means"—he continued in a voice that was soft and gentle; it made Emily think of a pediatrician or a nurse—"that offensive use of powers is very much frowned upon here. Come, sit. I won't harm you."

Emily moved over to the only seat across from Handshake, letting go of Teddy as she went.

"Who's the young lady?" Handshake asked.

She looked over to Teddy, who was busy dragging a chair over, and came to a snap decision. "This is my sister, Teddy."

"Ah, how cute," Handshake said without changing his tone in the slightest. "Very well. Miss Wright, do you know why you're here?"

"I . . . no?"

Handshake nodded. "That's okay. See, I'm an information broker. I buy and sell information. Which means that I have people who keep an eye on things in this fair city. You triggered a few things with your searches the other day, so we sent a feeler, and now you're here."

Emily nodded slowly.

"Don't worry, this meeting is really just to ascertain some things about you, about your goals," Handshake said. He glanced away from her and to his laptop. "From your searches, it seems as if you gained powers recently and were given a . . . non-Heroic starting point?"

"You mean, like starting as a, uh, not a Hero?" she asked.

Handshake made a noise at the back of his throat as if agreeing. "Exactly. Don't worry too much about it. Generally, the morality you start with is the one the power thinks is best suited to you. A lot of people start as Anti-Heroes, or as deep in the black as Vigilantes. I started as a Rogue and am still there now," he said.

Emily nodded, some of the tension in her shoulders bleeding out. "So there aren't any Villains here?" she asked.

He chuckled. "No, I'm afraid not. We have a few hotheaded individuals who live in Eauclaire. No big-name Villains, though, not for years."

"Right," Emily said. Her heart sank a bit. "Um. So you said that you didn't want to hurt me?"

"Of course not. Judging by your searches, you're trying to work your way over to becoming a Hero, of all things." He leaned back into his sofa, the smile he wore never so much as shifting. "Imagine if you become a Hero, and yet stay in touch with me? I have a few that are wonderful business partners. It's quite profitable on both sides."

"Why did you contact me, then?" Emily asked.

"I did more than that. I obfuscated your trail. Otherwise, the corporate Hero teams would pressure you into joining them. You're an attractive young woman, I'm sure they'd love to parade you around in tights and show you off to sell . . . sparkling water or something equally mundane."

Emily shook her head. That wasn't what she wanted, not at all. "So you'll tell me how to become a Hero?"

"For a price," he said. "One that is agreeable to both of us. That's my power, by the way. Hence the name."

She shrank back a little. "What kind of price?"

Handshake shrugged a shoulder, a languid, easygoing gesture. "That all depends on what you can offer me, and, more importantly, what you want to know."

CHAPTER NINE

Bearable Threats

Emily shifted on her seat. It wasn't an uncomfortable chair by any means, but the situation had her feeling antsy. Talking to a stranger was already a lot for her. Talking to someone who was a self-proclaimed Mask, a superhuman, was setting the butterflies in her stomach off in a whole new way.

"Um," she said. "I-I don't know what to ask. Maybe . . . maybe how to make my . . . you called it morality?"

Handshake nodded. "That's the commonly accepted term. There are others, more scientifically accurate ones, but morality covers the idea well enough. To advance, you need to complete quests. Those quests, in turn, are linked to your morality. A Rogue like myself mostly has quests that are about making connections and earning money. A person closer to the Heroic end of the spectrum will have quests about saving people. That information is free, by the way. I don't make a habit of selling things you can learn on Ikipedia."

Emily nodded slowly. "So if I want to change moralities?"

"Now, that information isn't as freely available," he said. "I could sell it to you for a small fee."

"Money?" Emily asked.

Handshake raised a hand and wobbled it from side to side. "Money is fine. I prefer favors and requests, but for something so simple, a bit of currency is more than sufficient."

"How much?" Emily wondered.

The man's smile didn't so much as twitch. "Two hundred."

Emily felt herself balking. "That's . . . a lot." She had some money. Her parents had given her enough to cover food and such for a while, and she'd worked all summer doing odd jobs to save up. She had enough to buy a few nice things, maybe some clothes and necessities for Teddy, but to lose a month's food budget on a bit of information . . . It was worse than paying for her textbooks.

"I can sweeten the deal for you, if you want. I have a gift for making sure that everyone is happy by the time it comes to shake hands." He turned to one of his laptops and clicked on a few things. "I have a comprehensive list of the kinds of quests someone who began as an Anti-Hero needed to accomplish to turn into a Do-Gooder."

"What kinds of quests?" Emily asked.

"That would be telling," he said. "As would the number you need to accomplish, and how to do so."

"I-I don't know," Emily said.

His smile twisted a little at the edges. "Miss Wright, I'm hardly your enemy here. In fact, I can be a great boon for you. Think of what you want out of your situation. If your aim is to become a Hero, then you'll need to chart a path toward that goal. I can help you every step along the way."

Emily crossed her arms to warm herself. "I don't want to be a Hero. I don't want to be a Mask. I just want to go to school and live my life, Mister Handshake."

The man chuckled. "I'm afraid that that opportunity is quite a ways behind you. Imagine what would happen if the right people found out about your current situation?"

"What?" Emily asked.

He nodded. "Oh yes. That information alone is worth quite a bit, you know. Some people on the lighter side of the line would love the prestige of capturing a Villain in the making."

"A Villain in the making?" she repeated.

"Oh, you might not be there yet," he said. "But the temptation might be there. Evil-aligned quests are always much easier than Heroic ones. It's why some would consider you a threat. More power only requires that you hurt a few people."

"I would never do that," Emily said.

He chuckled. "Of course not. But that's not what others might think on learning about you. Did you know that some have powers that allow them to see the powers and skills of others? What if, say, one of those people believed that your morality made you a risk and decided to . . . take care of you."

Emily closed her eyes. She wasn't the smartest girl ever. When it came to social things, she had always been . . . lacking. But she could put two and two together just as well as the next person.

Handshake had opened with a threat, one that succeeded in making her come here. Now he was trying to position her in such a way that she . . . what? Had to rely on him? Had to do favors for him, or else he would sell her out to some Heroes and watch from the side as she was arrested for *maybe* being bad?

She hadn't told him that her morality was set at Villain from the start. She had thought that it was only a bit of bad luck, but increasingly, she was beginning to think that it was a lot worse than she had imagined.

Emily opened her eyes.

"Mister Handshake, are you threatening me?" she asked.

The man's smile turned ugly. "My, Miss Wright, I'm a businessman. I only want what's best for both of us."

"Boss?" Teddy asked.

Emily didn't *know* what her . . . companion, summon . . . sister? was asking. But she imagined that Teddy saw the trap just as much as she did. She had to leave, to find a place to think, and maybe find another source of information.

She nodded.

Teddy grinned.

Emily realized that maybe she had made a small mistake at about the same time as Teddy jumped to her feet, and her chair went flying backward.

Between one second and the next, fur bristled all across Teddy's body, her clothes disappearing into the thick fluff of brown growing out of her. Then Teddy grew, and grew, and kept growing bigger.

An arm as thick around as Emily's torso shot forward and shoved Handshake into his sofa.

A paw came down on the nearest laptop, four-inch-long nails digging into and through the machine with a spittle of electronics being torn apart.

Emily froze as she took in the massive form of a grizzly bear leaning all the way across the table.

The paw on Handshake's torso twisted a little, and long white nails poked out and pressed into his button-up shirt.

The bear moved closer to him. "Did you threaten the Boss?" it asked with a voice that sounded like gravel being poured into a tumble dryer.

Emily's mind returned from its vacation in the little room at the back of her head, where she could scream as loud as she wanted, and snapped back into place. She took in the situation as quickly as she could and drew up a neat little list. At the top was the fact that Teddy was more bearlike than she had imagined.

"Teddy," she said. Her voice was surprisingly calm, like her mother when she'd found out her dad had purchased two-hundred-dollar hockey tickets using the family credit card.

The bear turned a head that had to outweigh Emily toward her. The face was huge, with canines longer than Emily's entire hand, but the eyes—those were Teddy's placid brown eyes. "Yeah, Boss?"

"Please don't kill Mister Handshake. This place has rules."

"Hmm. All right, Boss."

Emily nodded and turned to Handshake. The man's handsome face was a bit red, and she suspected that he was having a hard time breathing. "Loosen your grip on him, please. He can't talk," Emily said.

She felt a little like she did when she dove to the very bottom of a pool and just allowed herself to sink, like she was weightless and floating.

"Miss Wright," Handshake said.

"We're not going to kill you," she said, more for Teddy's benefit than the man's. "But, but you threatening me . . . that's not acceptable, Mister Handshake."

"I understand. I'm sorry," he said. His confident little smile was long gone, replaced by the sheepish look of someone caught red-handed. "I was trying to do the best for both of us?"

She didn't believe him, not one bit. "How does your power work?" she asked. "Do you even have a power?"

"I do!" he said. "I can make deals with people. I know what people want and what they'll accept in a deal."

Emily frowned at the news. "Then why did you threaten me?" she asked.

He swallowed. "I could get a better deal out of you if you're under pressure."

"And . . . and you didn't think I would be hurt by that?" she asked.

He froze up. "Um. It's more that I didn't think your friend would turn into a bear."

She crossed her arms again. "That's . . . Mister Handshake, you've been dealing with me in bad faith," she said.

The man started to tremble, especially as Teddy growled her displeasure.

"How about a new deal, then?" he asked. "I'm sure I can make it worth your while!"

CHAPTER TEN

Born Knowing

Teddy walked just a bit ahead of the Boss with her head held high and her chest puffed out. She was allowed to look so prideful because she'd done a good job.

That guy in the hidden bar place had been supersuspicious from the start. Asking the Boss for money and favors in exchange for information. She was pretty sure he was one of those capitalists she'd been warned about.

So at the first sign of him being crooked, she'd used her power and she put the fear of the proletariat—and of the Boss—in him.

Now they were on their way back home, and Teddy was sure that the Boss would give her something nice for all her hard work.

The Boss was a bit busy though. She had one hand up, holding a phone close to her face so that she could read all the information she'd gotten from the Handshake guy, while her other hand was safely guarded by Teddy's own.

"Found anything good, Boss?" Teddy asked.

The Boss made a humming noise. "I guess?" she said before looking up and sighing. The Boss was really dramatic that way. "All this information is . . . piecemeal? It's not set in a straightforward way, I guess."

"What's that mean?" Teddy asked. Information was . . . knowledge and stuff. It couldn't be straight or crooked or anything like that, as far as she knew. Maybe the Boss was being metaphorical again.

"I mean . . . um, there's a lot of little bits and pieces of . . . data? But it's not organized. When you open a textbook, things are all neat, and when you look something up, it's usually made to be easy to understand, or at least find. But we kind of just . . . took everything."

"Yeah, okay," Teddy said. "But we did good, right?"

"I-I don't know," Boss said. She looked over her shoulder as if she could see the coffee shop from where they were, but it was a couple of streets back already. "What we did back there, that was illegal. So illegal. We used a power to threaten someone. Before that, well, at least I had never used my power for anything. They could have accused me of being a . . . V-word, but not of any crimes."

"Yeah, but he was a capitalist," Teddy said.

"I-I guess," the Boss said. "I mean, he tried to extort us, but the right thing to do would have been to call the police, right?"

"Nah, you did okay, Boss," Teddy reassured. She squeezed the Boss's hand to make her feel better. "We even completed a quest."

The Boss blinked a few times, then her eyes wiggled through the air as if reading something. "Oh no," she said.

Teddy's smile faltered and failed. "What's wrong, Boss?"

"I-I didn't mean to complete any quests," the Boss said. "If I do the wrong ones, I'll be stuck as a . . . V-word for a long time." She pulled out her phone and scrolled over to a chart that Teddy couldn't quite make out. "I . . . think that to move up the morality thing, I need to only do certain kinds of quests?"

The Boss sounded really unsure to Teddy, so the girl slowed down and tugged Emily's sleeve down so that she could see the picture on her phone.

The chart was nice enough, with small words that Teddy knew already. It was also dead wrong. "Yeah, most of that's not right, Boss," Teddy said as she let go of the Boss's sleeve.

"P-pardon?"

Teddy waved at the phone. "Those moralities. Some of them are wrong."

"How do you know?" the Boss asked.

Teddy puffed out her chest some more. "'Cause I do," she said.

"You mean, like something you were, uh, born knowing? Because you're a summon?" Boss asked.

"Yeah. Like I know how to talk, and do my business in the bathroom, and I know how to be a bear real good," Teddy agreed. She could list off all the things she knew how to do all day if that was what the Boss wanted.

The Boss's expression twisted this way and that before her arms went loose by her side, and she let out another deep sigh. "I could have just asked you this entire time," she said. "I didn't need to look it up online and get into trouble and threaten Handshake." She tucked her phone away in her purse, and then used her now-free hand to rub at her face.

"It's all right, Boss, you didn't know that I know," Teddy said. She didn't like seeing the Boss looking all mopey and sad. Her job was to help the Boss, which meant making the Boss's life better. That meant that the Boss being sad was the opposite of what Teddy wanted.

"It's okay," Emily said. "I just— I think it's been a long couple of days."

That made sense. "Yeah. But don't worry, Boss, I'm here for you now."

The Boss actually cracked a smile, even if she did it while turning to look away from Teddy. "Thank you, Teddy," the Boss said.

Teddy couldn't have puffed her chest out any more without turning into her full size. "No problem, Boss! Hey, do you want me to explain things to you?"

"I . . . would appreciate that, yes," the Boss said.

Nodding, Teddy searched for a nice place to start her explanation. She decided to settle for the thing the Boss was confused about the most. "So, your rank, like on that chart, you wanna change it, right?"

"Yes," Boss said.

"Right. Well, that's easy. See, you get quests, just like I do, right? So if you do quests that fit with your rank, you'll stay there, but if you do some for other ranks close to yours, you'll eventually move over to one of those."

"I see," Boss said. "I guess that makes sense. Can you move up a lot? Like . . . faster?"

The Boss was already at Villain and she wanted to move up? Teddy searched her memory for ranks that were even more impressive. Super Villain and Mastermind were both close, but if she wanted to move fast . . . was the Boss aiming to be a Demon?

Teddy was very impressed. "Yeah, Boss. You just need to do really impressive stuff, like, way more than what the quest asks for."

"I see," the Boss said. "Okay. That's good. I can do that. We can do that."

Teddy grinned. She was being included in the Boss's plans!

"What about, um, the points?"

"Points? You mean like on your status screen?" Teddy asked. When the Boss nodded, Teddy brought up her own screen just to be sure.

Name: Teddy Wright		
Alignment: Villain, Little Sister		
Alias: None		
Level: 1		
Powers		
WereBear		
Rip and Bear	Rank 1	
Points		
Power Slots: 0	Skill Upgrades: 2	Skill Slots: 0

Two Skill Upgrade points. One from her mugging the other day, and the other from scaring the capitalism right out of that Handshake guy. "Right, so there are three sorts of points, right? The Power Slot ones give you a whole new power. You don't know what you'll get, though, like when you got the power to summon me."

"I think I've heard of that," the Boss said. "Some of the best Heroes have a bunch of powers."

"That's right, yeah. The Skill Upgrades one allows you to make a power's skills better. Like, once I unlock some skills for my bear power, I could make them better and stuff like that."

"Okay," the Boss said.

"And the Skill Slot ones, those unlock new skills for a power you already have."

A frown appeared on the Boss's forehead. "I don't understand that one, sorry."

"Ah, it's like . . . I could get a new skill that allows me to, uh, talk to bears. It would match with my power, but be a whole new skill."

"I guess I can see that?" the Boss said. She didn't sound like she saw the whole thing, but Teddy figured she would in no time.

They'd arrived at their destination, so Teddy slowed down and finally came to a full stop.

The Boss blinked a few times and looked around in confusion. "Why did we stop?" she asked.

Teddy pointed across the street to the Im Orton's they'd gotten lunch from. "We're here," she explained.

The Boss stared at the busy store, a look of confusion appearing and then passing with a roll of her eyes. But because she was the best Boss, all she did was mutter something under her breath, and then nod her head. "Fine. Might as well."

CHAPTER ELEVEN

A Queen of Sorts

Emily didn't exactly sleep well that night. The entire time had been spent curled up in a small ball so that the large towels she'd unpacked could serve as a blanket against the cold in her room. She listened to Teddy's steady snoring and tried to fall asleep to no avail.

She did sleep, eventually, but when she awoke, it was with bleary eyes and no energy.

At least it hadn't been the sound of her door slamming open as a team of Heroes barged into her room that woke her up. She'd had a few nightmares like that already.

She got dressed in a hurry, tacking a note to the inside door telling Teddy not to step out unless it was an emergency. She also left her number, just in case, and made a note in her own agenda to maybe find out if getting a phone for Teddy was doable.

Class started, and within moments Emily found herself zoning out. She wasn't thinking about literature and its impact on society, or the artistic merit of stringing words along in pretty ways. She wasn't even overly worried about the people sitting around her for once.

Her mind was focused on quests.

Now that she knew a bit more about how the system worked, she figured she could start to work on becoming something that wasn't a Villain.

It was, on the surface, rather simple. She just had to pick out quests that would lead her in another direction and do them.

Quest!

Fighting Good

Join the battle against the forces of good.

Reward: +3 Skill Upgrade points per Hero incapacitated or killed. Villain +4 per kill!

Accept? Refuse?

That was clear enough. The quest would make her even more of a Villain. Also, killing people was completely off the table.

New Quest!

The Black Queen

Begin to climb the societal ladder . . . with violence!

Reward: +1 Skill Upgrade point per person assassinated, socially outcast, or bullied into submission. Crime Lord +1 per rung climbed!

Accept? Refuse?

There were more things she wasn't familiar with. Societal ranks? She opened her agenda and added it to the "Ask Teddy" list. A few flips back to another list had her adding "Find a code" to her weekly list. She didn't want just anyone finding her agenda and knowing everything she was up to.

The Black Queen quest was off the table. She didn't want to become a Crime Lord any more than she wanted to be a Villain. Teddy had said something about points near the same rank sometimes allowing for sideways growth, though it hadn't been in so many words and there was a warning about capitalists in there, too, that Emily didn't understand.

The next quest was one that had her a bit more on edge.

New Quest!

The Queen with the Silken Sword

Become an outstanding member of your community!

Reward: +1 Skill Upgrade point per 10 people who recognize you as "good." Scoundrel +1 per 10 people who recognize you as "good"!

Accept? Refuse?

That had potential! She had to stifle the urge to smile, or else the people around her might begin to wonder why her mood had changed.

She could do that, she could help the community!

Sighing, Emily sat back and did her best to pay attention to the lesson. She would have to look up any notes left by students from the previous year, in case she missed anything important, but that was also something she could do.

In the back of her mind, she was planning out ways to join volunteer groups. Maybe she could pick up trash, or clean clothes at a thrift store?

She'd done things like that before! It would be easy once she figured out how to work it around her school schedule.

The points that she made from it . . . didn't really matter to her. She had a single Skill Upgrade point at her disposal, and she didn't mind having more or less; they were part of the thing causing her woes, and she decided that they could safely be ignored.

Class ended on a high note, the teacher announcing that the homework he was going to hand out would wait until next Monday.

Emily gathered her things, then patiently waited as the class emptied a bit so that she wouldn't be bumping into anyone at the door.

One advantage of suddenly being thrust into the world of Masks and Villains and such was that her anxiety about being around people had been, partially, replaced by a multitude of new and far more terrifying anxieties.

Emily plotted her course from her English lit class to the campus cafeteria. If she arrived late enough, they might not question her taking enough food for two, and there wouldn't be a line at the free food they served.

The rumors online said that it wasn't exactly . . . *good* food, but it was free, which counted for a lot to the student body.

After that she had an afternoon history class. She would need to look at the map on her phone to know exactly where that was on the campus other than the vague idea she'd gotten from her first tour.

Emily was still plotting ahead when she slowed to a stop outside the English building.

There was a crowd. Not the kind of crowd that appeared when foot traffic jammed or when people were gathering to protest something, but the sort of crowd that came together to collectively gawk at something.

It only took looking up a bit to see what the fuss was all about.

Jezebelle Winthrop

Defender, Level 1

Emily froze, a deer in headlights. The crowds shifted, bulging out like the sea rising, and somehow Emily was the place where it broke.

The woman under the name was a shorter girl, with short brown hair that fell down to her neck, a face that Emily might have called plain, and eyes that were a bit big but shone with mirth.

She had her hands stuffed in a denim jacket over a T-shirt with Hot Stuff's handsome face on it. Jezebelle was grinning from ear to ear, soaking in all the attention around her like a flower indulging in a heavy rain of attention.

And then she bumped into Emily.

"S-sorry!" Emily squeaked. She started to step back.

Jezebelle's hand caught her elbow.

For a moment, Emily thought that it was all over. Defender was a Heroic morality—she was done for.

Instead, Jezebelle only grinned wider. "You okay?"

"I'm fine," Emily said.

"Were you waiting here for me?" she asked. At Emily's quick shake of the head, she chuckled. "There's no need to be shy," she said.

"I-I'm sorry," Emily said. "I should . . . I should go." She clutched her backpack close, arms bunching up by her sides to ward off the attention. Jezebelle's hand loosened.

"Fangirls already?" she said as she walked on past.

The laughter had Emily burning up, but that kernel of anger warred with the relief of being free.

Who, she wondered, *was that?* Public Masks were common enough, but to go around on campus . . . She wanted to smack herself. Power Day was only days ago. She'd gotten her powers then—how could she forget so easily that others would be gifted powers on that day too?

So a new local Hero, then.

She paused to watch the crowd slowly moving on, the name of a potential threat hovering at its center.

Emily hoped that it wouldn't come to that. But if it did . . . maybe seeing the girl's smug, too-confident facade break when she came face-to-face with an angry Teddy would make things better.

She swallowed. That thought hadn't been very kind. There was no reason for her to dislike or distrust Jezebelle. They weren't enemies; they were only on different sides of a line that Emily planned on crossing.

That was no reason to be antagonistic.

CHAPTER TWELVE

Voluntary

Finding a place to volunteer was actually very easy.

Emily's first stop had been to a thrift store, not only to see if they needed some help, but also to pick up some essentials for Teddy: a few hoodies (Teddy found one with a bear on the front that she immediately grabbed, even though it was a men's hoodie and about four sizes too large) and some shirts and shorts and some pj's. Emily even found a few blankets and a blow-up mattress that had been patched up a few times. It was cheaper than buying a new one, though, so she added it to her stuff.

It took some pacing to build up the courage to ask the nice older lady behind the counter whether or not they needed help. As it turned out, the thrift store was operating just fine, but the soup kitchen across campus was usually staffed in part by students, many of whom had graduated.

Emily paid for her things, thanked the old lady profusely for the discount she added for "such a nice single mom," and walked out of the place with her face steaming and Teddy asking some very loud and inappropriate questions all the way back to their dorm.

The soup kitchen was a little building near the campus and set up in an old office block with some ratty apartments above it. The people waiting around for a bite to eat were surprisingly young. Not the destitute people Emily had been expecting, but students who were maybe on the wrong side of the poverty line.

Finding the person in charge was simple enough.

Mister Landcaster was a big, gregarious man with a voice like a foghorn and a personality to match. When an almost-hyperventilating Emily asked him if they needed help, he took one look at her, then eyed Teddy, who was swimming in her new hoodie, before he barked a laugh. "Girl! We always need the help!"

Emily and Teddy were ushered to the back rooms where a few other volunteers were setting things up. Mister Landcaster decided that she was too pretty and that Teddy was too young to be out and about with the ruffians, so they were set to doing the dishes in the back.

Emily expected Teddy to complain, but the girl took to drying with gusto. "I'm going to do my part to help my comrades," was all she had to say on the matter.

She chose not to look the gift bear in the mouth.

Doing the dishes was . . . surprisingly cathartic. The back rooms for the soup kitchen were a bit dingy, with old, cracked tiles. The water had to be stopped every few minutes so that the hot water tanks at the back could warm up a bit more, but it was all impeccably clean, and the place smelled like her kitchen back home when her mom had another cooking show phase.

The other volunteers chatted among themselves a bit, but they didn't force Emily to participate, something she wholeheartedly approved of.

It was a nice backdrop to work in, filling all her social needs for the year in the time it took for her to wash up a few dozen plates. She learned that someone called Abigail was pregnant *again*, and that her wife was very proud about it; that a scary Villain called Broccoli, of all things, had turned into some sort of sky pirate; and that the local knitting circle had lost a member recently because of infighting.

It was all quite titillating and interesting, and Emily didn't have to say a word other than to ask Teddy to help her take out the trash.

An hour or so in, she noticed that the water in her rinse bowl was getting a bit nasty. She flicked the tap off and took a deep breath.

"M-miss?" she asked one of the friendlier-seeming women who was chopping up carrots.

"Hmm? Yes, dear?" the lady asked without looking away from the machine-gun clatter of her knife tearing through vegetables.

"The dirty water, um, I can't just dump it in the drain, so do I, uh . . ."

The woman paused and looked up. "It's only soapy water? Bah, take it out the alley in the back. There's a big old drain by the trash. A bit of bone and some vegetables tossed down there won't cause anyone any harm."

"Oh, okay," Emily said.

She scurried back to the sinks and started to lift the heavy square bucket of dirty water out. "What are you doing, Boss?" Teddy asked.

"Emptying this out back. It'll only take a minute," she said through gritted teeth. Her arms were on the skinny side of muscly.

With wobbling steps, Emily carried the soapy water past the kitchen staff, who all carefully stepped out of her way, and toward the back door. She had to place the bucket down to open up the door, but that was simple enough.

The back alley was a bit like the kitchens. Old and dilapidated, but still fairly clean. The smell coming from the two dumpsters off to one side was a bit strong, but she figured that was the old vegetables and meats flung into it, nothing really bad, just a bit on the stinky side.

Emily had barely spotted the drain she was probably meant to use—a good thing because going back for more detailed instructions would have been mortifying—when some screaming from the far end of the alley had her turning around.

A man, one she suspected would stick out from any crowd, was running toward her. He had an outfit like some sort of renaissance actor, a long burgundy coat that flared out behind him, strange calf-length pants that showed off his white stockings and a dark green bandanna-like mask under a bicorne hat.

Above him, floating like a warning to all who would care to look, was a name.

Alea Iacta

Rascal, Level 1

Emily gasped, stumbling back as the man, the *Villain*, sprinted toward her.

He wasn't the one screaming though. That was the two people coming around the corner at a dead run after him.

Silver Fox

Do-Gooder, Level 3

Glamazon

Defender, Level 1

Emily felt her breath hitching as she stared at not one, but two Heroes coming down the alley toward her. The first was even one she recognized. Silver Fox was an older Hero, one who had changed his name over time to match his aging body.

He was supposed to have superstrength of some sort, able to throw cars and dodge shots from guns and such while keeping his mop of black-gray hair perfectly quaffed. His foxlike silver mask was on every bottle of men's shampoo in her parents' bathroom.

The other Hero . . . was a young woman in a denim jacket, a glittering mask over her face the only costume she had. Emily put two and two together. "Jezebelle?" she muttered.

And then the Villain was on her.

Emily squeaked and ducked forward, eyes squeezing shut as she expected a blow that never came.

Instead, Alea Iacta tore the bucket from her hand and laughed aloud as he spun by. "Thank you, milady!" he said as he ducked between the dumpsters at the far end.

A couple of gallons of soapy water crashed to the ground and splattered the front of her skirts, turning them lukewarm and wet while suds spread out before her.

The Heroes, like something out of a poorly plotted comedy, stepped into the water and, as one, lost their footing.

Silver Fox, for all that he was older, spun around in a way that was almost graceful before crashing onto his side and rolling across the dirty ground. His silver costume got stained, but he was up on his feet in an instant.

Glamazon wasn't nearly so graceful.

She tripped with a squeak, legs spinning and arms flailing as she tried to turn the spill into a roll. She succeeded, partially, and ended her tumble by kicking Silver Fox's legs out from under him.

Emily stared, arms still outstretched to hold on to a bucket that was rolling away. Her mind kicked back into gear with a squeal, and she turned around to run back inside. Not only was it the smart thing to do when people in masks started to throw down, she also had a very good reason not to be stopped.

Which is why she had a full-body cringe when Jezebelle called out. "Hey, you! Stop!"

Emily stood rigid, eyes staring longingly toward the back door of the soup kitchen.

"Damn," Silver Fox said. He had a deep baritone of a voice, one that had probably helped convince Emily's mom to buy his shampoos for her dad. "He's a slippery one, I'll give him that."

"Ugh, was that a pun, old man?"

Silver Fox snorted. "I'm meant to teach you all the parts of the trade. Banter's important too." A hand landed on Emily's shoulder. "Now, miss, would you mind if we asked a few questions?"

CHAPTER THIRTEEN

An Interrogation or Two

Emily didn't know what to do.

There was a hand on her shoulder, a hand belonging to an actual, bona fide Hero, and he was telling her to stop.

What if he knew?

She dismissed the thought. If Silver Fox knew she was a Villain, then he wouldn't be asking so nicely. He'd wait until she was in a holding cell or something before asking her anything. No, Silver Fox and Glamazon didn't know. All she had to do was play it cool, and she would be fine.

It was with a sinking realization that she recalled that she had never played anything cool in her entire life.

Emily turned around. There might have been something on her face because the Hero stared at her before carefully pulling his arm back and letting out a sigh. "Sorry, miss," he said. "Just have a few questions, nothing big."

"Oh—okay," she said right back. It sounded like the right thing to say.

He nodded, the fox mask he wore shifting a little with the motion. It was only a half mask, allowing her to see his eyes through a clear visor above it. "Did you get a good look at the Villain that ran past?"

Emily waffled. "Not . . . really?" she said. "Um. A bit?"

Glamazon stretched behind Silver Fox, then sighed. "Do we really need to question her?" she asked.

"She might have noticed something," he said.

"Just give her a fine for interfering or something, and get the cops to question her," the girl suggested.

"A fine," Emily repeated, feeling faint all over again.

Glamazon looked at Emily, her eyes narrowing behind her sparkly domino mask. "Hey, I recognize you," she said. "You were at the college earlier."

Emily swallowed. "Um."

"Oh?" Silver Fox asked. It wasn't just a noise, it was an outright question.

Emily wondered how hard it would be to get a power that would allow the ground to swallow her up.

"Can you tell us what you were doing out here?" he asked when she failed to reply to his prompt.

"Dirty water," she said. There was meant to be more after that, but she had a hard time finding the words.

"Can you elaborate?" he asked.

Emily nodded and gestured to the door behind her. "The . . . I work at this soup kitchen here. I came out to empty the dirty water."

The Hero's shoulders slumped a little and she had the impression he was smiling wryly. "I see. And then what happened?"

"Um. I heard screaming? A man, a Rascal? He ran by and bumped into me and the water"—Emily gestured to the still-wet and soapy ground—"and then you came and tripped."

Glamazon sniffed. "If you weren't so clumsy," she muttered.

"Glamazon," Silver Fox said, his voice a warning. "She's a civilian. You'll learn not to expect too much out of them with time. It's hardly her fault. I suspect that Alea Iacta has some sort of luck manipulation ability."

The Hero tilted her head to the side. "How's that? 'Cause she just happened to be here on time with soap water?"

"And his luck before, too. Also, we used to have Latin in school when I was closer to your age. I *do* know what his name means. It's a bit pompous, but it's a hint if I ever heard one."

Glamazon barked a laugh. "Showing your age there, old man."

"Showing your age doesn't mean you're showing your weakness," he said. Glamazon groaned, and if Emily wasn't completely mortified and wasn't in the same postal code, she might have groaned too. It was the catchphrase of his shampoo commercials, and it was cheesier in person.

Emily shifted on the spot a little. "Can . . . can I go?" she asked.

"Of course," Silver Fox said. "We'll just need your name and number. In case we need to call you up for anything."

She could do that much, and with a minimum of stuttering too.

Emily thought she was home free, when the door behind her opened up and someone jumped out. "Hey, Boss. You all right?"

Silver Fox and Glamazon both turned to stare at a bored-looking Teddy. The bear girl had her hoodie up, Emily noticed. Her ears were safe. That was only a small blessing because the girl took one glance at the situation and her entire face scrunched up.

"Who're these people?" she asked.

"Hello, little miss," Silver Fox said. "We were just asking your . . . Boss here some questions."

"What kind of questions?" Teddy asked. Her eyes narrowed and she stepped closer to Emily's side.

"Hey, kid, c'mon, the adults are talking. Do you want to see a light show?" Glamazon asked. Her hands sparkled as little motes of light flashed around her fingers.

Teddy stared for all of a second before dismissing her and looking up to Emily. "Who are these weirdos?"

"They're Heroes," Emily said. "Just . . . asking me some questions. It's nothing."

"Yeah, I can read," Teddy said with a gesture over their heads. "Are they making trouble for you?"

"N-no, it's okay," she said. Wiggling her hand a little to tell Teddy to stand down somehow backfired and ended up with the girl reaching up and holding on to her hand. Emily squeezed it and tried to meet Silver Fox's visor. "This is Teddy, she's a bit . . . uh . . ."

"It's fine," he said. "We were just on our way off, anyway . . . Here!" He reached into one of the pouches on the hip of his silver costume and pulled out a little card that he handed to her, and a second that he gave to a confused Teddy. "Have a good day, you two, and keep up the good work!"

Emily waved them goodbye and hoped they didn't notice the glare Teddy gave them as they left.

The instant the Heroes were around the corner, Emily thought she might faint. All the stress and anxiety—or at least, a lot of it—leaked out of her like a pierced balloon.

She stepped to the side, and, heedless of how dirty it might be, leaned against the nearest dumpster. She read the little card she'd received. On one half there was the Silver Fox logo. On the other, a tear-off coupon for some men's shampoo.

Teddy was glaring at her own coupon. "Wait, they were capitalists?" she asked.

Emily didn't even bother answering. She needed a moment. She needed a few moments. Maybe some moments spent lying down on her bed, face buried in her pillow, while screaming. But not screaming too loud, or else the people in the neighboring rooms would hear.

"That was certainly stressful!"

Emily jumped up and whipped around to see the top half of an unwelcome face poking around the back of the dumpster.

The words above his head were gone, but there was no mistaking Alea Iacta's mask and costume.

"Who's this one?" Teddy asked.

"Just a friendly neighborhood ruffian," the man said. "So . . . the men in tights are gone?"

"You . . . you . . ." Emily said.

"Me!" he said right back. "Thanks for the distraction, by the way. Turns out . . ." He stopped and pointed to the end of the alley the Heroes went down. Emily followed his finger and stared at the brick wall across from them. The alley obviously forked between two buildings. She could hear the cars and such on the street, but not see them. He went on. "Although you can come from that way, you can't leave that way." He pointed over his back with a thumb. "Bit of a dead end. I'm quite lucky you were there!"

Something in Emily clicked. "Teddy."

"Yeah, Boss?"

"You remember what you did to that man in the bar?"

"Yeah?" Teddy said.

"Do it to him," she said while pointing to Alea Iacta.

The Villain stared at the two. "What, is the tyke going to kick my shiiiiii— What the hell!"

Teddy's transformation into a grizzly bear, now that she wasn't hidden in the depths of a dingy bar, and now that Emily was so far past stressed that she couldn't muster the energy to care, was actually quite impressive.

One moment she was Teddy, a normal girl, a bit chubby and kinda cute when she wasn't asking uncomfortable questions about the values of communism. The next, she was taller than Emily while on all fours, her body covered in bristling dark-brown fur.

Alea Iacta stumbled back, but he couldn't move backward faster than a car-size bear could move forward, and he found himself rather quickly with no space to maneuver.

Emily had never intimidated anyone in her entire life, but she figured with Teddy helping her, she could maybe manage a little.

The Rascal's eyes were looking all over for an escape. Then Teddy's paw crashed into the wall next to him and her claws bit into the bricks.

His only other route of escape was through Emily.

She glared.

He didn't seem that impressed.

Do you wish to reveal your identity?

"Yes."

Alea Iacta's eyes slowly traced up from her face and to the words hanging above her. What little she could see of his face turned white, then went a bit green.

She glanced up, too, just in case.

The Boss

Villain, Level 1

"I . . . have questions," Emily said.

CHAPTER FOURTEEN

An Adorable Misunderstanding

Teddy didn't know what the weird guy did to anger the Boss. All she knew was that he was smaller than her, and not nearly as strong, and those two things made it real easy for her to pin the guy against the wall and keep him there for the Boss.

"I . . . have questions," the Boss said. Her voice sounded shaky, like she was holding back a whole lot of anger.

Alea Iacta—which was a weird name, but that's what it said above him—looked kind of pale. That was probably the right response. Teddy would feel kind of pale, too, if the Boss was angry at her.

"A-ask away," Alea Iacta said with false cheerfulness in his voice. "I live to serve, Lady Boss."

The Boss frowned at him. "Why were you running from those Heroes?" she asked.

"I swear, I was minding my own business, walking across the street, not bothering anyone. And then they decided to start screaming at me. That Glamazon girl? The one in the awful costume? She started throwing fireworks at me! So I hightailed it out of there. I didn't mean to run into you, I swear."

The Boss frowned harder and Teddy caught her cue. She took a deep breath in, then let it out as a low rumble deep in her chest. She even opened her mouth a little to show Alea Iacta her big bear teeth.

"You . . . you were just walking along?" the Boss asked. She sounded shrill, on the edge of either panic or of screaming. Teddy figured that Alea Iacta was about to make the Boss real angry now. Lying was against the rules. "Walking in costume?"

"W-well, maybe I was playing around with my powers a little? You know, I had a quest or two? Little things. Completely harmless. I didn't rob anyone who doesn't have insurance to cover it."

Teddy flexed her claws. They kind of hurt when they dug into the bricks of the wall behind Alea Iacta, but it was worth it to see the man flinching back.

"I might have used my power on people too!" he squeaked.

The Boss's eyes narrowed. "Your power? How does it work?"

The man waved his arms about. "You know how everyone is a little lucky?"

The Boss didn't seem impressed by his rhetorical question.

"Ah, well . . . I can take a bit of that luck and tuck it away for a rainy day, as it were. A pinch here or there from people on the street, you know?"

"And you used that to decide which alley to hide in?" she asked. Teddy hadn't thought of that. The Boss was really clever.

He nodded. "That's the gist of it, yeah. I used up a chunk of my luck to find a place to hide from the Heroes, and then I met you . . . how lucky."

The Boss seemed to deflate a little. "That sounds more truthful, at least," she said. "Can people sense you using your power on them?"

"Yeah," he said. "It feels like, uh, passing gas, but from everywhere? Giving people luck feels like the opposite, or so I was told."

The Boss's face went red with anger. Teddy didn't know what the guy said that angered her so much, but she growled anyway.

"Hey, hey, no need to worry, I'm an honest kind of guy. I'd never use my powers on friends," he said with a smile that even Teddy knew was fake as fake could be. "I just want to head on back home, maybe move to the next city over? I wouldn't want to mess with your turf."

"My turf?" the Boss asked.

The man swallowed. "Your territory. Your city."

"You don't need to move away," the Boss said. "I don't have any . . . turf. I just . . . I just want to do my own thing."

"Right, right, of course," he said. "I'm very, very sorry about bumping into you. Here," he said while reaching into his jacket. He pulled out a big wad of cash, all sorts of paper bills squished together in a heap. "I'll give you half my winnings for the day. That ought to make us even, right?"

"Half?" the Boss asked.

Teddy knew what that meant. She swiped a paw down, tore the entire heap of cash out of the man's hands, and pinned it to the ground.

Quest Complete!

A Muggy Afternoon

Reward: +1 Skill Upgrade point per person successfully robbed. Scoundrel +1 per item!

Awesome! The Boss must have known that Teddy's mugging quest was still active.

"Right, right, that's fair, sure," Alea Iacta said. "Take it all. It's what I deserve, right, Boss?"

"'Boss'?" the Boss asked. "Oh, right, the name. Sure, you can call me Boss if you want."

Understanding took a moment to appear in the man's eyes, but when it did, Teddy backed away. The Boss had claimed him as one of her own now. He was more new than Teddy, though, so he didn't have seniority or anything like that. Also, he was small and squishy compared to her.

Alea Iacta nodded, stood a bit straighter, and brushed off his costume front. "Right. Cool. So, ah. What do you want me to do, Boss?"

"Do?" Boss asked. She shook her head. "I don't suppose I could tell you to hand yourself over to the authorities. That would be hypocritical." She paused, then sighed. "Just go. And please, if you can help it, don't kill or hurt anyone. I don't want the Heroes coming around and asking a bunch of questions."

"I can be subtle," he said before adjusting his huge feathery hat.

Emily stepped back, too, and gestured toward the mouth of the alley. The words above her head flickered away, and she was back to being a normal girl who was also secretly the Boss.

"Wonderful, stupendous," he said. "If you don't mind me asking, Boss, what scheme were you running here?"

"Sc-scheme?" Emily asked. "None? I was working at the soup kitchen."

The man's eyes widened. "You were poisoning the food or something?"

"What?! No! I was doing the dishes."

He nodded. "Poisoning the utensils. Make it harder to figure out who did it."

"Just . . . just go, please," Emily said.

Alea Iacta snapped a salute and took off jogging toward the end of the alleyway. In a moment, he was off and heading out of sight.

Teddy figured her time as a bear was up, so she untransformed and returned to being just Teddy the girl. "That was well done, Boss," Teddy said. It felt a bit weird to go from taller than the Boss to a bunch shorter.

"Thanks, Teddy," the Boss said. She knelt over and picked up the bucket she'd used for the dirty water. "We should get back to work, I guess."

Teddy nodded and picked up the cash she'd successfully mugged. She didn't have much use for it, so she gave it to the Boss, who stared before pocketing it. "Cool. Are we gonna grab some food after? Maybe we can eat here?"

The Boss nodded. "I'll ask if they can set aside a pair of plates for us," she said. "They won't be impressed if we take any longer though."

Teddy nodded along. This little diversion had been fun, but her work drying utensils and plates for her comrades inside was just as important. She was glad that the Boss was conscious of the needs of the proletariat. Her book said that that was very important.

"Yeah," Teddy said. "Let's get back to work. We can continue plotting after we've had lunch."

CHAPTER FIFTEEN

A Cryptic Request

You girls did good work today," Mister Landcaster said.

Emily looked up from her plate of mac and cheese and mashed potatoes to take in the larger-than-life man standing above her, then she looked back down. Meeting his eyes for any amount of time was hard enough already, more so when she had a great excuse not to.

"Th-thank you, sir," she said.

"Yeah, thanks," Teddy said.

Mister Landcaster harrumphed. "I wish I had more to give you girls than a pair of warm meals as thanks, but that's what it's like in our line of work, isn't it?"

"It's okay," Emily said. "The, uh, work is its own reward? Would it be okay if we returned?"

He grinned at her, huge and proud. "Of course! Take one of the fliers by the door. They have our opening hours. Show up a bit before that and you'll be more than welcome to help."

"Thank you," Emily said.

"No, thank *you*," he replied. "Now, I'll be off. We need to get everything sorted out for tomorrow morning. You girls keep safe on the way back home."

"Yes, sir," Emily said.

"Sure thing, Comrade Landcaster," Teddy replied.

Emily watched the big man walk off while picking away at her noodles. They'd found a little corner at the back of the kitchen where they could have a bite to the tune of the volunteer cooks packing up and a radio in the corner blasting 24/7 ads between the occasional intermission of pop music.

"Today was fun," Teddy said as she scarfed down her potatoes. Emily didn't need to worry about Teddy being picky, not if the way she devoured everything on her plate meant anything.

"I guess it was," Emily said.

Teddy nodded along, spoon stuck between her teeth as she grinned up at her. "You check your notifications, Boss?"

Emily blinked. At first she thought Teddy was talking about her phone, but then it clicked. She hadn't looked at her quest messages in a bit. Nor had they bothered her during the latter part of the day.

It seemed that however the powers system worked, it at least had some common decency at times. "I didn't, no. Can you keep an eye on our surroundings?" she asked.

Teddy gave her a quick salute. "Of course, Comrade Boss."

Emily snorted a laugh and shook her head. At least her "sister" was kind of . . . cute, when she wasn't a car-size bear.

Quest Complete!

The Queen with the Silken Sword

Reward: +1 Skill Upgrade point. Scoundrel +1!

That was wonderful! Not the Skill Upgrade point. That was something she could do without. But the boost to Scoundrel—that meant she was a little bit closer to no longer being a Villain.

Scoundrel was still pretty bad, but, for Emily's purposes, it was a step up from outright Villain. People reacted to moralities in different ways. A Scoundrel was kind of scary, but a Villain was terrifying.

She noticed that she had another notification. It wasn't like she had a flashing thing in her sight, but more an . . . impression of something waiting for her attention.

Action Reward!

For turning another powered individual into a minion through threats, blackmail, and fearmongering, you have earned:

+1 Skill Slot!

Emily frowned even as the prompt faded away. "Teddy, what's a Skill Slot?"

Teddy looked up, her tongue currently out to lick her plate clean. She slipped it back into her mouth before answering. "Didn't I tell you that already, Boss?"

Emily felt herself flushing a little. Being told off by a girl who was a head shorter was a bit embarrassing, but it was Teddy, and . . . and Emily found herself surprisingly comfortable with the bear girl, more so than most people who weren't her mom, at least. "You did, but now I have one."

"Oh, that's good," Teddy said. "You can get a skill added to a power with one of those. Not a new power, though, just something tacked on. You get them for doing stuff." Teddy nodded sagely.

"I see," Emily said.

"You should use it sooner rather than later," Teddy said. "You'll have time to get used to it that way."

"I'll think about it," Emily said. She eyed her plate and pushed it over to Teddy, who took it with a happy little growl and tore into the leftovers with more gusto than Emily thought the food deserved.

Then Teddy was done and leaned back to pat her tummy. Emily picked up their plates and washed and rinsed them off at the sinks, adding them atop the pile of cleaned dishes they'd been working on all afternoon.

"Are you ready to go?" Emily asked.

"Yeah, coming!"

Emily and Teddy left by the front with as few goodbyes to the other volunteers as Emily could manage, and then, hand in hand with her strange little sister of sorts, Emily started walking back toward their dorms and what she hoped would be a good night's rest.

They were a couple of blocks along when Emily felt something buzzing at her side. "One sec," she said before gesturing to a bus stop by the nearest corner. It was empty, save for a few discarded cups left next to an overflowing garbage can.

She slipped in with Teddy and pulled out her phone from her purse. The number on the screen wasn't her home number, which meant it wasn't a number she recognized.

"Hello?" she said as she pressed the phone to her ear.

"Miss Wright," said an all-too-familiar voice.

She felt her blood go cold. "Mister Handshake," she said.

"Let's keep this short. I've secured this call as best I can, but that only means so much. I . . . have to ask for a rather em—" The man cut himself off to cough, rather violently.

Emily didn't know how to react to that, though she did pull her phone away from the side of her face as if that would do something. "Mister Handshake?"

"I'm well," he said. "Well enough? It doesn't matter. I need to talk to you in person, and soon."

"Why?" she asked.

"This line isn't secure," he said.

Emily bit her lip and looked down to Teddy who quickly yoinked her finger out of her nose and shrugged. "I . . . I think I'd like to know why anyway."

" . . . All right. As you can imagine, I keep some information about all my clients. It's stored on a very secure device, encrypted to all hell, with some power-tech thrown in for good measure. If you can't read my mind, you can't get into it."

"Oh— Okay," Emily said. She felt her stomach edging closer to a deep precipice.

"A few days ago, my laptop was destroyed, as you'll recall. I had backups, but they're not quite as secure. Someone took them and"—he stopped for another bout of coughing—"and they got the passcodes out of me. It's only a few weeks' worth of information, but the business we conducted is part of that."

Her stomach finally rolled over the edge and dropped. "What?" she asked faintly.

"That's why I want to meet in person. In my line of work, there's a certain . . . responsibility. See, someone crossed me bad, and now a lot of my clients, yourself included, are at risk. I need your help to settle things."

Emily felt her hand going numb so her other came up to cradle the phone close. Teddy looked a bit worried as her own hand was dropped. "I . . . okay. Where?" she asked. "Wait, no. Can . . . can we do something about it?"

"I hope so," he said. "I really, really hope so."

The line went dead.

Emily stood, cradling the phone for a few long minutes while screaming in her mind. Then it buzzed, and she found herself staring at the screen as an address and time appeared via text.

That very night, at a park on the opposite side of the campus as her. There was a note attached to the end of the text. "Come as your other self."

"Boss, you okay?" Teddy asked.

Emily took a deep breath in, then let it out slowly. "I . . . I don't know, Teddy. I really don't know."

CHAPTER SIXTEEN

Midnight Meeting

Emily understood that she should be going to the meeting with Handshake in costume. Or in some sort of disguise.

The only little problem with that was she lacked anything even remotely similar to a disguise.

A long search through all the clothing she'd yet to unpack found her wearing a pair of old cargo pants she'd used for gardening back home and a thick jacket over a simple T-shirt. With the collar popped and a scarf around her lower face to ward off the cold, the Emily in the mirror was at least partially hidden.

Partially. She figured it wouldn't take much for anyone to recognize her.

An old pair of sunglasses helped a bit, as did a tuque her mother had knit for her, but it was . . . not much of a costume.

That was okay. She didn't want to be in costume anyway. Getting a costume, a Mask persona, would mean admitting that she was part of the greater game of Heroes and Villains, while she knew full well that participating was the last thing she wanted to do.

Teddy, on the other hand, was a bit harder and easier to hide. With her big, oversized bear hoodie and a scarf around her face, the girl looked like a large brown marshmallow. The fact that she insisted on wearing her shorts meant that under the bundle of cloth from her hoodie were two thin little legs exposed to the air, ending in a pair of poorly tied hiking boots.

"Are you, uh, ready?" Emily asked.

"I'm always ready, Boss," Teddy said.

Emily smiled. At least Teddy's confidence was something she could maybe rely on. She extended a hand to the bear girl, who immediately grabbed hold of it. And then they were off.

The park the text directed her toward wasn't far. One side of it rubbed up against the college's campus, right next to where they had a few outdoor practice fields for soccer and such.

The sun was still up as she crossed the campus with Teddy, but it was definitely dipping down, and with it, the air turned just shy of cold. The people Emily crossed still in T-shirts looked to be regretting their choices, so she figured her overdressed state wasn't anything to comment about.

"When . . . when we see the people over at the park," Emily said. "We need to be careful not to, uh, make them know that we're . . . aligned the way we are, okay?"

Teddy nodded. "My name is already hidden," she said.

"Well, yes, but I mean, uh, don't go full bear unless things become dangerous. Even if Mister Handshake is . . . rude."

"Can I threaten him, at least?"

"I . . . suppose?"

Emily wondered if this was a side effect of her power. A few days ago, the thought of threatening someone would have horrified her. But now all she could think was that Handshake had brought this on himself by trying to extort her and by not minding his own business. Even the information he had given her wasn't worth all that much when Teddy knew more than he had provided.

They reached the edge of the park, and Emily realized that she didn't know where in the park she was meant to meet anyone. It was a rather large place, after all, with winding paths and a small patch of trees and bushes that had been trimmed and tended so that they weren't all that natural.

Stepping into the park, she paused, then set off down one of the winding cobbled paths snaking around the entire thing. She was only half an hour early, so there was a good chance that she'd get to meet Handshake as he entered. She didn't know how punctual a man he was.

It was while moving closer to the middle that Emily noticed a gazebo set up next to a little pond. The kind of scenic place that probably looked great on brochures about the city.

Someone was screaming from within the gazebo.

Perhaps not *screaming* screaming, she considered, but they were certainly talking at the sort of volume Emily would never dare speak at. A woman's shrill voice bled anger and . . . and Emily suspected that she was on the verge of tears.

She shared a look with Teddy. "M-maybe we can go around?" she asked.

"And check them out from over there," Teddy suggested as she pointed to a spot farther down. It was the kind of position where they'd be able to see into the gazebo without looking too suspicious about it.

Emily agreed wholeheartedly if it meant she could be spared having to talk to someone.

They moved around, occasionally peeking back to see what was going on in the gazebo. It was only when they were nearing the spot Teddy had indicated, lined up with the open front of the pavilion, that Emily could see what was happening within properly.

Her heart sank.

Handshake was there. He was dressed in far more casual clothes than he'd worn in the hidden area of the coffee shop, with one arm in a sling and both eyes obviously browned even though he wore a pair of shades to hide them. He even had a split lip.

Before him, bent over almost double with a hand on her hip, was a short woman with frizzy black hair. She had a finger hovering just before Handshake's face in a way that looked rather threatening.

Emily chewed on her lip as she wondered what she should do.

Unfortunately, Teddy came to the rescue. "Hey, lady. You gonna beat him up?"

The woman and Handshake both spun to look their way.

"It's okay," Teddy said. "He's a capitalist. They all want to steal your food and break your backs and stuff."

Emily pinched her eyes shut, wishing that she was back home being nagged by her mom about doing her chores or something equally mundane. Then she opened her eyes and faced the music. "I think that's enough, Teddy," she said softly. "Let's go see Mister Handshake, I guess."

The frizzy-haired woman stepped back from Handshake and looked between the girls and the man. "You know this moron?" she asked.

Emily swallowed, wilting and slowing down under the woman's steady gaze. "I . . . do," she said.

"What's the story?" the woman asked. Not to her, but to him.

He winced. "She . . . uh, is a new client. Very new."

"Like last week's Power Day new?" the woman asked.

"You know I don't divulge information about my clients so easily," he said.

The woman scoffed. "You keep clinging to those last tatters of professionalism, *Dave*, and we'll keep pretending that you're as competent as you'd like us to believe."

Emily squeezed Teddy's hand for reassurance and looked back toward the trees of the park. "I can . . . go, if you want?" she asked.

"No, stay," Handshake said. "She's . . . she's in the same situation as you."

Emily looked over to the woman and tried to see any signs that she was in any way special, but she couldn't spot anything obvious. If she had powers they were the more subtle sort. "Oh," she said at last.

"Dammit, Dave, she looks like she's a teen. And that one can't be older than fourteen." She pointed to Teddy.

Handshake shrugged, then winced as the motion moved his shoulder. "You know how it is. Trust me, my life would be easier if I'd never contacted her to begin with."

The woman scoffed. "Yeah. I'll bet. Want to fill her in on all the embarrassing details?"

Emily shifted. That was why she was here. Getting things out of the way sooner meant getting back home sooner.

"Yeah. God knows I'm going to have to explain this one a few more times. Do you have a phone that's on?" he asked Emily.

"Uh," Emily said.

"Yank the battery out," he said. "Or go drop it by the woods."

Emily stared at him.

"Look at her, you idiot," the woman said. "You can't just tell a girl to ditch her phone. Next you'll be telling her there are puppies in your white van."

"It's for security," he said.

"I will disappear your jewels," the woman argued right back.

Handshake blanched and looked over to Emily. "Never mind then. Look . . . what do you know about the Try Hard gang?"

"Um," Emily replied. "Nothing?"

He sighed. "Great. In that case, I'll have to start from the beginning."

"You can skip some of it," the woman added. "And since when do you hand out info for free?"

"Since the info dislocated my arm and punched three of my teeth in," he growled. "There are rules, and if those jackasses won't follow them, then they ought to suffer the consequences."

"So who messed you up?" Teddy asked.

Handshake shifted on his stone bench. "Let me tell you a bit about Homie and his crew."

CHAPTER SEVENTEEN

Homie and the Try Hards

Homie?" Emily asked.

She didn't mean for it to sound so surprised, but the word was just not one she'd associate with such a straitlaced-looking person as Handshake. He looked more likely to complain about anyone using the name than anything else.

The information broker nodded. "Yes. You might want to take a seat, I have a lot of information to deliver."

"You, um," Emily said with a look around, "you won't charge for it?"

"After what he did to me? No. The fact that he inadvertently put you at risk also means that he has waived any decent thoughts I might have had about him." Handshake rubbed at his stubble-covered cheeks with his uninjured hand. "It might make him want to come back at me if he learns, but I figure we're antagonistic enough at this point."

"Okay?" Emily tried. She scooted over to one of the wooden benches lining the edge of the gazebo and sat down. A moment later, Teddy hopped backward and plopped herself down next to her.

"Right," Handshake said. "Melanie, want to sit down too?" he asked.

The now-named Melanie shot him a glare, but stomped over to a bench halfway across from Emily's own, a spot that forced Handshake to turn ninety degrees to be able to face both of them.

"Thanks. So, Homie. Twenty-seven years old, male. Dropout from the local college. Gained his powers on Power Day last year while in his final year in the engineering program. Went from a nobody to . . . honestly, he's still a nobody. It's a minor miracle that he hasn't been locked up yet, but his rap sheet is pretty pathetic."

"He's a Villain?" Emily asked.

"He started with Dealer as a morality. Technically Gray, but as dark as Gray gets," Handshake said. "He's still around there now. His gang, the Try Hards, are a joke, on purpose."

"What do you mean 'on purpose'?" Teddy asked the question in the back of Emily's mind.

"They recruit from disillusioned college students, mostly well-off sorts who came in with a lot of mommy and daddy's money and no idea how to take care of themselves. They want to feel and look tough, and the Try Hards give them an opportunity to do that."

Melanie scoffed. "Their worst crimes on most days are things like painting shitty graffiti on walls and loitering. Sometimes there are noise complaints when they listen to music too loud. To be fair, it's shit music."

"They deal drugs, too," Handshake said.

Melanie's brows bunched together. "Hard?"

He shook his head in denial. "No. Soft stuff. Weed and a few party drugs. Legally gray."

Emily wondered what that meant. She knew that drugs like alcohol and marijuana were pretty dangerous but not illegal, and she knew there were worse drugs out there. If they weren't selling the really illegal stuff, then were they really doing something gray?

"They're directionless kids following some jumped-up idiot with powers," Melanie said.

"You'd think that," Handshake said, "but there's a method to their madness. This is the part that most people don't know. The Try Hards gang, if you even want to call it that, is part of a bigger group. One led by a Criminal who goes by the name Cement."

Melanie's face scrunched up in distaste. "That guy? I thought he did white-collar shit? The occasional protection racket."

"Homie is his top lieutenant," Handshake went on to explain. "The Try Hards are basically a kind of cover. They're also an arm of Cement's . . . organization. I don't like using the term, though; it's too strong. Cement has three or four knee breakers who work for him, but most of his income comes from nonphysical crimes. Blackmail, extortion, a bit of information selling. The kind of thing that the average Hero can't punch."

The woman sitting across from Emily shifted and glared harder, but she didn't say anything to that.

"That's, um, the man responsible for your . . ." Emily gestured at Handshake.

"That's probably it, yeah," he said. "I was snooping into his group. One of Homie's little pets got a power last week, and Cement seems to have moved a few things to hide someone, possibly another new Mask. He might have clued in that I was snooping on him. Or he just decided to take a bigger slice of the information-selling pie. Or maybe Homie's too big for his britches. I don't know."

"It doesn't matter, does it," Melanie said.

"No, not really. Homie has a drive with information on it that I think both of you would rather not get out into the public. And now you know."

"What . . . what are you doing about it?" Emily asked.

He shrugged his good shoulder. "Well, for one, I'm telling you two. You're the only Masks in the immediate area who are impacted the most."

"Dammit," Melanie growled. After hearing Teddy's growling, it didn't sound as scary as Emily would have thought. "Before anything else, give me the lowdown on their powers."

"Homie's powers are the stranger of the two. They're kind of hard to describe and can be rather esoteric. Also, he's been a Mask for over a year now, and even if he's Level One, he's been cultivating his power for a while."

"I know how it works," Melanie said.

He pointed to Emily and Teddy. "They don't."

The woman crossed her arms and leaned back in her seat. "Fair. Go on."

"So, Homie's power allows him to . . . permeate a room. The more time he spends in an area, the more he gets to know it. The location of items, where people and things are in relation to each other, and so on. It sounds weak, but then most powers that sound weak have a kick to them. His big advantage is that he learns how to use things in a room he's in. Spend time in a class and he'll learn from the books within. Spend time in a garage and he'll know how to . . . I don't know, change your oil? I don't think the effects are permanent."

"That's kind of impressive," Emily said.

"It gets worse," Handshake said. "If he stays in one place long enough, his control of the things there improves. He can set off lights, move things a little, operate machines, and so on. He has a few bolt-holes set up across the city for his use that he visits regularly to reinforce."

Melanie nodded. "Kind of esoteric, but I can see it being a pain in the ass to deal with. Is that all?"

"For him, yeah. His boss is a bit harder to pin down."

"Cement?" Melanie asked. "He controls cement. It's pretty simple."

Handshake shook his head. "He's Level Two. Cement control was his second power."

"Um," Emily said and immediately regretted it when their attention turned her way. "Sorry, but Level Two?"

"Each level a person gets unlocks an entirely new power," Melanie said. "But there's only one way to get a level, and that's by winning an Endgame."

Emily shuddered. "Oh. Right."

"Cement's first power isn't known. I can't even pin down which Endgame he was at. I can tell you that he only started moving in full after he got his cement control abilities. He tends to use them to cover himself in a foot or so of the stuff. It moves slow, but it's heavy, and his power lets it stay liquid."

"He's a bruiser. Able to take a beating and dish one out, but not able to move fast," Melanie said.

"Unless his first power was a movement ability, in which case your assumption could be dangerous," Handshake pointed out. "I suspect that his primary power is some sort of intelligence-gathering one. He's found blackmail material on some people who are incredibly secure about things. Or so I've heard."

"Something like your own power?" Melanie asked.

Handshake shook his head. "Mine's more about social interactions. Anyway. His name tells us a lot of nothing, his real identity is properly hidden, and his activities keep him in the shadows too. He's a proper Criminal, the sort that are kind of rare in this city."

"Criminals are rare?" Emily asked.

"They are here, love," Melanie said. "Us Hero types outnumber the bad guys three to one. It's not the place with the best ratio, especially not so soon after Power Day, but we're still far ahead of the curve."

"Oh, right." Emily felt a cold sweat breaking out on her back. Melanie was a Hero, then. A proper, bona fide Hero would break Emily apart the moment she learned what Emily's morality was set at.

"You okay?" Melanie asked.

Handshake sighed. "I was hoping to get you two working together," he said. "It would make you a whole lot more efficient out in the field."

"Ah, I'll . . . I'll see," Emily said. "What . . . what kind of things did you have about me on your . . . hard drive?"

"Just about everything I could learn about you," he said.

CHAPTER EIGHTEEN

Sisterportation

Emily had expected that getting home after heading out that late afternoon might . . . just not happen. She'd been worried about ambushes and potentially running into Heroes waiting to grab her and Teddy. Worse would have been running into Villains. The common media portrayal of what Villains were, of what they did, was . . . not pleasant.

She and Teddy were, of course, the exception.

A flick of her phone next to her dorm room door unlocked it, and Teddy squeezed past her and into the room.

Emily followed, pausing to take in the room. There were still some unpacked boxes stacked off to one side. They would have taken up a lot of room if she had any proper furniture other than her bed, her desk, her favorite chair, and a blow-up mattress sticking halfway out from under the bed.

Teddy was quick to slither out of her hoodie and crash onto the mattress the moment it was tugged out.

"Going to sleep already?" Emily asked.

It didn't take a genius to see that Teddy, even in her human form, had some bear in her. Including a love for sleeping long hours.

"Nah," Teddy said as she rooted around under Emily's bed and pulled out some bear-paw-covered pj's and a little red book. "Gonna read a bit, then I'm going to sleep."

"Oh, okay," Emily said.

She didn't have any homework to do or anything of the sort. She could have gone to sleep herself, but a glance at her phone showed that it was still only six. Far too early. And while she was mentally exhausted and her social batteries were utterly depleted, she was physically still full of energy.

Pacing didn't feel right, though, so Emily walked over to her bed, picked up a small blanket she'd bought at the thrift store, then curled up on her chair with the cover over her entire body, like a warm, little, depressed cocoon.

"What are we going to do?" Emily asked. She had two numbers on her phone now. Handshake's, and that Melanie woman's. The former had told her to call if she needed more information on . . . anything, really. The latter had told her to give her a heads-up if she planned on doing anything about Homie.

"I don't know," Teddy said as she rolled onto her back with her book held above her. "We could beat that Homie guy up and take the drive things back."

"Do you think we could actually do that?" Emily asked.

She truly doubted they'd be able to pull it off.

"Can't think of anything else," Teddy said. "What will happen if they, uh, open the drive things?"

"Then our lives are ruined," Emily said. Cement was supposed to be dangerous with blackmail and such. He could use what little information Handshake had gathered on her to make her work for him. Or maybe do worse things. Emily couldn't imagine what kind of things, but she was certain they were horrid.

"Yeah, in that case, I say we fight them."

Emily buried herself deeper into her chair. Could she?

"I think . . ." she began at last, "that we could maybe, um, try to take the drive back instead? Without having to, uh, fight?"

"Okay," Teddy said.

"You're okay with that idea?" Emily asked.

Teddy nodded and turned a page in her book. "Yeah, of course, Boss. It's your idea, yeah?"

Emily nodded slowly. It was that. "We'll need to be a bit stronger, I think," she said.

Teddy perked up. "Are we going to spend some points?" she asked. "I don't have any skills to spend my points on, though."

"Ah," Emily said. "You don't?"

"Nope. Just my base skill. I've got two upgrade points, but nothing to use them on," Teddy said. "Can't wait to do something so incredible that I get a new trait for my bear power. I bet it will be something amazing. Like a nose able to smell capitalism or something."

"Uh," Emily added. "That sounds . . . nice." She cleared her throat. "Status."

Name: Emily Wright	
Alignment: Villain	
Alias: The Boss	
Level: 1	
Powers	
Sister Summoning	
Create Sister	Rank 1
Points	
Power Slots: 0	Skill Upgrades: 3 Skill Slots: 1

She had the one point she could spend to unlock a secondary power . . . skill thing. And seeing as how she might need it soon . . .

Do you wish to spend a Skill Slot point on the Power: Sister Summoning?

"Yes," Emily said.

New Skill unlocked!

Sisterportation has been added to your Power's Skills!

Emily didn't feel any different when the notifications left. Then again, gaining the power at first hadn't felt strange either. "Status."

Name: Emily Wright	
Alignment: Villain	
Alias: The Boss	
Level: 1	
Powers	
Sister Summoning	
Create Sister	Rank 2
Sisterportation	Level 1
Points	
Power Slots: 0	Skill Upgrades: 3 Skill Slots: 0

That was a little different. Her Create Sister skill had ranked up and she now had a new skill . . . or maybe a trait beneath that. And the point she'd spent was now gone. "There's a way to see what a skill does, right?" she asked Teddy. She vaguely recalled doing that for her own skills once.

"Yeah," Teddy said. "Just say 'status,' then the name of the skill."

"Status . . . Sisterportation."

Her opened status screen shifted over to the side and a new box appeared before her.

Sisterportation
Sister Summoning
Level 1
Allows you to teleport a sister from anywhere in the world to your side. Instant use.
Activation: Voice command
Cooldown: Twelve hours
Max Sisters: One

"Huh," Emily said as she finished reading the description. "What does voice command mean?"

"Means you need to say something to make it work," Teddy said. She'd rolled back onto her belly to read, her chin resting on a pillow and her arms outstretched before her.

"Something like . . . Sisterportation: Teddy?"

Teddy disappeared from her spot on the mattress and reappeared right next to Emily . . . still in the same pose and three feet in the air.

The girl had time to go "Huh?" before crashing belly-first on the ground with a dull thump.

Emily scrambled off her seat, eyes wide and arms questing for something to do as she took in her summon's sprawled-out form. "Are you all right?" she asked.

"Boss, that hurt!" Teddy whined.

"I'm so sorry!" Emily said.

Teddy rolled around so that the full force of her pout could hit Emily dead-on. "My tummy squished," she said.

Emily looked the girl up and down, but nothing past her pride looked hurt. "I'm really sorry. I won't do that again."

Teddy sighed and rolled again, then again until she was back over by her mattress. "At least tell me before you do that. What if I was in the middle of sleeping? Or pooping."

Emily felt her cheeks warming at the thought and decided to save the new skill for emergencies. Not that it would come in handy all that often in other situations, she figured. "That was my only Skill Slot point," she said, changing the subject. "The rest of my points are all normal Skill Upgrades, and I'm not sure if I want to make this one better. It seems . . . good enough."

"Does it have restrictions on it?" Teddy asked as she resettled.

"Um. It has a twelve-hour cooldown and can only summon one sister at a time? Those don't seem that bad."

Teddy shrugged, a strange gesture when lying down. "The Skill Upgrades will probably just make that shorter or increase the number of sisters before doing anything fun."

"Is there a limit to the number of levels?" Emily asked. She was curious as to how many times she could upgrade the new skill.

"Depends on the skill," Teddy said. "Are we going to sleep tonight?"

"I guess," Emily said. A glance at her phone for the time showed it at just past seven. Still a little early. "I still have a lot of thinking to do."

"Yeah, I guess that's a Boss job," Teddy agreed. "You going to find a costume or something? If I get one, I want it to be red. And have bears on it."

"A costume," Emily repeated. She wasn't keen on the idea. Then again, she was less keen on the idea of succeeding against someone like Homie only for her identity to be leaked because someone saw and identified her. "We're going to need to find something," she said. "I don't even know where to start."

"Doesn't need to be complicated," Teddy said. "Maybe you can ask your other minion? He's supposed to be lucky, right?"

"Alea Iacta?" Emily asked. "Why would I try calling him? I don't even have his number."

"Doesn't the internet have people's numbers? And you could try calling him because he had a great costume. It was all fancy-like."

Emily rolled the idea around. "I'll think on it," she said. She had other things to look forward to. Class in the morning and then . . . and then maybe starting to act in the afternoon. She didn't have forever to wait until Homie started rooting around that drive.

She sighed. Her life had been simple, once.

CHAPTER NINETEEN

Teddy's Adventure in Costume-Finding

Teddy woke up from a nice restful sleep to the sound of the Boss's sock-clad feet thumping around. She peeked out of one eye and followed the Boss around with her gaze as the older girl moved around the room and packed a few things away in her backpack.

"Boss?" Teddy asked.

Emily paused, turning toward Teddy so fast that the towel wrapped in a big bun over her head swayed wildly. "Teddy? You're awake?"

Teddy shrugged. She hadn't decided on that yet. "What're you doing, Boss?"

"I'm getting ready for class. I have a history lecture this morning." The Boss gestured to some books, which were different from the books she usually carried around in her backpack. "I have another class right after. I should be back by about one?"

Teddy nodded and started to rebury herself, when the guilt of not helping started to gnaw at her. "Need help?"

"I'm okay," the Boss said. "Thanks."

"All right," Teddy said.

"And I don't think you'd be the best suited to help me with other things," the Boss muttered.

Teddy's ears twitched at that. "What other things?"

Emily froze, her face taking on a weird shade of red. Was she angry that Teddy had asked? "Ah. I meant stuff like the Homie thing. And finding a costume and . . . all that."

"Oh. Villain stuff," Teddy said.

"Yeah, that."

Teddy nestled back into her mattress and vaguely paid attention to the way the Boss was moving about in a hurry. Was the Boss late? That was unlikely. She probably wanted to arrive early to check the place out for any capitalist or Heroic traps.

"I'm off," the Boss said.

"Okay, Boss. Have fun," Teddy said with only one big yawn in the middle.

The door opened, the door shut, and the Boss was gone. Teddy also left as she sank back into a deep sleep.

Teddy awoke some time later, a bit of niggling worry working its way around her tummy unpleasantly. What had the Boss meant when she said that Teddy couldn't help her with her stuff? Did she mean that Teddy wasn't suited to being a Villain?

That was just wrong. Teddy was a perfectly good Villain!

With an irate huff, Teddy tossed her blankets off and stood on the wobbly surface of her mattress. Her bear-paw-print pj's were a bit of a frumpled mess, even though Teddy didn't move much in her sleep, and her hair was plastered all over.

First things first, she had to put on a good front. That's why she reluctantly went to the bathroom and showered, then changed into her everyday clothes. Cargo shorts, a cool T-shirt with the word *Bear* on it, and her hoodie decorated with an awesome image of a grizzly bear roaring on the front.

Now dressed to intimidate, Teddy moved over to the door and paused just before leaving.

She had people to find.

First, the Boss needed more information on that Homie wannabe, the guy who acted like he was some sort of Villain while only being a mere Dealer. Teddy already didn't have much respect for him, what with his lukewarm level of Villain and his weird name and the fact that he'd inconvenienced the Boss.

Finding him would be tricky, though, especially since the city was pretty big and she was only the one bear girl.

If only the Boss had more minions . . .

Teddy turned back into the dorm and rushed over to the Boss's laptop. Opening it up and typing in the password: Kitt3nsRb3st (which Teddy had seen the Boss typing in the other day, much to her horror; it was proof that the Boss had given in to the consumerist propaganda about the so-called glories of the feline as opposed to the far superior bear).

She paused when she found the search engine browser thing. Her first search "Where is alley lactate?" didn't help any, especially since autocorrect was trying to push some sort of milk-based conspiracy at her.

Her subsequent searches didn't help all that much until she landed on one in particular. A thread called "I'm Alea Iacta, Eauclaire's newest ne'er-do-well. AMA!"

Clicking on that showed her an entire thread of people mocking Alea Iacta, which while kind of funny, was also a bit rude. He was one of the Boss's minions after all.

It was only after searching through the entire thing that she noticed an interesting exchange.

User/Material-Sword
9 points Two days ago
> So Alea Iacta, you got any hobbies other than being a so-called ne'er-do-well? You know, something you could do that wouldn't be wasting everyone's time?
1 Reply:
> **User/Alea_Iacta_bEst**
> *−13 points Two days ago*
> Why yes, good sir! I happen to have a penchant for the theatrical!

The rest of that comment thread was all about making him look like an idiot, which Teddy thought was quite amusing. That one hint stuck with her though.

She pulled up the school's site, one that was saved in the Boss's favorites, then looked for a theater club of one sort or another.

"Found you!" she said.

There was a group that met on campus to do plays and such for free in the park. They practiced at one of the old school buildings.

Teddy noted the number on a piece of loose-leaf paper, tongue pinched between her canines as she made sure to write down all the numbers the right way.

Folding her note away, she stuffed it in one of her pockets, placed the computer on a page with nice pictures of bears so that it would be the first thing the Boss saw on opening up the computer, and then she scampered off toward the door.

She had a minion to track down.

Now a bunch more confident in her chances, Teddy left the dorm and headed down to the first floor. From there, it was out the door and down the street.

Teddy had no idea how the numbers on the old buildings worked, but that was okay because she found someone who could help. There were two someones, actually, a pair of people wearing nice red shirts and waving signs around so fast that Teddy couldn't read them.

They were chanting, though, and that was clear enough. "Down with the pigs! Down with the privatization of our futures!" one girl was screaming.

Teddy moved over to the woman and, when she didn't notice her, tugged at her jacket.

The screaming stopped as the woman looked down. "Hello, comrade," Teddy said. "I was wondering if you could give me directions?" She pulled out her note and showed it to the still-blinking girl.

"Uh. Sure?"

"Thank you. This is part of a mission to take out a filthy drug-peddling capitalist," Teddy said. She tried to remember the big points from her book. "He's a horrid person who sells drugs and doesn't share the profits with everyone."

Teddy got some good instructions, then with a final farewell and a pat on the back to her comrade, she was off and heading toward a building apparently known as the Old Theatre.

As it turned out, the building in question was a huge edifice with statue-decorated stonework all across its front and a billboard next to its entrance with a timetable on it. Teddy eyed that, looking past all the entries about band practices and debate clubs so that she could spot those about the theater club.

Unfortunately, she didn't know the time or the date, so that didn't help any.

With a shrug, Teddy yanked the doors open and stepped into a lobby lit only by the sunlight poking through the windows by the front. It was a clean place, but it smelled old, like polished wood and floor wax.

The lobby was divided up with a booth by the front, presumably for ticketing, and some passages off to the side to get to the bathrooms and such.

Teddy shrugged again and walked past the unmanned ticket booth and into a large hall where a few dozen rows of seats laid out in big arcs descended down to the base of a raised stage. The curtains were drawn up to the sides, revealing a platform with some discarded props lit from above by a gantry of pale lights.

There was a distinct lack of anyone around, but that didn't deter Teddy, especially not when she heard someone talking from the back of the stage.

She got to the edge, looked for a way up, and when she didn't find one, she grabbed the edge and pulled herself high enough to fling a leg over and roll up onto the stage.

"Jacob, you can't keep doing this," someone was saying. A guy's voice, deep and serious.

Someone chuckled in response. "Hey, you know how it is. The show must go on!"

Teddy grinned. She recognized the voice.

The Boss would be so proud of her once she rallied her fellow minion into helping!

CHAPTER TWENTY

Backstage Bear

Teddy swished a curtain aside and stepped backstage.

The area wasn't what she expected from the rear of a theater. There were big closets on wheels, and dozens of thick ropes coiled on the ground, reaching up to a bunch of pulleys mounted to the ceiling.

The floor went from a nice polished hardwood on one side of the curtains to rough plywood covered in colored tape on the other. Even the air smelled different; from clean and dull to the mixed odor of too-full trash cans and popcorn.

In the middle of all that were two guys. One was a tall, well-muscled Black guy and the other a reedy pale person who Teddy immediately labeled as Alea Iacta out of costume. They both paused to stare at Teddy.

"You don't need to stop arguing because of me," she said. "I can wait."

"Who are you?" the not–Alea Iacta guy asked.

"I'm . . ." Teddy stopped herself from saying any more. The Boss had been going on about secret identities for a while. "I'm Not-A-Bear-Girl."

"Oh, shit," Alea Iacta said. He took a long step back and away from Teddy, only for her to freeze him on the spot with a glare.

"You know this kid?" the guy asked.

"Yeah," Alea Iacta said. "I mean . . . no."

Alea's friend shook his head. "Kid, how did you get in here?"

"Through the curtains," Teddy replied.

"No, I mean in this building."

"Oh," she said. "I asked directions from some communist comrades."

Alea stepped up and tried a smile on. It was a weird-looking one, though, all nervous and uncertain. The Boss smiled like that sometimes too. "Are you, uh, here for me?" he asked.

"Yeah. The Bo— person we work for needs help," Teddy said very stealthily.

Alea's friend looked between the two of them, then with a grunt, he jammed a finger against Alea's shoulder. "You get your crap together, Jacob. Take whatever this is outside. In fact, you can stay outside while you're at it."

"Yeah, yeah, don't worry," Alea Iacta said. "I'm doing better, you'll see."

"Uh-huh," the big guy said. He turned to Teddy and looked her up and down. "You trust this idiot?" he asked.

"Not really," Teddy said. "But I can kick his butt if he tries anything."

He nodded. "Good. If he does do anything, you tell me and I'll pop his head right off his stupid shoulders, you got that?"

"Yeah, okay," Teddy said. "But I can do that myself."

He snorted and moved off toward the back of the room. "I've got my eye on you, Jacob."

Alea Iacta, whose real name Teddy presumed was Jacob, swallowed, looked to her, then swallowed even harder. "We need to talk," she said. "The Boss needs you for stuff."

"Ah, what kind of stuff?" he asked. "Because I have a life, you know. Things to do, people to see and all that."

"None of that matters," Teddy said. "The Boss is gonna be beating up some Dealer guy 'cause he stole something that kinda belongs to the Boss. Now the Boss needs a costume to beat him up in, and she needs cannon fodder."

"I could maybe help with the costume?" he said.

"You could help with both," Teddy assured him. "But I think the costume is more important for now. The Boss will need to move soonish."

Alea licked his lips and looked around the room for a bit. "Look, I don't know why you think I can help that much. I did my part to pay your . . . Boss back for what I did. That was it."

Teddy didn't like where the conversation was going. Alea Iacta seemed to be backing out of the deal he made with the Boss and that just wasn't cool. But Teddy was a clever girl, and she knew about the carrot and the stick.

"You can't just back out from helping the Boss," Teddy said.

Alea Iacta puffed his chest out and made himself bigger. He looked like someone shoring up all his bravery.

"Because if you don't help the Boss," Teddy continued, "I'll eat you."

If someone hit you with a stick, you ate them, and if they hit you with a carrot, you ate them and then the carrot.

Alea's bravery puffed out of him like a particularly squeaky fart. "I . . . I'll show you to the costume room," he said.

Grinning, Teddy followed him as he scurried off the one side of the stage and toward a corridor that jutted out of the back area. There were a few rooms with plaques over their doors telling people what was inside. It wasn't a particularly nice corridor, with pipes running along the ceiling and light coming from the sort of fluorescent bulbs that flickered just enough to bug Teddy's eyes.

"Here," Alea Iacta said as he gestured to a door marked "Costumes." It was between "Makeup" and "Men's" in the corridor.

"This is where the cool costumes are?" Teddy asked.

Alea Iacta nodded along. "Yeah. It's where I . . . borrowed mine. I figured if I was going to go test my luck, I might as well do it in style, you know?"

"Yeah, that makes sense," Teddy agreed.

Alea fiddled with the handle and it clunked open, then there was more fiddling as he searched for the lights against the walls inside. When they came on, it was to illuminate a room filled to the brim with all sorts of clothes on hangers and racks that ran against most of the walls. The far wall had a couple of stalls that Teddy guessed were for changing, like those at the thrift store.

"Do you have any idea how much trouble we could be in if we're caught?" Alea asked.

"No," Teddy said. "But the Boss needs a costume, so it doesn't matter."

"Might not matter to you, sure," he said. "But I'm in a heap of crap if people find out. Just . . . don't pick anything too ostentatious, all right? They might notice if something like that goes missing."

Teddy didn't know what that word meant, so she nodded and started looking over the costumes. Most of them were easy to dismiss right away. They were all old-looking, and while that was okay for Alea Iacta's own costume, it would probably look a bit silly on the Boss.

"Do you know what you're looking for?" Alea Iacta asked as he stood in the middle of the room with his arms crossed. "'Cause I do have things I want to get done today."

"Important things?" Teddy asked.

"I do have a job, you know," he said.

She looked over at him, his hands currently stroking the soft velvetness of a big ball gown. "Someone hired you?" she asked.

He huffed and looked away from her. "I'm hirable," he said.

"Did you use your luck powers to find a job?" she asked.

"You're too nosy for such a little brat," he said. "Now, what are you looking for?"

"I don't know," she said. "Something that will make the Boss look cool and intimidating and scary. Do you have any bear costumes?"

"Look, I won't pretend to know your Boss all that well, but the only bear costume we have looks like a mascot thing and . . . yeah, no, I can't imagine any girl wanting to look like that." He moved over and past Teddy, then kicked open a trunk. "Last year we did the *Greater Gatsby*. It was like the *Great Gatsby*, but if he had powers and . . . yeah, never mind."

Teddy moved over and peered into a truck full of folded cloth. Most of the costumes were simple and black, though some had very sparkly fabric.

Alea pulled out a very small dress, the kind that Teddy figured would only cover the Boss to midthigh. "Something like this, maybe?" he asked.

Teddy imagined the Boss wearing something like that, then dismissed the idea. The Boss liked wearing clothes that covered her more from what she'd seen. Looking back down, Teddy saw a mask sitting next to a fedora. It was made of a material that matched a loose suit beneath. "What's this?" she asked as she lifted both up.

"Uh," he said. "That's Baker's Hero costume. The writers shoved this whole side plot in with her and . . . yeah, never mind, it was kinda trashy."

Teddy held the costume up. It had straight-cut pants and a black vest. The Boss probably had a blouse that could fit under it all, and if it was a little loose on her, that was okay.

"Yeah, this will do," Teddy said.

"Really?" Alea Iacta asked. "I mean . . . yeah, great. Here, shove it in this." He reached over one of the racks and pulled out a bag, then he dumped its contents on the ground and pushed them to the side. A bunch of folded-up rain boots clattered to the floor.

Teddy shoved everything in the bag, then turned and pointed to a big jacket by the back. "And that too."

Alea looked up, then his face went strange. "That's a pimp jacket," he said.

"Is a pimp a kind of big predator?" Teddy asked. The jacket was very furry, after all. Though she didn't think there were that many purple animals out there.

"Uh . . . yeah, sure."

"Cool," she said. "I can use that for my costume."

Alea Iacta opened and closed his mouth a few times. "You know what, sure. You just talk to your Boss about it first." He took the jacket off the hanger, grabbed a big matching hat from above it, and shoved them into her bag.

In the end, the bag was full to bursting, with a sleeve trailing out behind it, but it all more or less fit.

"Okay," Alea Iacta said. "You're all geared up. Now please leave and never return."

CHAPTER TWENTY-ONE

Costuming Up

Emily walked into her dorm that afternoon with the same energy some people would arrive with at a resort or a fancy hotel. It was the joy of finally being away from too many people, and finally being able to enjoy the privacy of her own solitude.

"Oh, hey, Boss, you're back."

Emily sighed as she slipped in and closed the door behind her. Almost solitary.

Teddy was sitting on her bed, legs crossed and back against the wall while Emily's laptop sat open before her with its charging wire extended across the room, using Emily's chair as a suspension point so that it could reach all the way.

A deep Ritish voice was coming from the laptop. "The most ferocious predator of the northern Rockies of Anada, the grizzly is a predator with a surprising soft spot."

"You're watching a documentary?" Emily asked.

"Yeah," Teddy said.

"The male bear, when his mate seems interested, will mount—"

The laptop clacked shut. Teddy kept staring past where the screen had been.

"How was your day?" Teddy asked as she unfroze.

Emily eyed her suspiciously, especially the red tint on the girl's cheeks. "It was okay," she said. "Classes were a little boring, and the professor handed out a bit of homework due next week."

"That's cool," Teddy said.

"Have you been here watching . . . nature documentaries all day?" Emily asked. She didn't know if she really wanted an answer to that.

Teddy shook her head, then burst out from her pile of blankets. "I got you a costume, Boss."

Emily's mind took a moment to shut down, download some updates, then reboot. "You what?" she said at last.

By then Teddy had rushed across the room and come back with a pile of clothes squished between grubby hands. "Here, Boss."

Emily took the clothes, then set them on the bed as she took off her backpack and tossed off her shoes. Unfolding the costume revealed a black outfit that looked like a suit at first, but the pinstripes on the pants and the little vest screamed "1920s gangster." The suspenders and the little tie that matched them didn't help any.

And the fedora that Teddy plopped next to the costume quashed any hopes that it was something else.

"There's a mask, too," Teddy said as she reached into a pocket and pulled out a large black domino mask.

Emily looked at the clothes, then at Teddy. "Where did you get all this?" she asked. She didn't want to ask. She was terrified that the answer would be *I mugged it*. It was the kind of question where the answer might be a knock on her door as a pair of cops came over to ask some pointed questions.

"I found Alea Iacta," Teddy said.

Emily rebooted her mind again; clearly the first time hadn't been enough. "What do you mean you found him? How?" Had the Villain visited their dorm?

"I used the internet."

"He has his address online?" she asked.

Teddy shook her head. "Nah. See, I found out he's a theater guy, so I went to the theater and then got him to give us some costumes."

"Just . . . like that?"

Teddy frowned and looked off to the ceiling as she thought. "I had some help from some comrades."

Emily pressed her face into her hands. "Did you hide your identity? Wait, how did you get back into the room?"

"I asked comrade janitor," Teddy said. "And Alea Iacta didn't hide his identity. His name's Jacob. He looks kinda wimpy out of costume. Wimpier."

Emily gestured to the costume. "And you think this is . . . appropriate as a costume for me?"

Teddy blinked then looked at the costume. "Yeah. It's a Boss costume, and you're the Boss."

"I . . . I guess," Emily said. She didn't feel bosslike, but Teddy kept saying it, and it was her name, at least according to her status page. Maybe she should play it up. When she thought costume, the first thing that came to mind was the skimpy short-skirted outfits with boob windows that Heroes had worn during the seventies when Heroism became a big deal.

Emily could safely say that she wouldn't be caught dead wearing something like that.

The other option, the one she found a lot more acceptable, was the heavy armor worn by some of the more intimidating Heroes. But that sort of stuff probably cost a whole lot, and she suspected that buying that kind of equipment would put her on a list.

"Aren't we heading out in a bit?" Teddy asked.

Emily shifted. She hadn't made any sort of concrete plans for the evening yet. She knew that she had to do something about Homie, and sooner rather than later, but acting, actually going out and doing something was . . . It wasn't in her nature, especially not something that might be violent.

But then, if she didn't act, wasn't her future just as ruined as if she did?

"Yeah," she said. "I mean . . . yes. We're going to call Melanie and . . . and then we'll see."

"Cool," Teddy said. "I've got my own costume. I can get changed in the bathroom while you change here."

Emily hesitated, then nodded. Teddy was surprisingly kind about Emily's reservations about personal space. She watched the girl take a big bag with something purple in it into the bathroom.

She made sure the door was locked, then got dressed in a hurry. The costume fit almost as if it was tailored for her. She had to wiggle a little to get into the pants, but no more than when wearing some well-fitted jeans, and while the vest squeezed a bit, it wasn't in a bad way.

Emily stared down at herself and hesitated. How had Teddy found something that fit so well? Or was it Alea Iacta? Her cheeks warmed. Had he figured out what would fit just from looking at her? The most likely answer was that his power had kicked in and found something that just fit.

She slid the fedora on and then hesitated before putting on the mask.

The bathroom door slid open and something purple walked out.

Emily didn't know what to make of Teddy's costume. It was . . . it was a pimp outfit.

The girl had found a cute yellow summer dress that Emily recognized from their purchases at the thrift store, but she was wearing it over a pair of cargo shorts. That much was bizarre but acceptable.

The huge, fuzzy purple jacket and the hat with a brim that was half Teddy's height in diameter was . . .

"What are you wearing?" Emily asked.

"My costume," Teddy said. "It's a pimp outfit."

"I noticed," Emily said. "Do you . . . know what a pimp is?"

Teddy nodded, the huge brim flip-flopping like mad. "Yeah, it's a kind of big predator."

Emily felt her nose scrunching up against the inside of her mask. "I don't . . . I mean, technically. But I don't think that it's very appropriate."

"I mean, it's not brown," Teddy said. "But it's not that bad, is it?"

"It's . . . I think you'd look a lot better without the coat," Emily said.

Teddy shrugged out of the jacket. "All right. Can I keep the hat?"

"I . . . maybe the hat should stay too? We can find you a much nicer hat, I'm sure. Maybe a mask as well?" She was certain they could find a nice mask at the Dolla 'n' Mor' store. There were always masks for sale there, cheap knockoffs of Hero merchandise.

"Cool," Teddy said. "So we're going out like this?"

Emily looked down at herself, worked through the obvious consequences of stepping out of her dorm in the costume she'd be wearing while maybe committing a crime, and then decided that she really wasn't made for the whole Heroics and Villainy thing. As if it hadn't been obvious enough already.

"Okay. I think you can wear your hoodie over your dress. It'll hide your ears, too. And we can bring a backpack to put everything in. I'll . . . have to change out of all this. Can you give me a minute?"

"Yeah. I'll be in the bathroom again. Tell me when you're done, Boss."

Emily changed back into her normal school clothes, then tossed the costume into her backpack after emptying it. "I'm done!" she called out to Teddy while looking for her phone.

She had a call to make, and then, after that, they would be off to get themselves into a whole heap of trouble.

She was not looking forward to it in the least.

CHAPTER TWENTY-TWO

Plastic Bear Masks

E-Wright: Hello?
Mel: Yeah?
E-Wright: It's Emily. We met yesterday? I thought we could meet again?
Mel: Good timing.
Mel: There's a café on Main and Sixth. I'll be behind it.
E-Wright: Okay. Thank you. I'll see you soon.

Emily slid her phone into the pocket of her jacket and took a deep breath. The air outside was quite a bit cooler than inside, and not nearly as stuffy, though there was the dubious bonus of smelling like . . . well, like air in a city did.

"Where are we heading to, Boss?" Teddy asked. She had a hand in Emily's and was looking about with big motions of her head, mostly because her hoodie was cutting off her line of sight.

"Main," Emily said. "We'll have to take the bus."

"All right. I've never been on a bus before."

Emily smiled down at Teddy. It had only been a couple of days, but she'd kind of gotten used to the little summon being around. She still liked her privacy, and talking—even to Teddy—was a bit exhausting, but it was growing to be like . . . like talking to her mom or dad. Easier than with others.

She wondered as she started to make her way toward the nearest bus stop if that was just her getting used to Teddy, or if the power she had over the bear girl had anything to do with it.

Her new position of dominance seemed to ease her into liking Teddy as much as she did. Emily had never had power over people before. It was amusing.

She shook her head and banished the thought. It wasn't a very nice, or very Heroic, way of thinking. Power over others was just a disguise for responsibility. Teddy might have been her summon, and that might have meant that Teddy listened to her, but it also meant that Teddy's welfare was Emily's responsibility.

They arrived at the bus stop and sat down on the least sticky part of the bench while Emily fished out her phone and looked up the timetables for the city buses. They ran on a half-hour rotation across part of the city all day, but that schedule only worked as long as they didn't run into construction or roadblocks, and there were both of those everywhere all the time.

"You okay, Boss?" Teddy asked. She was looking at Emily with obvious concern.

Emily shifted her backpack a bit. "I'm fine?" she said.

"All right," Teddy replied. She didn't sound so sure of it, but she didn't look ready to push either.

The truth, Emily considered as she boarded the bus when it came around and stopped before them, was that she wasn't all that fine. Her hands would have been trembling a little if one of them weren't in Teddy's firm and somehow reassuring grip, and she had the impression that her insides were twisting about.

She had never dealt all that well with uncertainty. In fact, it was quite the opposite.

Now she was heading out to . . . do something. No plan, no idea, no expectation of what would go down.

She kept having to suppress her own imagination as it came up with increasingly dire predictions on what would happen to her, or of what she would have to do.

"It'll be fine," Teddy said a few moments later when they were both seated at the back of the bus where it was quieter.

Emily had paid for a pair of tickets in cash. Cash that they'd gotten from Alea Iacta and that she had counted out to nearly four hundred dollars in loose bills. Not an enormous amount, but enough to keep her afloat for a month or so. Teddy wasn't exactly expensive, but it did mean having to buy a bit more food.

Maybe if they did more volunteer work, they could skip having to buy a few more meals, and she could grab more free lunches.

Clothes would be a problem eventually, but those could be bought bit by bit over time.

So all that was left was finding a way to get Teddy into some sort of school.

Emily figured that that wouldn't be possible without some sort of bureaucratic help. That meant registering Teddy as . . . a citizen? Was that something that was doable? Emily didn't know the first thing about that.

If she approached one of the big Heroic organizations and revealed that Teddy was a summon, Emily was sure that they'd have some sort of precedent on the matter. She couldn't remember any Heroes with human-like summons, but there had been some with strange creatures before, and one notable Anti-Hero called the Stray Cat who had a flock of cats as part of her power.

All that was contingent on Emily being able to slide into a more Heroic disposition in a short enough time that it didn't look suspicious.

That, or she could wait until next year and pretend she'd gotten her powers then?

That didn't seem likely to work at all.

Emily was so deep in thought that she almost missed their stop and had to squeak out an apology to the bus driver just as he was about to shut the door and move on.

Stepping out onto a broad commercial street, Emily took a moment to reorientate herself, then started walking down the avenue.

There were a lot more people here, with shoppers and people look-ing through windows, and even the occasional mascot calling out for attention. A lot of the posters she saw called people's attention toward the reveal of new Heroes coming soon. That meant that there would be new merchandise hitting the shelves in a few weeks.

New merchandise meant new books and films and toys and cartoons for the kids. New Heroes tended to hog the spotlight for the month or two after Power Day, but they faded out for old favorites soon after.

Emily wasn't any more versed in the marketing side of things than that.

Some searching found a little dollar store that she pulled Teddy into. Emily always felt weird entering that kind of place with a backpack on, like she was there to rob the place even though she'd never had that kind of intention before.

A quick dip into the children's section at the back found an entire wall covered in Hero stuff, from knockoff gadgets and toys to generic costumes and—as she was hoping—masks.

The masks they had weren't anything special, just overlarge plastic domino masks and full-faced ones made to look like some popular Heroes. She recognized Silver Fox's visor, Melaton's sharp red faceplate, Wi-Fire's strange angular mask, and a few others besides.

"Look, a bear!" Teddy said. She was arm-deep in a rack filled with the more generic sort of mask.

"Can-can I see?" Emily asked.

Teddy nodded along and let go of her hand to better pull out the mask she'd found.

It was a big cartoonish bear face, done in browns and blacks with paint that had run a bit on the edges. Teddy pressed it to her face and looked up at Emily. "How do I look, Boss?"

"Intimidating," Emily lied.

"Cool. We should get this one."

She nodded along, then picked a few plain cloth domino masks, too. Then, because she was there, she went around and bought a few other things she kinda needed for the dorm. Mostly more utensils and some sealable containers that would inevitably find their way into the trash.

Emily didn't want to arrive at the counter with nothing but masks; that would have been far too suspicious.

Once everything was paid for, they left the store and shoved everything into Emily's backpack a few feet away from the entrance and off to the side where they wouldn't be in the way of the passing crowds.

"Okay," Emily said. "That's all we need for that. Now, um . . ."

"Now what, Boss?" Teddy asked.

"Now, I suppose we go find Melanie and see what we can do about . . . that man."

"You mean Homie?" Teddy asked.

Emily sighed and nodded. "I was trying not to say his name," she said.

"Oh," Teddy said as the realization hit. "You were being all sneakylike. I can do that, too, sometimes. Bears are real stealthy predators. That's why nothing attacks a bear. Because we're sneaky and we'd eat anything that'd try."

"I'm certain," Emily said. She reached her hand out and it was almost instantly grabbed by Teddy. "Come on. I guess we should get this over with."

CHAPTER TWENTY-THREE

Melaton

A little bit later and they were on the corner of Main and Sixth, a rather busy street with tight roads that probably predated the idea of cars and was rather cramped. A little terraced café sat on the corner, as Melanie had told her.

"This it, Boss?" Teddy asked as she eyed the café.

"We're supposed to go behind it," Emily said. "I think, um, maybe this way?"

A bit of exploring later and she found a tight little alleyway that led toward the back of the café. This was the second time she'd gone into an alley in a week—probably in the last few *years*, in fact.

The shadows cast by the buildings above them turned the already chill air much colder, and the stench of old leftovers warred with the buzz of flies, making the area rather unpleasant. Emily wondered what the people who'd seen them go into the alley thought they were doing.

"Hey, kids."

Emily gasped while Teddy spun around and moved to place herself between Emily and the voice.

There was another alley nearby, a sort of T-junction in the passages lit only by a rusty old light hanging off the wall. Standing just on the edge of that light was the rather short form of a woman with familiar frizzy hair.

The height, hair, and voice were enough to identify her, which was good because the rest of the woman was covered in a complex costume that fit her form closely. It was made of red leatherlike material with bumps where armored plates stood out under the cloth.

Her boots—which reached up to her knees—were covered in metal plates, the same as her gauntlets, though those only covered the tops of her hands. The knuckles of her palms and her fingers were left free.

There wasn't anything on Melanie that wasn't covered except for her mouth and chin, but even that was only exposed because her lower mask was undone and dangling to the side from a strap. There had to be a hole somewhere at the back, too, because her black hair was loose over her back and shoulders.

"Me-Melanie?" Emily squeaked. "You're Melaton?"

She eyed the woman, the Hero, and backed up just a step. Teddy growled at the woman in red, though what she could do against her was questionable. Melanie had a handgun strapped to one thigh and a large knife on the other.

The Hero crossed her arms. "I thought I told you to come in costume," she said.

Emily froze. "Um," she said before looking for words. "You . . . didn't?"

She had the impression Melanie was frowning, though there was no way to tell with most of her face hidden behind a visor. She reached down and Emily tensed until she pulled out a phone from a small pocket sewn just below her holster.

The light from the cell illuminated the alley for a bit and reflected off the opaque lens covering Melanie's face. "Huh. I didn't. My bad."

"Oh, okay," Emily said.

"You a big-shot Hero?" Teddy asked.

Melanie snorted. "I guess so. You never heard of Melaton?"

Emily knew her. Well, as much as she knew any celebrity. The Hero showed up in commercials for sportswear and there had been a controversy when Melaton knocked out a crowd of reporters.

"Uh . . ." Emily said.

Melaton sighed. "All right, kid, I figured you might be of some help. Handshake said you were okay, for the most part. And we're both after the same jerkwad."

"You mean going after Homie?" Emily asked.

"Pretty much," Melaton said. "Tell me right now, you in or not?"

"I . . . I don't know what you're planning on doing," Emily said.

The Hero grumbled under her breath, then nodded. "Yeah, okay, fair. I have a plan."

The silence after that lasted a few long beats until Teddy decided to fill it. "Yeah, what is it?" she asked.

"I'm going to find Homie, and then I'm going to give him some nightmares."

"That's . . . your plan?" Emily asked.

"Got a problem with it?"

That was not, in Emily's opinion, a plan. It was barely an outline! She put more planning into buying cereal—she didn't want the cashier to think she was too childish buying the tasty kinds, or too much of a prude if she bought the sort of cereal that was too healthy. "N-no, no problem," Emily lied.

"If you want to come along, I could use a bit of help, especially powered help."

Emily considered it. "What will we do if we find the hard drive?"

Melaton shrugged a shoulder. "We can give it to Handshake for some cash."

"It has a lot of . . . bad things on it."

"I'd be all for giving it to the fat pigs in charge, but there's some information on there about me, you know?" Melaton said.

"I, yeah," Emily said. "I think, maybe, if you don't mind, we could destroy it?"

The Hero's jaw twisted one way, then the other. "Yeah, we could do that. We'll see. You coming?"

What were the chances that Melaton would just remove the things about herself on the drive, then give it to her bosses? And then the fact that Emily was a Villain would be out in the open. She didn't have much of a choice. At least being with Melaton would allow her to maybe make . . . maybe not friends—that was going too far—but become the acquaintance of a Hero.

"We're coming," Emily said.

"Good. You got a costume? Because looking like a civvy is great if you're a nobody, but it's hardly intimidating," Melaton said.

"I do," Emily said. "But, ah, I need a place to change?"

Melaton looked around. "No one here," she said.

"The Boss doesn't like it when people see her naked," Teddy said.

Emily considered if she could turn around and run away from the mortification, especially when Melaton started to laugh. "And you don't mind, kid?" she asked.

"I get naked in front of people all the time," Teddy said.

Emily slapped a hand over her face. It was . . . kind of technically true. Teddy's grizzly form wasn't wearing anything but its fur, but that didn't count!

Melaton choked on her laughter. "What?"

"Is there a place we could change?" Emily asked.

The Hero nodded and gestured behind her. "There's a little booth back there. It's for changing in and out of costume."

"There are booths?" Emily asked.

Melaton nodded. "Yeah. Bit of a trade secret. You don't want some overzealous fan camping out in front of a booth. The creeps might put up a camera or something, and then I'd need to find and knock them out."

Emily tilted her head to the side, expecting to see a little booth, like a phone booth but hopefully with blacked-out walls, but other than a few dumpsters, there was nothing of note. "Um."

The Hero sighed and spun around to head deeper into the alley. "It's camouflage," she said before stopping next to a dumpster. A tug upward on a bar at the front, then a yank to the side, and part of the garbage container's exterior slid open, revealing a small white room with a bench and some windows on the walls that Emily couldn't see from the outside.

"Oh, wow," she said.

"Have fun. I'll be over there." Melaton pointed off to the end of the alley.

"R-right."

Emily ducked into the booth first, with Teddy waiting for her just outside. She undressed herself in a hurry, shoved everything in her bag, then got dressed—with only some reluctance—into her costume. Looking like a gangster from the twenties in front of a Hero was sounding like an increasingly dumb idea, but she didn't have much of a choice.

"I'm done," she said as she reopened the door. The window set into it allowed her to see an unaware Teddy picking her nose. The girl yanked her finger out and scurried in to change.

Melaton looked back, then moved her head up and down as if inspecting Emily. She squirmed a little under the gaze, but didn't move.

"Nice costume," Melaton said. "You able to take a hit?"

"Um . . . no?" Emily said.

"That doesn't look armored at all," Melaton added.

"It . . . isn't," Emily confirmed.

Melaton sighed. "Well, you'd better be good at dodging then."

"Right," Emily agreed. "So, once Teddy's done, we head out?"

The Hero nodded. "Yup. Will this be your first outing in costume?" At Emily's nod, she went on. "Oh. In that case, I might as well show you the ropes."

CHAPTER TWENTY-FOUR

The Ropes

Melanie . . . Melaton? Emily still wasn't sure how to address the woman. It didn't really matter, she figured. Either way, she seemed to know where she was going and took off with a steady stride, as if expecting Emily to keep up.

She had to jog to catch up. Melaton might have been half a head shorter than Emily, but that didn't mean it was easy keeping pace with her. Emily couldn't decide between walking quickly and jogging to stay even.

"You've never been out and about, right?" Melaton asked.

"N-not really," Emily said. "Um. You mean in costume, right?"

"Obviously," she said before reaching up and rubbing at her chin. "Right. This'll suck. I'm not the sort of person you'd want teaching you the ropes."

"That's . . . okay?" Emily tried. "I don't really want to be a, um, public Hero or anything. I just want to live my life."

"Humph. Yeah, that's fair. Can't even blame you. Chasing after Villains is a mess, dealing with corporations is a nightmare, and Endgames are complete shit."

"You've been to some?" Emily asked.

Melaton didn't reply for a while. "So . . . there are four paths you can take. For being a Hero, I mean. There are probably more than that, but it's easier to break them down, you know?"

"R-right."

They reached the end of the alley and Melaton stepped out into the foot traffic without so much as slowing down. Emily stumbled and stuttered after her, aware of every eye turning their way, of the expressions of surprise appearing on the faces of those around them and of the phones coming out of pockets to snap pictures.

"Um . . . um, uh," Emily said intelligently.

Teddy grabbed her hand and squeezed it. A look down at the big brown eyes half hidden by a cartoonish mask reassured Emily that she wasn't entirely alone.

"Get used to it," Melaton said. "And never slow down, or they'll start thinking that they can stop you for pictures and autographs and all that. It's not worth it, trust me. Even after knocking out the first ten idiots who think that being in costume means they can grab a pinch, they still don't learn."

"W-what?!" Emily squeaked. Did people really do that? Of course they did. She walked faster to stay close to the Hero.

"There are four paths, like I was saying," Melaton said. "The first, and probably the easiest at the start, is to join the Heroic Response Force, the HRF. They've got training and all that stuff. Their contracts are kind of shit, the pay isn't all that great, but it's government work, so the benefits are all right. They kind of demand that you participate in any Endgame that's in the country, though, and they're pretty heavily linked to the army."

"Um," Emily said. "I thought the army couldn't have people with powers?" she asked. It had been a big point in her history class.

"You drank the Ool-Aid if you think even a single country actually does more than pay lip service to that," Melaton said. "If you want to actually make a difference, then the government's a dead end. You practically need to fill out forms in triplicate to save someone from a burning building."

"That doesn't sound good," Emily said.

Melaton shrugged. "It is what it is. We're crossing here."

The Hero stepped out into traffic, the cars in either lane slowing to a sudden stop as she just marched across the street.

Emily bit her lower lip at the casual jaywalking, but the nearest pedestrian crossing was halfway down the block and the peer pressure was mounting, and Melaton was getting away and . . . and so she ran after the Hero with one hand over her head to keep her hat on, the other pulling Teddy along.

"So that's one option," Melaton said. "The other big one is going corporate. Just as much paperwork, but you can hire an agent and a lawyer to do it all for you. The pay is incredible too. I pull in six figures. The problem is that the pay matches the level of risk you take, and you need to be out in public a lot. One big screwup can ruin your career, and it's not like you can just rebrand."

"That sounds, um, interesting?"

"Meh. There're a lot of PR stunts and meet and greets and all that. Most corporations have entire teams that keep you looking presentable and coaches to teach you how to speak and all that. No swearing out in public either. That's a pain in the ass."

"Uh," Emily said. She didn't want to point out the hypocrisy there.

Melaton gestured to a building across the street, one that had a large billboard mounted to its side with an entire team of Heroes. Emily recognized Silver Fox and Melaton, of course. There were a few more besides: Wither, who had a rose in his mouth, White Knight in his knightly armor, and Peacemaker in her nurselike outfit. Emily didn't recognize the half-dozen others.

"That kind of ad? That's expensive as hell, but it sells your image, and then you can use that image to sell other crap. Only works if your powers are flashy or if you've got the personality for it," Melaton said.

"Oh," Emily said. "Then, um, maybe it's not for me."

"Yeah, you seem the sort to fold in front of a crowd. Not that there isn't a place for that kind of personality. Some guys really get their jollies off to shy girls."

Emily's face flamed.

"But yeah, I figure you'd panic the first time you forget someone's name at a conference or something," Melaton said. She pointed to another alley-way and walked in without so much as pausing. "The other options aren't all that great." Her voice echoed through the tight little passage.

"O-oh?" Emily asked.

"You can become a freelancer. That's like a corporate goon like me, but you do everything on your own. That's kind of locking you into being a B-rater forever. Some manage to go big, anyway. Wi-Fire is a household name, and he does all his own advertising and all that."

Emily nodded along. "Okay."

Melaton arrived at the end of the alley and stepped onto another street without pause. "Then there's the last option. The one we're doing right now."

"What's that?" Teddy asked.

Melaton looked down at Teddy. At some point the woman had covered her lower face with her mask and Emily hadn't noticed at all. "Vigilantism. Taking things into your own hands, government and laws be damned."

Emily squeezed Teddy's hand. Their walk turned quiet. They crossed another street, then slipped through another alleyway. The area changed. The buildings went from mostly commercial, to commercial with a sprinkling of normal apartment complexes mixed in.

Eauclaire was a nice city, with a decently large population. The college helped, as did the large Trans-Anadian highway crossing through the bottom half of the city keeping commercial traffic high.

It was meant to be a well-off city. That didn't mean it didn't have rougher sections.

The buildings they were passing took on an ugly look. Graffiti covered their walls, and more and more often there were homes with boarded-over windows and closed-down shops dotted along the street.

It was the kind of area Emily would have avoided normally. She didn't expect it to only be a few blocks over from all the shops and malls.

"This is Homie's area," Melaton said. "Look sharp, all right?"

"Oh, okay?" Emily said. She didn't know *how* to look sharp, but she'd try.

"What are we looking for?" Teddy asked. "Like, Villains and stuff?"

Melaton snorted. "I doubt it. Villains don't last long here."

"They don't?" Emily asked.

The Hero shook her head. "Nah. Think about it. How many new Heroes do we get every Power Day?"

"I-I don't know."

"Here? Two or three. Twice as many people who just want to mind their own business. And as for Villains? Maybe one every other year or so. They don't have time to get strong before they're completely swamped by Heroes. It's why it's so damned hard to get stronger. The best quests are those against an opponent of equal or greater strength. Being a Hero gives few opportunities in that regard."

"Oh," Emily said.

What did that mean for her? Other than that she had a lot of people who would be gunning for her if she messed up. That . . . wasn't ideal.

"We're here," Melaton said.

CHAPTER TWENTY-FIVE

Sleepy Time

Here" wasn't what Emily was expecting.

She'd developed a mental image of the kind of place a gangster would hang out. Maybe a sleazy bar, or a strip club, or some abandoned gas station. Maybe even a tenement building if they wanted to be subtle about things.

A perfectly ordinary-looking office building wasn't it.

"This is where, uh, Homie is staying?" Emily asked.

The office had a sign behind its front window reading Whitechapel Technical next to some generic stock vector art of a computer. It looked like any of a thousand shops Emily had passed by already.

"Nah," Melaton said. "Homie and his Try Hards are more of a street gang, if you can even call them that. I think the only reason he hasn't been nailed yet is that the crimes he does commit are so small they're barely worth noticing. At least, those that can actually be pinned on him."

"But he's a Villain?" Emily asked.

Melaton wiggled her hand in a so-so gesture. "He's a Dealer. It's not an outright Villain morality. If he were, he'd have been in a cell a long time ago, but as it is, his morality isn't outright illegal."

"There are illegal moralities?" Emily asked.

"Not really. But if you see someone with Criminal floating above their head, you don't just smile and wave."

"But . . . but just having the morality doesn't mean they've done any-thing," Emily said.

Melaton looked at her.

"I mean . . . aren't they still innocent until they've, uh, done something?"

The Hero shrugged. "Yeah, probably. But the moment they start displaying any sort of power, you know they've done something bad to get it upgraded. It's a better-safe-than-sorry kind of thing. Plus, nailing them gives you a few points. Grays, like Homie, are kind of a middle ground. Dealers can deal in perfectly legal stuff. Rogues too."

"Oh," Emily said. "Okay then." She hoped that the worry in her voice wouldn't register with Melanie, or if it did, that the older woman would assume maybe Emily was also in the gray area, and she was worried on account of that.

"So this place isn't where we'll find Homie, but it is where he launders some of his cash. At least, Handshake thinks so. We're going to go in and ask some people some very pointed questions."

Emily wanted to know more, but before she could begin to ask, Melanie moved forward and shoved her way into the office.

Emily and Teddy shared a quick look before following after her and setting off the bells above the door all over again.

The interior was pretty much like every other middle-grade office Emily had ever seen. A big desk at one end with a secretary behind it, some chairs, and a few small coffee tables near the entrance with stacks of *Mask Weekly*, *Inanity Fair*, and other magazines.

"You," Melaton said as she pointed right at the person behind the desk. "Who's the boss here?"

The young woman, about Emily's age, give or take a year, stared back wide-eyed and took a moment to respond. "The . . . the boss? Mister Sachar?"

"Sure," Melaton said. "Is he in?"

The secretary nodded furiously. "He's in his office."

"With anyone?" Melaton asked, and on getting a head shake in response she walked right past the desk and toward the back. "Cancel his meetings for the rest of the afternoon, then," she said.

"Um, we're all very, uh, sorry?" Emily said in a rush.

She had the choice between staying with the confused secretary and explaining things or continuing on with Melaton. She chose the latter.

The Hero moved on into the office proper and took one look at the few cubicles around the area before beelining toward a room at the back. Emily kept close, with her head down and her cheeks flaming. She hoped that none of the people working in their little boxes looked up.

The boss's room was a tight space, not meant to have three people suddenly walk in on the middle-aged man sitting behind an old computer screen. Mister Sachar was a corpulent fellow, with more than one chin and a gut that showed even when sitting down. It bounced a bit when the man jumped to his feet. "What's this?" he asked.

Melaton waited until they were all in before closing the door. Then, without so much as pausing, she launched across the desk and tapped the man midchest.

Sachar wobbled on the spot, his eyes slowly closing before he started to tip back. It was slow enough that Melaton had time to move around the desk and ease him into his seat.

"Is—is he dead?" Emily asked. She wondered if she had just witnessed a murder, but a rumbly snore from the man put paid to that.

"He's asleep," Melaton said. "It's what my power does."

Emily swallowed. "Right, right, that's what you do." Putting people to sleep with a touch didn't sound terribly strong, but Melaton had made a career from it.

"I can do more than that," the Hero said. "I'd keep it hushed up, but things won't make sense otherwise. So keep it to yourself."

"Keep what to myself?" Emily asked.

"This," Melaton said. She pressed a hand to Mister Sachar's forehead and her eyes rolled back. The woman swayed a little, random muscles across her body twitching minutely. Her lips moved and she even snorted once.

And then the Hero snapped out of it and took a long step back.

"What, what happened?" Emily asked.

"I think she went nuts for a bit," Teddy said.

Melaton rubbed at the side of her head like someone working through a headache, then gestured to the door. "Let's go," she said.

"Um, what?" Emily asked.

The question earned her a pointed glare that had her rushing out of the office ahead of an irate Melaton.

They breezed through the entrance, ignoring the secretary's confused questions, and then back out onto the street. Melaton took the lead again, taking them over to a nearby alley where she pulled out a phone and started tapping away at something.

"Um, Melaton? What happened?" Emily asked.

Melanie didn't look up. "Powers evolve. Mine felt rather awful when I got it. I can make people sleep. Big whoop. I'm a walking single-use cure for insomnia. It's not ideal. But then I took out some pretty heavy hitters in some spars and even a couple of people who went wrong. My power works absolutely if I can make physical contact with someone. No counters. Just a nice snooze. It's basically the perfect nonlethal takedown power, at least from zero range."

"Oh, okay?" Emily asked.

"But then my power got some more utilities. I was hoping for range, but instead I got dream-related things. I can see people's dreams if I'm touching them, and I can direct those dreams."

Emily put two and two together. "You can read minds?"

"I wish. I can see dreams. You remember some of your dreams?"

"A bit?" she said.

"I dream of eating things, and that I'm asleep," Teddy said.

Melaton snorted. "They're disjointed and messy and usually nonsensical. Lots of skipping around locations, and time isn't always linear. Normal dreams can loop the same thing over and over again, or be weird metaphorical nightmare-scapes. But I can push and nudge them, and sometimes see what's what."

"That's what you did in there?" Teddy asked. "That guy was snoring lots in no time."

"Yeah, pretty much. Which now means that I kinda know where he meets with Homie on a regular basis."

"That's . . . good?"

Melaton nodded. "He dreamed of picking up a load of cash, so I think that's where he gets the money that he then pays to his company for stuff before paying it back to Homie—probably all nice and legally on the return."

"And now we're going to . . . that place?"

"Yup. Hope you like pizza," Melaton said.

"Uh. I do," Emily said.

"Never had any," Teddy said.

The Hero stared at Teddy. "Huh. Well, all right. It's across town, though."

"How are we going to get there?" Emily asked.

"I'll call a taxi."

CHAPTER TWENTY-SIX

Just Along for the Ride

Teddy didn't know what was up with the sleepy lady getting them all to cram into some taxi, but the Boss didn't comment on it, so Teddy went along for the ride.

Her job wasn't to ask questions and stuff like that, it was to keep the Boss safe.

Going around all over with the Boss and the Melanie lady who was actually a Hero and who was also able to make people sleep was just part of that. She kind of wished that the Boss could have found someone who wasn't a Hero to pair up with, but that was okay. Less okay was the amount of walking they'd done. Teddy's legs were kind of short and stubby.

They were perfectly good legs, made that way so that her center of balance could stay low. But that meant that for every step the Boss took, Teddy had to take two. It was real tiring.

She relaxed into the taxi's seat. She got to sit in the middle seat, so if she perked up a bit, she could see the road out ahead over the mileage meter thing. The driver was being real careful, probably because she was clearly wearing a bear mask that put the fear of bears in him.

The ride was pretty quiet. The Boss didn't talk much at the best of times, and Melanie, who was also Melaton, was pecking away at her phone, clearly one of the sheep that had fallen for the capitalist cell-phone trap.

The silence was all right. It was also boring. "So where're we going?" Teddy asked. She'd heard something about pizza? She'd never had any of that, but she thought it was something she'd like to eat.

"Um," the Boss said. "We're going to the place with . . ." She looked over to the driver, then cleared her throat. The Boss was real clever that way. "We're going to see about buying a few slices of pizza and talking with someone."

"Oh," Teddy said. "All right."

The Boss smiled at her and placed a hand atop Teddy's head to pat her hair. It was real nice, like a hug for her head. It got even better when the Boss started to absentmindedly fiddle with Teddy's ears.

It probably made the Boss happy, too, because Teddy had great ears. They were her most bearlike feature when she wasn't actually a bear, after all.

She wondered what it would feel like for the Boss to play with her ears when she was big. Maybe while riding her into combat?

But the Boss didn't have any attacks that worked from afar . . . or from up close. So she'd need a gun or something.

Teddy didn't know why she knew what an AK-47 was, but she did, and she wished the Boss could ride her into battle while spraying capitalist pigs with a pair of them.

"Yeah," Teddy whispered.

"Hmm?" the Boss asked.

"Nothing," Teddy said. "I was just thinking about stuff."

"Oh, okay."

Melaton looked up from her phone as the taxi started to slow down. "We here?" she asked.

"Yes, ma'am," the driver said as he came to a full stop and the car pitched back and forth a bit. "That will be eleven fifty," he said.

Melaton slid a green twenty through the grating and stepped out. "C'mon, kids," she said. Teddy unbuckled herself—belt buckles were, in her opinion, stupid, but the Boss insisted—and scrambled out on the Boss's side.

The moment they were all out, the taxi clunked a few times, then sped off, leaving the three of them standing on the side of the road.

Teddy looked around. There was a meager field, with big bushes and long grass cut up by footpaths covered in cigarette butts to one side. It was squished between a row of homes with fenced-in backyards and the rear of what looked like a grocery store.

Closer by was a four-way stop with a cigar store on one side and a pizzeria on the other. She figured that the pizza place, with its nearly deserted parking lot, was their objective.

Most of the other buildings around were all little homes. The word *bungalow* came to mind, but Teddy wasn't so sure that these homes were that kind.

She sniffed the air, then sniffed it some more. Sure, it stank of cars and trash, but under all the stink was a heavenly smell that had her moving toward the pizza place as if in a trance.

"Kid's got the right of it," Melaton said. "That's the place."

Teddy barely noticed the Boss grabbing her hand and slowing her down so that Melaton could move into the pizza place first. The Hero held the door open from inside, so Teddy could slip in right after her.

Her nostrils flared. She took in a huge breath through her nose, and then Teddy almost fainted.

It smelled so good. Like grease and old cheese and raw onions and mushrooms. Just being there made her feel all clammy and delicious.

Then she took in the place. It had one table, with two little metal chairs, and a small sofa off to one side. There was a really old soda machine with a cracked front next to that, then the lobby place ended at a big wraparound counter.

She climbed onto her tippy-paws to look over the edge of the counter and at the wonders beyond.

There was a skinny guy in a stained white outfit, rubbing at his nose with a knuckle while the dough was being squished in some sort of vise. He pulled it out, all flat and wobbly, then spun it around a few times before dropping it onto a flour-covered metal plate and shoving the edges in with his knuckles.

That was neat, but the person who captured her attention was a huge man wearing an apron that couldn't wrap even halfway around his stomach. He had huge hairy arms that were flicking back and forth as he laid down a thumb-thick layer of pepperoni on a sea of tomato sauce. Then he reached into a bag and grabbed a double fistful of cheese that he dropped onto the pizza he was working on.

It was, in a word, art.

Teddy wanted one of those pizzas more than she'd ever wanted anything in the past two or so hours.

She turned to the Boss and hit her with the best bear-cub eyes she could manage. The Boss sighed and ruffled her hair. "We'll see," she said.

That was close enough.

"Hey!" Melaton called out.

The big guy paused in the act of dismantling some mushrooms with a big knife and no concern for his thumbs. "Yeah?" he asked before turning around and taking in Teddy's fearsome appearance, the Boss's cool costume, and also Melaton.

"We're looking for someone," Melaton said. "I think you might be able to help."

The big artist wiped his greasy hands with his apron as he came closer. "Maybe," he said. "Who're you looking for?"

Melaton shifted so that she was leaning up against the counter. "We're looking for a criminal called Homie," she said.

The guy at the back, the tall skinny one, dropped his pizza dough to the ground with a dull splat.

"Five-second rule!" Teddy shouted.

He didn't seem to care. The boy took one look at all of them, gasped, and bolted toward the back.

"Hey!" the big guy said.

"Crap," Melaton added.

Teddy didn't know what was going on, only that the boy running toward the back skidded to a stop near the door, turned to a pair of potato fryers, and dipped his hands into them.

He screamed as he whipped his arms out and twin whiplike gouts of boiling oil shot out toward the front.

Teddy jumped to the side and tackled the Boss to the ground and out of the way as the oily whips snapped at the air above her. A fine drizzle of oil splattered around them and Teddy winced as some of it landed on her exposed calves. It hurt a bunch! Like getting stung by a swarm of small, wet bees.

"Dammit!" Melaton said before she vaulted over the counter.

The big guy was screaming now and the door at the back slammed shut with a dull thump.

"Where'd he go?" Teddy asked. He'd tried to hurt the Boss. She'd eat him!

"You can't leave from the back," the big guy said. "He'll have to circle around."

Teddy scrambled off the Boss and rushed toward the front. She saw the Boss rolling over onto her knees, her eyes wide behind her mask as she looked around. The Boss was clever, though, she'd figure it out.

In the meantime, Teddy had a jerk to catch. If she did it right, she was sure she'd get a meal out of it.

CHAPTER TWENTY-SEVEN

Bearing the Burden of Being the Best Bear

Teddy barged out into the parking lot in front of the pizza place, took three steps, then paused to look around. Where, she wondered, was the oily jerk who'd tried to hurt the boss?

A noise from off to one side had her turning toward the path between the pizza place and the fence around the house next to it.

Teddy ran over in time to see the jerk flopping over the top of the fence and into the yard beyond just as Melaton ran around the back. "Where?" the Hero asked.

"Fence!" Teddy replied.

The fence was way, way too tall for Teddy to try and climb over it, and turning into a bear to go through it would take a bunch of time.

She pouted a bit when Melaton vaulted over the edge and landed on the other side with a shout of, "Stop, damn you!"

Taking to the streets, Teddy ran as fast as she could past the first house, then another, and finally a third where she saw the jerk running around someone's pool. Melaton was one yard back still.

That was her chance!

She darted toward the boy roaring as hard as her small human throat could manage.

The jerk stared at her, wide-eyed, then whipped his arm around in a big half circle.

Teddy only just had time to dive into a roll as a big splashing crescent of oil flowed past her head. "You jerk!" she called after him as her roll turned into a tumble and she ended up flopped on the ground as he continued to run.

Melaton landed in the same yard as them, so at least Teddy had won the Hero some time, but Teddy wanted to do a lot more than that!

Growling, she started charging after the two even as she turned into a big, fearsome bear. She made sure that her mask stayed on top of her bear form because the Boss said that was important. The elastic stretched a bunch, but it held.

The nice voice of that Ritish man who did all the documentaries rang in her head. "The North Merican grizzly bear can run at a top speed of thirty-four miles per hour. Compare that to the average human running speed of fifteen miles per hour, and the fearsomeness of a bear in full charge becomes even more impressive!"

"Holy crap! What the shit!" Melaton screamed as Teddy shot past her and through a wooden gate.

She was briefly disoriented as the barrier crumbled out of her way, but one sniff was enough to find the oil jerk. He took one look at her over his shoulder, said some very rude things, then bolted even faster.

"No! You're mine!" Teddy roared. Her bear-form roar was a lot more scary than her normal girl roar because the man's scent changed from someone who smelled like oil and pizza to someone who smelled like oil, pizza, and poop.

He jumped over one more fence, this one with chain links between metal posts. Judging by the way he hissed when he grabbed the top, he'd cut himself on the little metal twisty bits at the top.

Good! Teddy wanted him as hurt as he'd hurt the Boss. But more.

Chain links weren't meant to deal with a metric ton of awesome bear energy, and the entire fence bent over as Teddy crashed into it and shoved it down to the ground.

Oil-boy was still saying bad words while fishing for something in his pocket. And then he pulled out a lighter, spun around, and flicked it on.

Teddy roared as a gout of burning liquid burst out of the boy's hand and spattered over her coat. It wasn't normal fire that would just beat against her thick fur, but wet fire that sank in and burned through.

It hurt a bunch!

"Take that, you—" the boy began.

And then Teddy stood up on her hind legs and punched down with a big balled-up paw.

Bear beat oil.

Action Reward!

For defeating a powered opponent in a running battle, you have earned:

+1 Skill Slot!

Teddy slumped back down and started licking her fur over the spots that had been burned the worst. Most of it was on her shoulder and down her left forepaw. The fire stopped, but it still felt tender, and her fur was matted and burned. It didn't smell nice at all.

"Well done," Melaton said as she ran over. She was panting slightly, but seemed to be in good enough shape that it wasn't too bad. The Hero bent over the fallen oil guy and placed a hand over his head. "Watch out for me for a bit," she asked.

"Yeah," Teddy said.

The lights in the houses around them were all on, and at a glance, she could make out some people staring out of their windows, some of them with phones pressed to their ears.

That wasn't good.

The sound of someone coming up behind them had Teddy turning, but it was only the Boss. "Teddy!" Emily said.

"Boss," Teddy replied. "I got burned."

"Oh, oh no." The Boss ignored her own lack of breath and moved closer to Teddy to look over her wounds. She didn't touch them, but she did hover her hands over it as if she didn't know what to do. "Will it stay if you turn back?"

In answer, Teddy returned to her boring normal body, one hand up to make sure her mask was fixed over her face properly.

The Boss winced as she looked at the ugly skin over Teddy's shoulder and down the part of her arm not covered by her dress. "We'll need to put some water on that," she said. "Maybe some bandages."

"Yeah, okay," Teddy said.

"Is there anything I can do to make it better?" the Boss asked.

Teddy nodded. "Pizza."

"Pizza?"

"With lots of meat," Teddy confirmed.

"When you two are done discussing your meal plans for the evening," Melaton said, "we might have a few things to go over."

The Hero stood up from over the oil guy's knocked-out form and glanced around.

"Crap. We're going to have the cops here soon." She gestured to the Boss and to Teddy. "You two should head out. We don't need to bog you down with all the paperwork and the questions they'll ask. You didn't actually commit a crime or anything, but they'd bring you in on principle and then you'd need to fend off recruiters for the next week."

"I— That would be bad," the Boss said.

"It would," Melaton agreed. "Head out for a bit. I'll call you tomorrow, share what I got on our target."

"Oh, okay," the Boss said. "Um. Tonight was … well, it was educational?"

"Uh-huh," Melaton said. "It was that. You girls be careful, all right?"

The Boss nodded, grabbed Teddy's unburnt hand, and pulled her along.

"Are we getting pizza now?" Teddy asked.

It took a while for the Boss to reply. "You know what, Teddy? I think we are."

"Awesome." Double rewards!

"But we'll need to get changed first, and, um, maybe we can grab it to go and eat it at the dorm?"

That way they could go to sleep right after eating. The Boss was real clever. "Yeah, I like that idea," Teddy said.

"Good, good, and, um, Teddy?"

"Yeah, Boss?"

"Thanks. You did really well tonight."

Teddy grinned big and proud. Triple rewards! It was the best night ever.

CHAPTER TWENTY-EIGHT

A Perfectly Ordinary Day

It was a little strange to go from a day where everything felt like it was happening all at once, to a rather quiet day where Emily woke up, showered, went to classes, crammed some homework between breaks, then finished for the day around noon.

All perfectly normal, all perfectly ordinary.

She stopped by an Im Orton's on the way back to the dorm and picked up some doughnuts (not all honey-glazed . . . but a few of those) and a strong coffee to keep her going, then walked all the way back home.

Again, all perfectly ordinary.

Her room was a bit messier than she liked it, with a pair of very empty pizza boxes left on her desk, and a half-eaten box of fries scattered across the floor leading up to the mattress like an evidence trail, but Emily could ignore that.

Teddy was there, sleeping with her tummy exposed and her mouth wide open. Her entire belly was bloated, no doubt with the two large pizzas she'd devoured the night before.

"Teddy?" Emily asked once the door was closed.

Teddy cracked one eye open and stared at her. She mumbled something that could be vaguely made out as "Boss?"

"I bought doughnuts," Emily said.

Teddy's response was a painful groan before she tried to roll onto her side, then failed as both her tummy and the wobbliness of the mattress conspired against her.

"I'll, uh, put them on the desk," Emily said.

"Mm-hmm," Teddy said.

Emily paused next to Teddy's bed to look at her arm. The signs of the burn were still there, though they'd gotten a lot less obvious overnight. Teddy was a fast healer, then. That was great. Emily didn't know how they'd handle a hospital visit.

She set the box of doughnuts on her desk, then stacked up the pizza boxes to one side after checking to see if there were any leftovers (there weren't). Then, because she was in a cleaning mood, she picked up the fries flung all over and packed everything away next to the door so that she could put it out later.

Then, and only then, did she sit down, pull out her computer, and settle in to look up things while eating. She glanced at her usual haunts first, but even brand-new images of kittens and puppies being themselves didn't spark more than a passing "aww," so she moved on to looking at the local news.

Not from an actual news site, though. She wasn't made of gold, and those had paywalls. Instead, she found the sub-forum for Eauclaire.

The first post at the top had her blood turning to ice.

New Local Hero Melaton and Two Unknowns Take Out Pyromaniac Villain!

6.7K Up | 231 Down

"Oh no," Emily said. With nearly trembling hands she clicked on the link.

Local Hero Melaton and Two Unknowns Take Out Pyromaniac Villain!

Posted: Yesterday By: ArthorMac

Last night, at around 4 p.m., local Hero Melaton was seen chasing after an un-Masked young man who used fire-based abilities. The known Hero was accompanied by two others. A young woman who turned into a bear (Images!) and another who wore a '20s-style gangster costume and who didn't use any obvious powers.

The arsonist was apprehended when the bear Hero caught him and Melaton knocked him out.

Police have yet to comment, but Melaton's agent spoke up on Witter, saying that Melaton was glad to work with some new up-and-comers to take out a Villainous threat.

EDIT: More footage here.

More sources:

Eauclaire Gazette

Hero News Weekly

EDIT: And even more pics!

Posts sorted by: Best Rated

User/TheChub509

28 points Yesterday

Pro Tip: Don't piss off the bear.

User/SamMax

24 points Yesterday

That takedown was brutal. I wonder if it was legal? That's, like, a classic excessive use of force.

2 Replies:

> **User/Kat**

> *10 points Yesterday*

> Don't be an idiot. That guy tried to light her ON FIRE! Plus she's a minor.

> **User/TheWanterofAcogs**

> *8 points Yesterday*

> kid isn't even a registered Mask. Wtf was Melaton thinking bringing her along?

User/TheChub509

23 points Yesterday

Our new Heroes need names!

4 Replies:

> **User/MerlinS**

> *11 points Yesterday*

> Ursa Minor for the bear girl!

> **User/MomentKiller**

> *8 points Yesterday*

> Ursa Minor is a great name! What about the other Mask?

> **User/SomethingSomething-KidFriendly**

> *7 points Yesterday*

> Capone? The Head Honcho? Maybe something more feminine? Femme Fatale?

> **User/J-Giannuzzi**

> *6 points Yesterday*

> OMG yis!

User/HandshakesThrowawayAccount

18 points Yesterday

That's certainly a development!

User/ChaoticSky

17 points Yesterday

I want to give it pats!

2 Replies:

> **User/KentBoy**

> *14 points Yesterday*

> She would eat you. But it would be worth it!

> **User/KoalaTodd**

> *8 points Yesterday*

> She's so fluffy!

User/CrazyCoder

15 points Yesterday

Does anyone have anything on the bad guy in this case? Anything at all?

2 Replies:

> **User/Taveri**

> *7 points Yesterday*

> :(

> **User/TheWarriorDale**

> *4 points Yesterday*

> Not much to go on. Seems like his costume is a . . . cook? Looks rather dirty. Powers don't seem like direct fire control. More like control over a liquid fire? Napalm maybe? Range and speeds were okay, but not spectacular.

User/Deamion

14 points Yesterday

So . . . Ursa Minor merch when?

3 Replies:

> **User/BookishWyrm**

> *12 points Yesterday*

> My soul for an Ursa plushie!

> **User/ShaggyMelsa**

> *7 points Yesterday*

> She does seem very marketable. Plus she's a kid, how hard would it be to just get her to sign off on a contract to sell.

> **User/GreatOm**

> *5 points Yesterday*
> They'd need to join a corp team, then get an official costume, then have it be signed off on, and then . . . so yeah, give it like a month.

Emily lowered her head into her hands. There was just so much out there about them. Pictures and videos. She didn't doubt for a moment that some people were trying to un-Mask them already.

Her only saving grace was that they hadn't been too close to anyone and that the lighting was pretty poor. Most of the pictures were amateurish and poorly made, so maybe there wouldn't be enough to identify them.

That, and they'd been caught doing something Heroic, which was . . . okay?

Her phone buzzed.

With a sinking heart, Emily pulled the phone out of her purse and checked the number. Melanie's number was displayed right there for her to see, along with a message.

Mel: You free?

Emily took a deep breath and unlocked her phone to reply.

E-Wright: I am.
Mel: Good. Got some info, but I'm being grilled for yesterday. Sent it to HS to send to you. Check your mail.
E-Wright: Okay. Thank you.

Emily slid her phone to the side and opened her email client. It didn't take much to find Handshake's email. It was the only one she'd received all week that wasn't an ad for something or a likely scam.

The contents were surprisingly sparse though, just two addresses. Addresses Homie could often be found at. Tacked at the end was a rather unwelcome "good luck" from the informant.

Leaning back into her seat, Emily wondered just how wrong everything would go if she headed out there on her own (with Teddy, of course) and tried to tackle a Villain solo.

She didn't like her odds.

And how would Homie react to losing someone with powers who worked for him?

She bit her lip and fell back onto a breathing exercise to keep her heart rate down. If she couldn't take on the situation in one go, then she had to break it down.

First, she had to find out where Homie was. Then she had to corner him, preferably with an annoyed Teddy. Then . . . steal the drive back.

She'd need to be so stupidly lucky for all that to work out.

Something clicked in the back of Emily's mind and she spun around in her seat. "Teddy!"

"Mmm?" Teddy mumbled.

"Teddy . . . where did you say you last saw Alea Iacta?"

CHAPTER TWENTY-NINE

Harald

Harald was a simple kind of guy. He got up in the morning, ate his Orn Lakes with a bit of milk, went to the bathroom and showered—just like anyone else.

He even lived in a perfectly ordinary sort of place. A little apartment on the top floor of a tenement building. It was a nice place. The water was warm enough ever since they replaced the heater, and it was nice and insulated from the snow in winter. He even had a little parking spot for his Ivic out back.

If anyone asked, he worked the night shift at a grocery store, and sometimes the morning shift too. Nice, respectable but boring work. He was even on the payroll if anyone looked.

That was all a lie, of course.

An elaborate ruse set up by his boss.

He wasn't spending the night shoving cans into neat rows just for some Karen to come in an hour after opening and mess everything up. Not that he hadn't done that kind of work in a past life.

Nah. Harald was a boss. He was a cool cat. A playa. Not the top dog, but real close.

He had mad girls after him all the time, and his nights were spent at the Garter Belt, a little joint tucked away in the most interesting part of town where the music could be played real loud without bothering anyone.

It wasn't all fun and games, though. Sure, he had his Try Hards to impress. A bit of cash changing hands, some substances of questionable legality being tossed around and snorted off the backs of cute college girls who'd gotten tired of daddy telling them how to live, maybe a bit of planning on where to place the coolest tags.

It was all in good fun until the boss called in.

The last time was two days back. The boss had wanted him to hit up some guy out in a hidden bar somewhere. He'd rolled in with a few boys, knocked him around, and, as the boss asked, taken a machine off the guy.

It was sitting in front of him now.

The Garter Belt had a nice little basement. All bare cement walls and piping, but clean. It was where he had his office. Just a desk and a chair and a PC that hummed in the corner. Sometimes a guy needed a nice quiet spot away from all the music and noise.

He, of all people, could understand finding a place to call his own.

Harald didn't sit. He didn't like sitting down. Instead, he walked around the room. There were shelves with bits of stationery and printers and a few knickknacks. As he moved, he picked each one up in turn and set it back down. A stack of papers here, a book there, a stapler next to that.

It was just how he de-stressed as he waited for the boss to call.

He needed a bit of de-stressing. He'd lost one of his own subordinates the day before. A big takedown. It'd made the damned evening news. Oily Cheeks getting smacked down by a godforsaken bear of all things.

Harald had plans for that boy! He was supposed to add some legitimacy to their entire operation. Oily Cheeks wouldn't stay behind bars forever. Oh, sure, he was a bit gray, but the kid was clean. His worst infraction had been a bit of fooling around in high school.

But now he was tainted. He'd be watched, and they'd have his name and address, and the moment someone showed up looking too sweaty, or like they hadn't showered, they'd catch Cheeks in no time.

Harald kept on moving things around. He had a little cloth in his back pocket that he'd use to rub the dust off stuff. Dust always bothered him because he knew *exactly* where it was, no matter what he did.

He turned toward his desk. The phone rang.

Harald reached a hand over to the cordless and it snapped across the room and into his hand, the device turning on with the same motion. "Yo."

The voice over the line was muffled and grating, the kind of voice that made it just a bit hard to understand. There was no doubting who it was. "Hello, H."

"Hey, Big S. How are you?" Homie asked. Not Harald. He wasn't Harald when talking to the boss.

He winced a bit at the sound of cement rubbing against cement across the line. "Let's cover things one at a time. Do you still have the drive?"

Homie looked over to his desk where the computer he'd taken was sitting. The drive was in there. As much as he knew about computers from his power-granted osmosis, he still didn't want to risk popping it out and breaking it.

"Good," the boss said before he had time to say anything. "Then we can move on to the next step. I'll need you to bring the drive over to a specific address tonight. You'll be meeting a contractor I hired. I'll text you if it's the right person."

"Cool, cool," Homie said. "I can do that much."

"You've been dependable so far," the boss agreed. "This will almost certainly give us a leg up over the Cabal."

Homie nodded, and the boss, of course, saw that.

"Very well. The address should be on your burner phone. You know what to do."

"Yeah, yeah, no worries."

There was some shifting over the phone. "Now, what happened to your recruit? That is, if you can tell me anything more than what I saw on the news already."

Homie winced. "I really don't know. Or, well, I can guess. Cheeks went out and got himself caught. I don't know how they tracked him down, though. Might have shown off to some of the girls here. You know how women can be."

There was a groaning sigh. "Amateurish."

"He was new. Plenty of potential, but a bit of a pushover. Not a bad thing, but . . . yeah. His power wasn't all that great, at least. So no big loss there."

"I've yet to hear of an entirely useless power," the boss said. "It's a lost opportunity, but these are times of opportunity. We'll make back the loss."

"You think this was the Cabal?" Homie asked. He wanted a definitive no. The boss was, surprisingly, an honest guy. If he said it wasn't the shadowy freaks, then it was probably just some fluke.

"I can't say either way," the boss said. "Get me that drive and we'll know better."

Homie nodded again. "Can do. And, uh, you got anything on that Melaton woman? I looked through her Ikipedia profile, but it's not much. If she comes knocking, I want to be ready."

"I'll send you what I have. I'm afraid it's not much," the boss said. "I have far less on the other two accompanying her."

"They looked like sidekicks or something," Homie said. "Nothing to worry about, right?"

"I suppose not. Good evening, H. Stay safe, and keep an ear open for my next message."

"Will do, Big S."

The line went dead. A moment later, the inside of his desk buzzed. Homie's eyes unfocused as he read the text. Just an address, one that he memorized by repeating a few times while he flicked his phone over and had it land in its recharging cradle.

The drawer popped open and the phone within flew up and into his back pocket as he picked up the laptop with the drive and shoved it into a carrying bag.

He'd get the boss's work done, then he could put some of his smaller worries behind him for a time.

CHAPTER THIRTY

Gentle Persuasion

E-Wright: When can we meet?
Mel: Not any time soon.
E-Wright: But the drive?
Mel: I know. Still filling things out. Should be free by this evening. Calm your tits.

Emily shoved her phone away and stood up to pace. Time was ticking and it felt like . . . like waiting in line at the dentist's office, knowing they were going to tear out a cavity with their little drills and not being able to do anything about it.

Worse, at least the cavities were her own fault. The drive thing . . . wasn't.

"Are we going?" Teddy asked. She was all dressed up. That was, she had changed from her pj's to her cargo shorts and a hoodie and slid her boots on without tying the laces. Her costume was firmly stuffed into Emily's bag.

"Yes," Emily said. "Yes, we are."

Her dad had once told her that, sometimes, you needed to help yourself. That without making the effort to get something, you wouldn't get it, and that relying on chance alone was a complete waste of time.

She picked up her backpack and slung it over her shoulder. Then she stopped next to Teddy to tie her shoes before the girl sent herself spiraling down a staircase.

"Let's go," she said while extending a hand for Teddy to grab.

It was only when they were outside that Emily realized she didn't know where they were going. "Uh. Did you grab Alea Iacta's number?" she asked.

"Nope," Teddy said. "But I know where he hangs out twice a week."

Emily squeezed her eyes shut. "This isn't off to a great start," she said.

"It's that way," Teddy replied.

Seeing as how she was already almost certainly doomed, Emily just sighed and gestured for Teddy to take the lead.

A few minutes later, after crossing half the campus on a winding path that looped over itself a few times, and after asking Teddy if she was sure she knew where she was going, they arrived before the old theater building near the center of campus.

"This is it," Teddy said with confidence Emily was pretty sure she didn't deserve. They'd passed by the roads around the building twice before Teddy had finished retracing her route.

"You sure?" Emily asked. The idea of just walking into a building she wasn't meant to be in felt incredibly wrong on so many levels.

Teddy nodded and moved ahead, but pushing on the door did a whole lot of nothing. "Uh. It's locked."

"Oh well," Emily said. "Back home it is."

"Hey!"

Emily froze, but Teddy was a lot faster in turning around and looking toward the voice calling out to them. "Oh hey," she said. "It's the Black guy."

"Teddy!" Emily squeaked. "You can't say something like that."

She turned to see the person calling out to them was a tall young man with rather handsome features and a concerned look in his eyes. "Hello," he said to her before looking down at Teddy. "And hey to you."

"Hello, comrade," Teddy said. "I'm looking for comrade . . . Jacob. Do you know where he is?"

"Oh," he said. "And here I thought you were going to break into the theater again."

"Teddy!" Emily said. "You said you walked in!"

"I did!" Teddy said. "The doors weren't locked or anything."

The man raised his hands. "Wait, wait, she's probably right there. She just did a bit of trespassing is all. We had a meeting about it last night. The doors should stay locked from now on."

"Oh," Emily said. "Okay. Good. Um . . ."

"I'm Matthew." he said. "The director of the volunteer theater group, and I'm one of the senior members of the not-so-volunteer group. Is Teddy here your, uh . . ."

"My sister," Emily said. "She's my little sister. We were looking for Jacob?"

One of Matthew's eyebrows jumped. "Him, huh? He isn't here today. No practice. I . . . don't think he has classes right now. So he could be anywhere."

"Oh," Emily said. "Do, do you know where his dorm is?"

Matthew eyed her for a bit. "What's your relationship with Jacob? Because, I have to say, he's not the most . . . I don't want to talk bad about someone when he's not around."

"Emily is Jacob's boss," Teddy said.

Matthew perked up. "Oh. Yeah, I remember him taking on some work at that latte place. You should have said so. He pull a no-show?"

"S-something like that," Emily said.

Matthew shook his head. "I'll text him, ask him if he's in his dorm."

"Can . . . can you not tell him that we're coming?" Emily asked.

"Catch him unawares, huh? You give him an earful, all right. And if you want, you can send me his work schedule. God knows that boy needs some discipline in his life."

"S-sure," Emily said.

Matthew let her copy Jacob's address off his phone, then told them to stay safe before they went on their way.

Another trip across campus, this time led by Emily's phone, took them to an apartment building two streets over from the campus proper.

It wasn't the Quantum Mothman House, but it was a nice enough place. A bit older, a bit more run-down, and there was an uncomfortable number of cigarette butts left in the unmaintained grass next to a few bottles, but it wasn't . . . terrible.

Emily had seen worse. In movies.

She stepped into the stairwell that was the apartment complex's lobby, then found Jacob's room number on the mail slots to one side.

Three flights of stairs later, and they were at his door.

"Can I knock?" Teddy asked.

Emily was too busy catching her breath to deny her, so she watched as Teddy slapped the door three times.

There was movement on the other side, someone stumbling over something, swearing, then rushing over to the door.

It opened to reveal a lanky Jacob wearing nothing but a wifebeater and CucumberJoe Poly Pants boxers. Emily looked up and locked eyes with the boy who was holding on to a gaming controller in one hand and a set of headphones in the other. "Oh, shit," he said.

"Let us in, please?" Emily asked.

"Or I'll eat you," Teddy persuaded softly.

They were let into an apartment that reeked of sweat and soda and had so much dust collecting in it the edges of the floors were discolored. "What are you doing here?" Jacob asked. "I have a roommate."

"Is he here?" Emily asked.

"No. But still."

"I need your help," Emily said.

"No," was his immediate reply.

Teddy huffed. "The Boss was asking nicely. You need to do your duty for the proletariat and your boss by doing what she says."

Jacob backed up a step, both hands raised. "Hey, hey, none of that. Not in my own house. I saw what you did to that guy on the net, I don't want to get KOed by little Miss Teddy Bear over here."

"We don't want that," Emily agreed. "We just need your help with one thing. It's . . . there's an information broker who knows a lot about, um." Emily wasn't keen on lying, but she'd never been in a situation quite like this. "He knows a lot about all the Villains in Eauclaire. And he put that information on a computer, and it was stolen. We need to track it or else we're all in a lot of trouble."

Jacob's shoulders slumped. "You think there's stuff about me on there?"

"Probably?" Handshake definitely knew about Alea Iacta's more public stunts, she was sure.

"Come on, I wanted to spend the night being angry at the jerks on *Federation of Fables*."

"I'm . . . sorry?" Emily said. "We don't need much. We just need to know where to go. Where to find someone called Homie."

CHAPTER THIRTY-ONE

Ready Teddy

Teddy was ready.

The Boss had been real cool about finding a place to hide away and get changed while they were en route to the place where Homie was hiding from the Boss.

Sure, it had been in a public restroom by some gas station, but Teddy didn't mind. The place had really interesting smells in it.

So, fully kitted out with her fearsome cartoon bear mask and her yellow sundress with the pockets, Teddy walked next to the Boss while the Boss looked at her phone a bunch.

They'd gotten Alea Iacta to find out where Homie would be by tossing darts at a map on the back of a Thai place pamphlet. That was really cool, and some of the foods on that pamphlet looked real tasty too. Maybe they were like pizza.

Teddy added something to her list of things to do in life. It wasn't very long yet because she'd started it just recently after seeing the Boss make lists about all sorts of things.

Hers was so short she had it memorized:

1. Make the Boss happy
2. Sleep next to the Boss for a full day
3. Eat a capitalist
4. Eat food from every place to find out which one is the best
5. Go to a zoo with the Boss

Her life goals weren't going to get done if she didn't help the Boss catch that weaselly Homie guy, though. "We almost there, Boss?" Teddy asked.

"I . . . Almost, I think," the Boss said. "I don't think this is a very busy part of town."

It really wasn't. They'd been walking past a bunch of homes with the occasional apartment complex sprinkled in. There were stores and stuff, but they were all little things. A butcher's here, a hairdresser there. Nothing too cool.

"I think it's supposed to be there," the Boss finally said as she pointed across the street. She looked at her phone again, then nodded. "Yes, that looks like the right place."

The right place turned out to be a little corner store, of all things. It had signs out front for beers and stuff like that, and a couple of older guys sitting on a bench, both drinking out of some paper bags.

"Man, that's a lame place to make a Villain base," Teddy said. "When we get a supersecret base, it should be a lot cooler."

Emily made a noise that sounded like a really lame growl. Teddy was a bit embarrassed, but she didn't want to point it out to the Boss and make her feel bad about her growling. She'd show her how to do it later.

"Should we go in and try and see if we can find that Homie guy?" Teddy asked.

"I . . . no, not yet. Let me call Melanie first." The Boss moved over to the side and started tap-tapping some stuff onto her phone.

Teddy shrugged and plopped herself down on the curb so her legs could stretch out between two cars. She still had a good view of the corner store in case some fat capitalist tried to sneak out of it.

"Um," the Boss said. "Melaton is on her way."

"Cool," Teddy said. "So what's Homie look like, anyway?"

"Uh. I . . . don't know?"

"Huh," Teddy said. She stuck a finger in her nose to clear it out. "Well, maybe we should ask? We should know what our prey looks like."

"R-right, that's a good idea," the Boss said.

Teddy basked in the glow of occasionally having good ideas while she continued to wait. The Boss tap-tapped some more, then knelt next to Teddy to show her a photo. "This is Homie in costume," she said.

The photo wasn't the best. It was all smudgy and the angle was kinda lame, but it did picture some guy with a print bandanna around his lower face and a big blue beanie atop his head. His clothes looked like they were two sizes too big, and he had a bunch of chains around his neck for some reason.

"That's a lame costume," Teddy said. Even her pimp outfit had more flair.

A car pulled up to the corner store. It was impossible to miss, what with the heavy bass music thumping out of it and the lights mounted beneath that made the street below glow yellow. Teddy looked at the guy who stepped out of the car, then down at the photo.

The skin color was right, and the height looked right, but the bandanna was different and the beanie was green. "You think that's Homie?" Teddy asked.

"W-we need to hide!" the Boss said.

Teddy blinked up at her, then looked around. They were behind a pair of cars, only able to see because the loud car had parked itself directly ahead of them. "We are," Teddy said.

"Oh, oh right."

"So we gonna go get him?" Teddy asked.

"Um," the Boss said. She was hesitating, which wasn't good. Predators had to be decisive and strong.

"I could get him real fast, Boss. I bet his power's weak out in the open."

The Boss nodded, but put a hand on Teddy's shoulder when she started to rise. "Let me text Melaton first," she said.

Teddy nodded and stood up slower. "Tell me when you're done, Boss," she said.

"It's sent."

Teddy grinned a big bear grin. She took in a deep breath, then roared as she ran across the street.

She didn't see the truck until the Boss screamed and the truck's tires squealed across the pavement.

Homie was almost done. He'd gotten the chump driving him around to the right place and was pulling the laptop out of the back seat. All he had to do was give it to the guy waiting for him in the shop and he'd be done for the night. Then it was back to the club and to the ladies.

And then, because life hated him, he heard someone screaming from across the street.

He looked over to see some kid with a cheap plastic mask running across the street, her arms above her head with her hands stretched out like claws. She was going "Raaagh!" over and over like . . . well, like a kid pretending to be a bear.

He was ready to dismiss her when a semitruck came out of nowhere and thudded into the girl with a dull, meaty thwap that sounded loud even over the squeal of its brakes.

Homie stared at the scene, taking it all in. The fallen girl, the other kid with a mask on screaming behind her, the Truck-Kun Fantasy Delivery Service logo on the side of the van.

"Oh, shit," he said.

He was ready to tear off his mask and see if the kid was all right—he was a criminal, not an ass—when the girl turned into a bear.

"Oh, *shit*!" he said with a lot more emphasis.

The bear shook its great mangy head as if clearing it. It looked up to him and they locked eyes.

The bellowing roar it let out was a friendly reminder he'd skipped using the washroom before heading out.

Homie's ride bucked once as the driver put it into gear and blasted down the street while "Gangsta 'Ero" boomed out of its speakers.

He was left on the sidewalk with nothing between him and a ton of angry bear except for the bag holding the laptop.

He did the only sensible thing—he spun around on a heel and ran.

CHAPTER THIRTY-TWO

Garage

Homie wasn't much of a runner.

He wasn't in bad shape. His diet was a bit crap, and his exercise routine . . . nonexistent, but he was thin, with a great metabolism, and the drugs he took did wonders for his gut.

The fact remained, though, that he hadn't actually run for the sake of running since high school, and that was a few years back.

He was running now, running faster than he'd ever run before, all thanks to the motivational push that came from having a two-ton grizzly bear roaring after him.

The bear roared some more and redoubled its speed. All Homie could think was that nothing so big should have been able to move that fast.

And then he came around a corner, and his salvation was in sight. A garage, old and rather decrepit, with a couple of used cars parked out front. Its front door was wide open, and Homie could make out the rough shapes of a pair of mechanics tinkering on the underside of an old pickup.

It wasn't just any old garage, though: it was one he had frequented in the past, one that paid protection money to the boss, one that he had spent hours in while changing oil and fixing brakes in his normal identity.

It wasn't one of his safe houses or one of the places he knew well, but he'd spent time there, and that was enough.

He zigged and zagged around a few parked cars, darted across the street to the sound of someone honking at him, then bolted through the parking lot before the garage and into its poorly lit interior. "Move!" he shouted.

The guys working within took one glance at him, some of them looking like they were going to complain about his entrance. He could see the moment they saw the bear running after him.

They left with no protest.

Homie had all of thirty seconds to ready his power. Usually it was a slow process, like a seeping, invisible miasma that enveloped everything in a room and filled his mind with a hyperdetailed image of where everything was and what it was meant to do.

Now he let loose the floodgates and swamped the room with his power. The moment it reached the controls near the door, he tugged at them and the electric motor near the ceiling came to life.

It was far too slow. The bear hardly had to duck to slip into the garage. Still, now it had oil drums and stacks of tires in its way.

Homie swung an arm and made a tire tip off its pile and fall toward the bear, only for it to bat it out of the air. His power had barely been able to lift that much. He had to stall for time.

"Come here, ugly!" he called out as he set the laptop and its bag atop a tool chest.

The bear complied, rushing through tool trays and knocking over parts as it moved across the garage. Homie kept pushing at his power as he ran a circle around the back end of the room. There were a couple of cars parked there that served as great cover the bear couldn't weave around as quickly as he could.

As Homie's power finally started to fill the room in full and become more concentrated, he began pushing back against the bear while searching for something, anything, he could use to scare the creature off.

Unfortunately, there weren't any loaded hunting rifles tucked away for him to use.

The bear was getting a lot closer than he wanted when his power brushed against something he thought might help.

Each side of the lift holding up the truck in the middle had emergency release valves on it. They were big and heavy, and would spill out the fluid in the hydraulic jacks, but they needed to be undone by wrench.

There were plenty of those around.

Homie jumped onto the hood of a car, hopped over a swiping paw, and ran toward the far end of the garage while two wrenches flew across the room, unnoticed by the bear, and started to undo the hoses.

He ran under the pickup, grabbed a random tool from a rack, kicked a safety stand out from under the truck, then flung the tool back with a bit of guidance from his power so it rapped the bear on the head.

"Come at me!" he roared.

By then the mechanics were long gone, though there was someone panting and bent over double by the little office.

The bear smiled toothily at him and charged across the room.

The wrenches finished their work and the hoses came loose just as Homie pressed the down button with his power.

The bear's eyes went wide a moment before two tons of rusty old pickup came crashing down atop it.

"Boom!" he cheered.

The bear roared again, but it was pinned down nice and good. Still, one surprisingly long arm came out from under the truck, and if it wasn't for Homie's power telling him it was coming, it would have swiped him off his feet.

"Yeah, you stay there," he said. The bear didn't sound happy with that, but it didn't have a choice.

Even better, if it could turn back into a little girl, it would still be pinned under the truck.

"See you later," he said as he swaggered off. Then he saw a canister filled with oil.

He still had an Ippo lighter in his back pocket.

New Quest!

Removing the Competition

Take out the competition—permanently.

Reward: +3 Skill Upgrade points and +1 Skill Slot per powered enemy killed. Blackguard +3 per success!

Accept? Refuse?

The bear *had* been trying to kill him.

"Accept," Homie muttered before tipping the canister over. His power found a few gas cans at the back and helpfully flipped those over too.

Soon the entire garage was smelling like gas fumes.

There was still one person left in the garage, hiding away in the office, but he could tell them to run off at any moment.

"Bye-bye, bear girl," he said as he flicked on his lighter and let it fall.

The fire was . . . rather anemic. Just a small puddle on the floor that was far from impressive. He flung a few rags onto it and nodded satisfactorily when they lit up and the fire spread around.

The bear rumbled and shook under the truck. Homie almost felt bad for it.

Grinning to himself, he jogged to the spot where he'd ditched the laptop, then he pulled into the garage's lobby and office space to tell the last idiot lagging behind to get the hell out of Dodge.

And then he ran into another Mask.

It was the tall blond girl in the gangster uniform he'd seen earlier.

"Where's Teddy?" she asked. Her voice was a quivering mess, and her hands trembled.

"She's a bit busy," Homie said. "Just like you'll be in a moment."

He found that he still had some anger to work out.

She looked past him, then her attention snapped to the flames. "There's a fire," she said.

"Your bear friend's in the middle of it," he said. He rather enjoyed the way her eyes widened in horror. "Maybe you'd like to join her?"

He moved toward the desks at the front lobby. His power had tickled against a bat under the counter he could put to good use.

"You-you bastard," she said.

"Terrifying," he replied as he reached over the counter.

"Sisterportation," the girl said.

Homie looked over his shoulder, wondering what in the world she meant.

"Sisterportation . . . Teddy."

And then the bear was in the room with him, its fur matted down by hydraulic fluid and burned at the edges, but it didn't seem to mind that at all, not judging by the anger in its eyes.

"Oh shi—"

CHAPTER THIRTY-THREE

Victory

Emily stared at the very insensate form of Homie. The man was sprawled on the floor, arms and legs spread out every which way, his mouth wide open.

In any other scenario it would have looked as if he were asleep. That was, if he weren't fully clothed, and on a garage's floor with some rather distressing claw marks across his front.

"Want me to kill him, Boss?" Teddy asked.

Emily shook her head. "No, no, Teddy. We don't need to do that. We've won."

Action Reward!

For finding and defeating another powered individual through luck, brute strength, and more luck, you have earned:

+1 Skill Slot!

"Oh, I got a Skill Slot," Teddy said.

Emily nodded. "Good," she said before turning around and taking in the main section of the garage. It was getting a little smoky, but the fire was mostly contained to one big puddle on the ground and some rags. There were other liquids, though, and she didn't doubt they might be troublesome.

"Teddy, can you take him outside?" Emily asked.

"Sure thing, Boss."

The bear reached down and clamped down on the front of Homie's shirt before awkwardly dragging him toward the front door.

Emily left her to it and found a fire extinguisher by one of the doors.

The thing was nearly too heavy for her to lift off the ground, so she ended up rolling it on its rim all the way over to the fire.

She hesitated before spraying it though.

The case Homie had been carrying was still in the lobby, left on the ground when Teddy had knocked him clean off his feet.

She jogged over to it and opened up the bag to reveal a laptop. The drive. The source of her woes.

The temptation to keep it, to try and unearth its secrets herself, was there. In the end, she flung it, bag and all, onto the pile of rags burning the brightest and watched as the plastic case shriveled and burned.

"Boss?" Teddy asked from the doorway. The bear could barely fit her head through.

"One sec," Emily said. She pulled up the nozzle on the fire extinguisher and hosed everything down with whitish foam.

Was that enough to destroy the drive? She kicked the laptop over and eyed it for a moment. It was warped and melted on the edges, and she was certain that it didn't work anymore, but maybe some of it was still retrievable.

"Teddy, could you come here?"

Two or three cathartic minutes later, and the laptop was broken up in a few dozen pieces, the drive was not-so-carefully extracted, and Emily had vented her frustration by hammering into the still-smoking device with wild abandon.

"So, Boss," Teddy said. "Are we going to do anything about the cops?"

Emily whipped around and looked outside where a pair of squad cars were just coming to a stop.

"Where did you put Homie?"

"There's a bench out front," Teddy said.

Emily flung the drive into the laptop case, looked at the mess they'd made, then decided that it was mostly Homie's fault anyway. "Let's leave out the back," she said before leading by example.

No one got in their way as they left out the back and Teddy helped her over a wooden fence that blocked off someone's backyard.

Feeling rather self-conscious about the whole thing, Emily pulled Teddy along with her toward the center of the city and toward the campus.

It was only when she was halfway there and crossing over a little waterway that she finally ditched the bag and the drive. The bag went into a public trash can, and the drive splashed quite satisfyingly into the running water under the bridge.

Littering was bad, but . . .

But that was disposing of evidence, which was probably worse.

"How are you feeling?" Emily asked Teddy.

"I'm all right," Teddy said. "Got squished a bit, but nothing broke, I don't think."

"Oh," Emily said. "That's . . . good. Um. What do you want to eat tonight?"

Teddy blinked up at her. "Anything?"

"You did a lot of hard work today," Emily admitted. That, and if a nice meal could alleviate some of the guilt she felt for leading Teddy into trouble again, then it was worth any price.

Teddy licked her lips. "Fish. All the documentaries say that bears need to eat lots of salmon to get big and chunky. And I want to be the chunkiest."

"We can buy some salmon," Emily said. "Um. My dad used to grill fish outside. It was really good. But, uh, we can just stop by a nicer place and order some to go?"

"Sure!" Teddy said.

Emily patted the bear girl on the head, right between her fuzzy ears, then inspected her hand when it came back all greasy and covered in motor oil. "But you're going to shower first," Emily said.

"Aww, Boss."

The return to the spot where Emily had stashed their normal clothes, then the quick stop by one of the nicer restaurants to pick up a rather expensive meal, was nearly all done in silence. Teddy did talk a little, but mostly she was going on and on about *Cool Bear Facts*, which Emily found . . . surprisingly enjoyable.

"And all the coolest bears have two layers of fur," Teddy said as they finally, finally reached the dorm. Emily handed Teddy the food boxes as she unlocked it and opened up. "The long fur is to keep warm and make the bear look even bigger, even though bears don't need to look big because they are big."

"Uh-huh," Emily said.

"And the short fur, that keeps the bear nice and dry and clean. Which is why I don't need to take a shower."

Emily smiled down at the girl. "Shower first, then food," she said.

Teddy pouted, but she placed the food on Emily's desk and ran off to take a no doubt very quick shower.

Emily slumped into her seat and let some of the stress just . . . seep out of her. It was done. The drive was broken, the bad guy was caught. No doubt the police would have questions, but Emily was well and truly done with the life of a Mask. She'd be hanging up her costume for good.

Still . . .

Name: Emily Wright		
Alignment: Villain		
Alias: The Boss		
Level: 1		
Powers		
Sister Summoning		
Create Sister	Rank 2	
Sisterportation	Level 1	
Points		
Power Slots: 0	Skill Upgrades: 3	Skill Slots: 1

She had one Skill Slot available. A Skill Slot that could give her something that might be the difference between life and death. Homie had seemed ready to attack her, and when she'd frozen, Emily had thought herself done for until she remembered her Sisterportation skill.

What if her next skill was something equally lifesaving?

She hesitated a little, then gave in.

Do you wish to spend a Skill Slot point on the Power: Sister Summoning?

" . . . Yes," Emily said.

New Skill unlocked!

Double Trouble has been added to your Power's Skills!

She . . . had no idea what that meant. Two Teddys? That would be pretty troublesome. Would she need to get numbered shirts? No, that was silly.

"Status: Double Trouble."

Double Trouble
Sister Summoning
Level Max
Allows you to summon a second sister with Create Sister. Instant use.
Activation: Voice command
Cooldown: None
Max New Sisters: One

"Oh no," she said. "Status: Create Sister?"

Create Sister
Sister Summoning
Rank 3
Allows you to summon a sister, a being with power, who will aid and assist you on your path to Villainy. A sister has her own powers and stats that you may improve. Can be resummoned.
Activation: Voice command
Cooldown: None
Max Summons: Two

Emily sighed. That . . . had not been what she was hoping for. Not that she'd known what she'd get. Really, it had just been a pull of the gacha and a hope for something handy.

"You okay, Boss?" Teddy asked as she stepped out of the washroom. She was wearing a pair of towels and an oversized T-shirt that was all damp and wet. "Do you have indigestion?"

"No, Teddy," Emily said. "I . . . can summon a second sister now."

"Cool," Teddy said. "You should do that after we're done eating."

Emily blinked. "Why?"

"Less to share?"

She gave the bear girl a flat look that bounced off without doing any damage. "I'm not going to create a sister later just for you to have more to eat— Oh no."

But of course, it was too late once more.

CHAPTER THIRTY-FOUR

The Rules

When Teddy had appeared, it had been with a breeze that fluttered across her room and coalesced into the young bear girl. This time was no different.

The air shimmered and twisted, and Emily found herself raising an arm to shield her face a moment before, with a sudden exhale, there was now someone else in the room.

Skill: Create Sister successful!

"Hey," Teddy said.

Emily lowered her arm, the wind having stopped as suddenly as it'd started, and she took in the new sister she had summoned.

??? Wright

Owl Seeing Eye, Level 1

The girl was taller than Teddy, by maybe half a head. That still left her much shorter than Emily, even with the poofy white and brown hair she had. Big round glasses, perched atop a little nose, partially hid a pair of huge yellow eyes.

The hair and eyes were the only strange things, though; the girl looked rather normal otherwise. She had very pale skin, covered by a white jacket whose neck and brim was covered in feathery fluff, and perfectly ordinary Mary Janes on her feet.

The girl shifted, her shoes clicking together and her hands falling by her side. "Greetings."

"Uh, hi," Emily said.

"What kind of girl are you?" Teddy asked. "You don't look like any sort of predator I know."

The girl raised her head back and turned her head away from Teddy with a snooty little huff. "I'll have you know that I am a proud snowy owl. I am very much a predator. Who are you?"

"Owls are smaller than bears," Teddy said. "And bears are apex predators because they eat everything else. Plus, I'm the first sister, so you need to know the pecking order."

"Who cares which order you came in," she said. "All that matters is Big Sister's opinion."

"Ah," Emily said. She wasn't entirely sure how to act around the new girl, or any other stranger for that matter. The bit of tension between her and Teddy certainly wasn't helping. "Um. Teddy, be nice. Your . . . sister is new. And please, you should be nice to Teddy, too. I'm sure she can teach you a lot."

The girl nodded. "I can do that."

"You should name her, Boss," Teddy said. "Get it over with so we can all go to bed already."

"Uh," Emily said. The girl was staring at her now. Her eyes really were rather big; it wasn't just the glasses making them look that way. Not so big they would be considered abnormal, but certainly . . . large. "Maybe we should all get to know each other first?"

"I would love to get better acquainted with you . . . Boss?" The girl turned the last into a question.

"Yeah, she's the Boss," Teddy confirmed.

"N-no, you can call me Emily. You can both call me that unless we're in, um, costume," Emily said.

"It's a pleasure to meet you, Big Sister Emily," the girl said with a nod.

"Good! Um . . . Teddy, you present yourself first." Emily joyfully flung Teddy under the metaphorical bus.

Teddy crossed her arms. "I'm Theodora, but the Boss calls me Teddy because that's a cuter name and it's a kind of bear, which makes it more fearsome. I'm a bear girl. I like communism and helping the Boss, and I don't like it when people don't share. And I like fish and other foods and sleeping."

That was nice and concise. "Ah, I'm Emily Wright. I'm a student here studying English literature and history; I . . . don't know exactly what I want to become. I like . . . uh, looking at nice animals and quiet evenings at home."

The new girl made a little interested sound at that, like a cross between a faint whistle and a hoot. "That's very interesting," she said. "I like . . . I'm not certain what I like yet. But I suspect I'll enjoy furthering my education and learning many things."

"That's wonderful," Emily said. "I'm sure we could visit the library, or, uh, something like that."

The girl nodded. "Now that you're aware of my preferences, will you be naming me?"

"I, uh," Emily looked around. They had some food to eat, and not much else in terms of distractions. "Well, I, um, wouldn't want to give you a bad name. So, please tell me what you think, or maybe what you'd like to have as a name?"

The girl hummed and adjusted her glasses. "I don't know. Perhaps something that reflects my staggering intelligence?"

"Uh," Emily said. The only names that came to mind when thinking of owls were a little bit bizarre for a girl. "Maybe something like . . . Alex? For the library of Alexandria?"

"That is rather nice," the girl said. She said it with some hesitation, though.

"Or maybe Athena?"

She blinked slowly. "Like the goddess of wisdom?"

"Yeah," Emily said. "I think it's a nice name."

"I'll call you 'Tina,' " Teddy said.

"You will do no such thing," the newly christened Athena said.

Emily shifted. "We do need a non-Mask name. Not, not that I'm planning on doing costumed stuff."

Athena tilted her head to one side. "Fine. Tina when at home, then Athena when in disguise. That seems perfectly logical."

"Tina then," Emily said. She smiled a little. It was a relief, at least, to see that her new summon was mostly normal. A bit . . . tiny bit full of herself, but she seemed nice enough. "So, are you hungry?" Emily asked with a gesture toward the boxes of food. "We could eat while I . . . while Teddy fills you in on what's been happening?"

That actually ended up requiring some reshuffling of things. Emily had a little stool and her comfy chair, but that left one person standing. She didn't have any boxes strong enough for someone to sit on, and her nightstand was too heavy to move.

Teddy and Athena, as the two smallest, ended up squished together on Emily's seat while she took the stool and divided up their meal for two into a meal for three.

"Here you go," Emily said.

"Thank you, Emily," Athena replied as she slid the top half of one of the Styrofoam containers closer.

"So, uh . . . do you mind if I look at your stats while Teddy talks?"

"Of course not! I'm certain you'll be tremendously impressed by what I can do!"

Emily smiled at her while Teddy began a rather . . . exaggerated recounting of what had been happening, with some commentary about capitalists that Emily couldn't quite recall happening, but she set that aside. "Status: Athena?"

Name: Athena Wright		
Alignment: Villain, Little Sister		
Alias: None		
Level: 1		
Powers		
Owl Seeing Eye		
Owl Alone	Rank 1	
Points		
Power Slots: 0	Skill Upgrades: 0	Skill Slots: 0

That was similar enough to Teddy's own status, at least the first time Emily had looked at it. Terrible puns and all. If ever she needed a sign the system was cruel, it was right there.

"Status: Owl Alone."

Owl Alone
Owl Seeing Eye
Rank 1
Allows you to inflict growing suspicion, doubt, and paranoia on those around you.
Activation: Thought
Cooldown: None

Emily looked to the side, eyeing Athena as she carefully cut up her meal and ate it with careful little bites. That power seemed . . . ominous.

But Teddy's power was dangerous, too—that was no reason to judge one of her sisters poorly.

She hoped.

CHAPTER THIRTY-FIVE

Paranowl Activities

Athena woke up in the optimal sleeping position, her arms by her sides and her tummy flat on the mattress Big Sister Emily had graciously provided.

The only problem with sleeping that way was that her other sister took advantage of the position and was currently sleeping with an arm across Athena's back, a leg over hers, and her fluffy-eared head tucked between the mattress and Athena's shoulder.

Hideously irritating.

Big Sister Emily was scooting around the room, no doubt getting ready for a long day at school. Athena, in her wisdom, decided not to interrupt. She just rested, comfortably cuddled up next to Teddy, who was very warm, and listened to Big Sister Emily scurry about.

Emily paused next to the mattress a little bit later. "Um," she said. "Are any of you awake?" she whispered.

Athena turned her head all the way around to look up at Big Sister Emily. "Yes," she whispered back.

Big Sister Emily went a little pale, but she nodded. "R-right. Well, I'm off to classes. You two behave, okay?"

Athena nodded. Not very hard because her neck was already stretched to its limit. "Okay."

Emily picked up her backpack and left a moment later.

The room felt a lot quieter without Big Sister Emily there.

And then Teddy started to snore into Athena's ear.

Sighing, Athena began to extricate herself from Teddy's grasp, a surprisingly complicated ordeal since Teddy had a strong grip. She ended up having to lift Teddy's arm up and then roll out from under it, and even then, the bear girl's arm quested for something to hold on to.

Thinking fast, Athena took the pillow from Big Sister Emily's bed and stuffed it next to Teddy who grabbed it and hugged it close.

Her little—insofar as Teddy was shorter—sister was quite troublesome.

She stared down at Teddy while Teddy got to chewing the top of Emily's pillow. It was kind of cute, she supposed.

Athena found her glasses folded nice and neatly on the floor near the mattress, and slid them on, then she found her jacket and donned it, so she was protected by its warm cushiony interior.

The pajama pants she had were Teddy's; they were a bit wide at the hips and ended about midcalf. Her T-shirt didn't fit all that well, either, so it was nice to be back in something proper.

And then she found herself with a lot of nothing to do.

A whole room all to herself, at least until Teddy woke up. No computer to plan diabolical plans with, no books to read . . .

Athena decided to take an enthusiastic walk.

Walks were good for the heart and general health, and if she encountered anyone, she could display her staggering intellect in a more public forum.

Being the most clever of her sisters, she decided that getting locked out of the room wouldn't be very wise. So she found a package of loose-leaf paper from Big Sister Emily's school supplies and appropriated a page. Then she found a bit of tape, and she used both to cover the latch hole on the door. That way the door wouldn't lock behind her.

She was certain that if Big Sister Emily saw her she would be in awe of Athena's superior cleverness.

Stepping up, Athena pulled the door to their dorm closed behind her, a big smug grin on her face. One that faded when the taped-up contraption she'd jammed into one side slid down and the door clicked.

She tried the handle.

It was very locked.

She tried the handle some more.

Then she tried some knocking. "Teddy. Teddy! Wake up, you lazy bear!"

"Uh." Athena paused midbash to look up and around. There was someone there, a taller young woman, with mocha skin and a fashionable blouse over a pair of jeans. "You okay, kid?" she asked.

Athena composed herself, pushing her glasses up her nose and straightening her back. "I am fine," she said. "I may have locked myself out of my room."

The girl looked at the number on the door. "That's . . . Emma's room? The blond girl?"

"Emily, and yes, that's my big sister."

"Right. I'm Sam, from five-oh-five." She gestured behind her. "You, uh, here permanently? Because, you know, these dorm rooms aren't meant to hold more than one person."

Athena found herself in something of a bind. "I'm certain that Big Sister Emily has permission, probably."

"Uh-huh," Sam said. "Do you want to come with me? I'm sure there's someone from the staff downstairs. The janitor, at least. He might be able to open the door."

Open the door and reveal the mattress with Teddy on it. "I'm okay," Athena said.

"Come on, I can't just leave you out here," Sam said.

Athena frowned a little, then, very carefully, she wiped away the expression and replaced it with a smile. Her power came on, like a dimmer switch given the faintest little nudge. "I don't know. Honestly, I don't trust the staff here."

"You don't trust the staff," Sam deadpanned. She had a hand on her hip now and was looking increasingly unamused.

"No," Athena said simply. She turned the dial up on her power. "Would you trust them? Do you even know who they are, or what they've done?"

"Uh," Sam said. She looked past Athena, toward the elevators at the end of the hall.

"How much did you pay for your room? It wasn't that much, was it? Did you ever consider there might be a reason for that?"

"Well, no?"

Athena pushed her power up another notch. She watched, carefully, as Sam shifted her weight from foot to foot, how her hand dropped, and her confident stance turned to one of a mouse darting across an open field. But through all that, Sam never saw the smiling Athena as a predator. "Do you really think I'd be here if I didn't have permission? Of course not."

Sam licked her lips. "Yeah, I guess," she said.

"And if you go to the staff . . . you wouldn't want them to start looking around, would you? What if they . . . find something?"

Sam was sweating now, despite the cool air in the corridor. She was eyeing the shadows and the corners, then frowning as if to herself. She *knew* there wasn't anything there, nothing to be afraid of, that the staff obviously weren't out to get her.

The mere idea was ridiculous.

But Athena's power forced her to ask a simple "What if?"

What if the staff was malicious? What if they did look through her room? What if there was something hiding in those dark corners and in those shadows?

Athena held the dial on her power, keeping it steady. It was enough to have Sam doubt everything for now. She didn't need to be pushed any further.

"I'll be fine," Athena said.

The words, after nearly a minute of silence, made Sam jump. "Oh?"

"Aren't you going to be late to class?" Athena asked as she lowered the intensity of her ability.

"Ah, crap. Yeah, I should go. Are you sure you'll be okay here?"

"Undoubtedly," Athena said.

"Right, well, you keep safe and, uh, if the staff do anything, you tell me, okay?"

"Of course. Thank you, Sam." Athena waved the girl goodbye. She could have continued putting pressure on her—make her doubt her friends and her loved ones, make her terrified of the world and the government and of every lurking thing. In the end, Sam would only have one person she didn't doubt, and that would be Athena herself.

But that would take a lot of time and Athena didn't feel like doing that just yet. She still had to figure out how to get back into the room.

And then the door clicked open and Teddy stuck her head out into the corridor. "Hey," she said.

"Theodora," Athena said.

The bear girl yawned. "Why're you up so early, Tina?"

"Emily woke up already."

"Yeah, but the Boss is like that." Teddy rubbed at her nose. "You coming in?"

"I suppose. There's not much to do."

Teddy shrugged a shoulder. "You can sleep on the Boss's bed when she's not here."

That did sound nice. "Are there books?"

"Yeah."

It was Athena's turn to shrug. "Might as well, then."

She was sure Big Sister Emily would have all sorts of important tasks for her later, so until then, she could relax a little.

CHAPTER THIRTY-SIX

A Receipt for Ulcers

Emily arrived home with an odd sense of trepidation. She found Sam near the dorm entrance, the girl cocooned in a pile of blankets and eyeing everyone who entered with suspicion. That had Emily herself a little nervous, but she arrived at her room with no trouble.

She'd kind of expected to find a mess inside. Instead, Teddy was reading her red book while thumping her feet on the bed, and her new sister, Athena, was bundled up in Emily's favorite chair, a stack of Emily's schoolbooks on the desk next to her. "Big Sister Emily!" Athena cheered.

Teddy craned her neck back without actually moving from her spot on the bed. "Hey, Boss," she said.

Emily closed the door behind her and smiled at the two. "Hello," she said. "Um, how was your morning?"

"It was all right," Teddy said. "Real quiet. We need another computer so we can look at stuff while you're gone."

Emily, for the first time in her life, considered the benefits of a parental lock on a computer. "We'll have to see," she said. "Maybe I can find a used laptop somewhere. You can use mine on some days."

"Cool."

Athena extricated herself from her blankets. "So, Big Sister, are we doing anything Villainous today?"

"Uh," Emily said.

"Nah," was Teddy's reply. "The Boss has bigger concerns than just being a Villain. She's taking the fight to the pigs in charge."

"Um, it's not quite that," Emily said. "I . . . ah, don't really like doing Villain stuff. I'd much rather people see me, see us, as Heroes."

"Huh," Athena hooted. "Well, I'm sure we can do something about that. It'll be substantially more work, but we can do it, I'm certain." She nodded, and Emily had the impression there might have been a crucial misunderstanding there, but she couldn't quite pin what and how.

"So," she said, "I guess we have a few Mask things to do today. And we need to grab something to eat. Maybe we can stop by the thrift store again and buy a microwave, so we can cook stuff in here."

"What'll we cook?" Teddy asked.

"Um, just noodles and stuff," Emily said. She felt kind of bad—it was her duty to make sure Teddy and Athena ate well, but she wasn't exactly equipped for feeding them and so on. "And we can pick up some clothes for Athena. I don't think she'll fit in yours, Teddy."

Athena nodded. "That would be nice. Could we stop by a book place, too?"

"Oh, sure," Emily said. "There's a used bookstore around, I think. New books might be beyond our budget, but we can probably buy some secondhand."

Athena nodded along. "Sure."

Emily smiled at her . . . sisters again, then sighed as she took off her backpack and set it aside. "I have to make a phone call real quick. Can you guys be, uh, a little bit quiet for a few minutes?"

Athena nodded at her seriously, and Teddy gave her a lazy thumbs-up.

Emily fiddled with her phone for a moment. She didn't want to have to make the call she had to, but, well, she had to. Putting off that kind of thing was always so very tempting, but it wouldn't end well.

She unlocked the phone, then stared at the twenty-odd texts from Mel.

Mel: Hey.
Mel: Hey!
Mel: Did you just catch the H loser?
Mel: Yo?
Mel: Kid, answer me!
Mel: Holy crap, just saw the vid.
Mel: You're on the news. Again.
Mel: Well done!
Mel: Did you grab the D?
Mel: Oh, ewww.

Mel: Didn't mean it like that.
Mel: Sorry.
Mel: Is Bear okay?
Mel: There was a camera in the lobby place.
Mel: I'm trying to suppress things, but I don't have the pull for it.
Mel: Hey?
Mel: You alive?
Mel: Yo?
Mel: Call me.

Emily hesitated, her thumb hovering over the texts so long her screen ended up going dark. She sighed and unlocked it again, then tapped a few times until the phone was ringing.

She pressed it to her ear and waited until the click of someone picking up sounded. "H-hello?"

Some part of her wished she'd somehow gotten a wrong number.

"You!" Melanie's voice came through. "Wait. Give me a second." There was shuffling, and Emily heard Melanie telling someone it was an important call that she had to take.

"Um?" Emily asked.

"Okay," Melanie returned. "I'm away from prying ears."

"It's eyes," Emily said.

"What?"

"N-never mind," she said. "Uh, did you . . . want to . . . talk?"

"Do I? Yeah, girl, of course I do," Melanie said. Her voice grew louder. "What were you thinking? I know it worked out in the end, but . . . God, you're still just a newbie. Homie might be some small-fry punk but that doesn't mean you should have just run in there solo. And no, having a fourteen-year-old with you doesn't make it any less dangerous."

"I'm sorry?" Emily said. "I . . . he had the drive."

The phone rumbled as Melanie sighed into its microphone. "Yeah, all right. So do you have it?"

"The drive?"

Melanie scoffed. "I'm not asking about common sense—we both know you don't have that. Yeah, the drive."

"I destroyed it," Emily said.

"Destroyed how?"

"Um. We burned it, then smashed it a bit, but it was hard, so I tossed it in a river. Do you think that's enough?"

Melanie hummed. "I guess? Was it a solid state drive? Or one of those old ones with a disk? Mechanical ones are a lot more fragile. But . . . yeah, lighting it on fire and flinging it in a lake would do."

"Oh, okay, but . . . it's done?" Emily asked. "We're safe now?"

Melanie took a little while to respond, which didn't inspire confidence in the least. "Yeah, I guess so."

"Oh, good," Emily said. It was good. In fact, it was great. She could go on living a normal life, returning to working toward her goal of reaching a Gray morality, while figuring out how to take care of her summons.

It was all coming together.

"Hey, kid," Melanie said. "I think I might have a job for you."

Emily's eagerness petered out. "A-a job?"

"Yeah. Nothing too big, but it might help you. Your career's already taken off a fair bit. With some decent management, you could make it pretty big, if only locally."

"I don't think I want that," Emily said.

"Nah, it's good for you. Tell you what, why don't we meet for an early dinner? I'll tell you all about it. I'll send you the address, and don't worry— I'll pay the tab."

"What? No, no, it's okay, I . . ." Emily stopped when she realized that she was talking to a dial tone.

She lowered her phone, then glared at it when the screen lit up to show a texted address and time.

"Are you okay, Big Sister Emily?" Athena asked.

"I'm fine," Emily lied, though for once it was a small lie. "Just fine. So are you guys ready to head out? The stores close at five, so if we want time to see what they have, we should leave soon."

Teddy groaned and rolled off the bed, and Athena hopped off her chair.

"We can grab something to eat, too," Emily added. It gave Teddy's step a bit of pep.

Why couldn't all her problems be as simple to understand as her sisters?

CHAPTER THIRTY-SEVEN

Bonding

So you two can pick out whatever you want as long as it's not too much, okay?" the Boss said.

Teddy nodded. She was real good at following orders, but she had to show she was the best, not only to cement the chain of command, but also to teach her new sister how things were done. "You got it, Boss," she said.

The Boss had brought them all to the same thrift store where Teddy had gotten her awesome hoodie and the dress that became part of her costume. In fact, most of her clothes, except for her underthings, were bought here.

The Boss said that secondhand panties were evil, though, so they didn't get any of those. Teddy figured they should have bought a few. There had to be a way to weaponize some of the granny panties she'd seen, but if the Boss said no, then it was no.

The Boss had a few things to look at, so with a little wave to the pair of them, she moved off and left them in the shop all on their own.

Teddy spun around and took in the sea of racks and clothing, no two garments alike. "There's a lot of stuff to look through," she said.

"I suppose," Tina replied. "So do we just go around and pick out any outfit we happen to like the appearance of?"

Tina always had to use big words where small words would do, Teddy noticed, but it wasn't that big a deal. She mostly knew what the bigger words meant, and if she didn't then she could guess. Bears were great at guessing. "Yeah, pretty much," she confirmed. "I found this by looking really hard." She tugged at the front of her hoodie, the one with a big bear on it.

"Then perhaps I won't look that hard," Tina said.

Teddy blinked. What was that supposed to mean? "Look, skirts and stuff," she said as a sort of distraction. There were, indeed, skirts and stuff hanging off a rack. Tina moved over to them and brushed her hand past a few as if feeling the fabric.

"I don't know if I like skirts," she said at last.

"Yeah. I'm more of a shorts person, but I'm a bear, so I don't get cold."

Tina nodded. "Snowy owls also don't get cold much because of our superior downy feathers."

"Meh, feathers are like lamer fur," Teddy said.

Tina gave her a flat look. "Can your fur make you fly?"

"Can you fly?" Teddy asked.

Tina huffed and moved on past the first row of skirts, then stopped at the second. These were a lot more serious, done up in browns and pastel colors. "What about these?"

"You'll look like a librarian," Teddy said.

Tina nodded. "Good. I bet I can find some nice blouses to go with them. It'll make for an exceptionally smart outfit."

Teddy shrugged. She didn't care how smart her outfits looked, only that they were comfy.

Tina ended up being really hard to shop with. She'd poke and prod, and hum and hoot over each choice before picking something. Teddy's method of just grabbing everything that looked cool was way more effective.

"So, Teddy, since you've been around longer, can you tell me about Big Sister Emily?" Tina asked after a while. She was busy trying on some jackets, but they were all made for women that were a lot bigger than Tina, and she ended up looking very silly in them.

"Yeah, I guess," Teddy said. "The Boss is pretty cool. She gets real excited a lot, and her words get all mumbly. I think she's a bit shy, though."

Tina let out a low "hoo" of exasperation. "We'll need to fix that."

"Fix? The Boss isn't broken," Teddy said.

"I'm aware that she isn't broken, but she does seem to lack self-confidence. We can make her even better."

Teddy gave her a look. "I'm not sure what you mean. The Boss is fine the way she is."

Tina shook her head. "Haven't you seen how the Boss doesn't want to do evil things?"

"Yeah."

"That's because she lacks the confidence to do them," Tina said.

She might have sounded entirely sure of herself, but Teddy wasn't sure she bought it. "I don't know. The Boss might not want to do evil things because she just doesn't feel like it."

"She's a Villain," Tina said. "Doing evil things is in her nature. Of course she wants to do them. I bet the only reason she doesn't is because she's shy. Can you imagine her giving an evil monologue?"

Teddy really couldn't. "I guess not. So if we're gonna help the Boss be more confident . . . wait, how are we going to do that?"

Tina hummed. "I don't know."

Teddy felt her shoulders slumping. "But you just said you wanted to."

"I didn't say that I was aware of all the answers. I'm not knowledgeable about everything," Tina said. "I suppose we could just be very supportive of her?"

"Like, tell her she did good when she does something evil? Not good in, like, the opposite of evil way, but good in the . . . uh, did right way."

Tina nodded. "That could work. It sounds a bit slow, though."

"That's all right. The Boss's plans aren't meant to be real fast. I think she's playing the long game."

Tina slid one thing onto the rack and pulled off another. "She has a long-term plan?"

"Yup," Teddy said.

"What is it?"

"I don't know."

Tina's eyes narrowed, and since they were really big, that was a lot of narrowing. "Then it's a secret long-term plan."

"Yeah, I guess," Teddy agreed.

"That's really cool," Tina said.

Teddy nodded. It was really cool. She pointed to a blouse. "You should get this one."

Her new sister looked at it for a moment. "It's very red. I don't know if I like red."

"You should like red. Capitalists don't like that color. They have this whole thing called a red scare. It spooks them."

"Are capitalists dangerous?" Tina asked.

Teddy nodded. "Oh yeah. Very. Even the Boss said that capitalism can be bad."

"Well, if Big Sister Emily said so." Tina picked the blouse off the rack.

"But I'm going to look into these capitalists myself. You sound like you're nervous about them."

"A bit? They steal your food and they have these invisible hands," Teddy explained. "It's real creepy."

"I think that's enough stuff," Tina said as she tossed the blouse atop her pile of clothes. She didn't have all that much as far as Teddy could tell. A few skirts, some blouses, and a few other things, like pj's that were all flannel and fluffy, and a poofy white scarf made of some sort of fur.

Teddy helped her carry some of the stuff, because she was a bear and bears were stronger than owls. Not that Tina could even turn into an owl. Her power was all mind-gamey and kind of boring.

They had to wait by the entrance for a while, the woman behind the counter eyeing them the entire time, but then the Boss showed up and everything was okay again. She paid for the clothes, because they lived in a failed system where taxation and disproportionate monetary compensation were still a thing, and then the Boss reached down and grabbed each of them by the hand.

"Where are we going now, Boss?" Teddy asked.

"I think we should take all this back home. If you feel like changing, that'll be the best time," Emily said. "And then we have someone to meet later. She's paying the tab, so eat as much as you want."

"Really?" Teddy asked.

"Oh yes," Emily said. "She sprung this on me, the least she can do is cover some of the food bill." The Boss didn't look too pleased, but Teddy didn't mind.

"Then let's go home," Teddy said. "I need to make a big poop to make room for all that food."

For some reason, the Boss sighed real hard.

CHAPTER THIRTY-EIGHT

Nom Nom de Guerre

Emily hadn't spent all that much time in Eauclaire before. Oh, sure, it was only an hour's drive from her hometown, and it was one of the closer cities, but they had everything they needed in town.

The only reason to come to Eauclaire was to visit some of the more niche shops, or to visit the college. There was a decent hospital, too. She might have been born there, maybe. She would need to ask her mother to confirm that.

The point was, Emily didn't know the city enough to be able to pinpoint all the nicer restaurants and other places like that. So she was a little surprised when she followed the address Melanie had given her all the way to a strange building set on the corner of a street just a couple of blocks away from the shopping district.

This was on the western side of Eauclaire, where the more affluent houses were, and the nicer neighborhoods.

Maybe that's why the restaurant was so fancy . . . and yet strange.

The Railroad was a two-story building, made of red brick, with some nice landscaping around its entrance. That much was perfectly ordinary. The large train engine sticking out of the front wasn't ordinary in the least though.

It was a big red steam engine, situated as if the restaurant had grown around it.

"Cool," Teddy said.

"Is that normal?" Athena asked.

Emily shook her head. "It isn't," she said. "I'm kind of surprised I never heard of it."

She started toward the front door, tugging her sisters along with her. All three of them were plainly dressed, though Athena's outfit made her seem a bit more formal, or like someone trying really hard to look like a businesswoman.

They were greeted at the door by a pimple-faced teen in a butler's outfit. "Hello," he said in a voice straining not to crack. "Do you have a reservation?"

"Um," Emily said over the clink of cutlery. "Maybe? Under 'Melanie'?"

"Family name?" he asked with the tone of someone trying hard to be taken seriously.

"I don't know?" Emily said.

He looked at her, then back down. "Well, there is a Melanie," he said.

"Ah, um, does she have black hair and, uh, a loud voice?"

He nodded reluctantly. "Let me ask the lady. What are your names?"

"Emily," she said.

The waiter left, leaving her and her sisters standing awkwardly in the lobby. All the people at the nearest tables were dressed sharply and looked important. She could only imagine what they thought of her and her sisters in such plain clothes. Maybe she could return home and change? But she didn't have anything too nice to wear, let alone something to give to her sisters. They'd stand out no matter what she did.

"Right this way, miss," the waiter said as he returned.

They crossed a room full of little booths that partially hid the people having their meals, then walked alongside the parts of the train engine resting in the middle of the restaurant until, finally, they reached a spot with a rounded booth that had a curved bench around a table.

Melanie was there, sitting back with a pair of empty glasses before her. "Hey, you're finally here," she said. "The Hero of the day!"

Emily nodded and eyed the rounded bench. There was plenty of room for her sisters and herself. Teddy slid in first to place herself between Emily and Melanie, then Emily and finally Athena sat down. Teddy was just tall enough to place her arms on the table.

"Um, so, hi?" Emily began.

Melanie grinned at her. "Yeah, hi," she said. "Who's the new munchkin?"

"I'm Tina," Athena said as she tilted her head up and back. "I'm Big Sister's sister."

Emily looked for the right words, then settled on doing her best. "She's like us. That is, uh, Teddy, you, and me."

"Huh," Melanie said. "You know, at this rate you're building up an entire team."

They were interrupted as a new waiter came by and filled their cups with icy water, then left a few menus on the table.

Emily eyed the two normal menus and the two kids menus, then pushed the latter toward her sisters. "I-I guess. I don't plan on having a whole team or anything."

"Hmm," Melanie said as she leaned back with her menu in hand. "You should maybe think on it. Speaking of . . . did you think of what you'll be doing?"

"You mean, from now on?" Emily asked. "Um, no, not really."

"You should. This time of year is pretty ripe for new names to show up and market themselves. It's the only time where the big names chill out for a bit and don't mind others hogging the limelight before they jump back in it."

"Um," Emily said.

"Just think about it, yeah?" Melanie said.

Emily nodded, then turned to her sisters to help them choose. It also meant putting off her own choice, which was fine. She hated picking things off a menu. She never knew what she would like.

"They have fish sticks," Teddy said. "That's good, right?"

"I guess," Emily agreed.

"But look." Teddy pointed to the picture next to the fish sticks. "They look like little animals. What if they give me some that look like bears?"

"I'm sure they'll taste just as good?" Emily tried.

Teddy pouted up at her, but she returned to the menu, so Emily turned toward Athena, who was glaring at hers.

"Did you decide what you want?"

"All the things on here are for kids," she said.

"Um. Yes?"

Athena glared harder. "I'm too old for these things," she said.

Emily looked at the menu for a moment. "You don't like . . . spaghetti and meatballs? Or, uh, miniburgers? Look, that one comes in a little cardboard train."

"What?" Teddy asked. "You get to eat a train? That's awesome."

Emily rubbed the top of Teddy's head and pretended not to notice the flash of envy across Athena's eyes. She'd give Athena some affection, too, if that's what Athena wanted, but Emily wasn't so sure yet. Athena was a lot harder to read than Teddy. "You can choose from my menu, if you want," Emily said.

"Right, well, while you guys pick," Melanie said. "I had a chat with our handsome friend about big H and the drive. He's pretty happy with you, you know."

"Oh, um, that's good," Emily said.

"I won't ask how you found H, but yeah, good work. Kinda why I wanted to bring you here to celebrate, you know? One less Villain on the streets. Though I think you made a few idiots in the community jealous."

"Huh?"

Melanie shrugged. "The world of Heroes isn't as pretty as it's made out to be. We're all competing for relevance, and there are only so many Villains to beat down. There's a lot of petty infighting and shit like that."

"Really?" Emily asked.

"Oh yeah. Those who just want to look good for the cameras can pick up little quests here and there, but those who want to be big-time Heroes, they need worthy opponents. Those aren't all that common. The world's an increasingly peaceful place, and that means fewer opportunities. So you and Teddy here nabbing that guy, that got some people really annoyed."

"But they could have gotten him themselves?" Emily asked.

"Don't bring logic to a fight about feelings. It'll only get you stabbed," Melanie said.

"If anyone tries to stab my sister, I'll stab them right back with their own logic," Teddy said.

Melanie snorted. "You go, bear girl," she said. "But, yeah, I didn't invite you here for nothing. There're a couple of things we should talk about."

"Like what?" Emily asked with growing trepidation.

"Well, first, we need to talk about Cement. He reached out to our handsy friend, arranged for a meeting and everything. A nice face-to-face. I'm not going to be there, too many other affiliations, but Handsy might invite you. He'll pay you, of course. Make sure to gouge him."

"I-I don't know if that's a good idea," Emily said.

Melanie shrugged one shoulder. "Up to you. The other thing I want to talk about is your future. Or your lack of it. You kinda made a small splash, you and teddy bear here. I was thinking that maybe it would be a good time to show you around."

CHAPTER THIRTY-NINE

A Mouthful

Emily looked at the menu with eyes that weren't quite focused. She wasn't paying it any attention. Rather, she concentrated on other things.

Most notable was Melanie's offer.

Emily had to think of which potential path would lead to her and her summons seeming the least suspicious. That, and which path would take up the least time. She already had a lot more on her plate than she'd expected to.

Her plans had been to lead a quiet college life, get a degree that could help her find a nice quiet job, and then live as a lone bachelorette with about eight very cuddly, quiet cats.

Those dreams had collapsed a while ago. Her quiet college life was in shambles. She hadn't even done all the homework due in a few days!

Emily shifted her grip on the menu, then carefully turned the page. She kind of wished that she was looking at images of kittens instead of pasta and steak. Those would at least calm her beating heart.

She had to refocus.

Melanie's offer would put them in the spotlight. That . . . might not be the greatest thing there was, but it had potential. They could come out as Heroes, then slink back out of the limelight. People would assume the pressure was too much or something.

Maybe they could do a few nice acts, cement themselves as good people in the community?

She nodded. That made sense.

The problem was joining a corporate team or anything like that would mean placing themselves in a position where they'd be asked a whole lot of questions, some of them uncomfortable.

What were her other concerns?

Handshake's . . . thing. He wanted her for something. Backup, maybe? Some sort of intimidation thing when meeting with Cement? That made some sense. She herself wasn't very intimidating, but Teddy could be. Especially when she was in her bear form.

Was she strong enough to take on someone who could move cement around with his mind?

Emily would rather not find out. Even in the best-case scenario, Teddy would complain a lot if she got wet cement caught in her fur.

"Ma'am?" Emily jerked up to see that she was the center of attention. A young waitress was staring at her, notepad in hand and a patient smile on. "Your order?"

"Oh, oh, uh, sorry, I'll have . . . what she's having," Emily said with a finger pointing toward Melanie.

"A second lobster and filet mignon plate then," she said.

Emily blanched. That sounded expensive. But then, Melanie was the one footing the bill.

"And you, miss?" the waitress asked Teddy.

"Yeah, I'll have the fishy sticks, but not if they look like bears."

"Um, noted," the woman said. She had a bit of a smile that she hid from Teddy by raising her notepad. "Anything else?"

"Yeah, I'll have the train meal, too." Teddy pointed to an image of a cardboard train with a chicken breast and fries and cheese.

"That's a full meal," the waitress said.

Emily waved her arms to try and dispel the comment. "It's okay. She, uh, eats lots. Weird . . . metabolism?"

"Yeah, I got the best meta."

The waitress nodded. "Of course. And to drink?"

"I'll have a pint of vodka."

Emily wanted to press her face into her hands.

"Um," the waitress said. She looked over to Emily and Melanie.

"It's best when served really cold," Teddy explained. "Maybe with some ice?"

"She'll have juice. Any sort of juice," Emily said.

The waitress nodded rapidly and turned to Athena next. Fortunately, the owl girl just ordered some chicken risotto with a glass of grape juice.

"So," Melanie began when the waitress walked off. "Actually, wait, you never told me about the new girl."

Athena leaned forward so that she could better meet Melanie's gaze. "I'm Big Sister Emily's little sister," she said.

"Ah, so she knows everything, right? Because I just assumed back there."

Emily nodded. "She knows, yeah." She wasn't going to admit that Athena had her own power, not when she herself wasn't familiar with it yet. She had to remember to test that, actually.

Bringing a notebook around with her was growing to be a priority. She had so many little things to remember all the time—it was getting to be too much.

"Cool," Melanie said. "So there's this thing where the corps and the government grab all the newbies and jumble them together. It's a semi-public thing. So no press, but plenty of press."

"That doesn't make sense," Teddy said.

"It kinda does," Melanie returned. "When we say that the press is somewhere, it usually means that they're there in force. Cameras and reporters and all. Now they're aware of the event, if you want to call it that, but they're politely told not to show up. So lots of paparazzi hide around the planned routes and take 'in action' photos. They're big sellers. It makes the new Heroes out to be pretty active."

"Will we get to beat up some other Villains?" Teddy asked.

Emily's heart constricted at the "other," but she realized that Melanie would probably assume Teddy meant "other than Homie."

"Probably not," Melanie said. "Heroes are kinda awful at law enforcement."

"Really?" Emily asked.

"Oh, don't get me wrong, they act as a decent counterbalance to the police, but most don't have training, and a lot of powers are too lethal for proper policing. Even then, most police calls are simple things. Speeding tickets, the occasional accident, some domestic disputes. You don't need someone in a cape to show up to every fender bender."

"Then why're you keeping the Heroes around if they're not helping the proletariat?" Teddy asked. Her eyes narrowed. "It's some capitalist ploy, isn't it?"

Melanie snorted. "Pretty much. There's a lot of money in marketing. Lots of donations and Heroes make the politicians standing next to them look great. That, and there is a need for Heroes. Endgames can't and shouldn't be tackled by normal folk. Actual Villains with strong powers are downright terrifying if you're a normal person, and some Heroes bring flexibility to situations that the police just can't manage."

"It sounds as if the world isn't quite used to the idea of there being some who are just better at things," Athena said.

Emily looked over to her little sister. That was a weird sentiment, and one that certainly didn't mesh with what she'd been taught before.

"Something like that," Melanie said. "It's a weird situation to be in, but it's not like you can just tuck away every person with powers. Some places have tried that—it doesn't end well."

Emily nodded. She still had a few questions, but the waitress returning with some drinks put an end to that. The girls each got a glass of juice, and then the waitress set down two very fancy glasses before her and Melanie. She left without a word, leaving Emily staring at her drink.

It had a little umbrella, and crumbs around the rim, and the drink had a few colors still mixing within.

"Neat," Teddy said.

"Um, what is it?" Emily asked.

"You're over eighteen, right?" Melanie asked.

"I . . . yes," Emily said.

The woman shrugged, flicked the umbrella out of her drink, and took a sip. "Then enjoy."

Emily hadn't ever really tried drinking anything alcoholic before. Oh, maybe a sip from her dad's beer when she was little, but that was so far back.

But then, she was already pushing way past her comfort zone, with acts of Heroism, and fighting, and surrounding herself with the kinds of people she'd never expected to befriend before.

Maybe continuing to try new things wouldn't be so bad? She'd certainly dreamed of being far, far braver than she was.

Carefully, she picked up the cup and brought it close to sniff at it. The drink smelled sweet, and like alcohol.

Emily made up her mind.

She took a sip.

And then she almost gagged at the taste, while Melanie broke out into uproarious laughter.

Maybe new things weren't for her after all.

Everyone Poops

Athena grunted as she took on her sister's full weight. Teddy, for all that she was about as big as Athena herself—a bit shorter even—was heavy.

It probably had something to do with the way her belly was protruding, making the bear on her hoodie look almost three-dimensional. "You're fat," Athena remarked quite sensibly.

Teddy's head turned around and she leveled a flat gaze at her. "No, you're fat."

"I am not," Athena said. She patted her perfectly flat stomach. "See. Nothing." She reached out and poked at Teddy's stomach. "But here it's full of food."

"Don't poke it," Teddy said. "It's not ready to come out."

Athena heard Big Sister Emily sigh from behind them and she turned her head all the way around to look up at the taller girl. "Please . . . just . . . watch what you're saying?" Emily asked.

"I was talking about needing to poop later," Teddy said.

"Yes, I know. We all know," Emily said.

"Well yeah, everyone poops," Teddy said.

Athena poked Teddy again. "Big Sister wants you to stop talking about poop," she said.

Teddy shifted. "Oh. Well, she could have just told me that."

Emily walked around the two of them and to the door to their room, which she opened up for them. "Okay, everyone inside," she said.

Athena helped drag Teddy over to the mattress, then paused next to it. "Want me to dump you here?" she asked.

"Yeah, I need to sleep this off," Teddy said.

"Oh no," Emily said as she closed the door. "No sleeping before taking a quick shower."

Teddy groaned. "But I took one . . . recently."

Athena's eyes narrowed. "What's recently mean?" she asked.

"Like, yesterday, maybe?" Teddy glared. "You never took a shower in your entire life. You're probably covered in summon goop or something."

"I am not!"

Emily coughed, cutting the argument off before it could really start. "You're both taking showers. Come on, start finding some clothes. Put your dirty stuff in that box over there and . . . and we'll find out where the cleaners is tomorrow. Thank God it's Saturday."

There was some running—and in Teddy's case waddling—around for clean clothes and stuff, then because she was the fastest, Athena jumped in the shower first. When she came out and let Teddy in, it was to find Big Sister Emily at her desk, looking at her laptop.

"What are you looking for, big sis?" Athena asked.

"Oh? Ah, I'm looking at the profiles for some of the new Heroes," Emily said.

The screen was on some flashy site, with a few images of people in strange costumes. They were mostly bright and colorful and very high-tech. "All right," Athena said. "Does it have anything to do with that conversation with Melanie?"

Emily nodded, then paused. "Um, do you know who Melanie is?"

"A woman who paid for our food and tried to get you drunk?" Athena asked. It was a good thing Big Sister hadn't drunk that drink, or else Athena would have had to do something rude to the Melanie woman.

"She's a Hero. An actual Hero. From some company. Her name's Melaton. She can make people fall asleep."

Athena flinched back. "A Hero? Why would we want to be near one of those?"

"Um, because she helped us with Homie?"

"Does she know that we're Villains?" Athena asked. She made sure to enunciate the word with all the gravitas it deserved.

Emily shook her head really quickly. "No, no, she doesn't. She thinks that we're Heroes too. Or, at worst, Gray?"

Athena understood. Big Sister was being very clever, as expected of her, and was beguiling her way closer to the Heroes. She'd no doubt spring some sort of trap on them and murder them all in a frenzy of violence and destruction. Athena only hoped she could grow strong enough by then that she would be helpful.

"I see what you're doing," Athena said. "It's very impressive."

"Thank you?" Big Sister Emily said. "I'm just looking at the profiles for these new Heroes before we meet them. I think we could maybe push back some suspicion by being close to them."

Athena agreed. "Of course."

"Um. I . . . don't know if you can be present for that? They don't know you, and you don't have any sort of costume. You'd stand out."

Ah, so Big Sister wanted Athena not to stand out. "With my power, that's probably for the best. Teddy is much better at that kind of thing."

Emily nodded. "Good, good."

So when Athena did go to this . . . event thing, it would be out of costume, to help in her own way. Her sister was really turning out to be a top-notch strategist.

Athena adjusted her glasses so that they flashed, and she held back a bout of manic laughter.

Teddy trampled her way out of the bathroom looking all bedraggled and wet, then she flopped onto the mattress. "I'm sleeping now," she said.

"Ah, okay," Emily replied. "My turn in the shower, then. Good night . . . in case you fall asleep."

"Yup! Good night," Teddy said.

"Mm-hmm," Athena agreed as she too went over to the mattress and lay down tummy-first. She slid her glasses off and carefully set them under the nightstand so no one would step on them.

Sharing a bed with Teddy wasn't all that great—Teddy moved a lot in her sleep, and she snored, and she liked cuddling up into Athena's side and drooling all over her—but it wasn't awful.

Once they'd taken over a decent part of the country, they would be able to afford a big bunker, or a secret base, or maybe a gothic mansion on a hill somewhere, and then Athena would get a bedroom all to herself, with lots of bookshelves and stuff.

"What are you thinking about?" Teddy asked.

Athena twisted around so she could see Teddy's face. Her eyes were closed, but the bear girl was obviously still awake. "I'm thinking about later, when Big Sister becomes a big-time Villain."

"Oh, that's cool. She wants to become more than just a Villain, though," Teddy said. "I think she wants to become a Super Villain, or maybe a Demon."

Athena's eyes widened. "Whoa."

Her big sister was aiming high.

"Yeah. It's pretty cool," Teddy confirmed.

"Do you think . . . do you think she'll need our assistance?"

Teddy snorted. "Yeah, of course. She can't turn into a bear on her own or . . . uh, make people a little bit nervous?"

"My powers do more than that," Athena said.

"Sure," Teddy said.

Athena poked her in the tummy, eliciting a groan. "Don't be mean. It's against the rules."

Teddy stuck her tongue out, but flinched when Athena raised her hand for another poke. "Yeah, yeah, I get it. We'll need to be a lot stronger to help the Boss is all I'm saying. I'll need to turn into, like, a much bigger bear, and you'll need to be even scarier."

"Even scarier . . ." Athena said.

She wondered if she could do that.

Was she scary already?

Probably not. She was a skinny tallish girl, with big glasses and near-white hair. None of that sounded scary. She couldn't even make a disappointed face like Big Sister could. That face was the scariest thing she'd ever seen.

Athena could rely on her power, of course, but that felt like it wasn't enough. Or maybe it was more of a crutch.

No, Athena would need to work on being scarier.

Or maybe she could work on her overall presentation.

She imagined herself looking really cool, posing as people fell into nightmares all around her.

"Yeah," she said.

Emily came out of the bathroom with a towel around her head, yawned, then trudged over to her bed. "Good night, Teddy."

"Night, Boss," Teddy said.

"Good night, Athena."

Athena smiled up at her big sister, the sister she was going to make so proud. "Good night, sis."

CHAPTER FORTY-ONE

Knots

Emily set her pen down and looked up to her screen. There was a nice wall of text before her, and about eighteen different tabs open on her browser from when she'd gone down a rabbit hole during her research.

Her homework had been pretty simple, but Emily figured that it was okay to go above and beyond. She needed to shore up some points now in case they ever had any sort of group work later in the year. She had never had a good presentation in her entire life, and she doubted that would change.

With a sigh, Emily closed her laptop and let her hands rest upon it. Doing her homework had been her last excuse not to get going. If she didn't leave soon, she might be late, and that was practically unforgivable. "All right," she said.

"What's that, Boss?" Teddy asked.

The bear girl was on Emily's bed, legs over the edge and arms held out above her with her precious red book in hand. She was nearly a quarter of the way through it by now.

"I said all right," Emily repeated. "I think I'm almost ready to get going."

"Cool!" Teddy said. She snapped her book shut and sat up. "I'm already ready."

That was true. Teddy had her yellow dress on, cargo shorts and all. Her plastic mask was smiling up at the ceiling from atop Emily's pillow. "That's great," Emily said. "You should get in your hoodie to hide all that."

Teddy nodded and jumped to rush over to her hoodie, which was lying in a corner on a pile of clean clothes. As it turned out, there was a small laundry room on the first floor of the dorm, so Emily had some clean things, at least.

She considered training Teddy or Athena to clean her clothes, and maybe pick up her room, but that felt a little mean.

She'd probably still do it, because washing up was very much the opposite of fun, and it was just about the only way she could use her powers for something that was actually useful.

Emily stood up, stretched a little, then looked at her notifications.

She had a lot of pending quests, well over a dozen. Most she dismissed without a second thought. Any that mentioned killing or maiming were struck out right away. Those that wanted her to rob people could go too.

It left her with a few choices that actually seemed interesting.

Quest!

The Queen with the Silken Sword, Continued

Become an outstanding member of your community!

Reward: +1 Skill Upgrade point per 10 people who recognize you as "good." Scoundrel +1 per 10 people who recognize you as "good"!

Accept? Refuse?

That one was easy enough to agree to. She'd done it once, and doing it again seemed straightforward. The upgrade points would probably be wasted on her, but she could use the push toward Scoundrel.

New Quest!

The Thorn Among the Roses

Convince the local Heroes that you are one of them.

Reward: +1 Skill Upgrade point per Heroically aligned person who recognizes you as an ally!

Accept? Refuse?

That one was . . . well, it would serve as a way to tell how well she was blending in with the Heroes she was to meet. No push to Scoundrel, but none toward Villain, either.

"Hey, Big Sister Emily?"

Emily looked over to Athena. The owl girl was wrapped up in a pile of blankets, something that she and Teddy both seemed to enjoy doing. "Yes?" Emily asked.

"Is there anything you need me to do while you head out with Teddy?"

Emily shook her head. "No, I don't think so. You can just, uh, stay here, if that's what you want."

Athena pouted, but only for a moment before wiping the expression away. "But I want to help," Athena said.

Moving close, Emily dropped to her knees next to Athena, then hesitantly placed a hand on the girl's head. "Thanks," she said. "But I think Teddy and I can handle this bit. You can do your own thing."

Emily imagined that the girl would appreciate a day off, all on her own.

"I'll leave my laptop here, and . . . well, we don't have that many books. We can pick some up next time we head out."

Athena nodded. "All right, Big Sister Emily, I'll do my own thing. I won't let you down."

That was a rather strange way of putting it, but Emily could live with it. Her sisters seemed to have a few bizarre idiosyncrasies at times. Athena with her odd determination to seem smart and mature and Teddy with . . . Teddy could probably serve as the basis for a psychiatric thesis, actually. She had a lot going on in that bear head of hers.

"I'm superready!" Teddy said as she posed in her hoodie.

Emily cracked a grin, then stifled it before she could offend Teddy. "Good! I'm just going to get my pack, and put my shoes on . . . and then retie yours, and then we're off."

"You can't even tie your shoes?" Athena asked as she poked her head out to look at the messy knots holding Teddy's boots on.

"I can! Knots count as tying!"

Emily shook her head and dropped before Teddy. She tapped her lap so the girl put a foot onto it. "Before we go," she said as she started to pick away at the knot, "you have a Skill Slot to spend, right?"

"Yeah, I've got two," Teddy said. "Should I use them to get stronger?"

Emily nodded. "Sure. Better now than later. But, ah, maybe just use one, to see what we get? We can save the other for later."

"Cool!" Teddy said. She stared off into space, then grinned huge. "Oh, cool! My new skill is the best!"

Emily set Teddy's foot down, then tapped the other. "What's it called?"

"Iron Bear!"

Emily wondered what that entailed, then remembered that she could look for herself. "Status: Iron Bear?"

Iron Bear
WereBear
Level 1
Allows you to turn your fur into iron spines for a period of one minute.
Activation: Thought
Cooldown: One hour

"Wow," Emily said. "That sounds impressive."

It did sound somewhat impressive. Not terribly imaginative, but certainly interesting. She imagined that it would make Teddy quite a bit more fearsome, and perhaps a little more dangerous.

"Yeah!" Teddy agreed, the pride in her voice and demeanor obvious. "Can I put some points into it? I wanna turn into an Iron Bear more often."

"Um. Sure, but maybe save a couple in case you unlock another, better skill?"

Teddy nodded. "Yeah, yeah."

"All done," Emily said as she placed Teddy's foot down. She brushed her pant leg and climbed to her feet. "Are you all ready?"

Teddy nodded.

"Good. Now, once we get there, don't threaten the Heroes, or anyone else, and try to be nice. Remember, we're trying to pass ourselves off as Heroes. I think Melaton will be around, so she can help us if we have questions. It'll go well, I'm sure," Emily said.

She really, truly, hoped that was the truth.

Emily picked up her backpack next to the door, then turned to make sure Teddy was following her. "Okay," she said. "Athena, we'll see you later, all right?"

"Of course," Athena said.

"Um. Bye?"

With that awkward exchange out of the way, Emily took Teddy by the hand and headed out.

CHAPTER FORTY-TWO

Buckle Up

Emily pulled out her phone while the elevator hummed its way down to the first floor. It stopped on the third floor and a pair of young men stepped in, but other than eyeing her briefly, they never spoke directly to her or Teddy, so she happily ignored them in favor of checking her texts.

There was one from Melanie, telling her to meet up by the parking lot next to the park on campus.

They reached the first floor and were out of the dormitory a moment later. "I'm going to end up being really fit if I keep having to walk so much," Emily said.

Teddy looked her up and down in much the same way the boys in the elevator had. "That's not so good," she said. "If you want to find a good mate, you need to have healthy fur, and a nice big store of fat." She patted her tummy. "Like this."

Emily didn't trip over her own feet, but it was a near thing. "T-Teddy, you're not, um, looking for a boyfriend, right?" Emily asked.

There was a world of unsaid questions that followed. Emily had kind of left Teddy, and now Athena, to her own devices, but she had never wondered how much either of them knew about how . . . things . . . worked.

She could vividly remember the horror of her mom explaining that kind of stuff and could only imagine the nightmare of explaining it all herself.

"What? Nah. Boys are yucky."

"Yes," Emily agreed right away. "Yes. Boys are real yucky and you should never let any of them so much as touch you, okay?"

Saved!

More or less.

"All right, Boss," Teddy agreed.

Emily felt a little cheap. She'd caught herself admiring some of the guys in her classes already, and she could imagine a more charismatic, less awkward, and less socially idiotic version of herself maybe, sorta, flirting with some of them. But her little sisters could wait until they were in their thirties before worrying about that as far as she was concerned.

They arrived at the park in due time, Emily's preoccupied mind making the trip feel rather short.

She only had to look around the parking lot for a minute or so before she spotted Melanie leaning against the side of a little red sports car. She was in costume already, and if it weren't for the way the park was deserted despite it being a weekend, Emily imagined that there would've been plenty of people gawking.

Emily pulled Teddy a ways away and toward a little restroom building. "Let's get changed real quick," she said.

Teddy had it easy when it came to changing. She took her mask out of her hoodie pocket, then slid the hoodie off, and she was done.

Emily had to practice her dexterity in a little stall, doing her very best not to touch anything. Sliding into a pair of tight pants while hopping on one leg and avoiding mysterious stains left her jealous of her bear summon.

They stuffed everything into Emily's backpack, and then, because they couldn't leave that behind, put the bag onto Teddy's back before heading out.

Melanie looked up when they came close. "About time," she said.

Emily knew they were at least ten minutes early, but that was cutting it pretty close. "Sorry," she said. "We had to get changed."

"Mostly the Boss," Teddy said. "I could just go around as a bear, but that would intimidate too many people, and the Boss wants us to be all Hero-like."

"Uh-huh," Melaton said. She flicked a thumb over to the car. "Get in."

Teddy hopped in without argument and bounced around on the back seat while Emily climbed into the passenger seat and buckled up. "Teddy, can you manage your seat belt?"

"I don't think I want to," Teddy said.

"You'd better listen to your Boss," Melaton said. "Cops can be jerks about that kind of thing. It doesn't matter if you can take a tank shell to the face and come out of it looking windswept, they'll still fine you for not having your belt."

Teddy frowned. "Fine you what? Money?"

"Yeah, obviously."

"I bet these buckles are a capitalist ploy," Teddy said.

Melaton turned around to stare at Teddy, her elbow resting on her seat. "Buckle up, or I'll put you into naptime and then your Boss can buckle you herself."

Teddy pouted but did as she was asked. She complained about the oppression of the proletariat the entire time, but she did it.

"So, um, where exactly are we going?" Emily asked. Cursory research the night before on WriteIt had revealed that a lot of people knew about the event, but there wasn't any concrete information about where it would take place, or who would participate, exactly.

"First, we're stopping by the Heroic Response Force's headquarters. Eauclaire's HRF is one of the smallest around, but they still have a few hidden access points, because they need to justify their budget somehow."

"Okay?" Emily tried.

"That means you'll be meeting everyone else in some boring room. You'll be given the rundown of the rules, then one or two of them, whomever the government got their hands on, will lead the lot of you out and about on a big tour of the city. There might even be some vans to shuttle you around for maximum coverage."

"That doesn't sound too bad," Emily said.

Just a simple stroll through the city. She could do that.

No problem.

It would all be fine.

She wanted to go back home.

"You all right, Boss?" Teddy asked.

Emily swallowed, reminded herself she wasn't alone, and nodded. "I'm fine," she said. Having Teddy with her was . . . not quite like having her mom along, but it was similar. Someone she could rely on.

She knew that she was relying on a preteen communist werebear, but she could deal with that whole issue some other time.

"You're going to be meeting some interesting folk. Most will probably be around your age. Power Day tends to aim for younger people. Your sister back there is probably about as young as they come. Some might be older," Melanie said as she passed a car at a speed that was probably unsafe.

"Oh, okay," Emily said. She wondered if it was too late to return.

"The government types won't stop trying to recruit you. Hell, the corporate ones might push you toward them."

"Huh?" Emily asked.

"Yeah, because the HRF Heroes don't do nearly as much public relations stuff. They have paychecks as long as they serve and a nice retirement package. Corporate Masks need to show off to the public. So if you're with the government, you're no longer competing for attention."

"Oh," Emily said. That was more cutthroat than she'd imagined. "All right. And the others?"

"Don't know if there will be any independents other than you, actually. I got you in as a favor. Well, a favor that pays me real well."

"I . . . don't understand?" Emily said.

Melaton smiled over at her. "Don't worry, you'll figure it out."

CHAPTER FORTY-THREE

Crisis of Personowlity

Athena, unlike her slightly older and far more foolish bear of a sister, was terribly clever. At least, she certainly thought she was clever, and since she was the cleverest person she knew, that counted for something.

It's why she waited a whole fifteen minutes after Big Sister Emily was gone before slipping out of the room. She used a piece of paper and some tape to make sure the door didn't lock behind her. She didn't even mess it up this time.

Sure, someone could now steal from Big Sister Emily's room, but if anyone did that, they'd have to face her, and Teddy's, wrath.

Athena made sure she was nice and presentable, looking like a proper young woman in her blouse and skirt with a nice sweater vest atop it all. It . . . felt like the right thing to wear?

She made her way to the elevator, then down to the first floor while thinking about it.

She was clever enough to know what was happening to her, why she couldn't pick between one thing and another, and why sometimes she felt weird feelings when thinking about Big Sister Emily.

Athena was having a crisis of personality!

It was perfectly normal, at least according to the things she'd looked up on the internet. She was, sorta, at the age where she was supposed to feel rebellious.

Not that she actually felt rebellious toward her big sister, of course.

No, it was that she had come to this world with a certain style of clothes she felt didn't represent her, not the way she wanted it to.

It wasn't just the clothes. It was everything.

Teddy was better off than her. The bear girl was, well, a big bear girl who had things she liked and things she didn't like. It was all nice and simple.

Athena didn't have anything so clear-cut to rely on.

That was obviously because she was an owl, and owls were far more intellectual than mere bears. But then . . . that also meant that with her superior intellect came a whole lot of uncertainty.

She stepped out, then hesitated before turning toward the deeper part of the city and starting her trek.

Athena would ask her big sister how she wanted her to act, but . . . but that didn't feel right either. Big Sister Emily was the best, the greatest person ever, and no doubt a Villain who would terrify the world, but Athena . . . Athena wanted to make Emily proud for who Athena was.

So she'd find out. She'd learn how to be the best Athena there was, and Big Sister Emily, who was the best, would accept her with open arms, and hugs, and pats on the head. Unless new-Athena wasn't into that (which sounded highly doubtful).

Her current plan didn't have much to do with finding herself, though. No, Big Sister Emily had given her a mission! A sort of optional mission, if Athena was reading her correctly. She wanted Athena to be there when the Heroes went out and about, as backup.

Searching online had revealed that a bunch of people thought maybe the Heroes would be going around that afternoon. But then a leak came out that it would be tomorrow instead, so people were doubting it. Athena knew better, though.

All she needed to do was get to the center of the city, then follow after the Heroes. There would probably be a crowd, and even if there wasn't, she could just make everyone around her more suspicious than she was to the eyes of the Heroes.

Simplicity itself.

A plan so simple couldn't fail, of course. That's why Athena grew increasingly confused as she kept walking through the city at a nice, brisk pace, without ever actually seeing the center of the city.

In fact, the houses and shops she was passing looked increasingly dilapidated, and she was beginning to have the impression she might, maybe, have perhaps gotten herself a tiny bit lost.

But that wasn't possible. She was an owl! A mighty predator of the air! Able to hunt down even the smallest rat through feet of snow!

She swallowed and looked around. Her feet were getting tired, and her legs were achy. There were some people on the street, but they looked rather intimidating to approach.

Athena didn't want to give up, not so soon after leaving.

She considered going back, and then she came to a terrible realization.

She had no idea which way her home was.

Balling her hands into fists, Athena continued onward. Eventually, she reasoned, she'd find the middle of the city. All she had to do was keep moving. Maybe she could find a phone to call Emily with?

But then Emily would cancel all her plans, and she'd be really disappointed in Athena, and she'd think Athena was dumb. That was not an option.

She turned a corner, then paused. There was a bar there, with a lot of big guys standing out front in leather jackets next to big motorcycles. Athena hesitated, but with a bit of shored-up courage she crossed the street (looking both ways, because she was smarter than Teddy) and continued on her way.

There was a nice inviting alleyway there, one that would get her away from the biker people. She didn't need to be nervous or anything, the darkness was the natural habitat for an owl like her.

"Hey, girl, whatcha doing here?" the sleaziest voice Athena had ever heard asked.

She felt her blood go cold as she looked up at a man dressed in what might have been a nice suit once. Now it had weird, wet stains down its front and smelled so strongly of alcohol and puke she recoiled even a dozen paces away.

"Ah, don-don't be afraid," he said as he wobbled closer. He had a baggie in one hand, something sloshing within it, and his voice was on the wrong side of slurred. A drunkard?

"Go away," Athena said.

"Aww, don't, don't be like that," he said. "Cute thing like you."

She was cute, but she didn't want to hear it from this guy. She glared over at him, then started pushing her power toward him. Just a little—enough to make him nervous.

The man blanked, glancing around uncertainly before he looked back at her. "Do you want to come with me?" he asked. "It's . . . it's not safe out here for a young lady."

Athena took a long step back.

"Real not safe," he said as he wobbled toward her.

"Oy!"

Athena jumped and spun halfway around. There were three men at the entrance of the alley. Three big guys in black leather, with big beards and bigger scowls. "Look at you, drunk at this hour," the biggest of the lot said. "Piss off, man."

"I was . . . I was just being nice to the nice girl," the guy in the suit said.

The bikers looked at one another, then, at some unknown signal, two of them stepped up and passed Athena while the big one moved toward her.

For a moment, she thought she was in big trouble.

Then he dropped to one knee. "Hey there, kid. You all right?" he asked.

Athena didn't know how to react. " . . . I'm fine," she said.

The man smiled through his big beard. "Yeah, you look like a brave girl," he said.

Athena nodded. Of course she was. She hadn't actually been afraid, merely . . . surprised. "I am," she said.

"Are you lost?" he asked. "Because me and the boys, we wouldn't mind taking you home, or letting you use the phones over in the pub?"

"I'm . . . a little misplaced."

The man roared with laughter. "I think we've all been there," he said. "Come on, we'll find someone to give you a ride back home, and maybe you can try the fish and chips, yeah?"

CHAPTER FORTY-FOUR

Heroic Introductions

Teddy yawned as Melaton pulled them into a parking garage, then stopped the car before a ticket booth. She fished around in a cup holder until she found a card, which she swiped over the screen of the automatic barrier.

When it rose, she drove past a few rows of cars, then past a second barrier and down a floor. "We should be pretty alone around here," she said.

Teddy wasn't afraid of tight spaces, quite the opposite, really, but she still felt as if the ceiling was pressing down on her as they sank deeper into the garage. Too much concrete and pipes, not enough grass and trees.

Melaton swung the car around into an empty bay and put it in park. "Right, let's go," the Hero said as she started to unbuckle herself.

Teddy was faster, though, unclicking her belt in no time at all, and bouncing out of the back of the car to land next to it with a smack of her boots on the ground. The Boss was the last out, but that was okay—she needed to make an entrance, sorta.

The Boss extended a hand down to Teddy, who grabbed it, then they both followed Melaton. They reached a heavy-looking door, one with a keypad next to it that Melaton poked at for a bit. A buzzer sounded; the door opened.

"All the way down," Melaton said as she pushed through the doorway.

There was a long, long hallway, with pipes in the ceiling and lights every few paces. Their shoes plap-plapped along the ground, the sound only interrupted when the door clunked shut behind them. It was a real boring tunnel, but at least it didn't smell like gas, like in the parking place.

The end had another door, this one requiring more tapping away at a keypad before it unlocked.

Teddy was expecting more tunnels, like any proper hidden base should have, but instead it opened into a perfectly ordinary corridor, with white walls and a plasticky floor. Teddy didn't even have time to look around before the Boss's hand tightened.

Two men were coming their way. Men in white-and-gray uniforms and bike helmets with visors over their eyes. They were armed, but their guns were tucked away in hip holsters, and they didn't look too threatening.

Both of them had badges over their shoulders and chests, with little maple leaves and the initials HRF on them. "Melaton," one of them said. "Right on time. Can you follow us?"

Teddy held on to the Boss and followed after the two guys. They didn't smell like Heroes, but they were wearing bright costumes, which was never a good sign. Bright costumes were like the bright frogs in her nature shows: eating the people wearing them would be a lot of trouble.

They followed the men around a couple of bland corridors, then stepped into a much bigger room. This one had a lot of doors, and off to one side, a dozen chairs and a whiteboard. There were more guys, and some girls, in white-and-red costumes.

"Please, take a seat," the guard said before moving on.

The seats, some of them, at least, were occupied. One had that Glamazon girl they'd met that one time in an alleyway. Her costume had changed—there was a lot more spandex and neon now.

Next to her was an empty seat, then a guy in a dark trench coat. He wore bandages around his head and hands, and a big pair of goggles. Teddy figured he was pretty weird.

A woman paced at the back of the last row of chairs. She was in a tight orangey suit, with a bunch of black-brown spots on them. The only part of her face visible was her mouth and chin; the rest was covered by a sleek helmet with cat ears atop it.

And there was one last man, squatting over a chair that didn't look like it could support him at all. He was a huge guy, covered in metallic armor decorated with golden bands. His helmet was full-faced, a big metal bucket with a visor at the front. He was so wide he took up two spots, his armored hands—both as big as Teddy's head—resting on his knees.

"Damn, that one's built like a brick shithouse," Melaton whispered.

Teddy frowned. "Why would you want to live in a house made of shit bricks?"

The Boss tapped Teddy on the head. "S-so, um, now what?" she asked.

Melaton pointed to the back of the room where one wall had a window in it. "I'm going to the break room for coffee and gossip. You, in the meantime, find a seat, listen to some boring instructions, and then try to make friends."

"Oh, oh, I . . . I can do that. Maybe," the Boss said.

Teddy patted her on the thigh. "You'll do great, Boss."

Teddy wasn't sure what the whole thing was about yet. The Boss wanted to blend in with the Heroes more, which was totally okay—it would make their inevitable betrayal all the easier—but Teddy didn't like they were kinda stuck with all of them in one room.

Even a bear didn't go after an entire wolfpack on its own.

Still, the Boss was real clever, so she probably knew what she was doing.

Teddy reminded herself not to insult the Heroes or anything, even if they ended up being disgusting capitalists.

Emily and Teddy picked some seats way off in the back, near the big guy in the black-gold armor. He turned their way, his armor scraping around his neck. "Hey," he said.

The Boss swallowed audibly. "H-hi."

"Hey!" Teddy said right back.

"So, which one of you called me a brick shithouse?" he asked. His voice was real cool, all rumbly and deep.

"That was Melaton," Teddy said. "But it's stupid because you don't look like a house, you look like a person."

The man snorted. "Cute. I'm Slaymaker," he said.

Teddy approved. "That's a cool name," she said, then whispered, "I'm, uh . . . Boss, what's my fake Hero name?"

The Boss shifted on her seat. "Um, Ursa Minor? That's the name a lot of people use online."

"Ursa is 'bear,' right?" Teddy asked.

The Boss nodded. "It is. Ursa Minor is a constellation of stars."

That was supercool. "Yeah, I'm Ursa Minor," Teddy said to Slaymaker. "I turn into a bear."

He nodded. "That's kinda neat," he said. "I punch things hard."

Teddy huffed. She could do that too. It was hardly impressive. Bears were known for their incredible swiping prowess. She bet she could outslay Slaymaker any day of the week. His name was cool and all, but he was still just a Hero.

Teddy was going to ask Slaymaker if his power was really just punching people—given what she knew about powers, they were usually a lot more complicated than that—but she was cut off as a weird man stepped into the room and walked up to the whiteboard at the very front.

The Boss gasped.

Teddy was too busy staring at the guy. He had a big helmet on, with a bug-eyed visor, and a pair of articulated metal antennae sticking out the top. He was wearing a lab coat over pajamas, and he had big fluffy moth slippers on his feet with their own antennae wiggling about.

Unlike most of the Heroes around, this one had his nameplate up.

Quantum Mothman

Paragon, Level 4

"Who's that?" Teddy asked. He was probably important. Only important people could get away with looking so silly.

"That's *the* Quantum Mothman," the Boss said. "He has a lot of powers and has been around for a long time. He's kind of a local celebrity."

Teddy shrugged. Just a big-time Hero. Probably a bit too big-time for the Boss to face off against, for now, but still. She'd keep her eyes on him in case he tried any funny business.

The Quantum Mothman cleared his throat. "Yes, hello, everyone," he said. "I'm me, this is an introduction, and now let's move on to the important parts, yes?"

He tapped the whiteboard and a bunch of words appeared on it, including a map of the city with a red line running through it.

"This is the city, yes?" he asked. No one answered for a moment. "Well, yes. This is your route. You will be given phones. Don't lose them, please. A bit fragile." He gestured to the side and a box appeared in midair. And then it fell to the ground with a crash. He stared at the box, which had opened to spill out a few phones.

Teddy snorted.

"Hmm, yes," he said.

CHAPTER FORTY-FIVE

Hoo You Are Deep Inside

The nice biker guys took Athena into the pub and one of them helped her up and onto a tall stool by the bar. "There you go, little miss," he said.

The lady behind the bar looked at Athena, then at all the guys in their big leather jackets. She gestured at Athena. "Where the hell did you guys find her?" she asked.

One of them rubbed Athena's head. "Ah, we found her in the alley out front. The little miss is a bit lost. You got a phone she can use?"

The bar lady raised an eyebrow and her lips—painted red with a smear of makeup—twisted to one side. "Give me a minute," she said.

Athena took that minute to look around the bar.

It was a strange place. Everything was made of old wood, and the lighting was rather poor. An old jukebox off in one corner was playing a raspy country sound that was crooning out of some speakers linked together by trailing wires. It wasn't loud enough to drown out all the talking and laughing.

There were posters, here and there, for beers and bikes, most of them with very chesty women with blond hair and big lips on them. There were a lot of guys in the room too. Sitting at tables, standing together in little circles, almost all of them with a big mug in hand or sometimes a brown glass bottle.

An enticing smell caught Athena's attention and she turned to see what the guy sitting a few stools over was eating. It was some sort of slab of meat, with a brown sauce over it and a handful of fries on the side. It looked disgusting and smelled heavenly.

"Hey, Su!" the nice biker who'd helped her called toward the kitchen. "Get the girl something to eat while you're at it. She looks hungry."

Athena felt her cheeks warming up, but that soon subsided. She had no reason to be embarrassed. It was only food. "So do you guys just hang out here all day?" she asked.

The big guy laughed, and some of his friends joined in. "Nah, of course not. We've got work and jobs. But once in a while it's nice to step back and have a drink with the boys."

Athena nodded. That made sense. She liked hanging out with Emily, and also, sometimes, Teddy. "That's cool. You guys seem really nice."

He smiled down at her, looking really smug. "Hear that, boys? I was called nice."

One of his buddies snorted. "Best compliment you've gotten from a girl since before your mum kicked you out!"

There was some laughter at that, and her new friend took on a look of mock offense. He turned back to her. "We'll get you nice and fed, call up your parents, then see you home safe, all right?"

Athena could see a couple of problems with that. "Um, all right," she said. "But I don't have parents."

There was some frowning at that. "Why's that?"

"I live with Big Sister Emily," Athena said. "She's the best."

"And she let you out on your own?" he asked.

Athena shook her head. She didn't want these people thinking Big Sister Emily wasn't a good big sister. "No. She had a big important thing to do today, so I wanted to help and . . ." Athena looked away. "I got a little lost."

One of them patted her back. "It's good you wanna look out for your sister," he said. "That's what we all do for each other. Not that anyone with half a brain would mess with us."

Athena pouted. "I wish people didn't want to mess with me," she said. She was taller than Teddy; why couldn't she be just as fearsome? Even her powers, which were kinda cool, didn't feel as useful as Teddy's.

When Teddy went out to help Big Sister Emily, she found costumes and new minions. When Athena went out to do the same, she almost got attacked in an alley.

It wasn't fair. She was an owl, a smart apex predator! She was meant to be more clever and more useful. She sniffled, then pouted harder to keep the tears in.

The bar lady, Su, returned with a cordless phone in one hand and a plate in the other. She took one look at Athena, then glared at all the guys around her. "Oy, you dimwits, leave the kid alone!" she said before placing the plate before Athena. "Here, you eat this. It'll make you feel better."

Athena snorted some snot back in. "Thanks," she said. She picked up a fork, then eyed the steak and potatoes and gravy on her plate. It all smelled really nice. "You're really kind," she said.

"Bah, think nothing of it. These idiots might look and act like meatheads, but they're all right," Su said.

Just like Teddy, really.

Athena began chewing her way through the rather cartilage-filled steak, occasionally slicing bits off with a knife while the guys who'd helped her chatted about motorcycles and spectacular accidents and things she suspected they were exaggerating.

They sounded so cool.

She wished she could be as cool and useful as them . . .

Athena blinked. She was being an idiot.

Turning, she found the guy with the biggest beard, which she suspected was a sign of importance, and tugged at his sleeve.

He paused in listening to one of the other guys telling a story about how he got into this big fight with some thugs and bent her way. "What's up, little lady?" he asked.

Athena swallowed. "Hey, could I be as tough as you guys?" she asked.

The man blinked, his beard twitched, then he roared with laughter. He patted her head, then sat on the stool next to hers with one elbow on the bar. "So you wanna be tough, eh?"

Athena nodded. That would be for the best.

He rubbed his chin, mouth working left and right. "I dunno. You're a bit small to be tough."

She balled her fists together. "There have to be other ways to be tough!" she said.

The big guy chuckled. "Well, half of it's looking the part, I guess. People don't wanna mess with folks who look like they can hold their own in a scrap."

Athena nodded. In her mind she was making notes. Her superior intellect hadn't brought her as much good as she would have hoped. She'd need to supplement it with more toughness. And if this guy was right, that meant looking the part.

A glance around the room revealed a lot of really tough-looking guys. They were big and muscly and tall. She probably couldn't be those things. But they all wore leather and black clothes and stood around in weird ways. "I'll need a nice jacket," she said.

The guy laughed. "Sure! I think we might even have something out back."

"And what's the other half?" Athena asked.

"Huh?"

"The other half to being tough." She wanted to know the full secret, not just part of it.

"Oh, that's all in your head. See, you get a lot of pansies coming around with nice Arlies and new coats, all puffed up and tough-looking, but when it's time to throw fists, they're all cowards. Don't matter how strong they are, they don't have the bal—brains for it."

He gestured into the crowd.

"But some of these guys? Some are old, some are weak, but when they take a knock on the head they get right back up and swing back twice as hard. It doesn't matter if you don't know how to fight. That's not part of being tough. Being tough means even when the going gets hard, you're always ready to go harder."

Su snorted. "What kind of half-brained idea is that?" she asked.

Athena wasn't paying attention to the bar lady anymore though. She was imagining herself—in a cool leather jacket, of course—wiping the blood off her mouth as she stood up to defend Big Sister Emily from some disgusting, no-good Heroes.

It didn't matter she wasn't as hard to put down as Teddy, not as long as she could keep up the fight.

"Yeah," Athena said. "Yeah! I can be tough too."

Su rolled her eyes. "You going to call your parents, kid?"

"Ah," Athena said. "Um . . . I don't know Big Sister's number," she said. Her very recent lesson about toughness kicked in. "But that's okay. I can walk all the way back home, no problem."

The big bearded guy shook his head. "None of that. You know where you live?"

She nodded. "Yeah."

"Ever ride a hog?"

She shook her head. "No?"

"Well then, missy, it's gonna be your lucky day. I'll grab some of the boys. They don't need much of an excuse to head out and around town." He gestured to her plate. "You finish off your meal, all right?"

"Thanks!" she said.

CHAPTER FORTY-SIX

Endemic

Quantum Mothman—no, even in the privacy of her own mind, Emily had to give the name the right emphasis—*the* Quantum Mothman was in the same room as her. It was a bit heady and crazy to think that she was sharing space with a real-life celebrity.

Though, to be fair, Melaton was also a local celebrity, but that wasn't the same. Melaton was small potatoes compared to the genius at the front of the room.

"Yes, well, ah," the Quantum Mothman said. He turned toward the board as if seeking guidance, then turned back to them, the antennae on his head wobbling about with every gesture. "Hmm, yes. Please, tell us your name, and about your power. Not going to be a big dangerous patrol, but it's still best to know."

He pointed to Glamazon first, probably to start at his far left.

"I'm Glamazon," Jezebelle said. "I can produce balls of light. Low kinetic damage, slow-moving, but very bright."

Quantum Mothman nodded. "And the endemic portion?"

Jezebelle looked around. "The what?"

The scientist gestured around with his hands, but no one seemed to understand. "Powers! All powers are multifaceted. They have useful aspects and less useful ones. Most come with a social function. This is called the endemic. Very dumb name. Misleading. Some powers are immediately social; they tend to gain smaller side benefits that match over time. Others are based upon physical changes. These are material powers.

Your balls of light. They're material. If they make people fall asleep, then that's endemic. Think of it as corporeal versus cognitive."

Emily found herself paying rapt attention. It wasn't every day she got a lecture from such an incredible figure.

She supposed that her power was more material. As was Teddy's. And Athena's was probably more endemic, though they hadn't really tested it yet.

"Right," Glamazon said. "I guess I don't have an endemic bit."

Quantum Mothman shrugged. "It will come. All my powers have developed both, though not at the same speeds."

"How do you get more than one?" the man in the trench coat and wrappings asked.

"Win an Endgame," Quantum Mothman said, his jovial voice turning serious. "It rewards you with an additional power. That is all. Your name?"

"I'm Hindsight," the man said. "I can see what happens a few minutes ahead if I focus."

"Precognition? Simulation? Other mechanism?" Quantum Mothman asked.

"Ah, I think it's a simulation?" Hindsight said. He didn't sound all that certain.

The Quantum Mothman nodded along. "Yes, plausible. Will have to test. Affiliation?"

"I'm with Nimbletainment. I just signed on this past week."

The older Hero made a humming noise and his antennae twitched about. "Will see then. Corporate Heroes don't get as much studying. More money, less science. Sad, but understandable. Next!"

The woman pacing behind the chairs looked up. "I'm Cheatah. Spelled C-H-E-A-T. I can move faster than most. And my, ah, endemic thing allows me to cheat."

Quantum Mothman's head tilted to the side. "Interesting. Vague, though. Yes, can keep it to yourself. No harm."

"Thanks," Cheatah said as she continued to pace.

"Good! Now you, in the large armor," Quantum Mothman said with a gesture to the man three seats to Emily's left. It was the big guy Teddy had been talking to.

"I'm Slaymaker," he said. "Independent. I can hit things hard."

Quantum Mothman's head tilted to one side, then the next. "Yes. I believe you. And you, little one?"

"I'm not little," Teddy said. "I'm a bear. And I'm, uh . . ." Teddy looked at Emily, but before she could say anything, Teddy remembered her new name. "I'm Ursa Minor."

Glamazon "aww"ed.

"Very well done," Quantum Mothman said. "Don't recommend the very young to participate in too many things. Best to take it slow, build up to it. Become very fearsome later thanks to accumulated points. Still. And you?"

Emily didn't jump. She'd had . . . maybe a whole minute to prepare. That wasn't nearly as much as she wanted, but it certainly was more than nothing. "Hello, I'm, uh, the Boss."

She cringed. Saying it out loud like that was so lame.

"The Boss," Quantum Mothman repeated. He didn't have an ounce of judgment in his voice and that somehow made it worse.

"Y-yes?"

"Not certain?"

Emily nodded, then shook her head, then used her voice. "Y-yeah, I mean. Yes, I'm certain that's my name."

"And your power?"

"I can, um, teleport others to me? But only people I'm close to."

The Hero hummed. "Interesting limitation. Usually comes with greater power to compensate. Built-in social aspect, too."

Emily nodded along. He *was* the expert on the matter.

"Yes, well, good," Quantum Mothman said. "Now that you know one another's names, please pay attention to this map." He flipped the whiteboard over to reveal a detailed map of Eauclaire. There was a route marked through it all in red. "This is your path. The map is on your devices, with a tracker. No getting lost."

"Should we expect anything on the route?" Hindsight asked.

The older Hero shook his head. "Nothing big. Mostly publicity stunt. Crime rates fairly low at the moment, unlikely to run into crime-in-progress. Perhaps minor Villains or ne'er-do-wells testing out powers, but even that isn't likely. Just follow the route. Sign autographs if willing. Smile at cameras. This is more to get to know one another."

Emily kind of wished there would be more crime to tackle. It sounded far easier than trying to talk and socialize.

Quantum Mothman clapped. "Okay. Time for you to go. Doors are that way. Goodbye."

And just like that, the Hero flounced off, hands buried in his coat and head ducked low as he power walked away.

For a long few moments, all the Heroes—and Emily and Teddy—sat around, the air filling with an air of uncertainty.

Glamazon was the one to break it. "Well, all right," she said as she jumped to her feet. "Let's head out, shall we? I kinda know my way around here, so follow me . . . ah, unless you guys want to use the facilities before we head out?" She bent over to pick up the box of phones Quantum Mothman had brought and hugged it before her.

"I don't need to poop," Teddy whispered to Emily. It was more of a stage whisper. One that everyone heard.

Emily contemplated just dying as she endured the looks from all the Heroes. "We-we're good to go," she said.

"Cool," Glamazon said. She grinned at them, then gestured to the far end of the room. "Come along!"

"How do you know your way around?" Hindsight asked as he started walking next to Glamazon.

The group formed up in a sort of row. Glamazon and Hindsight at the front, Emily and Teddy in the middle, and Slaymaker right behind them. Cheatah, for her part, lingered at the back, detached from the rest.

"I'm joining up with the good guys," Glamazon said. "I got the whole tour."

"The HRF are all right," Hindsight said. "But their wages are a bit poor for my tastes."

"It's not about the money," Glamazon said.

"The marketing contracts aren't much better," he added.

Glamazon huffed, hands clamping onto her hips. "It's not about that, either. It's about setting an example and making the world a better place."

Emily eyed the back of the woman's head. She'd seen Jezebelle lapping up attention before, and be rather . . . rude as a sidekick. Part of her really doubted that Glamazon thought the way she said she did.

They crossed a few intersections, the floor tilting down as they went. Emily had the impression that they were heading deeper and deeper underground, not helped by the way everyone in the group stayed quiet for a while.

Finally, they reached a small chamber with a pair of guards standing at attention. They looked like people who had been checking their phones moments before.

Glamazon tucked the box with the phones under her arm, then started handing them out. "One each," she said.

"Thank you," Emily said as she took hers. It was a sleek little flip phone, of all things. Old-school, but it looked new. Maybe it was tougher than a standard smartphone? Or more disposable?

"Does it have games?" Teddy asked as she poked at hers.

"I don't think so," Glamazon said. "It's a work phone, so the folks in charge can keep track of you and so you can call for help. Just press the red buttons on the side for anything."

"Wait, this thing is some sort of tracker?" Teddy asked. "That sounds like some sort of capitalist trick to get people to keep working for lower wages."

Emily patted Teddy on the back and pulled her aside before she could really get started.

Once everyone had a phone and Glamazon looked appropriately smug about keeping things more or less organized, she led them to a door by the back. "All right, let's go!"

CHAPTER FORTY-SEVEN

Economic Theory According to Teddy

Patrols were *so* boring.

If it weren't for the Boss holding her hand the entire time, Teddy would have flopped to the sidewalk for a quick bearnap already. All they were doing was walking.

Walking!

She could do walking at home.

Teddy knew she wasn't being fair. The walking at home wouldn't be the same as the walking here. They weren't walking to get anywhere, they were walking to be able to walk next to a bunch of boring Heroes so the Boss could look less suspicious and stuff.

It was all real clever, but Teddy was a girl of action. If she wasn't sleeping, eating, or doing her business, then she ought to be helping the Boss or helping her comrades in the proletariat.

That gave her an idea.

Teddy looked at all the Heroes around her.

There was the big Slaymaker guy in his kinda-cool armor. He seemed like a levelheaded kind of person. When the others stopped for autographs, he was right there with the Boss and that woman in the cheetah costume telling people he wasn't interested.

The other two, Glamazon and Hindsight, were lapping up all the attention, making themselves look bigger and more important like . . . like a couple of big fat aristocrats getting bigger and fatter off the proletariat's admiration.

The only thing people should get big and fat on, Teddy believed, was the shared work of their comrades—and lots of fish.

The defacing of people's private property was over now, and they were back on track to go nowhere. That meant Teddy could either be bored, or she could be a good bear and make the best of it.

"Hey, Slaymaker guy," Teddy said. "Are you a capitalist under all that armor?"

The big Hero looked way down at her, then shook his head. "No? Not really. I haven't given it that much thought."

Teddy frowned. What would a capitalist Hero look like?

Probably someone who wanted to grow stronger on the oppression of those beneath them, instead of supporting the people. It would have to be a Hero who placed their own popularity and fame and money before the needs of the people they were supposed to be Heroing. Also, according to what Teddy knew, they'd probably be fat.

"I think if you were a capitalist Hero, you'd be all like 'I'll save you, miss, but only if you pay me and we can take pictures and stuff after.'" Teddy said.

Slaymaker snorted. "Uh-huh. And what would the better kind of Hero do?"

Teddy needed to think about this, too. She was a communist *Villain*, not a Hero. "I think," she began slowly, "that a communist Hero would put the needs of the community first. They'd be a Hero because it's something only they could do, but they'd know fighting Villains isn't something that needs to be done if you can stop the Villains by, uh, addressing the things making them Villains . . . yeah. And they wouldn't need much from the community, because they'd live just like a normal person."

"That's surprisingly eloquent," Cheatah said. "I don't think people would want to risk their lives being Heroes just because it's the right thing to do, though. You need more than that. Fame and money fill that gap."

Teddy pouted. "That's stupid."

"I don't know, kid," Hindsight said. "I think I'm on the other side here. I'm a corporate Hero. Does that make me evil?" he asked.

"Obviously," Teddy said. "Not good evil, just lame evil."

Hindsight shook his bandage-wrapped head. "What? Being a Hero isn't evil, kid."

"No, of course not," Teddy said. Villains like her were evil. Heroes, like she said, were just stupid. "But if you're a Hero just to make a bunch of money and feel more important than other people, then you're the worst kind of Hero."

Teddy had the impression that Hindsight was glaring at her, but she was right, so he could glare all he wanted. The only person allowed to feel more important than others was the Boss.

"Kid, I think you're delusional. You can't expect people to do anything for free."

Teddy patted her dress where her red book was tucked away. "I read this thing, by some guy called Karl Mark, and his friend Fred Angel, and they say that if you want to be happy with the work you're doing, you need to see yourself in it. I think he meant like, uh . . . Boss, what's the word for a thing that's another thing, but not literally that thing?"

The Boss blinked a few times. "A metaphor?"

"Yeah, thanks," Teddy said. "Karl was talking about a metaphor. Like, can you see yourself being a lame Hero who only does stuff for money, or are you an okay Hero who does stuff to help people and because it's what you like doing?"

Hindsight went quiet, which meant that Teddy had scored a bunch of points. "I didn't come here prepared to debate a damned preteen on economic theory," he muttered.

"I suppose that's one of the reasons Villains are so bad, right?" Cheatah asked. She seemed much more interested in this conversation than anything else so far.

"Nah," Teddy said. "See, Villains, the good Villains"—she squeezed the Boss's hand—"they do Villain stuff because that's who they are, it's who they wanna be. They don't do it for money. The money they take is to do bigger things. And they don't just hurt people because they can, they hurt people to be able to do even more stuff later. Villains are the ultimate communist ideal."

The Heroes were all silent, no doubt awed by Teddy's superior reasoning.

"Um," the Boss said. "T— Ursa Minor can be a bit opinionated, but she means well."

Yeah, that was right!

"Uh-huh," Hindsight said. He shook his head and looked past them all. They were nearing another intersection, Glamazon leading the way with a few sparkling balls hovering by her side and around her openly worn nameplate. "Let's pause here."

"Need a break?" Glamazon asked. "We've been walking for a while."

Hindsight moved over. The intersection was cut into a hill, so the corner they were on didn't have any buildings, but instead a steep incline with an old lamppost atop it. The dirt was all smushed in a diagonal path that people had probably been using as a shortcut since forever.

A bench sat next to the lamp, one that Hindsight used. He placed his hands between his knees and lowered his head. "Let me use my power," he said. "It'll make scouting a little easier."

"All right," Glamazon said.

For some reason, the Boss was letting Glamazon lead them. It was weird, since she wasn't a boss like the Boss, but Teddy didn't question it much.

No one seemed to mind Hindsight just sitting there. To be fair, Teddy's legs could use a break. Bears were not always long-distance walkers.

Teddy plopped herself down on the grass next to the Boss, arm reaching way, way up to keep a hold of the Boss's hand. She was still pondering cool things, like how she'd get to be real smug at Athena later when they got back home, when Hindsight jumped on his bench and let out a low gasp.

"You all right?" Glamazon asked.

Hindsight scrambled to his feet. "That way," he said, pointing off to the side.

"What? No, we're meant to go that way," Glamazon said with a gesture in the other direction.

The Hero shook his head. "No, you don't get it. There's a Villain over there. I saw it."

"What?" Glamazon said. She was pulling her phone out already. "I'll call it in."

"Never mind that!" Hindsight said. "We have to stop them." He turned to the others, the Boss included. "Come on, quick!"

"Oh no," the Boss said.

Teddy didn't see it as much of a bad thing. Beating people up was one of her favorite things to do. "Let's go, Boss! We're gonna be big ol' Heroes today."

CHAPTER FORTY-EIGHT

Unwise

Emily was very much uncertain. She didn't know how wise it was to run toward a problem, as opposed to away from it.

For one, while she was surrounded by an entire group of Heroes, these were Heroes with no real training.

Glamazon seemed to be the only one with an idea of what she was doing, probably from having gone on patrols with Silver Fox. The others? Hindsight was blatantly focused on his own wallet, Slaymaker a bit brutish, and Cheatah seemed rather skittish at best.

Teddy was the only one Emily found herself trusting, which was probably why she held on so tight to Teddy's hand as they ran after the others.

She could have refused, could have turned around, and if asked later, she would admit that turning around would have been the brightest thing to do right then. But the peer pressure, the sudden urgency, and the shot of adrenaline to her spine all precluded thinking too hard about what she was doing.

They came around a corner and the group slowed down.

The street seemed perfectly ordinary at first glance. Cars parked by the road, a few people moving about, shops lining one side, a rocky outcrop on the other side of the street with a wide sidewalk cut into it.

It was definitely a nicer, if older, part of Eauclaire.

In the middle of the road was a very plain Onda Ivic the size of a small house. Its wheels straddled both sides of the road, wider than two people side by side, and the top of the car was nearly ten feet up.

"What the?" Glamazon said.

"Size manipulation," Cheatah said with certainty. She and Slaymaker were the only ones not obviously panting.

Hindsight pointed to one of the stores ahead of the oversize car. "Jewelry store."

Emily looked at the shop, a small place tucked in between two other stores, both high-end clothing shops. At first she couldn't see anything wrong with it, then she noticed the small rack of bars carefully set aside next to a glass pane on the sidewalk leaning against the building.

The shopfront's windows were missing.

"Crap," Glamazon said. "I need to call this in!" She started to fumble with her phone.

"Let's move in," Hindsight said.

"They could have hostages!" Glamazon hissed after him.

"One guy, and he doesn't," Hindsight said.

"How do you know?" Glamazon asked.

Hindsight paused and stared at the taller woman. Even with his face entirely covered by bandages and his goggles, Emily could tell that he was looking incredulous. "Because I can see the future?"

"Oh . . . right. I'm still calling this in." She turned to the side, pressing her phone to her ear.

The others, Emily included, didn't seem to know what to do.

"Okay," Hindsight said. "We should split this up. I'm not a heavy hitter. I think . . . The Boss, you're like me, right? You can teleport people?"

"Y-yes," Emily said. "Just T— Ursa Minor."

"Then we send in Ursa and Cheatah. They're both fast and can hit hard. Slaymaker, you take the middle." Hindsight flicked his hand, and a baton cracked out from his sleeve and deployed to its full length. "Let's go!"

There was no time to argue, or contest, or do anything.

Teddy laughed a very disturbed and excited laugh and charged ahead, arms out by her sides in a T and her little legs pumping as she took off across the street. Cheatah just sighed and shot off after Teddy. The woman was fast. Not impossibly fast, like some speedsters, but she moved like she could have been in the Olympics, overtaking Teddy in a second and making it across to the shop before anyone else.

Just as Cheatah was getting close, a bunch of spinning bits of glass flew out of the shop, then popped into six-foot-long shards that the speedster only narrowly dodged before they shattered.

A ladder sprang out of the front of the building, someone hanging on to its end before the whole thing shrunk down.

The Villain, if they were an actual Villain, rolled as they hit the road, then bounced to their feet.

Emily had all of a second to take in their costume.

It wasn't that impressive.

They had ripped jeans, a construction worker's belt, and a pair of what looked like sturdy steel-toed boots. Their face was entirely covered by a motorcycle helmet, and they had a jacket that might have looked cool, in a sort of punk way, if they didn't have a big off-white cushion strapped to their torso by a few chains.

The Villain was a rather short man, which made the costume look a bit silly and, frankly, cheap.

Small Package

Mischief Maker, Level 1

Small Package froze in the middle of the street as he took in all the people standing around, all the people in costumes.

"I'm an apex predator!" Teddy roared as she bolted at him.

The man ran forward, took something out of his pocket, and flicked it forward, where it turned into a full-sized electric scooter.

With a hop that looked practiced, Small Package landed in the scooter's seat and twisted the throttle to full.

Emily watched Teddy turn into a bear, but her sister's first swipe missed the man entirely.

Cheatah started to run after him, but the scooter was surprisingly fast.

And then, out of nowhere, Slaymaker exploded forward, a burst of flame roaring out of the back of his costume even as his fist's armor expanded and clanked until it was twice as big.

Emily saw Small Package's eyes grow wide as he tried to jump off his scooter.

Slaymaker's fist rammed into the spot where the front wheel of the scooter met its body with a crunch of breaking plastic.

Small Package went flying with a scream.

The cushion strapped to his chest burst, turning into a full-size mattress, yellow stains and all.

The Mischief Maker bounced off the cushion he'd been carrying around his neck, then rolled onto the street.

He was no more than ten feet from Emily.

"Sisterportation: Teddy!" Emily screamed.

Small Package rolled to his feet and was starting to run again when Teddy, in all her grizzly glory, appeared before him.

"Soviet Smash!" Teddy roared as she rose to her hind legs and punched Small Package in the face.

Small Package flipped, rear over teakettle, and smacked into the ground helmet first with a crack that sounded distressingly painful.

Action Reward!

For teaming up on a fellow Villain and taking him down, you have earned:

+1 Skill Slot!

His legs thumped into the ground, and Emily was genuinely worried he was dead before the man groaned and tried to turn over.

"Don't touch him," Hindsight warned. "I didn't see if his power works on people. I don't think so, but better safe than sorry."

Emily nodded and approached Teddy to pat her side. It was always a little strange to casually pet a bear that outweighed her so much, but it was still Teddy under there.

"Did I do good?" Teddy asked.

Emily was quick to nod. "Very."

Small Package groaned again and reached up to grab on to his helmet. Glamazon rushed over. "Don't!" she said.

The thief paused and groaned something else.

"The cops are on their way. Unless you want your identity leaked all over, I'd keep that helmet on. We'll have you in an ambulance soon enough," Glamazon said. "There are a lot of us, and only one of you. Don't try anything."

Hindsight hummed something. He looked happy, though, bouncing on his toes and all. "That was a nice bonus to an otherwise dull afternoon."

Slaymaker and Cheatah walked over. "I felt rather useless there," Cheatah said.

"You got him to run, sloppily at that. You did your part," Slaymaker said. He was rubbing at his fist, the armor having returned to its normal size. "Did you get anything from it?"

"Yeah," Cheatah said. "Don't feel like I deserve it, though."

"Take it. Early rewards are important." Slaymaker looked over the street. The huge car blocking it off was shrinking, and the people who had been hiding before were coming out to gawk, though they were still staying away. "We made a mess," he said.

"Nah," Hindsight said. "No injuries, except for this idiot, and no major property damage except for some glass. It's what insurance is for. Plus, it's a jewelry store. They're practically asking for it."

Glamazon shook her head. "Well done, guys. We might have to give statements, so let's just call this patrol done and stick around here for a bit? I'll ask that the bigwigs send over some drinks or something."

"Could go for a cold one," Slaymaker agreed.

"Drinks that can be drunk in public, when a kid's part of the group," Glamazon gestured to Teddy.

"Can I have vodka?" Teddy asked.

Emily held back a little laugh at the expression on Glamazon's face. Maybe . . . maybe being a Hero wouldn't be that bad.

And then Small Package spoke. He was crying, of all things, chest twitching and convulsing. "They said it would be good. They said I would be safe."

"Who said that?" Slaymaker asked.

"Maybe we shouldn't—" Hindsight began. What they shouldn't was never clarified, though.

"The Cabal. They said I'd do well," Small Package said.

Emily had a sinking feeling in her gut.

CHAPTER FORTY-NINE

No Rest for the Not-So-Wicked

Emily hadn't disliked the patrol. Sure, it'd really put her social abilities to the test, and it was hard and not something she'd want to do often, but it wasn't as bad as she'd feared. It was like going to the dentist. The anxiety of going was often worse than the experience itself.

She couldn't say the same about the postbattle scene.

Once they'd secured Small Package with a pair of cuffs, and after a van from the HRF arrived to help secure him, she and the other Heroes were left on a street crawling with police and EMTs.

There weren't any injured, and there wasn't any fire, but they still had firefighters looking around. Police cordoned off the street, and none of the Heroes were allowed to leave until they'd been asked a few dozen questions by a bored detective.

Emily was afraid the police officer might discover something, but the questions had been perfunctory and simple. Apparently, there had been plenty of footage of the entire event from a dozen angles, and the detective let slip that it was a pretty clear-cut case. The only person hurt was the criminal, and even that seemed negligible.

And so the young Heroes were then faced with a far scarier prospect than talking to the police: the media.

For every ambulance and police car, there was a news van, and it seemed more reporters were on the scene than government employees.

Emily tugged Teddy after her and tried to find a spot to hide away from the cameras. In the end, her savior came from the phone she'd been given. It buzzed and displayed a message saying that extraction was available if she wanted it.

Extraction, as it turned out, was a free ride in the back of a cramped van with Slaymaker and Cheatah.

"Just the four of us, huh?" Slaymaker said as Emily jumped in and then helped Teddy climb up. Teddy's legs were too short to make it up into the back without her first sitting on the edge.

"Um, I guess," Emily said.

The armored man shrugged huge shoulders. "Figures. Hindsight and Glamazon both seem to enjoy the limelight more than I think is healthy."

"They're Faces," Cheatah said.

Emily settled down in a seat opposite Slaymaker and three seats down from the cat-themed Hero. "Faces?" she asked as she helped Teddy buckle in.

"Heroes that work in the public eye a lot. Big, flashy. They sell a lot of merch and spend a lot of time doing image things," Cheatah said. "The other Heroes, at least the others that are active, they tend to be the ones carrying the brunt of the duty."

"Oh," Emily said.

"At least they don't need to costume up as much," she said. "And some are famous anyway. Like Melaton."

"Melaton isn't a Face?" Emily asked.

"Have you seen any interviews with her? She swears like a sailor half the time and seems like she's one rude comment away from punching out a reporter."

That . . . sounded about right.

The rest of the trip was done in relative quiet. Slaymaker pulled out a phone from somewhere in his armor, and Cheatah nestled into her seat and closed her eyes.

Even Teddy was pretty quiet, leaning all the way over so that she could rest her head against Emily's side while she moved Emily's arm over her shoulder like a blanket.

The van stopped eventually, and Slaymaker squeezed his way out the back.

On exiting, Emily found herself in a familiar parking garage. Melaton was nearby, leaning against the back of her car with a cigarette pinched between two fingers. Emily glanced around, but there wasn't anyone telling her where to go or what to do, so she helped Teddy out of the van and wandered over to Melaton. "Um, hi," she said.

Melaton blew out a plume of smoke from . . . not a cigarette, but a thin cigar. "You can't stay out of trouble, huh?" she asked.

"It wasn't our fault," Emily said.

The woman shook her head. "Want a ride back to the park?" she asked.

"That would be nice," Emily admitted. She knew it was only early evening, but she felt like . . . well, like she'd been out doing social things all day.

Melaton slid her cigar back between her lips and shoved off the back of her car. She strode over the trunk, stepped onto the top of the driver's seat, then fell down behind the wheel. "Come on."

Emily scrambled to get into the passenger seat, using the door because the idea of stepping on the car so casually felt superoffensive. Teddy got into the back seat and buckled up with no protesting. She seemed tired, which was completely fair. She'd worked hard.

"Same place?" Melaton asked.

"The park? Yes, please."

"Hmm." Melaton backed them out, then took off with a squeal of burning rubber. In no time at all they were violating traffic laws and heading over to the park. "We had something of a live feed going on," she said.

"Oh?" Emily asked.

"Negative points for following along with Hindsight's shit plan, but otherwise, good work."

Emily sank into her seat. "Was that normal?"

"Nah. We get maybe two, three Villain attacks a month, at most. It's worse this time of year, of course. Calms down, and by midsummer—" Melaton cut herself off as she changed over two lanes without so much as glancing back. "By midsummer it's quiet as hell for us. Endgames are generally rougher by then, though."

"Oh," Emily said. "Okay. And, ah, do you know what the Cabal is?"

They almost rear-ended a truck as Melaton's head whipped around. "Where'd you hear that?"

"The Villain, Small Package? He muttered something about that."

"Damn," Melaton said. "Just pretend you didn't hear anything. It's for the best. And get rid of those phones."

"Okay," Emily said. She took out the phone she'd been given, and lacking a place to put it, set it in a cup holder. A glance behind showed Teddy snoring through Melaton's driving, so she'd need to grab her phone later.

They made good, if quiet, time to the park. Melaton didn't bother parking properly, not when there were so few cars around. "You two stay safe, all right," Melaton said. "You did good today. You've got loads of potential. If you wanna do anything with it, then . . . yeah, I could show you around some more."

Emily felt her cheeks warming, so she acted, stepping out of the car, and shaking Teddy awake before taking the girl's phone and leaving it on the back seat. "I . . . I'll think about it," Emily said. "Um, thanks for today?"

"No problem. I'll be sure to swing a bit of cash your way. The way you're caring for the kid, I figure you'll need it."

"Thanks," Emily said again. Talking about money was just as uncomfortable as ever. "Bye."

She watched Melaton drive off while Teddy leaned into Emily's side, and then it was off to the public washrooms to get changed. As soon as they were out and heading back, Emily noticed how Teddy was flagging, and she couldn't ignore the gnawing guilt in her stomach anymore.

"Teddy, want a piggyback ride?"

"A wha?"

Emily knelt down, put her backpack on Teddy, then got the girl to hop onto her back.

At first, Teddy giggled and cheered Emily on, but soon her burst of energy ran out and she nestled into the crook of Emily's neck and went right back to sleep.

Emily had an odd moment of quiet where she could contemplate her day. It was . . . strange, but satisfying, too. She could get used to the idea that she was someone who *did* things.

They arrived at the dorm with only some trouble, mostly from Emily's back straining at the weight. Teddy was definitely on the heavier side.

Getting her phone out to open the door was tricky, but she managed, and soon enough they rode up the elevator and walked to their room.

Emily set Teddy down, the werebear yawning hugely as she stood next to Emily.

Emily opened the door and stepped in, then she froze.

Two things jumped to her at once.

First, where and when had Athena gotten herself a leather biker's jacket?

And second, and more disturbing, why was Alea Iacta lying on the floor in the fetal position?

CHAPTER FIFTY

Riding Owl Night

Athena didn't think she'd like the motorcycles at first. They were big, and really noisy, and they stank a lot. But the nice biker guys gave her a cool leather jacket and a less-cool helmet that was a bit too big for her, and then they sat her down behind this big, mean-looking woman who had a huge "hog."

It turned out that, after a couple of minutes of hanging on for dear life, she got used to the roar of a dozen bikes all rumbling down the roads as one big unit, and soon she was laughing and sticking her arms out like wings to catch the wind.

The ride ended way too soon with the gang stopping by close to the dorms. "Here we are, kid," the big lady whose hog Athena was on said.

Athena jumped off, making sure not to touch any of the hot parts because one of the beard guys told her she might get burned if she did. "Thank you," she said as she took off the helmet.

The lady took the helmet, then ruffled Athena's hair.

"Will you be okay, little lady?"

Athena nodded. "I'll be fine. Thanks."

With a few more goodbyes and a lot of thumps to her back, Athena was off and heading back home. She kinda hoped that Big Sister Emily wasn't there yet, because if she was, then that might mean Athena would maybe be in a bit of trouble.

Not too much trouble, though. Big Sister Emily was the best, and she wouldn't punish her little sisters too hard when all they were doing was trying to be the most Villainous Villains they could be.

She arrived at the dorms and waited until someone was approaching the doors before making her move. The young man eyed her as she grabbed the door to keep it open, and he seemed about to protest, so she blasted him with her power and slipped past while he looked up and around as if he'd seen something in the dark.

Athena fiddled with the zipper on her jacket as she rode up to the fifth floor, then it was straight to Big Sister Emily's room.

It took all of a second upon entering for her to notice that something was wrong.

There was no big sister in sight, not even an annoying Teddy. Instead, a strange guy was standing with his back to the door.

Athena pushed the door shut behind her while her eyes narrowed.

Big Sister would have told her if she was expecting someone, so this guy . . . this guy was trouble.

"Hey," Athena said. She pulled the reins off her power and started carefully flooding the room with just a tiny, tiny bit of it.

The man spun around and looked at her. "Oh, uh, hey," he said. He said it *very* guiltily.

"Who are you, and what are you doing here?" Athena said. This would be a great opportunity to test her newfound confidence. She just had to keep in mind all the cool tricks her biker friends had taught her.

"Uh, yeah, I'm a friend of Emily's?" he tried.

Athena scoffed. Even Teddy was a better liar. She puffed out her chest, brought a hand up next to her chin, and struck an intimidating pose. "I don't believe you," she said.

The man blinked dumbly, clearly taken aback by Athena's scariness. "Uh, right. Look, I'm sorry I just walked in, but the door wasn't even locked."

Athena made a note not to mention that to Emily. "Who are you?" she asked.

"I could ask the same," he said. "You're not the bear girl."

So . . . he knew Teddy. That was nothing. "I'm Big Sister Emily's strongest sister," Athena said.

Technically, since she was the only sister in the room, she was the strongest in every sense. That didn't matter, though. Athena started to press in with her power.

The changes weren't obvious, but they were there. He shifted a little, eyed the door behind her, then rubbed at the side of his neck with nervous energy. "So, uh, do you know when Emily will be back?" he asked.

Athena's eyes narrowed. "How about you tell me who you are?"

"Look, kid, I don't know you, and frankly, I don't trust you, okay? I just . . . I just need to talk to Emily."

Athena sighed. "I understand," she lied. Her power started to press in even more. "Big Sis should be back any minute now. Do you want something to drink? Maybe something to eat?"

She pressed her power, wrapping it around so he'd doubt any food they had, then, when he hesitated and took a small step toward the door, she latched her power onto that and made the idea that something bad was behind that door feel very, very real.

"Uh," he said. "I should, um."

"Sit down," Athena said. She tried another pose to see if it would help. "Come on, it's safe in here. But you might not want to go out."

"What? Why not?"

She shrugged with false nonchalance. "It's a dangerous place out there? All sorts of scary people." Athena's grin was predatory. "So many dangerous things."

The man started to sweat.

"And that's how I figured everything out," Athena said. She tried to keep the pride out of her voice, but she'd done such a good job and she knew Emily would be proud, so it was hard.

The weird man, who'd called himself both Jacob and Alea Iacta, was still on the floor, though he'd moved over so his back was to the wall and his knees were drawn up to his chest. She stopped using her power on him as soon as Big Sister Emily told her to, because she was obedient like that.

"So," Emily said, "you left the dorm to go help us, then you ran into some biker gang . . . accidentally joined them, then came back here and did . . . that to Alea?"

Athena nodded. "Yes. That sounds about right."

Emily took a deep, deep breath. "Okay," she said.

"I did good?" Athena asked.

"You . . . uh, sure."

Athena beamed. "If you want to question him, he's all softened up."

Having Teddy help with the interrogating would have been nice, but the werebear was currently cocooned in a bunch of blankets on the edge of Emily's bed, and the only help she was providing was some background noise from all her snoring.

Emily walked over to her chair, spun it around so that she was facing the weird guy, then sat down. "Okay," she said. Then to make sure, she said it again. "Okay. Al— Jacob. Jacob, can you tell me why you came?"

The man nodded. "I . . ." His eyes looked around, a bit nervous and crazed. "I met some people. They contacted me, said they knew what I was up to. Said they could help. But, but they sounded suspicious."

"Go on."

"I used some of my power, did a few coin flips. And . . . they're bad, real bad. And they know a lot about me."

"Who are they?" Emily asked. "Do you have a name or anything? How did they contact you, and why did you come here?"

"Here's safe," he said. "I looked around, and I found your place. Heard someone talking about you, followed them for a bit. Just got lucky. I'm out, though. Ran out of luck when I found the room and got in."

"The door wasn't locked?" Emily asked.

Athena tensed a bit, then she nodded. "Must be his powers," she said. "Hmm."

"I need . . . I don't know. They could be anywhere? They could be listening right now. I need more luck, more to be safe," he said.

"Who are they?" Emily asked.

"The Cabal. They called themselves the Cabal."

CHAPTER FIFTY-ONE

An Undisclosed Chat

Emily sat on her favorite chair, pulled up a blanket, and covered her shoulders with it.

It was a small comfort, but a comfort nonetheless.

On the bed sat Teddy and Athena. Athena was swinging her legs to burn off energy and Teddy . . . was still snoring. That was fine.

In the middle of the room, sitting cross-legged with his head bowed, was a very nervous Jacob, idly twiddling his thumbs and occasionally looking up to see if Emily was still watching him.

She was, but not with any bad thoughts in mind.

Not many, at least.

Having a boy barge into her room was a big no-no in her book. She cleared her throat and the boy flinched. "What can you tell me about, um . . . you called them the Cabal?"

"I don't think saying their name out loud's a good idea," Jacob said before glancing around.

Emily looked to Athena. That was her power at work, she bet. "Fine, then let's call them something else. The, um, the Clowns."

Jacob huffed a laugh. "All right, all right, I can do that. The Clowns, then. Yeah, I like it."

"So," Emily continued, "the Clowns. What happened?"

"I didn't do nothing," Jacob said, instantly on the defensive. "Hardly used my powers, just minding my own business. You know, you and the bear girl kinda scared me, so I was on the watch for trouble, keeping my head down. Then I get this letter addressed to me."

"To you as you, or you as in your, uh, persona?" Emily asked. She wasn't entirely sure about the whole persona thing yet. She could imagine some people were very different in and out of costume. She shook her head, setting the stray thought aside.

For all that the situation was a little tense, she had still been through a long day and was looking forward to doing like Teddy and going to sleep.

"Both," Jacob said. "It was addressed to both. It had a bunch of stuff about me too. And it said that I should contact these people on a website."

"Like Acebook Messenger?" Emily asked.

"No, no, like, this weird HTTP site. Just a bunch of letters and numbers for an address. I went, and as soon as I opened the site it opened up this chat thing. That's all there was on the site. Just the chat."

"Okay?"

Jacob nodded. "Then this person started writing to me, asking me questions. I asked them who they were and they said they were the Cab— Clowns."

"That's it?" Emily asked. That was rather underwhelming.

Jacob hugged himself. "I thought so, too, you know? Started telling them off. But they started offering me things, telling me stuff."

"Could you be any less precise?" Athena asked with a huff.

"I mean, they said they could help me become the greatest Villain ever, that I could be strong and cool. There's, like, fan clubs for some Villains, you know? And they offered money for stuff. I mean, it sounded kinda good?"

"You trusted them?" Emily asked.

He snorted. "Of course not," he said. "But they said they were, like, the top dog of Villains around here, that they run the show. 'Course, I know you're around, so that can't be true, right?"

"Right," Emily said for a lack of anything smarter to say.

"That's right," Athena said with a whole lot more enthusiasm. "Big Sister Emily's the top dog of Villains here. If she were a dog, she'd be one of those really big ones."

"Uh . . ." Emily said.

"So, I have this thing I can do, with my power. You used it on that map, remember? To pinpoint things. I can use it to flip a coin, see if something's a good idea or not. It takes a lot of luck, though. But the Clowns, they have me cornered so I figured it's no big loss. I flip, and it's bad. Real bad. So I leave my dorm, and I see some people looking at me."

"So you came here?" Emily asked.

What were the chances that he was followed? She felt a cold pit growing in her stomach. They didn't have much fighting power in the room, and any help they could get was a long way away.

"I was sneaky about it," he said. "Took the bus, left my phone behind, then I lucked out and found a new jacket. You know, a disguise."

"And you weren't followed?" Emily asked.

Jacob shrugged. "I mean, I don't think so. It took a bunch of luck to get here. I heard someone talking about you, and they moved to this building, and I slipped in behind them. I don't have anything the Clowns could track me with, I don't think."

Emily shifted within her blankets and then let her head thump back against the rear of her chair. "Do you have any idea who the Clowns really are?"

"No? Not really. They're bad news, though, I know that much." He sat up, then with a grunt got to his feet and looked around. "So, uh, I'm guessing I can't sleep here, right?"

Emily sighed as she slid out of her blankets. "No, you can't," she said. "Athena, can you keep an eye on him? If he tries anything stupid, tell Teddy to eat him."

"Yes, Big Sister Emily," Athena said.

With a pat against her pant leg to make sure her phone was still there, Emily walked to the door and then out of the room. She was still in her socks, which got her feet cold on the tiled floor of the corridor, but it wasn't too bad.

She made sure there wasn't anyone around, then made her way to the end of the corridor where a little window overlooked the street out front.

Thumbing her way through her contacts, Emily found herself standing there with her finger hovering over the call button to a rather familiar number.

Could Melanie help at all?

She pressed the back button. The Hero was nice, but she had told Emily to forget all about the Cabal.

Another name and number came up, this one a number that Emily was even more hesitant to call.

She weighed the very few options she had, then pressed dial.

The phone rang twice before someone picked up.

"Hello," a man's voice said over the line.

"Mister Handshake?" Emily asked.

"Ah, hello," he said. "I didn't expect you to call me. How are you doing this evening?"

"I'm well, thank you. Look, I . . . there's something I want to ask you about, but I'm not sure how safe it would be to ask at all."

"That's a surprisingly common issue in my line of work," Handshake said. "There are a few solutions. We could talk around the issue. We could meet in person. Or we could speak over a more secure method. There are a few systems online that are, for the most part, quite safe."

"I . . . yeah, that might be for the best," Emily said.

"You have a school email, right? I'll send you a link. You should be able to open the site on your phone. If that's all, I'll talk to you shortly."

"Right, thank you." Emily pulled the phone away from her ear and hung up. A moment later her email client pinged her and she was navigating over to a strange site. There was a button to connect to a room with one other person in it called H-Shake.

She joined.

"Hello?" she asked.

"Hey there. So, this isn't all that much better, but the communication is about as encrypted as it can be under these circumstances."

"Okay," Emily said.

"Is this about the offer I sent to you via Melaton?"

"No, no, it's not that," Emily said. "It's about . . . do you know anything about a group of people called the Cabal?"

The line was silent. "Where'd you hear that name?" Handshake finally asked.

"So you do know something." It was nice to have some sort of confirmation that something fishy was going on.

"I won't pretend that I don't know anything. Nor will I actually say anything about them. Not without compensation."

She bit her lip and shifted to the side. She had almost forgotten that Handshake's entire job was dealing with information. "Okay," she said. "What about, uh, safe houses? Do you know a place where you could hide someone?"

"I do," Handshake said. "Are you in trouble?"

"Not me. Look, I . . . I want to explain things, but I'm not sure if I should do that for free, not to you."

"Ah, the age-old problem of context coming with a price tag. All right. How about I let you hear about a job I might have for you, and in exchange, I'll tell you what I can?"

CHAPTER FIFTY-TWO

Complicated Conversations

What's the job?" Emily asked. She regretted asking the question even before it left her lips. But she didn't see any loss in actually asking.

Handshake's voice had a hint of laughter in it when he replied. "Nothing too complicated. I'm meeting with someone. Name starts with C. You took out one of his buddies?"

Cement. He was talking about Cement. Emily hugged her phone closer to the side of her head. "Okay? And you want me to . . . what?"

"I'm going to be meeting him alone. Which . . . let's say I'm not all that confident about it. I bet you can imagine why. I've still got a bit of a limp, you know?"

"I'm not equipped for dealing with that kind of thing," Emily said. "Nor are my sisters."

"Sisters, plural?" Handshake asked.

Emily felt her lips thinning into a line. "I misspoke."

Handshake snorted. "Sure. Would you be interested in coming?"

Emily shook her head, even if he couldn't see the gesture. "No. It's way too dangerous, and you haven't offered me much."

"What if I tell you the meeting is about a subject you're near and dear to?"

Emily's heart froze, and for a moment she found it hard to breathe. Had Cement copied the drive? Had someone retrieved it in that river and brought it to him? "What?" she asked.

Handshake cleared his throat. "The Cabal."

Emily blinked. "What about— You mean Cement wants to know about them too?"

"It's more than that. He knows some things I don't, and I know some he doesn't. It's a trade. And an excuse to get back on the same page, or at least to set aside some of our . . . mutual antagonism."

Emily paced back and forth before the window, considering. Would this be any more dangerous than her last excursion? The obvious and immediate answer was a resounding yes. Going out with Heroes was a risk, but if they discovered her, she would be arrested or worse.

Going out to confront a Villain. An actual, scary Villain? That was a whole lot worse.

"I don't like it," Emily said.

"I can up the ante a little," Handshake said. "I want to know what you know about them too. And I can offer you other things. Money, information. Not too much, mind you. What you know might not be worth that much to me."

Emily swallowed. "I'll think about it."

"My meeting is tomorrow evening. Think about it until then. It's one grand per powered head that comes to help. And I'll tell you what I know about the Cabal. A name you shouldn't be repeating if you can avoid it. It's unique enough to stand out in a normal conversation. "

"I know," Emily said. "We've been calling them the Clowns."

"Hah! That's brilliant. Anyway, I'll text you the address for the meeting place. Be there, or don't." The line went dead with a happy little chime.

Emily contemplated throwing her phone, but she held back. Shows of violence like that were just not her.

"Need help?"

Jumping, Emily looked up and found herself staring, wide-eyed, at Sam. "H-hey," she said. "Uh, no?"

Sam tilted her head to the side. "You sure? You don't look great."

"I'm okay," Emily said. "Just a, uh, hard phone call."

"Anything to do with the people in your room?"

For the second time in far too short a while, Emily's blood went cold. "What?"

Sam rolled her eyes and gestured over her shoulder with a thumb. "I'm not deaf. Or blind. You've got two kids staying with you."

Emily licked her dry lips. "They're my sisters," she said.

The girl nodded. "Yeah, all right. You having trouble because of them? I did some babysitting before—it's a real nightmare sometimes."

"N-no, nothing like that. My sisters are . . . actually, they're pretty nice. A bit, uh, well, sometimes they act up, but they're mostly nice."

"All right, cool. So if that's not it, what is it?" Sam crossed her arms. She didn't look like someone ready to move away.

"It's . . . ah. Is there a place you can take someone? Someplace that's discreet?"

"Someone like who?"

"A boy?"

Sam's eyebrows shot up. "No shit. You know they don't really mind if you have a boy— Oh, your sisters. Yeah, you wouldn't want to be banging your boyfriend with the kids in the room."

"What?" Emily asked. Her brain caught up, her face caught fire. "No, no, it's nothing like that. We're not, no."

"Hey, it's all right. Where do you think half the weird noises in this place come from?" Sam let her arms drop and moved a little closer. "There's a couple of places, you know, for folks feeling a little adventurous. I heard that the roof's pretty popular for that kind of thing."

Emily shook her head. Her ears were burning still. "I swear, it's not like that."

Sam grinned. "Fine. What are you looking for?"

"Just a place a friend can stay the night." Emily examined her shoes.

"Uh-huh," Sam replied, doubt tinged with humor. "All right, a place to send a friend. There's a motel a little ways away that might work. If your friend's really cheap, though, there's the library. It's got study rooms that are open all night. Glass walls, so no space for funny business, but you can rent one out for a dozen dollars, and if you fall asleep with a book open in front of you, the librarians won't bother you."

That . . . was a better answer than what Emily expected. "Thank you."

"Hey, no problem, love," Sam said. She winked at Emily, then headed over to her own room. "You knock if you need anything. Though I charge a lot for anything babysitting related, okay?"

"Thank you," Emily repeated.

Sam waved her off as she slid into her room, the door clicking shut behind her.

Emily took a deep breath and moved over to her own room. The door unlocked with a swipe and she stepped in to find Jacob pacing back and forth while Athena glared at his back. "I, ah, found a place for you to stay," Emily said. "For the night, I mean."

"Yeah?" he asked. "Is it safe?"

"It's . . . safe enough?"

He frowned. "I don't know if that works for me, you know?"

She nodded. "I know. But you can't sleep here."

The young man scratched at the back of his head. "All right, yeah. That'd be a bit . . . Fine. Where?"

"The library. You can rent a room to study and they don't mind if you fall asleep there. Just . . . pretend to study something. Or actually study something, I guess."

"And what about our Clown problem? What are you doing about that?"

"Big Sister Emily doesn't need to do anything about it, punk. It's not her problem, it's yours."

"Athena," Emily said. She couldn't fault the girl, though; she was thinking something very similar. "I'm going to be . . . meeting someone tomorrow. I might have more by then, maybe."

"That's not enough."

Emily glared. "It'll have to be," she said, then she cleared her throat and reined in her anger. It wasn't like her to let that out of its bottle. "Sorry. But I'd really not be comfortable with you staying here."

"You heard my sis," Athena said. She gestured to the door. "Get out of here, punk."

Jacob huffed, half exasperated and half amused, if Emily had to guess. "Fine, fine. I'll go take a nap at the library. Maybe actually do some of my classwork. God knows, I'm behind already. I'll call you tomorrow, all right? Just as soon as I find a phone."

"Sure," Emily agreed. She escorted Jacob out the door, then, once it was shut and he was gone, she leaned her head against the wall and took a moment to breath. "That was . . . something."

"You were awesome," Athena said without so much as an ounce of sarcasm. It helped, a little.

"We need to get ready . . . for tomorrow."

Athena sat up. "Ready for what?"

"Trouble. Ready for a whole lot of trouble." Emily moved to her bed, then sat on the edge so as not to disturb Teddy too much. She didn't look forward to moving Teddy onto the mattress. The werebear was heavy, especially as dead weight.

Athena grinned, toothy and vicious. Then she adjusted her glasses with both hands and lost any semblance of being threatening. "I'm always ready most of the time. Are we going to go out in costume to kick butt?"

"Not quite," Emily said. "And you don't have a costume."

"I have a cool jacket," Athena said. "And I have some pants. We just need a mask."

Emily patted Athena's hair down. It was a nice, soothing gesture, for both of them, judging by the way Athena's eyes fluttered shut. "All right. More help wouldn't be amiss. And . . . do you have any points to spend?"

"Not yet," she said.

"That's okay. I'll spend what I have. Teddy can do the same. We'll be as ready as we can be. And maybe things will go all right." She continued running her fingers through Athena's hair until she'd convinced herself of that lie, then Emily got up. "Right, go get changed. It's time for bed."

"Owls are nocturnal."

"And little sisters are diurnal. Get your pj's. You can change while I drop this bear in bed." Emily sighed. "We'll need our sleep, I think."

CHAPTER FIFTY-THREE

Healpats

The first order of business the next day was classes. The weekend was over, and Emily couldn't ignore her school schedule any longer. She had to keep her grades up, and that meant paying attention in her lectures and doing all her work.

It was . . . surprisingly difficult to sit in the back of the class and listen to a lecture about some long-dead author's work being dissected for meaning that the author had probably never intended for anyone to read into it.

It was empty. Not as exciting as the conspiratorial late-night phone calls with info brokers and the day spent patrolling the streets with real live Heroes.

It was, essentially, not as fun as doing the whole Hero thing, even if the Hero thing was terrifying.

Emily returned to the dorm after class and found both of her sisters cuddled up together on the mattress, hugging each other close. Athena was wearing her leather jacket over her pj's and Teddy was drooling into her smaller sister's hair.

She sat on her chair after setting her backpack to the side and made herself comfortable as she thought.

Was it worth it?

The risks were high. The rewards were kind of pitiful.

And yet she still wanted to do it.

"Was Teddy right?" she wondered to the near-empty room. Had the system given her Villain as a morality because she wanted that kind of freedom?

She kind of doubted it, and eleven in the morning was not the right time for navel-gazing. There were more productive things she could have been doing.

"Status."

Name: Emily Wright		
Alignment: Villain		
Alias: The Boss		
Level: 1		
Powers		
Sister Summoning		
Create Sister	Rank 3	
Sisterportation	Level 1	
Double Trouble	Level Max	
Points		
Power Slots: 0	Skill Upgrades: 4	Skill Slots: 1

She had points to invest, and a few things to think about. Notably, her Sisterportation power. It was at Level 1, whereas Double Trouble, the power that gave her Athena, was at Max. The obvious conclusion was that some skills were direct passive upgrades and didn't have any way to improve.

She could put points into Sisterportation, likely cutting down on the cooldown to use it, which was admittedly pretty high. But before that.

Do you wish to spend a Skill Slot point on the Power: Sister Summoning?

Emily nodded.

New Skill Unlocked!

Healpats has been added to your Power's Skills!

"Status."

Name: Emily Wright		
Alignment: Villain		
Alias: The Boss		
Level: 1		
Powers		
Sister Summoning		
Create Sister	Rank 4	
Sisterportation	Level 1	
Double Trouble	Level Max	
Healpats	Level 1	
Points		
Power Slots: 0	Skill Upgrades: 4	Skill Slots: 0

Emily flicked her fingers at the screen, wishing it gone, and it disappeared. She tried to open her skill status page the same way, but it didn't work. "Status: Healpats."

Healpats
Sister Summoning
Level 1
Allows you to heal minor injuries or sickness with an application of pats to a sister's head.
Activation: Physical contact
Cooldown: 600 seconds

That sounded like it had a lot of potential. She raised a hand and patted her head, but nothing happened. So it didn't work on herself, which was too bad—she could use some magical healing every once in a while.

It was probably worth investing in, at least a little.

"One Skill Upgrade point to Healpats," Emily said.

Healpats has reached Level 2!

Cooldown reduced to 540 seconds!

She considered the change. That was handy. "Another two points to Healpats."

Healpats has reached Level 4!

Cooldown reduced to 420 seconds!

That was seven minutes between healings, and as far as she could tell, those healings were relatively weak overall. It was better than nothing. If she found some time, she could work on doing a few more quests to reduce that to something more useful, but she wouldn't look a gift horse in the mouth.

With a sigh, Emily got up before her legs fell asleep under her, and she moved over to her sisters. She shook their shoulders and smiled as they blinked awake.

"Hey, girls," she said.

Athena was the first to wake up. "Sis?"

"Yup," Emily said. She pushed Athena's hair out of her face. "You especially, we need to get you costumed up. I think we'll be going out for a mission today, and . . . and I think it would be a good idea if we talk about it properly before heading out."

Athena yawned, stretched her arms and legs out to push Teddy off her, then climbed to her feet. "Proper communication is key to successfully leading a Villainous life," she said as she fumbled with her glasses.

"Something like that," Emily agreed. She shook Teddy. "Hey, wake up, sleepy bear. You've been in bed for over twelve hours."

"That's it?" Teddy asked as she looked around blearily. "That's not much."

"I don't think anyone else would agree," Emily said. "Come on, we have to get ready, and then we'll be grabbing a bite to eat later, all right?"

Teddy scratched at her exposed tummy, then nodded. "Yeah, all right." She rolled over and got up as well. "What's for breakfast?"

"Lunch, actually," Emily said. "It's a bit late for breakfast."

Teddy frowned, thought about it, then nodded. "What's for lunch?"

Emily stood up. "Lunch is for after the two of you get ready. Athena, we have some things around to make a costume for you. A temporary one, at least. Teddy, can you pack yours up in a bag to go?"

"Yeah, sure thing, Boss."

"Can I keep my jacket as part of my costume?" Athena asked. "I want to look tough."

Emily looked at the rough old jacket. It was thick enough leather, with steel studs on the collars and lapels. It looked very nineties punk, but it likely offered more protection than her own costume. "Sure," she said. "First things first, though. I want to start with you, Athena."

"I've been thinking about this, as I do with all things," Athena said. "I should get a wig."

"A wig?"

Athena nodded, then gestured to her hair. It was on the paler side, and rather distinct.

"Ah, that's fair," Emily said. "But I don't have anything wiglike around. I guess . . . a hat? I think I have a baseball cap somewhere."

Athena nodded. "That might work for now. Oh, and I'll need a really big mask because I have glasses."

"Ah, right. Maybe a scarf then? Something to cover the lower half of your face?"

"Can it be really long and cool looking?" Athena asked.

Emily got up and moved over to her drawers. She had a few scarves, thick and woolen to tough out the winter's chill. She found a nice red one. It wasn't too long, but on Athena it might well be as tall as the girl. "Here, how's this?"

"All right!" Athena said. "Red's a tough color. And I'll need pants, too. And big boots."

"I've got boots," Teddy said. "You can't have boots too."

Emily pat Teddy on the head. "It's okay. You can both have boots. There's nothing wrong with that."

Teddy blinked. "Hey, can you do that again?" she asked as she grabbed Emily's hand and brought it down atop her head again. She frowned. "No, it didn't work this time."

"Ah, I got a new skill," Emily said. "Healpats. I think we just triggered it." Emily looked at her palm, but it didn't feel any different than usual. "How did it feel?"

Teddy frowned. "You know when someone runs their fingers through your fur?"

"N-no?" Emily said.

"Oh, right. Well, it felt like that, but warm. It's nice." She grabbed Emily's hand and placed it on her head again. "Is there a cooldown or something?"

"Yeah, about seven minutes," Emily said.

"Hey! It's my turn to get patted next," Athena said.

"There aren't enough pats out there to heal whatever's wrong with you," Teddy said.

"Teddy," Emily said, "I thought you of all girls would be keen to share?"

Teddy blushed and looked away. "Yeah, all right. Fine."

Emily shook herself and pulled Athena closer to her drawers. She tapped one near the bottom with a foot. "Can you check through your clothes for something simple to wear? I think in this case it might be best if you just go unnoticed."

"I can do unnoticed," Athena said. "And if someone does notice me, then I'll make them notice all sorts of other things instead."

"Yeah," Emily said. She tried on a smile and looked around her room, memorizing where everything was, just in case. "All right. Let's get everything ready. We have some shady guy to meet before we head out."

"And lunch," Teddy said.

"And we need to grab lunch," Emily agreed.

CHAPTER FIFTY-FOUR

Questing for a Bear

The Boss hadn't told Teddy what was up yet, which was kind of annoying, but also okay. It was the Boss's prerogative to tell her little sisters the things she thought they had to know.

Still, Teddy was real curious, even if she was distracted by munching through her second lunch wrap.

The Boss, Teddy, and Athena were all sitting in a corner booth of the Im Orton's nearest the campus. It was a quiet enough spot even if there were lots of people sitting at other tables. Most of them were either talking to each other or staring into their phones anyway.

"So, Boss, what're we up to tonight?" Teddy asked.

The Boss, who was a real slow eater, paused in the act of blowing over a spoonful of soup. "Oh, right," she said. "We're, ah."

She looked around, as if to make sure that no one was snooping.

"It's all right," Athena said. "If they snoop, I'll scare them off." She puffed out her chest and sat up taller.

Teddy wasn't sure if she liked it when Athena acted all tough. That was Teddy's job.

"Right. So, we're going with Handshake to meet Cement."

"Handshake? That limp guy? And Cement . . . that's the other guy's boss, right?" Teddy asked.

"Can someone fill me in, please?" Athena asked. "I think it would be best if all of us were on the same page."

The Boss nodded. "Handshake's an information broker. We . . . did some things for him after he did some dumb stuff. Now we're going to help him out because we want to track down the . . . Clowns."

"Clowns?" Teddy asked.

What did clowns have to do with anything?

"I'll explain that bit later," the Boss said. "It's enough to say that we're going to be meeting Cement to learn what he has to say about the Clowns, and then Handshake will tell us more. After that . . . after that I don't know. We'll have to see from there."

"I'm sure Big Sister will figure it out," Athena said as she patted Emily's shoulder.

"The Boss is the boss," Teddy agreed. She tossed the last of her wrap down her mouth and chewed it up. "So we heading out now?"

"We have plenty of time to finish eating," the Boss said.

Teddy looked at her side of the table, which had plenty of wrappers, but none with any food in them, then she looked back up to the Boss and prepared her best bear-cub eyes.

"If you eat any more, we'll be rolling you all the way to the meetup," the Boss said.

"You could piggyback me," Teddy said.

"I don't think my back could take that," Emily said. "Although I imagine all the running around we've been doing lately will be great for my waistline."

Athena finished up her chicken salad, and then the Boss, swayed by Teddy's powerful bear-cub gaze, gave Teddy the rest of her soup, which Teddy slurped away. It made for good tummy padding atop her wraps.

Soon the three of them were off. Teddy was happy, the walk was fun, even though the Boss didn't let her piggyback again because Teddy had "legs that work just fine."

She skipped ahead because it was her duty as the Boss's protector to keep the Boss safe. If a car ran off the road or something, Teddy could cushion the Boss by turning into a big fluffy bear.

Still, for all that, it didn't leave Teddy with much to do, so she decided to take a peek at all her available quests.

New ones would appear all the time, and old ones would poof away as the opportunities for them passed. Even old ones that were accepted would leave after a while of not being completed.

The system wasn't random. It was very serious and calculated and had a bunch of numbers and stuff behind it.

Teddy wasn't good at numbers.

New Quest!

Bearing the Brunt

Be the best guardian!

Reward: +1 Skill Upgrade point every time you save an ally. Scoundrel +1 per save!

Accept? Refuse?

Meh. That was a lame quest. The points were fine, but becoming a *Scoundrel*? Did the system think Teddy was *lame*?

New Quest!

She Who Bearies Her Enemies

Put an opponent down with extreme prejudice.

Reward: +1 Skill Upgrade point every time you knock out an opponent. Villain +1 per knock-out!

Accept? Refuse?

"Boss, what's a 'prejudice'?" Teddy asked.

The Boss frowned. "It's when someone does something that's very . . . emotional, I guess. Like passing a law that doesn't just make something illegal, but also has a really steep punishment."

"So, like, extreme prejudice would be lots of feelings about something?" Teddy asked.

"I guess so. Where did you hear about it?"

Teddy shrugged. "Flavor text."

So knocking out an enemy while being real feely about it? Teddy could do that.

Quest accepted!

Good! Another way for Teddy to get even stronger. Soon she'd be getting some crazy skills too. Like . . .

Teddy tried to think of something appropriately cool and bearlike. It was real hard, though, because bears were already the coolest.

Maybe some superroar? Or wings. She'd heard about drop-bears, and they had to drop from somewhere, so there had to be some sort of flying bear out there.

New Quest!

Polar Opposite

There is stealth in boldness.

Reward: +1 Skill Upgrade point per 100,000 people who believe you are a Hero.

Accept? Refuse?

Teddy hummed and tapped her chin. That seemed to line up real well with what the Boss was doing, what with the whole acting bits. It really wasn't the sort of quest Teddy wanted to be doing, but points were like lunches: you took them where you could get them.

Quest accepted!

Teddy figured they had a few minutes left until they got to the place they were heading to, so she looked at one last quest for the road.

New Quest!

In Pawsetion

Acquire a suitable weapon and use it.

Reward: +1 Skill Upgrade point!

Accept? Refuse?

She shrugged. Why not?

Quest accepted!

"Teddy?" Emily asked. "We're almost there. Do you want to slow down a bit?"

Teddy stopped until the Boss was by her side, then she walked next to Emily, opposite where Athena was. That way, if the Boss felt like handing out more of those wonderful Healpats, she could reach both sisters with ease.

The Boss pulled out her phone and looked at it for a while, her free hand in Athena's grasp so at least one of her little sisters would be leading her.

Teddy didn't pout because Athena got to lead the Boss. She was pouting for other, unrelated reasons.

"This is it, I think," the Boss said as she gestured to an alley between a pub and a laundromat. It wasn't that bad as far as alleys went. Teddy had been in a lot of those lately, and she ranked this one, with its discarded newspaper rotting in the corner and empty pizza box halfway in, as a seven out of ten.

The Boss moved over to the very back of the alley, then to a metal door under the escape ladder fixed to the wall of the laundromat. The door opened with a tug, revealing a small tiled room with a light dangling from the ceiling and a single stool in the middle.

One of the walls had a bricked-over doorway, and some of the tiles were of different colors. Teddy thought it looked like a bathroom, but without the bath or toilets or sinks.

"I guess this is where we change?" the Boss asked.

She didn't sound so sure.

"Athena, ya wanna blast the place?" Teddy asked.

Athena nodded and glared into the room for a while. "There you go," she said. "If anyone was peeping, they're busy clawing out their eyes now instead."

Teddy's little sister's powers weren't as cool as turning into a bear, but they were pretty neat. "I'll go first," the Boss said.

Athena and Teddy looked at each other as the door closed. They nodded.

It was nice working with someone who knew keeping the Boss safe was the most important thing. For all that Teddy found Athena a bit much sometimes, she was an all right sister.

She leaned her back against the wall and crossed her arms, looking real tough as she waited for the Boss to get ready. Soon, they'd all be out and being the best Villains they could be.

CHAPTER FIFTY-FIVE

The Uncomplicated Art of Subtlety (According to Athena)

Athena had never seen Handshake before, so she wasn't sure what to think of the guy before he showed up.

When he did, it was by pulling into the alleyway in a car that looked like it was relatively new. Not new in the sense that it was cool, though. It was a white four-door sedan that could have belonged to any brand. It was the most boring car Athena had probably ever seen a hundred of.

The car came to a rolling stop before them, then the front door opened and a man stepped out.

Handshake, like his car, looked boring as heck.

He wore jeans and a sweater vest, all in muted colors. His hair was cut in a boring nonstyle, and he even slouched. He was like the living image of a boring person. If it weren't for the bandages covering him, and the domino mask perched over his nose, Athena might have dismissed him out of hand.

"He doesn't look so tough," Athena said.

The man came to a stop in front of his car, silhouetted by the head-lamps with his hands shoved deep into his pockets. "Boss, Teddy," he said. "Or should I call you Ursa Minor?"

"That's my name when I'm being a fake Hero," Teddy said.

Big Sister Emily placed a hand on Teddy's shoulder.

Athena remembered what Big Sister Emily said. Handshake was an information broker. He'd take all the information he could, so they had to be real subtle about things. It was a good thing that subtlety was Athena's specialty.

"And . . . who's this?" he asked while looking at Athena.

"Just a friend of the Boss," Athena said. She crossed her arms, leather jacket creaking with the motion. "You can call me Athena."

"Athena? Like the ancient Reek goddess?" He raised a hand out of his pocket and rubbed his chin. "Goddess of crafting, inventions, war, pottery, owls—often associated with wisdom. I wonder which aspect you're supposed to represent?"

"If you pay me, I might tell you," Athena said.

Handshake snorted. "I might just," he said before turning to Big Sister Emily. "I didn't expect three of you. Presuming that our littlest goddess here is coming with us?"

"She is," Emily said. "It's . . . nice to see you?"

"You don't need to lie on my account," he said. "If everyone's ready, hop in. We can talk tactics on the way to the hotel." Handshake turned and walked back over to the driver's side. "Coming?"

Emily pushed Teddy toward the back of the car, so Athena started walking around it, passing behind and taking note of the car's plates before shuffling past the plume of stinky smoke from the exhaust. She hopped into the seat behind Handshake's and pulled her belt on.

She had to tuck it behind her because it passed right in front of her face.

"You mentioned a hotel?" Big Sister asked as she buckled herself in.

"I did," Handshake said. "Nothing fancy, I'm afraid. We, that is, the lot of us and our guest, have a conference room scheduled for us at the Oliday Inn."

"Isn't that a little public?" Big Sister asked.

"That's the idea, yes. We're presuming that neither side wants to get the public involved. That means keeping a low profile. At the same time, having it be in a public place like this imposes some civility on both sides."

"I think I get it," Big Sister Emily said. "I don't really like the idea of being seen with a Villain, though."

"Ah, yes, your Hero persona. I wouldn't worry. I'm not a well-known face in the public, but in our world, people on both sides of the figurative fence know of and use my services."

"Our world?"

"The world of Heroes and Villains," Handshake said. "The real one, not the whitewashed and cleaned version the corps and government want people to see. I suppose calling it a *world* is a bit much."

"I guess?" Emily said.

"It's more of a community, separated from the rest of the world. And every year, on the same day, the community grows." Handshake leaned forward to see if any cars were coming from the road the alley opened up to. When it was clear, he drove out and merged with the traffic.

"Is it really separate from the rest of the world?" Athena asked. "We still need to eat, and some of us go to school and stuff like that."

Handshake nodded. "That's true. But a lot of powered individuals, myself not included I'm afraid, think that they are . . . I suppose superior would be the right word. Greater than normal people. More talented, or gifted, or deserving."

"That makes sense," Teddy said.

Athena blinked. "Aren't you a communist?" she asked.

"Doesn't mean I'm an idiot," Teddy said. "If all my comrades could turn into cool bears, then it wouldn't be a problem, but only I can do that. So I'm a little bit special. But that doesn't mean I deserve more."

Athena rolled her eyes. "Right, whatever. I guess it makes sense people with powers would think they're better."

"It's not an entirely illogical viewpoint," Handshake said.

They turned off the road and into a big parking lot next to a tall but squat building with a big entranceway covered by an awning where a young man in a too-tight suit was standing. Handshake pulled the car to a park way off in a corner of the parking lot where it would be hard to spot, then he shut the car off.

Everyone got out.

The early evening was turning a bit chilly, and Athena sort of wished she had mittens on to cover her hands, but those wouldn't have been tough looking. Instead, she shoved her hands in her jacket pockets and wiggled them around to keep the blood flowing while she followed the others to the hotel.

The guy at the front—the valet?—jumped when he saw them coming and hurried to open the door for them. "W-welcome to the Oliday Inn," he squeaked as they passed.

"This way," Handshake said as he walked right across the lobby without so much as a glance around. Not that there was much to see. The lobby had some fake plants and a big desk behind which sat a person with a smile on their lips but not in their eyes.

The few customers were all on benches next to a "Free Wi-Fi!" poster. None of the customers noticed the four of them moving by.

The conference room they were going to meet the bad guy in was on the second floor. Handshake took the stairs, despite there being a perfectly usable elevator.

They walked down a corridor, then slipped into a room where Handshake turned around to face them. "Please close the door," he said.

Athena, being the last one in, took a moment to look around first. It was a conference room all right, with a big table in the middle and a stack of chairs against one wall. "All right," she said before pulling the door shut.

"No, this isn't the room we'll be meeting Cement in," Handshake said. "That'll be deeper down. But I figured we'd cover a few things first."

Big Sister Emily nodded. "I was hoping we would," she said.

"Wonderful. First, let's look over the terms of our contract," Handshake said.

"Our what?" Teddy asked.

Handshake smiled. "Our contract. I wouldn't have you come here without first outlining the terms."

"Sounds like some capitalistic nonsense to put you on top," Teddy said. "Do you need some elitist lawyer sort to read it?"

"Um," Handshake said.

Athena stepped up and caught his eyes. "What are your terms?" she asked while making the darkened corners of the room ever so slightly more suspicious.

Handshake's smile never wavered. "Our currency today is information. In exchange for guarding my person during the following meeting, and the short period subsequent to that meeting, I will be giving your group all the information about the group known as the . . . I think we called them the 'Clowns' to avoid speaking their name? As well as a thousand dollars per person who came to guard me. I have that much in my car. Do remind me later."

Emily nodded. "Yes, that's what we want."

"Brilliant! Then in that case I think the deal is sealed."

"Hey, wait," Athena said. "Don't we know a bit about them too? If we tell you, and what we know is better than what you know, we'll be doing work for free."

Athena really hoped she hadn't just foiled one of Big Sister's plans. But then Emily nodded and she felt better. "Athena's right," Emily said. "What if information on its own isn't enough? The money is nice, but, um, we want more." Athena's big sister altered the deal, her voice trembling with barely suppressed anger.

"What more could you want?" Handshake asked.

Emily paused, then her eyes set and she looked very determined. "The location of a safe house in or around the city. And, of course, some monetary compensation for our role guarding you."

Handshake tapped his chin. "I could do the safe house if you allow me access to anyone housed in it. Assuming someone does use the location within the next . . . call it thirty days?"

Emily considered, then nodded. "Okay."

"Then let's shake on it," Handshake said. "Your protection, to the best of your ability, in exchange for one thousand each, the location of a safe house that I have access to, valid for thirty days, and information on a certain group code-named the 'Clowns.' "

He reached out his hand.

Emily shook.

And then something tightened around Athena's heart.

CHAPTER FIFTY-SIX

Tense

What was that?" Emily asked. She felt a shiver running down her back, from right at the base of her neck and flowing along her spine, as if someone had pressed an icicle against her bare skin.

Handshake's smile never so much as twitched. "Did you think I was one of those brave idiots that fakes having a power?" he asked.

She ran her hands up and down her biceps for warmth while her mind raced. Handshake had mentioned once that his power allowed him to form deals with people, but beyond that she couldn't quite remember all the details.

Teddy stomped over to Handshake, eyes narrowed and fists clenched. "What'd you do to me and the Boss?" she asked.

"Hey, he did it to me, too," Athena said.

"And her," Teddy added.

Handshake raised his hands in surrender. "Nothing much. I merely enforced the contract that we agreed to. As long as everyone abides by the terms stipulated, we will all get our just remunerations in the end."

"What's that even mean?" Teddy asked. "Use normal-people words."

"It's nothing you need to worry about," Handshake said. "As long as you protect me, and your Boss tells me what she knows about our current target of curiosity, then I'll be obliged by my power to fulfill my end of the bargain. Likewise, you'll want to fulfill your own end."

"What?" Emily asked.

"It's nothing too bad," Handshake said. "My power will help you carry out your end of the bargain. Little nudges and hints. And it'll discourage you from purposefully failing to meet your obligations."

"How?"

He shrugged a shoulder. "A bit of foreboding here, some twitching there. Nothing too intrusive."

"I can give you plenty of foreboding if you want," Athena said. She was glaring at the man, and Emily had the impression the lights in the little conference room were turning dim and the shadows in the corners were elongating.

"Hey now," Handshake said. His smile remained, but his voice did waver ever so slightly. "You're meant to protect me, not attack me."

Athena huffed, and the room snapped back to normalcy so quickly that Emily wasn't entirely sure she'd actually noticed anything.

Handshake looked at his wrist and hummed. "We should get going. We're a minute shy of when our meeting is meant to begin, and I don't want a reputation for being tardy." He adjusted his jacket, shifted the tie beneath a little, then patted down his slacks before heading for the door.

Emily felt her fists tightening by her side, and she wasn't sure what to do or, for that matter, what she was feeling.

How could he just spring that kind of thing on her and expect it to be okay? She . . . she was angry? Not angry-angry. Emily wasn't the sort to throw fits. Those always attracted way too much attention, and Emily had never handled attention well.

When she was angry, at least when she was angry when younger, she would just bottle it away and let it fade. That was the calmest way to deal with it.

But then, she'd never been angry because someone was threatening her and her sisters.

She shook her head. Summons, not sisters.

"Come on, girls," she said. If she didn't have a choice, then she didn't have a choice. It still left a bad taste in her mouth and made her stomach roil in displeasure. Emily didn't know what she would do. Even a strongly worded comment felt like too much, but she . . . she didn't like being taken advantage of.

She didn't quite glare at Handshake's back as she followed him, but the look she gave him was certainly very stern.

They exited into the corridor to find a group of three men walking by in clothes that didn't suit the hotel. The place was a nice, clean establishment, not one that fit the raggedy, either too-tight or too-loose clothes of the three men.

Emily let her arms drop and wiggled her fingers. Each hand was promptly grabbed by a summon.

"Are those the ones we're meeting?" Teddy asked. Her voice was just low enough that the three didn't seem to notice. They moved over to a door farther down, then slid into a well-lit room, leaving the door open behind them.

"I think so," Emily said.

Handshake paused before the entrance, twisted his jaw left and right, shrugged a few times, then refixed his smile in place. "Are you ready, girls?" he asked.

"You didn't say there would be three of them," Athena said.

"I expect that only one of them has powers. Cement *is* the only remaining member of his group that has powers. At least, as far as I know. And we're a floor or two above any cement. We should be rather safe."

"Don't know if I believe you, hand guy," Teddy said.

Handshake turned his smile to her, but instead of saying anything, he pushed into the conference room.

Emily let go of her summons' hands. Teddy moved in first, then Athena ran her hand through her hair and followed with her jaw set.

Being the last one in, Emily pulled the door shut behind her.

The trio of men, though really none of them seemed to be any older than their midtwenties, were all gathered at one end of the conference table. One of them was on the ground, toying with some wires connected to a laptop sitting atop the table. Another had his feet on the surface and was cleaning out his nails with the tip of a knife, and the last was sitting back, head nodding to the beat of a bassy song that was pouring out of his headphones. He had a mohawk, but it was pressed down in the middle where the headset cut across his head.

"Good afternoon, everyone," Handshake said as he pulled out the seat opposite the three men. "I assume you're the representatives Cement chose to send?"

The one with his legs on the table snorted. "Yeah. That's us," he said.

The contrast between the prim and proper Handshake and the three of them couldn't have been clearer.

Emily stood toward the back of the room, nearly out of sight of the others. Teddy took a spot between her and Handshake, and Athena pulled out a chair, then placed her own feet on the table. Though that meant she was almost falling out of her chair just to reach.

"Man, you brought kids to this thing?" the one Emily assumed was the leader asked.

"If we're all civilized and act with decorum, then there's no harm in that, right?" Handshake asked.

"I'm not going to kick a kid's teeth in," the leader said. "But still, man, just not cool, you know? What if I wasn't such a Paragon?" He waved his knife around in a circle. "Could do some nasty things to them. Powers or no."

"Perhaps," Handshake said. "I presume that none of you are Cement?"

"Nah," the leader said. "The boss thought it'd be wiser not to show up in person. That's what he's here for." He gestured to the one still on the ground with his knife.

"Yeah, yeah, nearly done," the man said. He stood up, a wire in hand, then plugged it into the laptop's side. "Let me just log in and all that."

A minute passed in awkward silence, with only the shuffling of the guy listening to music to fill the void and the occasional machine-gun clack of the laptop's keys. Then the computer was turned around and pointed in their direction.

The screen had a large "S" on it, white over a black background. The light next to the webcam was on, blinking a steady red.

"Greetings," a deep baritone said from the machine. "Handshake . . . the Boss, and if I'm not mistaken, Ursa Minor. I'm unfamiliar with your other companion."

"You can stay that way," Athena said.

"How very feisty," the man said. "Well then, I do believe we're all here for business—perhaps we should get to it?"

"Indeed," Handshake agreed. "Are your own companions trustworthy enough to discuss these things?"

"You can speak freely," Cement said.

"Brilliant. Now then, as per our previous agreement, I'm here in the flesh, meeting with you and some of your representatives. Are you ready to begin?"

The laptop was silent for a moment. "Yes, I think I am. Let's try and see if the two of us together can uncover a little bit about the Cabal, and if we can see about freeing Homie from his cell."

CHAPTER FIFTY-SEVEN

Inattention

D o you want to begin?" Cement asked.

Emily shifted her weight from foot to foot, but she did so slowly. The last thing she wanted was for people to stare at her, especially not the three punks across the room. They were exactly the sort of people her mother had warned her about. Bad boys who no doubt tried to use their charms to turn proper young women into too-young single mothers.

Or something like that. Her mother's warnings had always been a little disjointed.

In fact, Emily imagined her mother would be pretty . . . emotional about Emily essentially having two kids of her own.

She shook her head, set all those thoughts aside, then refocused.

"I don't mind starting," Handshake said. "At least, I can go over the history I've uncovered, then you can fill in what you can. And then we'll wrap it up with the latest information?"

"That sounds perfectly fair," the voice over the laptop said. The three men behind it were listening, and they were quiet, but they didn't seem to be enjoying themselves.

Handshake leaned back into his seat and rubbed a knuckle over his still-smiling lips. "Very well, then. The earliest signs that the Cabal exist actually come from Merica. That's not terribly surprising—their entire Heroic system is a bit more of a mess than here. The Cabal shows up in a few searches on some forums from Ew Ork, and E-Troit."

"North, then," the voice said.

Handshake made a meaningless gesture. "Mostly, yes. The posts generally talked about them as a group that showed up and asked people of a more . . . Villainous persuasion if they'd be willing to serve a greater cause. Recruitment, essentially."

"Anything from actual members?" Cement asked.

"One moment, I'm going over things chronologically," Handshake said.

"Ah, I see. Forgive my interruptions then. Go on."

Handshake's smile quivered. "The majority of the forum posts go nowhere. Lots of speculation and little else. Though some of those original posters can be linked back to local Villains, all minor, who were eventually captured and arrested. It's a little later that it gets interesting."

Handshake leaned his elbows on the table.

"See, that's mostly from ten to eleven years ago. There are two other sources that came out of the woodwork a little later. One a Rascal who had a sort of online journal. He detailed being approached by the Cabal, being offered some assistance, and eventually joining them. He stopped mentioning them, but his crimes spiked in intensity, and he suddenly found himself with a lot more equipment than before. He'd post images of it. New costume, some gear. He became a real local terror."

"And then?" Cement asked.

"Brought down by a local Hero. Captured. Died while behind bars. The other interesting lead from that same period never mentioned the Cabal before her arrest. Once she was behind bars, though, she squealed."

Cement hummed. "I imagine that didn't last long?"

"She recanted the next day. But some of what she said went on record and stayed there. She claimed that her robberies were made under the instructions of a group called the Cabal, that she had met with a Villain from the group and was acting on their behalf."

"I imagine she died?" Cement asked.

"She volunteered for an Endgame. Shortened prison term. Didn't make it out," Handshake said. "After that, we have sporadic mentions of the Cabal over the years, but they're infrequent. Their MO seems fairly simple. They target low-level, bad-morality beginners, offer them deals they can't refuse, then use them to commit some crimes. I can't find links between those. They seem almost random."

"Strange. Why get a Villain working for you if they won't use them for anything useful?"

"I thought as much. I have a few hypotheses. Perhaps there's an initiation phase, or some sort of hands-off training? They seemed to be the ones behind a few high-profile Villains, but those almost always end up captured or killed at the hands of a Hero."

Cement was quiet for a while. "Is that all you have?"

"For the Cabal's past? Just about. I have a lot of circumstantial information. The costumes they hand out might be from the same place and person. They may have been using the same payment system for a while before they switched to dead drops. I suspect they have at least one teleporter in their ranks. And, of course, I have more recent news, but you first."

"Very well. I was not approached by the Cabal. I think I might have been too successful at keeping my identity to myself, or perhaps I'm merely not interesting enough. They do seem to employ more . . . flamboyant sorts."

"That does seem to be their MO," Handshake said. "That, or the more subtle powered individuals they hired don't make as much noise."

"That's a possibility, yes. Either way, they never came to me. They did come to Homie."

Emily twitched. That was the man she and Teddy had knocked out and basically handed to the cops. The one who had the drive she'd gone through so much trouble to protect. Was he part of the Cabal?

"They approached him some weeks ago. Just a simple offer to talk, discuss his future and so on. Nothing threatening, not at first glance. We discussed it and decided to fish for more information. When that came back with nothing but vague allusions, I decided to deny their offer."

"Did they continue to pressure him?" Handshake asked.

"They did just that, yes. A small threat, but a threat nonetheless. We continued stalling, of course. Hemming and hawing. They seemed intent on making Homie more of a . . . household name."

Handshake leaned forward. "What do you mean by that?"

"Public stunts, robberies in broad daylight. More violent attacks against the few unpowered local gangs. They wanted him out in costume setting up protection rackets on every business in the city."

"I see," Handshake said. "They would provide some assistance, I imagine?"

"Location of police, windows of opportunity, lists of potential recruits to Homie's gang. Safe houses. The works," Cement said.

Handshake crossed his arms on the tabletop and nodded. "I see. That fits in with what I know. I've recently discovered that people on . . . our side of the fence aren't the only ones approached by the Cabal."

"Oh?"

"Indeed. Though they don't name themselves as such, an organization very similar to the Cabal tends to approach Heroes. Nearly all of them are approached by the Cabal at one time or another, though I think they're a bit more subtle with Heroes, especially those with governmental ties."

"And what do they offer the stalwart Heroes?" Cement asked.

"Villains. They offer them Villains. The locations of robberies in progress, along with footage of the Villain in question in action and plenty more information. In exchange, they steer the Hero toward accepting certain contracts. Product placements, ads, different patrol routes."

Cement sighed loud enough that it was picked up by whatever mic he was using. "They're running both sides of the game."

"Or they're trying to," Handshake said.

The room was silent for a while. "This has been enlightening. Thank you, Handshake. I appreciate you coming here."

"And I appreciate the information I've gleaned. May I ask what you plan on doing now?"

Cement chuckled. "You could certainly ask, but it would cost you to know. Not that I've made a choice yet. I think this is the end of our meeting."

Handshake nodded and stood up. "Well then. It was enjoyable conversing so peacefully. I do hope you keep me in mind for any future questions."

"Naturally."

Handshake gestured to the door, and Teddy stomped over and opened it up.

They were about to leave when Cement spoke up. "Miss Boss."

Emily froze. "Um. Yes?" she asked.

"I haven't forgotten what you did to my subordinate."

"Pfft," Athena said as she took her feet off the table. "Big talk from a guy who's hiding behind a screen. You couldn't touch a hair on the Boss's head if you tried, you fake Villain."

"Your own subordinates certainly have a high opinion of you. Perhaps we will see if it's well earned one day. Until then. Goodbye."

The screen flickered and the image was replaced by a gray square where Cement's "S" had been before.

Emily swallowed, looked to the three guys at the end of the room who were just then getting up, and scurried out after the others.

CHAPTER FIFTY-EIGHT

Call

You did good back there," Handshake said.

Emily looked at the back of his head. They were back in the hotel's parking lot, heading . . . not toward Handshake's car?

"I mean, there wasn't much action, but you did your part," he said as he came to a stop next to a minivan near the back. Bending down, the older man fumbled under the edge of the car, then pulled out a set of keys with a happy jangle. "Get in," he said.

"Why aren't we using your other car?" Teddy asked as she jumped in the back.

"Car bombs, my dear. Well, that and trackers—it's easier to follow a known car and so on. This might seem paranoid, but it's really not that complicated to set up. Both cars are rentals anyway. Under false names, of course."

"O-of course," Emily said as she hopped into the passenger seat. There was something there, something she sat on and had to bounce up to avoid. An envelope with "The Boss" written on it.

"That's yours. Two thousand. I know, we agreed on three, but that was before I realized you had a plus one. You'll get the rest soon enough. Oh, and a key and the address to a safe house. It's not exactly comfortable living, but it's out of the way and safe." He bounced on the driver's seat and fit the keys in the ignition. The van came on with a rumble. "Want me to drop you off at the same place I picked you up?" he asked.

"Uh, sure," Emily said.

"Good! Feel free to use that changing spot, by the way. Once I give one up I consider it compromised. Or don't use it, if you have even an ounce of paranoia in you."

Emily nodded. She didn't know whether she agreed or not; she just nodded because it was something to do. The envelope came open, and she stared at twenty neatly pressed bills. They looked . . . overwhelmingly small for the amount of money they held.

She wondered if she had ever had as much in her hands at once before.

It was going to be handy. The girls could use more clothes and some things, and she had to think of their education. She doubted they could go to a school, but maybe she could get them educational . . . stuff to teach them with? Homeschooling or something.

It wouldn't be fun, she imagined, trying to sit Teddy down to do anything like that. Athena probably wouldn't be as bad.

"Boss?" Handshake said.

Emily jumped. "Oh? Sorry, I was . . . sorry."

"It's fine," he said. "I asked you if you wanted to tell me what you knew of the Cabal, that's all."

Emily rubbed her hands together, then stopped. She didn't want to look nervous, even if it didn't take a genius to figure it out. "I . . . When we captured that man. Small Package? He . . . Wait, I'm supposed to negotiate for something first, right?"

"Oh, let me do the negotiation," Athena said. "I'll have him giving you everything he owns in no time."

Handshake waved a hand through the air. "Now, now, we can always put that off. Or perhaps we could say that I owe you a favor."

"Five favors," Athena said.

Handshake snorted. "Two. Final offer."

Athena leaned forward until she was bent over Emily's seat. "I say we sic Teddy on him until he gives us what we want."

Emily shook her head. "N-no, two favors is fine. It's not much besides and . . . and why aren't you buckled in?"

"Ah," Athena said. She fell back and Emily heard her belt clicking in place a moment later.

Taking a deep breath, Emily began again. "When we took out Small Package, I was near where he fell, and he mentioned something about the Cabal. That was my first clue, I guess. Then . . . a friend came to my place to hide. He was invited to join the Cabal, but his power told him that it would be a bad idea."

"His power?" Handshake asked.

"Um, I think that would cost a lot more than two favors," Emily said.

"My, my, for someone so new, you do make a lot of interesting friends, you know? Most people outside of a Heroic organization couldn't boast about knowing so many powered individuals."

"The Boss gets around," Teddy said.

"T-Ted— Ursa Minor!" Emily said. "Don't say that like that."

The bear girl in the back blinked dumbly at her. She didn't get the double meaning. Emily couldn't blame her, but it was still a little embarrassing.

"I'll explain later." Way, way later.

"So are you happy with your remuneration?" Handshake said. "I'll of course make sure that the remainder is available as soon as possible. We can arrange a dead drop, or I can have it sent to an address of your choosing. Perhaps a PO box? Though those are traceable if you don't know what you're doing."

"It's fine," Emily said. She took the bills out of the envelope and tucked them away. "Thank you."

"No problem," Handshake said. He flashed her a smile, but she didn't know if it was any more genuine than the one he always wore. "Was that all the involvement you've had with the Cabal?"

"Um. Just about, yeah," Emily said. "I did ask someone else about them, but they told me to forget about it."

"Hmm. If they're in the know, then they'll either let slip that you know more than you should, or they're against the Cabal, or just neutral and they might keep the fact that you asked to themselves."

Emily hoped that that was the case. Melaton had seemed nice . . . enough. More or less.

They pulled into the same alleyway where Handshake had picked them up and the man put the van in park. "Before you go," he said.

Emily paused, hand on the handle to leave. "Yes?"

"If I ever need you again, for things similar to what happened today, would you happen to be available? I might have more work suitable for you and all your . . . companions, no matter how many there happen to be."

She held back on the urge to gulp and give anything away. "I . . . might be willing," she said. "I guess we could keep in touch?"

Handshake nodded to her. "Brilliant! In that case, I'll be sending you a text with the location of the remaining money I owe you within the next day or so. Until then, you three have a fine evening."

Emily stepped back and watched Handshake back the van rather awkwardly out of the alleyway and into traffic before driving off.

She let a long breath out. "That's done," she said.

"That was kind of boring," Teddy said.

"Yeah," Athena agreed. "But it felt like it was real important stuff. So it couldn't be all that bad, yeah?"

"I suppose not," Emily said. "Who wants to get changed first?" she asked.

"Are we heading home?" Teddy asked. "I could use a nap."

"I was thinking maybe we could grab something to eat. Just fast food."

"I could use a snack too," Teddy changed tracks. "I'll get changed first!" The bear girl darted into the little changing room tucked away under the fire escape, leaving Emily alone with Athena.

Athena slid her hands into her pockets, then leaned against the nearest wall. She might have looked cool if she were taller than Emily's shoulder. "What're we going to do about the C-word people?" Athena asked.

"In the best case," Emily said, "nothing at all."

Teddy opened the door to the changing room, half out of her costume and with Emily's phone in hands. "Hey, Boss, this is ringing."

Emily felt her heart sinking. She took the phone and looked at the unfamiliar number on it. She tapped the call accept button. "Yes?"

"Oh, oh, thank God," Alea Iacta's voice came through. "I need help."

Emily considered hanging up and pretending there was nothing going on. But a look to her summons put paid to that. Not only would it be cowardly, it would be cowardly in front of the two people whose opinion she was starting to really care about. More than she cared about the opinion of people she barely knew, which in hindsight was probably more than she should have.

"What is it?" she asked.

"H-hey, no need to rip my head off," Jacob said.

"J-just tell me what's going on."

"I'm being chased. A Hero. Some flashy girl I've never seen before. I think the Cabal tipped her off. I need help bad."

Emily knew she would regret it. "Tell me where you are."

CHAPTER FIFTY-NINE

Catching the Mouse

Emily walked at a decent clip, her sisters . . . summons . . . keeping pace by walking fast with the occasional bit of jogging thrown in. Some part of her knew she had to slow down, that it wasn't kind of her to be heading off so quickly.

Another part of her didn't care.

Ever since Power Day, Emily had been tossed around, with new revelations, and near . . . perhaps not death, but certainly near-something-awful experiences. Not to mention suddenly finding herself in the position of what was essentially a single mom.

She took a deep breath and let it all out in one long exhale.

"Boss, you okay?" Teddy asked.

Emily nodded. "I'm fine, Teddy," she lied. "It's just . . . All of this has been a lot, you know?"

"That's okay," Teddy said. "You've got me to help. And Athena, too, I guess."

"There's nothing to worry about, sis," Athena added. "If anything bugs you, I'll handle it. And maybe Teddy can, like . . . stand by and try to look smart while I do that."

Teddy's head snapped around and she glared at Athena, who stared right back, smug as an owl that'd caught a mouse.

"Thanks, girls," Emily said.

She really did have to refocus. If Alea Iacta was in trouble, what would happen?

Her parents had taken her to a few psychiatrists over the years, mostly to help her through her anxiety. She'd never stuck with any one of them for very long. The meetings always made her too nervous. It was only later she could appreciate the irony in that.

Still, some had given Emily a few tricks that she still used.

One was to break things down into their worst possible scenarios. What *would* happen if Alea Iacta, if Jacob, was captured?

He'd probably squeal and tell the Heroes she was a Villain. That was bad.

If he died, then . . . that would also be bad. She'd be safe, but down an ally. Also, he'd be dead, which wasn't optimal. She didn't like him much, but she didn't want him dead.

What else? She couldn't imagine a scenario worse than the Heroes, and the Cabal, learning about her and her sisters.

So that was what she had to prevent.

If she arrived and an entire team of Heroes was there, what could she do? Other than maybe stalling them, Emily couldn't think of anything. Even that was asking for a lot.

If everything was in the worst possible situation, then there was nothing Emily could do. That was . . . not actually comforting at all. Maybe ditching that shrink had been a good idea.

She swallowed and kept moving. The closer they got to campus, the more people were out on the streets, and the more people stopped to look their way. Some seemed to want to gravitate toward them, but she suspected Athena was doing something if the way they looked spooked meant anything.

Emily bit her lip. She couldn't do anything to stop the Heroes.

Maybe she didn't need to stop them outright.

If there was one thing she could say with certainty about Alea Iacta, it's that he was slippery. Slippery and lucky.

"I have a plan," she said.

The girls looked up at her, eyes filled with naive curiosity.

"When we arrive, we need to slow the Hero down. She thinks we're Heroes. So we ask questions, and we try to lead her the wrong way, and we do our best to stall her. Give Alea Iacta time to run away and escape."

"We could beat her up? That'll give him plenty of time to run," Teddy said.

Emily shook her head. "No. Not . . . not unless we don't have any other choice. In fact, don't beat anyone up unless I specifically tell you to, okay?"

Teddy nodded. "Sure thing, Boss."

"I think I could use my power to confuse her," Athena said. "I can be really subtle when I want to."

"That's probably okay," Emily said.

Her phone rang. She had to hop as she fished her phone from the tight pockets of her costume's pants.

The moment she pressed the phone to her ear she heard Jacob panting. "Where the hell are you?" he hissed.

"I'm near campus. Where are you?" Emily asked.

"You know the Sleep Late station? With the gas and that little corner store? Cute redhead at the counter? I'm behind there. Hurry! I'm nearly out of juice and this girl just won't stop."

Emily picked up the pace a little. She knew where he meant, more or less. "Who is it?"

"I don't know!" Jacob said. "Oh, crap. I have to go. Look, there are a bunch of old factory buildings, like, two blocks down. I'll be there. It's quiet. Less people. Hurry!"

Emily stuffed her phone in a jacket pocket and reached her hands down. Both of her summons grabbed on without having to be told. The people ahead of them were dodging out of their way. She supposed that was normal. Seeing Heroes running by meant there was trouble ahead.

They arrived at the gas station Alea Iacta had mentioned, and Emily jogged to a stop on the edge of the parking lot and looked around while letting go of her sisters to place her hands on her knees. There was no sign of any Heroes or, for that matter, Alea.

That didn't mean much.

"I think it's that way," Emily said as she pointed.

They moved around the side of the gas station, and through the alley at its back. There was trash tossed around, and a few bags of it looked like they'd been slashed open where they were stacked next to some dumpsters.

All across the ground were faint, glimmering sparks, most fizzling out with little wisps of smoke, others still burning bright.

"Pretty," Teddy said.

"That's someone's power," Emily said. It had to be. That, or someone had been setting off fireworks in the alley just before they arrived.

"Makes it easy for us," Teddy said. She pointed to the end of the alley, where the sparks veered off to the left.

Emily had to admit she was right. "Let's go," she said.

They darted out the back, and across a narrow road set next to an old redbrick building. A factory of some sort, one that looked to be about as old as the city itself.

There were a few more sparks near one side of the building, so they rushed over to that. Around that corner was another old, narrow road set between two rows of old buildings. Some were still in use, though the factories were closed for the day. Still, newer cars were parked here and there, and past some frosted fences were forklifts and semitrailers parked next to stacks of wood and shipping containers.

"There!" Teddy pointed.

A glance that way showed one building, in worse repair than the others. Its heavy wooden door was chained shut, but there were windows next to it, broken and surrounded by shards of glass.

Lights sparked and flickered within, like sparklers going off, but without any of the accompanying noise.

"Good eye," Emily said as she ran over. One of the windows had a milk crate set under it, and it looked as if a lot more of the glass had been broken to make it easier to jump in. "Teddy, want to go in first?"

"Give me a boost!" Teddy said.

Emily got on the crate, then with a grunt, lifted Teddy over the lip of the window, careful not to let her touch the glass.

Then it was Athena's turn, with Teddy helping and hindering as best she could.

Emily jumped in last, landing on the dusty hardwood floor and looking around. The factory had a low ceiling with wooden beams running across it, and it smelled like mold and mothballs. A few heavy brackets mounted on the walls and floor hinted at where equipment had been before, but the place was otherwise empty save for some abandoned boxes.

"Come back here, you bastard!" someone screamed. Female, high-pitched, angry.

Emily looked to her sisters.

"I guess we go that way," Teddy said.

"I guess so," Emily agreed.

They didn't quite run. Not on flooring that was so uneven, and in a place where the lighting was so bad. Still, they made good time crossing the main floor and arriving at a loading dock. There was a mechanism in place for a large elevator, though it was missing, leaving the two floors above them visible through the hole.

Sparks flashed from above, racing ahead in complete silence.

"Stairs," Athena said. She grabbed Emily and Teddy and pulled them forward. "I've got the eyes for this, no worries."

When they reached the top floor, it was to find a familiar pair running circles around each other. Alea Iacta was diving behind pillars and using boxes as cover, always moving just as the one attacking him looked the other way and avoiding the flying sparks by a hair.

In the center of the room was Glamazon, the woman in her spandex armor, anger writ large on what was visible of her face, and around her, a storm of sparks and flaring lights.

"Okay," Emily whispered.

Now she just had to get Alea out of the factory and subdue an angered Hero.

Easy.

CHAPTER SIXTY

Being Clever

Emily took in the situation as best she could. That was, she took a moment to breathe in, heart racing from running around and climbing up the stairs.

Glamazon screamed something incoherent, her arm swinging forward with a straight punch that launched a cascade of sparks.

They were nice sparks.

Bright. Shiny.

They were pretty and glimmering, like raindrops sparkling off a streetlight, and they glowed a myriad of colors. Beautiful colors, some of which Emily was sure she'd never seen before.

She took a step closer, trying to see the sparks better, but they escaped around a pillar and out of sight.

Emily gasped and screwed her eyes shut. Her arms snapped out and, on instinct, caught her sisters by the shoulder.

She had been forming a plan, and then the sparks . . . that had to be some sort of power. Like turning someone's brain into a cat's while wiggling a laser pointer before them. She licked her lips and crouched down. "Be careful," she whispered, eyes still closed. "Those lights are dangerous."

"But they were pretty," Teddy whined.

"You idiot. They're a trap," Athena said, as if she hadn't stepped toward the lights too.

"Give me a moment. I need to come up with a plan," Emily said.

Her goal was to get Alea Iacta out of the room, but as it was, she didn't think there was another exit but the one they'd taken, and Jacob didn't look athletic enough to jump out of a window without hurting himself.

That meant either talking Glamazon down, or distracting her enough that Jacob could get away.

Glamazon roared. "You complete ass! Just come out already! I'm tired of running after you!"

"She says a lot of bad words," Teddy said. "You're only supposed to talk about asses when you're pooping."

Emily sighed and opened one eye. Glamazon didn't seem to have noticed them. She was crossing the room, disappearing and reappearing behind pillars. Emily glimpsed someone else move deeper down the factory. Glamazon didn't miss it, either, firing off a glowing barrage.

Emily shut her eyes. "Okay. Okay," she said.

There was no way that they'd be able to distract Glamazon long enough, not by just showing up and talking.

Although.

"Athena," Emily said. "Can you confuse her?"

"No problem, Big Sister," Athena said. "I just need to know more or less where she is. I can keep one eye closed."

"Good," Emily said. Her spur-of-the-moment plan was fairly simple. She'd let Athena distract Glamazon and . . . and hopefully that would be enough. If Jacob could run away, then maybe Emily could intercept Glamazon and pretend to be . . . well, herself, coming over to help. She pulled out her phone and prepared to text Jacob.

She paused.

"We should probably get to cover first."

"That's real clever," Teddy agreed.

The three of them moved over to some wooden crates collecting dust to one side. Emily had to squat to keep her head below the edge of the boxes, something her summons didn't have nearly as much trouble with.

"Okay," Emily said. "Athena, you distract her. Teddy, when I move over to Glamazon to talk to her, turn into a bear, just in case. And, while she's distracted . . . Athena, can you grab Alea Iacta's attention?"

"Sure," Athena said.

"Good, then lead him to the exit and tell him to just run away. We can call him later or whatever." Emily shifted a little. She really had to start exercising more if squatting for a minute was so much of a strain. "You girls got that?"

They nodded.

Emily smiled. "Then, Athena, start as soon as you're ready."

The owl girl leaned forward, her head sticking out of the side of the crates to fix onto Glamazon.

Her power, Emily knew, was about as subtle as they came. There were no lights, no flashes, no noise. One moment Glamazon was using language that wasn't appropriate around children, the next . . . she was still swearing, but now she was looking around a lot more, and her voice took on a waver that sounded just shy of fearful.

"Come on out, d-dammit!"

Emily licked her lips and pulled up her phone, one hand up to hide the screen's light. She sent a text to Alea Iacta:

E-Wright: Get ready to move soon. We'll cover for you. Run.

Somewhere, way off in the far end of the factory, a phone jingled.

Emily wanted to smack herself.

"There you are!" Glamazon said.

"Uh," Athena said. "I was trying to be subtlelike. I'm not done yet."

Emily bit her lip. With one hand against the nearest crate, she lifted herself up just enough to see Glamazon moving deeper into the factory. "Okay, okay," she said.

She was not the best at doing things with any sort of spontaneity. She glanced over to the stairs leading down. It was still possible to run away, maybe catch Glamazon after she caught Alea Iacta. But by then there might be cops on the way.

"Stay here," she said.

Emily stood up and quickly moved over to the opposite side of the stairs from her sisters. She saw Teddy backing up from the crates and bending forward, her hands on the ground and her back arched. Emily gave her a thumbs-up, then stepped up toward the middle of the room.

The lighting was poor. What little illumination there was came from between the boards placed over the windows and from the glowing embers left from Glamazon's power all across the floor. Emily could still make out Glamazon in her bright costume in the dark. She cleared her throat. "Glamazon?"

The woman spun around, twin trails of hissing sparks shooting out toward Emily.

She eeped and ducked down, narrowly avoiding the sparks.

The sparks that fizzed and popped with such cute noises. Emily found herself turning, a faint smiling coming up onto her lips despite the thumping of her heart.

She wanted to see them spit and sputter.

Emily shook her head and took a quick step away from the sparks, her eyes fixing onto Glamazon with some effort. "Glamazon!" she called. "It's, uh, the Boss. We met already?"

Glamazon paused, her hands hovering below a pair of new sparks. "The girl with a kid?" she asked.

"Um, yeah, that's me," Emily said. "I, uh, heard a disturbance? Yeah, and I came to see what was going on."

"In costume?' Glamazon asked.

"I heard it a while ago," Emily excused herself.

The Hero didn't look convinced. "And you tracked me here?"

"You, uh, left sparks all over?" Emily said. She gestured behind her, where she could still see the reflections of the sparks on the pillars and walls around her.

"Oh," Glamazon said. "Right . . . So what are you doing here?"

Emily worked her mouth as she searched for an answer. In reality, she really just wanted to be back in her dorm, studying ahead and maybe watching kittens fighting over string on Outube. "I really don't know," she said. "Uh, you looked like maybe you needed help?"

Glamazon huffed, hands on hips. "Trying to steal some of the glory? No, no, it's fine. I'd do the same. Yeah, I could use a bit of help. That jerk keeps hiding."

"What jerk?" Emily asked.

"Some two-bit wannabe Villain," Glamazon said. "He was seen going around and using his powers on civilians. Just want to lock him up, is all."

"How did you know where he was?" Emily asked.

"What do you mean?"

Emily shifted. "I mean . . . was he in costume? Did you find his real ID and track him? How did you know he'd be wherever you found him?"

Glamazon shrugged. "I've got sources."

"And how did they know?"

The Hero glared. "Look, do you want to help me or play twenty questions?"

Emily would have much rather played twenty questions, but she supposed that wasn't an actual answer she could give. "Okay, let's go see if we can find this, uh, guy?"

Glamazon nodded. "Yeah. Male, white, about twenty to twenty-five, more or less. Five foot . . . eh, four? He looks pretty short."

Emily thought she heard someone muttering from somewhere in the dark. "Okay, well, uh. I guess we can both go in different directions. If you find him first, call me, and I'll come over to help?"

"Can you manage on your own?" Glamazon asked.

"I got all the way here, didn't I?" Emily asked. She pointed off to one side, guessing that it was the direction where Jacob wasn't. "How about you start that way, and I'll go this way. And, um, did you call the police yet?"

"No, not yet. They don't like false alarms. And they steal some of the spotlight, you know?"

"Right, of course." She tried on a smile, then after a brief hesitation, set off to pretend to capture Jacob.

Or something.

Making things up as she went was not her strong suit.

CHAPTER SIXTY-ONE

Confidence

Emily pulled her phone out and tapped the power button to light the path ahead of her a little better. She had the impression that Jacob was somewhere around where she was, but she couldn't be entirely sure.

If he was smart, he was sneaking his way out.

That would be the optimal solution, to find that he was clever enough to run away while she was talking to Glamazon. She didn't think she'd be that lucky.

She moved past a pillar. It . . . felt weird to not be afraid. She should have been worried about Glamazon, but she wasn't. The girl's sparkles were a nuisance, but not that much of a threat. And although she was walking into a darkened factory, with cobwebs hanging off the corners and shifting shadows everywhere that her phone's flashlight didn't reach, the only thing Emily expected to meet in the dark was Jacob's terrified face.

It was . . . refreshing, to not be afraid.

A lot of her life had been ruled by that, the constant fear that something, some*one*, would pressure her, make her act on the spur of the moment. Now that it was happening all the time, she was . . . definitely not getting used to it.

On the other hand, she had a lot more power now, a lot more control over things. It was refreshing.

Maybe the confidence wasn't earned. Maybe she needed to sit down and wait for the adrenaline to wash away.

Or maybe it wouldn't be entirely bad to be confident, at least when she had the mask on.

Emily's light slid past something pale, then she brought it back and watched as Jacob blinked dumbly at her. "So there you are," she whispered.

"Emily?" he asked. "Oh . . . hey? Did you get rid of that crazy one? With the fireworks?"

"No, she's still looking for you," Emily whispered. "Don't talk so loudly."

Jacob nodded and shifted so that he was standing properly. Emily raised her phone and looked past him. There was only a dead end beyond, a sort of chamber stuck to the side of the main factory floor. "You know, I thought I was screwed there for a bit."

"You might have been," Emily said. "We're going to distract Glamazon. You need to get down. Do you have any luck left?"

"Fresh out. I was running on fumes already, and I spent what I had left getting this far." He stood and leaned forward to see past Emily, but she pushed him back. He was in jeans and a dark gray hoodie, enough to serve as sorta-camouflage in the factory, and it was probably one of the things that had stopped Glamazon from spotting him so soon, but it wouldn't do for him to just step out.

"Fine," Emily said. "I'll move over that way"—she gestured off to her left, toward another room—"and then call for Glamazon to come over. You run for it. If Athena follows you, you do as she says, all right?"

"And then what?" he asked. "Where am I supposed to go now?"

"I don't know," Emily said. "Hide somewhere and call me later."

"This isn't even my phone," he said.

Emily blinked. "You stole it?"

"It was just lying there . . . on the passenger seat of some guy's car. He has a cute girlfriend—her pic's on the background."

"I-I don't care. Just . . . get back there and wait." She stomped off, making sure to flash her light around as if searching in case Glamazon looked her way.

Somehow, it was so much easier to work with her little sisters than with someone like Alea Iacta. She couldn't decide if it was because they listened to her or if he was just an idiot.

She found another chamber, like the one Alea Iacta had been hiding in. There were boxes and enough corners that a dozen people could have been hiding there. Emily bounced on the spot a few times and unlimbered herself before taking a deep breath.

"Glamazon!" she called back.

"What?" came the echoing reply.

"Over here!"

The Hero ran over, sparks forming and sputtering in the air around her. Emily pointed into the chamber. "I think he's in here."

"What? You see any footsteps?"

Emily blinked and looked down. Her feet traced a path back to where she'd been, the dusty floor leaving little to the imagination. "No?" she said. There weren't any leading into the chamber.

"Hmm, he's a sneaky bastard. I think he's been jumping onto things to hide the traces, and it's not dusty everywhere, you know?"

"Uh, yeah," Emily said.

"You saw him in there?"

Emily nodded, then hesitated. She didn't want to be caught out in a lie. "I think so? Was he, uh." She flashed her light deeper into the chamber and made out a few rough piles of dust-gray cloth. "Was he wearing a gray shirt?

"Yeah. Gray hoodie."

"Then I think so."

Glamazon fired a few lights into the chamber, bigger ones, that served as decent flares. "It's a dead end," she said before raising her voice. "We've got you now, you dumb bastard!"

Emily moved up with the Hero until she paused.

"You're more of a close-range type, right?"

"Huh? N-no, not really?"

Glamazon's mouth set into a firm line. "Me neither. I know some martial arts, and my sparks can sting like mad when they're fresh, but that's about it. Stay close, then, I guess."

"Right," Emily said. She had to stay close one way or another.

She . . . probably shouldn't have placed herself in the middle of any sort of action. Her power was more of a minionish one, even if her minions weren't very expendable-looking.

She didn't like thinking that way at all—it felt wrong.

Something rustled way off behind her, and Emily started to turn before remembering that Jacob was meant to be running.

Glamazon's head rose and she started to look behind.

Thinking fast, Emily pointed ahead. "What's that?"

Glamazon blinked. "It's a box?"

It was, in fact, a box. "He could be . . . in it?"

Glamazon looked at Emily, even with half her face covered, the doubt was easy to read. The box was far too small to hold anyone.

"Uh, never mind?"

Something scuffed the ground behind them, and this time they both turned to see Jacob, in the middle of the factory, arms pinwheeling while some piece of wood skittered underfoot. She imagined that he'd tripped. Which meant that his luck really had run out.

"Got you!" Glamazon shouted even as her sparks raced out across the factory and smacked Jacob in the back.

He yelled, his flailing turning wild before he crashed to the ground.

Glamazon tugged something out from the back of her costume, and for a moment Emily thought she had a gun until she saw the yellow cap on the end. "Media's going to eat this up," Glamazon said. "Worth every penny."

Emily's eyes closed. "Sisterportation: Teddy," she muttered.

A grizzly appeared before her. "Boss?" she asked.

Glamazon turned.

Teddy was a lot faster.

A paw the size of Glamazon's head came around with a heavy swipe. Emily flinched back as the paw smacked Glamazon with a dull thump. She only just caught the Hero's feet flying out from under her.

It ended as soon as it started. Glamazon landed with a cough.

At the other end, Jacob scrambled to his feet, glanced back, then took off running.

Athena slipped out from behind her hiding spot and rushed over, only pausing to pick up Glamazon's Aser on the way.

Glamazon coughed, then rolled over. "What the hell is wrong with—" she began.

Then Athena fired the Aser right into the Hero's chest. She convulsed, twisting this way and that.

"S-stop!" Emily said. "Stop, Athena."

"Ah, but this is kinda fun," Athena said.

Glamazon coughed and raised a hand. Sparks appeared around her.

Athena pulled the trigger again.

"Um," Emily said. She swallowed, took in the confident, almost smug look Athena was giving her, then moved up to stand above Glamazon. "I'm sorry about that," Emily said. She was surprised that the quiver was gone from her voice. "That was my bad."

"Did, did you just double-cross me? What the fu—" Glamazon spasmed again. "Stop that!"

"Swearing is rude," Athena said.

Emily doubted Athena cared all that much. "I'm really sorry. I think my . . . sisters mistook you for a Villain."

"What?" Glamazon said. She rolled over, trembling arms going under her so that she could get to her feet. "What's that supposed to mean?" She glared as she stood. "You're just trying to get the Villain for yourself, aren't you? And who the hell is that?"

Athena glared right back. Teddy growled, filling the factory with the low rumble of her anger. "Look, you sparkly, no-good Hero," Athena said. "We're the only ones who know you're here. Big Sister said that it was all a mistake. So you shut up and accept her apology, all right?"

"Or what, you brat?"

"Does anyone know you're here?" Athena asked. "'Cause the way I see it, it would be really sad if people learned that some Villain got rid of you while you were off on your own."

Glamazon swallowed.

Emily placed a hand on Athena's shoulder. She tried on a smile for Glamazon, to reassure her. "It wouldn't come to that, right?"

CHAPTER SIXTY-TWO

Imposing

Glamazon's expression shifted, from a bit of reluctant fear, to a sort of arrogant sneer that immediately made Emily's stomach twist. "You wouldn't dare," she said. "You have any idea how much your morality would drop if you pulled that kind of thing?" Glamazon pointed a finger right at Emily's face. "I don't know what kind of game you're playing, but it won't work with me."

Emily almost took a step back to move out of the way of Glamazon's finger.

Almost.

Instead she smacked the hand away, the pain in the back of her wrist nearly as surprising as the flash of anger that ran through her. "D-don't," Emily snapped. She swallowed, reining in the sudden outburst of anger. "Don't poke at me like that. And don't . . . do whatever it is you're doing."

Glamazon glared and stood a little taller. The woman was imposing, in a way that no one wearing colorful spandex should have been. "You just made me lose that jerk. I would have caught the bastard by now." She poked Emily in the chest.

Emily took a deep breath and ignored the sore point right where Glamazon's finger had struck her. "Did you pay for that opportunity?" Emily asked.

"What?" Glamazon asked.

"Did . . . you . . . pay?" Emily asked, every word enunciated carefully. "Alea Iacta is low-key, for the most part. He's been hiding for some time, even, keeping his head down. But he got an offer that he refused. And then you appear out of nowhere, knowing where he was even when out of costume."

"Wait, do you know him?"

"Shut up," Emily said. Her hands shook by her side until she felt Athena grab one and squeeze. "Are you with them? The Cabal?"

Glamazon looked away, the same expression Emily's sisters had when they were lying flitting across her features. "What are you on about?"

"How much did it cost you?" Emily asked. "Or what did it cost you? Did you have to pay at all? How did it work? Did they just tell you where to find him?"

"I don't know what you're talking about," Glamazon said.

Teddy growled, low and rumbling from right behind Glamazon. The woman jumped and seemed to notice for the first time that, for all intents and purposes, she was surrounded.

"Tell me," Emily said. "Now."

It was strange seeing someone twitch back, as if Glamazon were one of her sisters caught with her hand in the cookie jar.

Emily felt her brows knitting together. "I won't ask again."

The factory's darkened corners grew deeper, and the low rumble from Teddy's throat amplified, drowning out even the faintest of noises from outside.

"God, what the hell is wrong with you?" Glamazon whispered. "W-we're meant to be on the same side."

"That's what I thought too," Emily said. "But I'm not so sure now. Not when you might be one of those people who paid for a little glory. What did Alea Iacta do that was such a big threat to you, or anyone else for that matter?"

"He's a Villain!" Glamazon said.

Emily's teeth snapped together and she bit back a growl of her own. "You chased him across several blocks while he was hiding after being blackmailed by the Cabal. You fired off those sparks of yours all over the damned place, in public. I'm sure you know how distracting those lights are. Did you make sure there was no car traffic around?"

The flash of guilt suggested a no to that question.

"As far as I can tell, you're the one acting like a menace here," Emily said. It wasn't quite true, but she had Glamazon in a bind, and while Emily knew that pressing harder wasn't the wisest thing to do, she couldn't think of anything else. "So tell me about the Cabal."

"I . . . I don't know what you're talking about," Glamazon said.

Emily stepped forward, dropping Athena's hand so she could stand right in front of the Hero. She was shorter than Glamazon. She didn't feel it though. "Jezebelle. Tell me."

The Hero cursed under her breath, but her shoulders deflated as she did. "Look, they said I had to keep things to myself."

"If you don't tell them that you told me, then it won't be a problem," Emily said.

"Why do you want to know?" Glamazon said.

"Because they're Villains. Villains operating in my . . . in this city."

Glamazon shook her head. "No, no, they're not Villains. Silver Fox told me about them. They help Heroes for a small price."

"And they help Villains, too," Emily said. "They're playing both sides."

"I don't believe you," Glamazon said.

"That's your problem," Emily returned. She almost let out a very inappropriate laugh. It was such a dismissive thing to say. She should have been mortified—instead she felt a thrill run down her spine as Glamazon flinched.

"God, what is your problem?" Glamazon said.

"I'm beginning to tire of being messed with," Emily said. "I'm thinking that maybe I should start doing something about it." She licked her lips. "We can start by having you tell me what you know."

"I don't know much, all right," Glamazon said. She crossed her arms and glanced around. "Just— They texted me. I asked Fox about it, and he said they were legit. They wanted me to do this sponsorship thing. The price was . . . I mean, not the best, but not bad either? And they told me where that luck guy would be today. And they were right."

"You'd really go so far to protect someone who only gave you that much?" Emily said.

Glamazon huffed. "At least one of us understands the concept of loyalty."

The Hero twitched, her breath coming in gasps, and her eyes widened to an almost comical size before they rolled up into the back of her head and she crumpled to the ground.

"What."

"Ah, oops?" Athena said.

Action Reward!

For defeating a powered opponent by intimidating her into unconsciousness, you have been awarded:

+1 Skill Slot!

Emily blinked at the prompt, then waved it away before eyeing the still-breathing form of Glamazon on the ground before her. "Did . . . did you just knock her out?"

"Not my fault," Athena said. "She's all weak and stuff. Barely even pushed."

Teddy warped and shifted, turning back into a girl in a butter-yellow sundress and plastic bear mask. "Bit of a coward, that one."

Athena nodded. "Weak."

With a sigh, Emily stepped back and shook her arms. There were pins and needles running through her whole body, as if she'd been on the verge of fainting herself.

"You were really cool, though, big sister," Athena said. "Superscary."

Teddy nodded. "I thought she was going to poop her capitalism right out of her."

"I . . . what does that even mean? No, don't answer that—it's rhetorical," Emily said. "We should probably leave."

Athena gave Emily a big thumbs-up and Teddy skipped forward to take Emily's hand in hers. "Home it is! We can call that idiot guy and tell him he owes us one."

"Right," Emily said.

She'd have to call Handshake, trade that bit of information for something or other. And he'd promised her the location of a safe house. That might come in handy.

As for Glamazon, Emily figured she could take care of herself.

Emily wiggled her hand toward Athena. As soon as the girl's hand was in hers, Emily turned and made her way out of the factory.

The sky had darkened even more while Emily and her sisters had been inside, turning to deep blue.

Home wasn't far away—just a few blocks to the college, and then a walk over to the dorms. Still, Emily couldn't walk over dressed the way she was. They found a spot near another factory, as abandoned as the first and with a broken-down bathroom on the first floor. Changing in a hurry, soon the three were walking home in the dark.

Emily swiped her phone over the panel next to the dorm's door, then she practically stumbled to the elevator and up to her room.

The moment she saw her bed she crashed into it and gave up. Life was too much sometimes.

She could figure out what to do with the sinking realization she was more of a Villain than she expected in the morning. Or maybe, if she was clever about it, she could do nothing about it and pretend that she didn't turn mean when under pressure.

She doubted it was going to be that easy.

CHAPTER SIXTY-THREE

Triple Threat

Emily woke up to something heavy and warm pressing against her side. Then she felt something breathing near her back.

Blinking, she stretched her head up and looked down through bleary eyes to see two bodies taking up what little room was left on her bed. Teddy was sprawled out, one leg over Emily's, the other folded over the side of the bed. Her elbow was digging into Emily's stomach and her head was pressed back into the nook between Emily's shoulder and neck.

A turn to the side revealed Athena rolled up in the fetal position and hugging Emily's free arm close.

She sighed. This kind of behavior wasn't appropriate.

It was kind of comfortable, though, and warm. She shifted until Teddy's elbow moved off her, then, ever so slowly, she sank back into a dreamless sleep.

When she woke up again, it was to daylight slipping in through the one window in her room. Groaning, Emily tried to move, but at some point the girls had turned around and were now clinging onto her from both sides.

She stared at the ceiling. The last day had been . . . a lot.

Threatening someone, running after Alea Iacta, the whole thing with Handshake . . .

Today was, Emily decided, going to be an ordinary day. She had classes in the afternoon, and maybe she'd take some time to text her mom. She hadn't in a couple of days, and she knew how her mother could worry.

There was one big advantage to everything, though.

Name: Emily Wright		
Alignment: Villain		
Alias: The Boss		
Level: 1		
Powers		
Sister Summoning		
Create Sister	Rank 4	
Sisterportation	Level 1	
Double Trouble	Level Max	
Healpats	Level 4	
Points		
Power Slots: 0	Skill Upgrades: 1	Skill Slots: 1

A new Skill Slot. Essentially, a new free skill. An upgrade to what she had. If things followed a set pattern, there was a chance the new skill would mean another sister, another person to care for.

Teddy growled in her sleep and buried her face deeper into Emily's side.

Maybe a third sister wouldn't be that bad, Emily reasoned.

Do you wish to spend a Skill Slot point on the Power: Sister Summoning?

Emily stared at the prompt for a long time. She would have to use it eventually, and by many a measure, sooner was better than later.

There was . . . a feeling of safety that came from her sisters. It wasn't something literal, she knew, more . . .

They trusted her? They believed in her fully and entirely. No one had ever done that before.

Sure, her mother cared, and her dad would give her a pat on the back and tell her to try her best, but their words never quite matched their actions. They were always watching and wary, in case something went wrong.

And Emily couldn't blame them. A lot had gone wrong. She was physically and socially clumsy at the best of times. There wasn't much she had done that hadn't flopped the moment she had to talk.

People, the complexity of conversation, kind of terrified her.

She was better now. A little more confident. Enough to try and live on her own, to try the college life.

That had been how high she'd raised her bar.

But now? With her power? With her sisters?

Maybe it was just the stress talking, or maybe it was the constant little victories but she felt . . . better. More assured of herself. She didn't like some of it, but . . . Emily smiled up at the ceiling.

Another sister would be nice.

"Yes."

New Skill unlocked!

Triple Threat has been added to your Power's Skills!

Triple Threat
Sister Summoning
Level Max
Allows you to summon a third sister with Create Sister. Instant use.
Activation: Voice command
Cooldown: None
Max New Sisters: One

Just as she suspected. Every other skill was related to creating a new sister. That was handy to know. Maybe the pattern would change later, but that wasn't a concern for the moment.

Emily wondered if she should wait. She was wearing the same clothes as the day before, was tucked under some blankets with two limpets resting on her, and she probably had terrible bed hair.

It wasn't the greatest first impression to make.

But then, her other sisters didn't seem to care at all.

"Create Sister," Emily intoned.

She was feeling excited as a burst of light heralded the arrival of a third sister.

The excitement turned to confusion as a second burst of light appeared next to the first.

The remains of the excitement ran into a brick wall with the advent of a third burst.

Three girls faded into view.

No, Emily realized. Not three girls, but one girl three times over.

They were shorter than Athena, and just a hair taller than Teddy, with gray hoodies and jeans over plain black sneakers. The little rounded ears atop their heads bore some resemblance to Teddy's, but the large poofy tails behind them—gray and covered in dark rings—were entirely different.

The girls all blinked as one, locked eyes on the bed, then smiled bright and goofy, showing off little fangs that poked out from the rest of their teeth. "Cuddle pile!" they screamed as they launched into the air.

"Wait!" Emily said, but they were already at the apex of their jump.

Three small but fortunately light bodies crashed into Emily and the girls, a disproportionate number of elbows and knees flailing around.

Athena woke up with a protesting hoot and Teddy growled, kicking out.

Somehow, after a few moments of confused scrambling, the chaos settled.

Emily found herself with two arms wrapped around her neck and a new face hovering right before her. "Hi!" the girl said.

"Uh," Emily replied. "Hey?"

Another head popped into Emily's line of sight, ears twitching and big eyes blinking fast. "Hi!" the second head said.

"Hi?"

"You already said hi," the first girl said.

"I . . . did?"

She felt the air being pressed out of her lungs as the third girl climbed onto the back of the one atop her and peeked over her sibling's shoulder. "Yeah! You did."

Emily was about to ask that they get off her when Teddy roared and jumped to her feet right on the edge of the bed. "You guys are waking me up!" she said. "Get off!"

Then the bed shifted and Teddy fell, but not before grabbing one of the new sisters and pulling her down with her to crash onto the mattress on the floor with a heavy "oomph."

Emily scrambled to look over the side, which made the girl hugging her squeak and roll off onto Athena. "Are you okay?" Emily asked the pile of limbs on the ground that was partially Teddy, partially one of the new girls.

"I'm fine," Teddy grumbled.

"Yep! I'm good!"

Emily sat on the edge of her bed, rubbed her eyes, then sighed. "Okay. We're all awake now, I guess. Can . . . can you line up? Please?"

"Me?" the girl still clinging to Emily asked.

"Yes, please," Emily said. "We need to, uh, figure things out."

Like how she was going to house three more sisters. Or how she'd feed them. Or buy clothes for all three.

Emily's heart sank.

Looking back up, she noticed that all three of the new sisters were standing in a rough row, shoulder to shoulder and all wearing identical grins. "Okay," Emily said.

Athena came to sit beside her and rested her head against Emily's shoulder while rubbing her eyes, and Teddy turned over and used Emily's legs as a backrest.

Emily took a deep breath. "Okay," she repeated. "Um. I'm Emily. This is Teddy, and this is Athena."

"Hi!" all three girls said at the same time. "I don't got a name yet."

"Right," Emily said. "We'll have to find three names for you." Maybe some sort of thematic name? She couldn't go calling them One, Two, and Three.

The girls blinked, then shook their heads. "Nope, there's only one of me."

"Huh?"

"Yeah!" the middle one said. "That's me," she said, pointing to the girl next to her. "And that's also me." She pointed to the other side.

"You're clones?" Emily asked.

"Nope! I just got three bodies."

"But . . . there's three of you."

"Yeah. Three of me."

Emily tried to wrap her head around that, but there weren't enough digits on the clock for thinking that hard. "Okay? So . . . do you, like, know what you're thinking?"

"I always know what I'm thinking. It ain't usually much."

"No, I mean, what the other . . . you are thinking."

"But there's only one me."

Emily gestured at the three girls before her. "But you have three bodies."

They nodded. "That's right," came the chorus.

Emily stared for a moment, then let herself flop back down. "I haven't slept enough for this."

"Cuddle pile!" came three cheers before Emily was swamped. Then Teddy and Athena started fighting for room atop her too.

She had the impression it would be a long day.

CHAPTER SIXTY-FOUR

Trinity and Toaster-Kun Kissing in a Tree

Trinity?" Best Sister Emily asked.

She tilted her heads. "Trinity," one of her repeated. It was a very nice name. Best Sister Emily was good at finding good names.

"She can be called that," Less-Good-But-Still-All-Right Sister Athena said.

"Yeah," Scary Sister Teddy replied. "That name sounds cool."

"I could be cool," she replied from two mouths. The third was busy picking her nose.

Best Sister Emily nodded. "Trinity can be cool if she wants."

Trinity nodded all her heads, then she leapt forward to hug Best Sister Emily, but Scary Sister Teddy bonked her head and sent her flopping to the ground.

"Teddy!" Best Sister said. "Don't be mean."

Trinity watched with four eyes as Teddy pouted and crossed her arms. "She's hogging all the hugs. She's getting, like, three times as many as us."

Best Sister shook her head. "That's not how it works, Teddy. Be nice, please. The last thing I want is for my sisters not to get along."

Trinity nodded with all heads. Bullying was bad. Especially when it was one of her that was getting bullied. Hugs were good. Especially when it was one of her that was getting hugged. Life was simple that way, just like her.

Best Sister Emily got up, glanced at the alarm next to the bed, then nodded. "All right, I have classes in a bit. I need to head out. I'm not putting anyone in charge or anything like that. I just expect all of you to behave nicely, okay?"

Three sisters (and five heads) nodded. Emily went around, giving each of them a hug and a pat. She gave Trinity twice as many as everyone else, though, which was nice.

One of Trinity's bodies followed Best Sister around. She really hoped that Best Sister needed her help, that she could repay all the hugs with niceness.

One of her wandered off to the bathroom. She hadn't really inspected all of their home yet, and her last self stayed with her other sisters, smiling at them while she absently rubbed her tail to smooth out its long hairs.

Soon enough, Best Sister had her backpack on and was out the door. Trinity was pretty sure she didn't notice Trinity following behind until she reached the elevators. Trinity waved to Best Sister, but Best Sister just leaned her head against the wall of the elevator and pressed a button. Did she not see Trinity at all?

Soon, that body was left all alone in the corridor.

"Hey," Teddy said. "So what are you anyway?"

"Me?" Trinity asked. The her that was with her other sisters refocused a little. "Um. I'm a raccoon girl."

"Raccoons are a kind of bear, right?" Teddy asked.

"Maybe?" Trinity said over the sound of the toilet flushing. Watching the water swirl around was fun.

"You have three bodies, right?" Athena asked. "Does that mean you need to eat three times as much?"

"I guess," Trinity said. She did have three tummies. "But I'm good at finding food and stuff for myself."

The her in the bathroom was sticking her head under the tap; that is, until water went up her nose and she started sputtering and choking. The her in the corridor looked around, then with a shrug, walked over to a door with a staircase sign on it. Inside was a staircase. She wasn't entirely surprised by this. She headed down, her quest for fun and food beginning.

"Do you like sleeping?" Teddy asked.

Trinity nodded. "I like sleeping with others," she said. "It's nice and warm and safe."

Teddy frowned at that, then shrugged. "Yeah, all right. But we share the blankets equally."

"Are we really just going back to bed?" Athena asked.

"You have anything better to do?" Teddy asked her.

Athena pouted. "No, but still."

Huffing, Teddy stomped back to the bed, slithered under the blankets, then poked her head out at the top and fluffed up Best Sister Emily's pillow.

Athena crawled up and over Teddy, then flopped on her other side.

Grinning, Trinity bounced up and crashed into the pair of them. The her that was drowning in the bathroom coughed a bunch, closed the tap, then stumbled into the bedroom to join the cuddle pile forming on the bed.

She wondered how many bodies were required to form a proper cuddle pile. At least three, she guessed. But making one all on her own wasn't any fun. So it had to be four. Four was the minimum.

The her that was stomping down the stairs finally made it to the bottom, where she encountered another door. Opening it revealed a lobby on the first floor, with the elevator next to her, and the door leading out to a little corridor.

She wouldn't wander outside yet. First she'd look for food and fun inside the building.

With a few sniffs, she took in the scent in the air, then zeroed in on something that smelled really nice. Grinning, Trinity bounced over to one of the big rooms adjoining the corridor.

It was a kitchenette of sorts. There was a fridge, and a table with shiny things. Some guy was yawning while staring at one such shiny thing. He had a butter knife in one hand, and a jar of something brown in the other.

Trinity walked over to him, because that's where the nice smells were coming from.

The boy blinked, then looked down at her. "Uh," he said. His eyes looked really crusty and baggy, like he could use a nap of his own.

"Hi," Trinity said. "Something here smells nice."

"Just . . . making toast," he said.

Trinity was intrigued. She kept staring.

Something popped, and she jumped a little and stared at the shiny thing in front of the guy. It was very impressively shiny. With buttons and knobs on the front, and two pieces of golden bread sticking out of the top. It smelled heavenly.

The guy looked at her a bit more, then he pulled a plate closer, put the bread on it, and spread peanut butter on the bread.

Trinity stared the entire time. "So, uh, you . . . got ears?" he said with a gesture toward her head.

"Yeah, I'm a raccoon girl," she said. She tried to make her eyes big. "Can I have one?" she asked while her tail wiggled behind her.

"So . . . that cosplay, or you a supe?"

"I have cool powers, yeah," she said.

The guy nodded, then succumbed to her stare and gave her a piece of toast while muttering, "I'm too hungover for this." He wandered off, but Trinity didn't care. She had her toast and it was just as delicious as she had imagined from the smell.

After licking her fingers clean, she looked up at the machine that had made the toast. It had a little tag on the front: "Quantum Mothman House toaster." If this place was that, then the thing had to be a toaster.

It was beautiful.

There was a bag full of sliced bread next to it, and the big jar of peanut butter was still on the counter.

She had successfully scavenged for food!

Getting up on her tippy-toes, Trinity pulled the toaster closer, then tugged at it to yank the cord at the back. She hugged it close, enjoying the warmth still coming from inside it and the smell of burning breadcrumbs.

Just to be safe, she placed it back on the counter, then put the peanut butter in her hoodie pouch and the bag of bread on top of the toaster before grabbing everything.

She passed by the guy again on her way to the elevator.

"Uh, where are you taking that?" he asked.

"To the cuddle pile," Trinity said.

The elevator was tricky to work with. She didn't know what floor her room was on, and so she just went up one floor at a time and snooped until she recognized their floor. It was made easy by all the posters and signs taped to the doors and walls.

When she found the right floor, she flounced over to the door of their room, but it was locked. One of her lying atop the cuddle pile got up and trudged over to the door to open it up for herself.

"What's that?" Teddy mumbled.

"It's a toaster," she said as she walked past and set it on the table. "It makes delicious toast."

"Huh," Teddy said.

Soon though, Teddy and Athena were both watching as two of Trinity set up the toaster, put the bread in, then waited until the toast popped out. They could make four slices at once, which was one less than there were sisters in the room. It was nearly perfect.

* * *

Some hours later, when Best Sister Emily returned, one of the first things she did was stop by the entrance to sniff the air. "What's that?" she asked.

Then she noticed the toaster, the empty bag of bread, the empty tub of peanut butter, and all her sisters piled up on the bed with round tummies in a glorious cuddle pile.

"What the heck?"

Single with End Unseen

Emily's classes had gone well enough. She was still in the early phases of the school year, where half the lessons were simplified to the point of near absurdity. She found her mind wandering a lot more than it once had, but in her defense, she had more things to ponder.

Trinity was . . . a lot.

Emily had a little less than two thousand dollars from Handshake, and another thousand owed to her. That was . . . not nearly enough money to do anything. She was essentially a single mother of five. When buying clothes for herself, even with her rather conservative tastes, she could rack up a two-hundred-dollar bill with no issue. Food for herself probably cost about ten to twenty dollars a week if she indulged mostly in ramen noodles and cheap meals.

If she took all that, and multiplied it by six to count herself and her sisters, that was . . . a significant amount of money. She could maybe cut some corners here and there. Maybe find a part-time job. Those were popular for students . . . she hoped.

Class ended and she wasn't sure she had absorbed even half the lesson. More reason to find time to study later.

Emily had about as many friends now as she did when she started the school year, and twice as many reasons not to speak to anyone. So she rushed back to her dorm. She'd need to feed her sisters, threaten them into taking their showers, then do some homework, and maybe study ahead. She needed to call Alea Iacta, too.

And then she opened the door to her room.

On her desk was an empty jar of peanut butter next to a shiny silver toaster marred by peanut-buttery fingerprints. A bread bag was left on the floor, seemingly licked clean of crumbs.

The suspects to that particular crime were all conveniently piled up on her bed, with exposed tummies and arms and legs poking out every which way.

"What the heck?" Emily asked, quite reasonably.

Trinity . . . one of Trinity at least, popped up over the others and grinned. "Hello, Best Sister!" she cheered. "Do you want to join?" Another Trinity wiggled over to the side, exposing a more or less Emily-sized space on the bed.

"No," Emily said. "No, I don't think I do." She closed the door. "Where did the toaster come from?"

"Found it," Trinity said.

Emily made a note never to let them talk to a police officer. "And where did you find it?"

Another Trinity rubbed at her eyes. "Downstairs?"

"You stole the communal toaster?"

"It was just there," Trinity defended herself. "The bread and butter, too. It's ours now."

Emily forgot some of her troubles, mostly because she had much bigger ones to deal with. "All right, everyone off the bed," she said.

There was a lot of grumbling at that.

Emily pointed to one of the dirty Trinitys, then to the bathroom. "In the shower."

"Shower!" the girl said before running over. Emily had been expecting a bit more trouble there, but she could live with not having to fight over that.

"Right. Teddy, you remember when I showed you the washing machines?"

Teddy slumped. "I don't want to clean stuff. It's boring."

Emily pointed to her bedsheets, currently stained with what she dearly, dearly hoped was only peanut butter. "Then you should have said something before eating on my bed. You're the oldest here."

Teddy grumbled, but she started pulling the sheets off.

"Athena, go wash up, then help Teddy," Emily said. She turned to the remaining Trinitys. "You two, pick up all this mess."

"Aww," she said in stereo.

Emily glared, then noticed that the toaster was missing. "Where is the toaster?" she asked, quite sensibly.

That was when a loud sparking snap sounded from the bathroom and the lights flickered out.

"Oh no," Trinity said. "I died."

"You what?" Emily asked. The room was darker, but not so much that she couldn't see the confused look on both of Trinity's faces. A form glowed next to Trinity, and another body, dressed the same as the other two, appeared. "What?" Emily asked again.

Did she have four Trinitys now?

"I died," all three said. "Mister Toaster didn't like the water."

Emily walked over to the bathroom, threw the door open, and took in the room at a glance. The shower was still running, water splashing down onto the smoking form of a very shiny, very soapy toaster. "What?" Emily repeated. She almost absently shut the faucet.

"It's okay," the Trinitys said. "I can't die while I'm still alive."

Emily was developing something of a headache.

"Does this mean I don't need to do the laundry?" Teddy asked.

Someone knocked at the door.

Taking a deep breath to cool down, Emily stomped over and opened the door just a crack. She came face-to-face with Sam, the girl from one room over. "Yes?" she asked.

"Yo! Power's out for you, too, huh?"

"Yeah," Emily said. "Do you, uh, know what happened?"

Sam shrugged. "Someone tried to charge too many toys at once? I dunno. I'll take the stairs down a level. There are a bunch of dudes there who would love to show how manly they are by resetting the breaker."

"Do you know how?" Emily asked.

"Yeah, I'm not an idiot. But I'm not crawling through this place's basement with no lights either. I'll let some bonehead do it for a smile and a wink." She looked past Emily. "You all right? You look frazzled."

"I'm . . . perfectly all right," Emily lied.

"Right . . . well, stay safe and all that."

"Yeah, thanks," Emily said. She closed the door and turned to stare at five entirely unabashed girls. She couldn't even find it in her to chew them out. "Never mind the laundry," she began. Teddy cheered. "For now. At least until the power returns." Teddy pouted. "We . . . need to figure things out for Trinity, and . . . yeah."

"Oh!" Trinity said. "My power is that there's always three of me. So when I die I get to live again. I don't have to do laundry or anything, I just need to die and I'll have clean clothes again."

Emily didn't know where to begin with that. She decided not to.

"You know what? I'm fine with that. Does it always spawn a new you . . . near you?"

"It's not a new me, it's just more of me," Trinity said. "I think I get a bit more dumb when there's less of me. Maybe. It's really hard to tell." All three of her held their chins. "Should I die two more times so that I don't have to shower?" She frowned. "But I *like* showers."

Emily considered the value of suicide as a way to avoid having to take a shower, then nixed that plan. "No, no, please don't do that. In fact, try not to die?" She didn't expect to have to add "no dying" to the house rules, but there she was.

The power came back on, the lights switching on with a snap. "Aw, dang it," Teddy said. She grumbled and picked up the blankets again.

Emily eyed Trinity up and down. "Do you know what all of you sees?"

Trinity blinked all six eyes. "Yeah?"

"Even when another you isn't around?"

"But all mes are me."

"Right," Emily said. "So can one of you go with Teddy and Athena, just to keep an eye on things, and another . . . part of you can stay here and tell me if there's trouble?"

"I can do that!" Trinity cheered. "Can we hug while we do that?"

"How about one of you showers while the other you stays with me, then you switch."

"Whoa, I'll be doing three fun things at once!"

Emily was worried.

She found her way over to her bed and sat down with a sigh. Trinity climbed up onto the bed, then shifted around so that she was sitting on Emily's lap, both hands around her waist. "Comfy," Trinity muttered.

Emily started patting Trinity's head, as if the girl were an oversized, bony cat. She did have very soft little ears. There were . . . a lot of things to take care of. A whole heap of them, really. Emily wasn't sure where to even start.

Still, things were relatively quiet, and she enjoyed quiet—quiet was good.

"We need to get you a costume," Emily said absently.

Trinity gasped and looked up at Emily, eyes wide and almost glowing with excitement. "Can I be a bandit?"

"A . . . bandit?" Emily asked. "Like, the house-robbing kind?"

Trinity nodded. "Bandits are cool because they find all sorts of things. I can be a great bandit. With a big bag to put all the things I find in."

Emily paused in her patting of Trinity's head to rub at the bridge of her nose. "You know what? We'll see."

CHAPTER SIXTY-SIX

Costume Shopping

Emily had a bit of money. Not a ton, not even enough to make anyone suspicious, but enough to get by for a little week or two. Maybe.

Having a . . . significant number more mouths to feed made that bit of cash pretty meaningless.

Still, she felt that her sisters deserved a break, and they were going out to have some fun. Costume shopping was a nice, calming way to spend the day.

They paused by a corner store, and Emily splurged a little on six slushies. She regretted it as soon as the last one was out of her hands and being slurped up by a Trinity who was already shaking with the start of a sugar high.

A problem for later. Maybe if she walked around enough, her three(ish) sisters would be able to bleed off some of that energy by the afternoon. "Right! On to the costume shop!" Emily said.

She couldn't help but hold back a smile as her squadron of little sisters formed up around her. Teddy, of course, took the lead, marching ahead and walking as if she was about three feet taller and owned the entire sidewalk.

Athena kept to Emily's side, one hand hanging on to Emily's while she tried hard not to look like she was observing everything around them. Emily hoped no one noticed the way Athena's head would turn too far when she was looking at something behind them.

And Trinity walked next to Emily—and ahead of her, and behind her too. The raccoon girl wasn't wandering around too much, not while occupied by her slushie. It was a little weird to hear three straws being slurped at exactly the same time, but Emily figured anyone passing by who heard that would dismiss it as coincidence.

The costume shop wasn't exactly in Eauclaire's nicest street, but it wasn't far from it. It was a relatively large building, with some Halloween stuff in one window and mannequins in uniforms in the other. Emily supposed that with October coming around soonish, it made sense that a place like this would start switching out their merchandise already.

The store, in addition to costumes, also sold work uniforms and equipment. Nurses' smocks, retail uniforms, and a few odds and ends. There was a dry cleaning service, too, at the back.

Emily gave it fifty-fifty odds of it being some money laundering front, because even with its two niches, there was no way it had enough customers to justify the size of the place.

"Okay," she said as she walked in with her gaggle of sisters. The girl behind the counter stared at the kids with the sort of horror reserved for retail workers on minimum wage that were about to have a story-worthy day. "We're going to behave."

"Yeah, yeah, no worries," Teddy said.

"No. Big worries," Emily retorted. She pointed to Teddy, finger all ready to waggle. "No threatening anyone, no running around, no complaining about capitalism or pushing the communist . . . whatever . . . onto anyone. Be civil. You're the oldest of my sisters—you should act mature. I trust you."

Teddy pouted at first, but by the end, her chest was puffed with pride.

Her finger turned to Athena. "No scaring people. You're a clever and observant girl. I'm sure you know what kind of behavior I'd frown on."

Athena nodded. "I can do that. Or . . . not do that. Yeah, no problem."

"Good. And, Trinity. I want . . . one of you with each sister, and one with me, okay? Also, no stealing."

"All right!" Trinity agreed. She only spoke from one of her, which was great because talking from three bodies simultaneously was just a little too creepy.

Emily nodded as she lowered her finger and straightened her back. She was getting really good at getting her sisters to listen. Not that they'd do what she said.

Holding on to Trinity's hand, Emily moved off toward the rows of cheap costumes, eyeing the sweaters and dresses and, most importantly, the price tags. "So . . . what sort of costume are you thinking of?" Emily asked.

"I know just what I want," Trinity said.

"Really?"

The raccoon girl nodded. "I want to be a burglar."

"A . . . a burglar?" Emily repeated. She remembers then Trinity's earlier remark about wanting to be a bandit.

"Yeah. They're the best. They get to take things, and keep them; they stay up late, which is cool; and they play tag with the police all the time."

"I'm pretty sure you have at least one wrong idea there," Emily said. "But . . . all right. I can see a burglar outfit working."

They crossed over a row, past cheap police uniforms, skimpy nurse outfits, and copies of the costumes worn by some of the more popular Heroes. Finally, Trinity gasped and pointed to a costume wrapped in a clear plastic box. Emily smiled as she tugged it off its hook. It was a simple costume—barely a costume at all, really. A shirt, with black and white lines across it, and a bandanna. It also came with a large bag with a dollar sign sewn into the side.

"Is this it?" she asked.

"Yeah," Trinity said. "But it doesn't come with pants."

"And no mask," Emily said. "We can grab a mask. I think I saw some plain ones a row over."

There were masses of domino masks, in all sorts of colors. Trinity ended up selecting a dozen because, at fifty cents each, Emily couldn't argue against having more. The fact that no two were the same color didn't matter much.

If anything, it would help tell Trinity's bodies apart while they were out in costume. Maybe they could get some scarves, too?

There weren't any changing rooms, but Emily looked at Trinity, noted how tiny she was, then picked the smallest-size mask they had available. "We'll have to try them on at home," she said.

"Yeah! Can't wait!" Trinity cheered.

Emily rubbed at her head, then froze when she felt her phone buzz within her purse. She fished around for it, then frowned at the unknown number on the display. "One sec, Trinity," she said. "Can you make sure your sisters aren't up to anything?"

"Athena is chasing Teddy around with a mask of Enry Ord on," Trinity said.

"The car guy?" Emily asked.

The girl shrugged.

Emily accepted the call, then pressed the phone to her ear. "Hello?"

"Hello, Boss," came a smooth voice. It interrupted itself a moment later, a racking cough that sounded just shy of painful. "You are in no danger, not from me."

Emily felt herself going tense, and she squeezed Trinity's hand. The girl looked up to her with guileless eyes, then frowned around them. "Who is this?" Emily asked. "I'm not anyone's manager." She wasn't the best liar, but she figured that was an easy enough one to make.

"This, my dear, is the one you know as Cement. Don't panic, we don't need you being afraid."

Emily felt her heart attempting to thump its way out of her chest. "What do you want?"

"I'm done for," he said plainly. "Do you have a good memory for numbers? I might not have forever."

"What?"

The Villain rattled off a few numbers, then an address. "Can you remember that?"

"What is it?" she asked. It sounded like something within Eauclaire, but she didn't know the city well enough to know where exactly it was.

"That, my dear, is one of my safe houses. The first number is for the safe behind the portrait of the *Fighting Emeraire*. You can't miss it."

"Mister, uh . . ."

"'Mister C' works."

"Mister C," Emily said. "Why are you telling me all this?"

"I don't know how much time I have left, but I'll tell you what I can while I'm still able. The Cabal is moving into this city. My city. Not that my reign was ever as strong as I would have liked. They are, in a word, bad news, even to people not on our side of the morality line. They've gotten to me. I only made it out because I had a shaft hidden under the floor. It doesn't matter. Soon, this city will be yours to rule."

"Rule?" Emily asked.

"Is that not what you are? A ruler, a boss? You are as all Villains are, aren't you? Soon the board will be cleared, and a new opponent will be sitting opposite you. It's early, yes, but for the good of everyone, Eauclaire needs a proper Villain in place. I wanted that to be me, but as I said, my time's up."

He coughed again, and it sounded worse, far worse.

"Black Shield, Thunder Clot, and Spin to Win. They're stationed here, and they're Cabal."

"I don't understand," Emily said. It didn't make sense for him to be telling her all that, not out of the blue. "I'm not a . . . you know."

"Oh, you are. You have potential, too, more than I ever did. I might be able to win you a little bit of time. Use it well."

The line went dead.

Emily had a bad feeling about the call, a really bad one.

CHAPTER SIXTY-SEVEN

Entirely Fine

The sisters went to the park next to the college, the same one where they'd met Melaton that one time. It was all sunny and bright, with green grass underfoot and plenty of room to run around in, and that's exactly what Teddy's sisters were doing.

Tina was huffing and puffing as she ran after one of Trinity, arms outstretched as if that would help her catch their newest little sister. But Trinity was really fast, so Teddy didn't think Tina had great odds.

Teddy kind of wanted to join in, but it was her job as the biggest and best sister to keep an eye out for the others. That, and the Boss was sitting on a park bench, bent forward with her phone dangling between her knees. She looked like she was thinking real hard.

The bear girl moved closer to Emily, then backed her butt up to the bench and jumped backward so she was sitting by the Boss's side. The Boss looked at her, and her lips twitched up in a smile that didn't quite reach her eyes.

"Are you okay, Boss?" Teddy asked.

"I'm fine," Emily said.

Teddy pouted when the Boss returned to staring at the ground.

Her sisters were still having fun. Athena had pinned one of Trinity to the ground and was laughing a proper Villain laugh as she tickled Trinity into submission. The raccoon girl's other two bodies were giggling so hard she was having a hard time running to the rescue of her third, who was writhing on the grass.

Teddy refocused on the Boss. The Boss wasn't feeling great, that much was obvious. So, with a bit of stretching, Teddy brought her arm up and started patting the Boss on the head. "There there," she said.

"Uh," Emily said. "What are you doing?"

Teddy continued to pat the Boss. "Making you feel better."

The Boss sighed, but it was an amused sort of sigh, so that was good.

Then she looped an arm around Teddy and pulled her into her side. It was a weird hug, and Teddy still had one arm straight up because there was no room for it otherwise, but she figured that was okay. If the Boss was giving out hugs, then things couldn't be that bad.

"Thanks, Teddy," Emily said. "That's nice of you."

Teddy preened. "Yeah, that's what I'm best at. Making sure the Boss is happy and stuff."

Emily laughed, then started to rub circles over Teddy's back. "Do you mind if I talk a bit?"

"Sure," Teddy said. "What do you need to rant about?" Ranting was, of course, a time-honored tradition for all Villains; monologues were especially common.

"It's not so much a rant," Emily said. "Just . . . Cement's message"—the Boss had told Teddy about Cement's call—"is weighing on me a lot. I don't trust him, of course. He's a Villain, or near enough. As hypocritical as that might be to say."

It wasn't, Teddy thought. Villains didn't trust other Villains most of the time; it was perfectly natural.

"I think the Cabal are a bigger problem than Cement, though, and he's basically giving us information on them for free . . . if he's telling the truth."

"You think he's lying?" Teddy asked. Lying to the Boss was a terrible, terrible thing to do. Only little sisters were allowed to do that, and even they risked disappointed looks when they did it.

"I think it would be in his best interest if we weren't around to mess with his plans anymore," the Boss said. "But . . . I don't know. Call it an instinct? Something is telling me that he was being honest. Or at least mostly honest."

"We could send in one of Trinity to see if it's a trap. If it is, she can tell us, and no one important will be hurt," Teddy said. She was quite proud of that idea. It was really clever.

The Boss shook her head. "I don't like the idea of sacrificing one of my sisters on a whim, Teddy, even if Trinity has an interesting relationship with the concept of, uh, dying."

Teddy shrugged.

The Boss stopped rubbing Teddy's back eventually and fiddled with her phone. She started by checking her messages. A bunch of them were from the Boss's mom (the GrandBoss?) and hadn't been answered yet. The Boss read them faster than Teddy could, then she sighed and went back to the phone's main page and opened a news app.

Teddy was soon a little bit bored. Sitting next to the Boss was nice and all, but it wasn't superfun when the Boss wasn't paying her any attention, and the others looked like they were having all the fun. Trinity had pinned Athena to the ground and were attacking her with tickles while she kicked and punched and giggled a bunch.

Then the Boss gasped, and Teddy started. She looked around, but couldn't spot any trouble, not until she looked at the Boss's phone and read the article the Boss had stumbled onto.

Local Hidden Villain "Cement" Captured by Glamazon and Silver Fox Team-Up!

Today, around noon, the intrepid new Hero Glamazon, as well as local celebrity Silver Fox, teamed up to capture a Villain known only as Cement.

Cement was an active, if discreet, Villain operating within Eau-claire for well over a year, mostly focused on white-collar crime, but he is suspected of organizing and leading a gang of drug smug-glers and sellers operating within the very heart of the city.

The arrest came after a short but decisive battle on Elm Street, leaving part of the street unusable.

"He was arrested," the Boss said.

"Looks like it," Teddy replied. He must not have been all that good of a Villain, then.

The Boss stood up suddenly. "So he was telling the truth. At least . . . partially. Teddy, we might have to go see that house he mentioned, before the police and everyone else gets there."

"Oh?" Teddy asked. "We're not in costume, though."

Emily nodded. "You're right. Let's go home. We need to pick things up real quick before heading out." She cupped her hands to her mouth. "Girls! Tina, Trinity, come on."

The others untangled themselves, then ran over, Trinity looking bright and happy, despite one of her six eyes being black on the edges and her clothes looking a bit rumpled. Athena, on the other hand, didn't look happy at all.

The Boss didn't seem very impressed, but Teddy didn't say anything. If it were up to her, and she weren't responsible for looking over her smaller sisters, she'd have been in the tussle too.

"Right," Emily said. "We need to hurry home."

"What's going on?" Athena asked.

"That Villain who contacted me? He was arrested today, probably just after calling me. He gave me the location of some stuff he thought I might need. I was going to ignore it, but with him being arrested, I don't think it's fake."

"So we're going to sneak over and grab something," Athena summed up. "I can do that. I'm very sneaky."

"I'm more sneakier," Trinity said.

"You are not!"

"Girls," the Boss snapped, and both Trinity and Athena flinched. "Not now. We'll have plenty of time to test your . . . sneakiness later. For now, we need to get back home, and sooner rather than later."

Everyone agreed to that, and Teddy knew that Trinity was looking forward to putting on her new costume.

Still, Teddy wondered if they had time to stop by that doughnut place on the way home.

The Boss nodded, then headed toward the exit of the park, all her little sisters jogging along to keep up. It seemed, at least to Teddy, that the Boss was in a hurry to act.

That was actually kind of cool. The Boss was really growing into her role as the Boss. She was becoming more . . . bosslike, and she was a whole bunch more scarier. Teddy imagined that in a few weeks, the Boss would be terrorizing the entire country, or at least the city.

She couldn't wait—it was going to be so much fun!

"Hey, Boss, can we stop at that coffee place?"

"No, Teddy, we're in a hurry."

"What about on the way back?"

"I . . . guess? It depends on what we find," the Boss said.

Teddy shared a grin with her sisters, and a silent bit of communication passed between them. First they'd help the Boss as best they could, because they were all good sisters. And then they'd reap the rewards: snacks and hugs and naps for everyone.

CHAPTER SIXTY-EIGHT

Breaking and Entering

Emily opened the door to her room, then stumbled back as all her little sisters pushed and shoved to be the first in. She stepped in after them and closed the door behind her. "Okay, everyone, we need to grab our costumes. We can't get changed here."

"What about me?" Trinity asked. "I've never put my costumes on."

Emily considered it, then nodded. "One of you get changed. That should be enough to know, I guess."

"Yeah!" two of Trinity's bodies cheered. They tore into the bag with her costume, then ran into the bathroom.

Emily listened to the click of the door, then started to move herself. Her costume wasn't exactly hidden. Rather, it was tucked in a plastic bag along with Teddy's costume in one of her drawers. Athena's was too large to fit, at least the jacket part of it.

"We're going to need to get you a new mask," Emily muttered as she looked at Teddy's bear mask. The plastic was a little warped on the sides and there was a crack along one ear. Just normal wear and tear on something made so cheaply.

"Oh, can I get one made of steel?" Teddy asked. "With knives for fangs?"

"I . . . don't know if we have the budget for that," Emily said.

She stuffed things away in a duffel bag, including Athena's leather jacket, then stood up and looked to the Trinity sitting on the edge of her bed. "I'm still getting changed," she said.

"All right, take your time."

Trinity nodded.

Emily had a minute or two to waste, so she booted up her laptop, then it was on to Oogle for a quick search. Black Shield, Thunder Clot, and Spin to Win, the three Cabal members Cement had mentioned, were all identified as Heroes.

The news said Cement had been captured by Glamazon and Silver Fox, but the news could be lying, especially if the Cabal controlled those two as well.

Black Shield's presence online was nearly nonexistent. There was an article or two, but they always had the Hero as part of a larger group. A young woman, in tight black spandex, standing at the rear. Her costume had some armor over the chest and knees and shoulders, black on black, with a few dark-gray highlights. The Hero's weapons were the only things that really stood out.

Emily clicked over to an Ikipedia page to check out the weapons and frowned. The Void Shields. Some Gadgeteer tech shields that could fire lasers. They were both basically gauntlets with a big teardrop-shaped shield, the point ending five inches past the Hero's knuckles, and the rounded part only about as wide as her forearm.

Her power was listed as "Black Shield Creation," but Emily had no idea what that meant.

Thunder Clot was a different story. He was a much louder sort of Hero. Plenty of participation at local hospitals, visiting sick children, doing volunteer work, baking cookies for some charity work.

Thunder Clot was an average-looking man, if on the thinner side. A bright yellow costume over a dark blue skintight suit. The armor looked high-tech, and he had some screens on his forearms. His helmet was a cross between an army hat and a bicycle helmet, with a yellow-tinted visor attached to heavy headphones.

There was plenty about his activities, and some footage of him firing lightning bolts at a mugger out in the open, but that was it. Emily didn't get the "Clot" part of his name. He was a speedster, though, the way he reacted almost instantly.

And finally, there was Spin to Win.

They were the strangest of the three. A person in a suit and tie, one that was different at every appearance they made, the only common thread being how bright it was, and the wild patterns of the cloth. They had something of a business-man-clown look going on.

They—Emily didn't know if they were male or female, Spin to Win seeming to change from picture to picture and event to event—had a large, hovering wheel behind them with an arrow in its center. The wheel was always divided into sections, each one labeled differently. Things like "fire" and "gravity" were written on the pie slices.

The consensus, from what Emily saw, was that they could "spin" for a new power, but they didn't have a choice on what they landed on.

"That's a terrible power," Emily muttered. Of the three, Spin to Win wasn't the most public, but they didn't exactly hide from the camera either. They had a lot of Villainous takedowns to their name and had participated in at least two Endgames.

"Sis!"

Emily turned to see two Trinitys stumble out of the bathroom. The one in her new costume stepped up and placed her hands on her hips with a big, proud smile.

The costume suited them. A green scarf over a black-and-white shirt, a green domino mask over her eyes, and a big bag with a dollar sign hanging by her hip. The shirt matched Trinity's tail, which was fluffed out behind her in plain sight.

"You need a beret," Emily said. "But other than that, you look great."

"All right!" Trinity cheered. "Now I need to get changed again, yeah?"

"That's right, and hurry it up. We'll be heading out as soon as you're done." Emily turned back to her laptop—after glancing to make sure her other sisters were behaving. Teddy was catching a nap and Athena was leafing through one of Emily's course books. Her next search was the address Cement had given her.

Plugging a nearby address into a map site let her find the right street. Eauclaire being as small as it was meant that the place wasn't too far away. A quick walk past the more commercial area and into part of the city filled with housing developments from the seventies. The kind of place with cookie-cutter homes in cul-de-sacs, like where Emily had grown up.

"I'm done!" Trinity said from the bed as another Trinity opened the bathroom door and stumbled out.

"Okay," Emily said. She shut down her laptop and stood up. "Teddy, wake up, sweetie. Athena, are you ready to go? Good! Trinity, don't wander around too much, all right?"

Emily led her troop of sisters out of her room again, and into the elevator where they boarded with a single boy who, when faced with five girls staring at him, seemed about as uncertain as Emily usually felt.

The ride down was fast, though, and soon they were back out onto the streets and heading more or less northward.

Emily didn't have the keenest sense of direction, but she could keep track of which way was which if she put in some effort.

The trip was mostly spent keeping her sisters in line. Teddy was being a little bossy to the others, which, while somewhat helpful, wasn't very nice. Athena kept pulling ahead, and Emily only had so many hands and eyes to keep track of Trinity.

Maybe half an hour later, Emily found herself approaching the street where the home Cement had pointed her to was. "We can't just walk up to it," she said. "We're going to need to either costume up and . . . walk in, or we can try being a little sneaky."

"I can go in on my own," Trinity said. "Just one or two of me, while I stay with you."

It wasn't a terrible idea. The problem was trusting Trinity to properly communicate what she saw. Still, it wasn't as risky as moving into the house herself.

"There should be some room behind the homes," Emily said. Most of the lots had fenced-in backyards, and past those was a section of forest before a highway leading into the city. Plenty of room to sneak past.

Emily found an alleyway to change in, a little nook where someone could hide away for a second or two. They took turns getting changed, and when all of them were in their costumes and her stuff was tucked away in a duffel bag hidden in a corner, Emily led her sisters to the backstreets and into the little strip of woods, with cars whooshing past just a hundred feet away.

"All right," Emily said when they reached the right house. The backyard was plain, with nothing but a firepit in its middle and a little gazebo in the back to make it stand out. "Trinity, you're up."

The girl nodded, then two of her bodies fell down next to the wooden fence and she boosted herself over it to crash on the other side with a thump. "I'm okay!"

Emily sighed and helped the second Trinity up and over the fence. "Good luck."

"I'm still here," the Trinity staying behind said.

"Right, right," Emily replied.

She wondered where her life had gone so crooked that breaking and entering was more of a chore than anything else.

CHAPTER SIXTY-NINE

Tippy-Toe Thief

Trinity, the sneakiest sister, walked across the lawn with little tippy-toe hops.

Well, two of her did. The last was standing with Best Sister Emily, but she couldn't help bouncing up and down on the balls of her feet. It wasn't fair that only two of her were getting exercise. If she wasn't careful, one of her might not get enough, and she could become one-third fat.

The two of her that were sneaking across the lawn stuck out her tongues and bit on the ends as she skittered across the yard and to the back of the house. She hoped that no one saw her, because if they did, Best Sister Emily might not be very impressed.

Then again, she had picked out a real clever costume.

See, she looked like a burglar, so if anyone saw her in her striped shirt and with her mask and poofy tail, they'd just think she was a trio of thieves, not a singular Villain. It was foolproof!

"Okay," Trinity said, the one next to Emily. "I'm at the house."

"All right," Emily said. "Now we need to find a way in. Can you check the door for alarms?"

All of Trinity nodded. "Can do!" she said.

One of her peeled away from the house's wall and zipped over to the balcony at the back. There was a fence around it, and a gate at the top of the stairs leading onto the balcony itself. The underneath was covered by a trellis fence and was filled with dirt and old rotten leaves that looked like they'd be hard to rake out.

Trinity hopped up, grabbed the lower edge of the fence, then squeezed up onto the balcony right next to a barbecue grill. Then her butt stayed stuck.

"Uh-oh," Trinity said.

"What is it?" Emily asked.

"Butt's too big," Trinity said.

Her other body near the house looked around, and with a happy "Aha!" she found the perfect tool for the job: a big old spade left halfway under the balcony. She snuck over to it, grabbed the spade shovel, and with a big overhead swing, bonked her body in the behind until she popped onto the deck.

"I'm near the door," she told Emily.

Trinity squeezed her face in up against the patio door and squinted as best she could to make out things within the house.

"Um, Emily? What's an alarm look like?"

Best Sister Emily blinked. "I . . . genuinely have no idea. I suppose . . . look for a box near the door, with wires on it, like a sensor?"

Trinity started looking for just that.

Meanwhile, her other body next to the balcony surfed through her quests. It was fair that her other sisters had a few more skills—they were older, of course—but that didn't mean Trinity wanted to stay behind forever. She needed to work hard to catch up!

New Quest!

Trash it!

Wreck things as only you can.

Reward: +1 Skill Upgrade point per home trashed. Mischief Maker +1 per success!

Accept? Refuse?

Well . . . that did sound fun, even if it wasn't very Villainous. Trinity accepted it, but then started looking for a quest that fit Best Sister's Villainous tendencies a bit better. It wouldn't do for one of her sisters to merely be a Mischief Maker!

New Quest!

Torch it!

Burn it all down.

Reward: +1 Skill Upgrade point per home burned down. Scoundrel +1 per success!

Accept? Refuse?

She shook her head. What was the point of that?

New Quest!

Thieve it!

Take what isn't yours.

Reward: +1 Skill Upgrade point per $1,000 of goods stolen. Villain +1 per success!

Accept? Refuse?

That was more like it!

Trinity finished looking around the door for any alarms. There was a thing, a small white box next to the door. She wasn't sure if that was it or not, but she didn't want to take any chances and ruin her reputation as a thief before it even started.

"I'm going in through a window," she said.

"All right," Emily replied.

Now Trinity only had to figure out how to get in through a window. There was one not too far from the door, leading into what looked like a kitchen. She scooted over to the barbecue and pulled it closer, the her that was below helping by pushing it from the ground.

Once it was up against the wall, she clambered up, and was thankful that she was so small, because otherwise the whole thing might tip over.

The window was all old and rimmed with some bare gray metal. There weren't any convenient latches on the outside for her to tamper with.

What she needed was something to break the seal.

Conveniently, she still had her butt-shovel.

She passed it up to herself, then wobbled atop the barbecue before ramming the edge of the shovel under the glass. She was aiming for the little crack at the bottom, where she'd be able to leverage it up.

Instead, the window exploded.

"What was that?" Emily asked.

"Uh," she said. "The window's open now?"

She shrugged all her shoulders, then poked the glass away from the windowsill. The damage was done; she figured there was nothing to do about it now.

The her that was under the balcony searched around and found some sort of plant-covering tarp stuff, which she passed up to herself. It was muddy, but she didn't care. With the tarp along the bottom of the window, she slid in and through the window, this time without her behind getting stuck!

Trinity slithered over a sink, then landed on her hands on the ground and flipped around to land in a crouch in the middle of a little kitchen area. There was an island in the middle, a fridge and stove to the side, and she could make out the dining room farther in.

"I'm in," she cheered next to Emily.

"Well done," Best Sister Emily said.

Then Trinity preened as she earned herself some celebratory headpats. She'd done good!

"What am I looking for?" she asked Emily.

Emily hummed. "Give the house a quick tour. I think I might need to move in there myself. Or maybe not, but before anything else, we should make sure that it's clear."

Trinity nodded all three of her heads. "Just the me that's inside then," she said.

"Yeah," Emily replied.

Trinity started to sneak around the house. The trick of it was keeping her weight on her backfoot, and only shifting it after her front foot had already made contact with the ground, that way, she didn't make tap-tapping noises as she walked around.

"Keep an eye out for paintings," Emily said.

Trinity hummed and nodded her understanding even as the her that was inside opened the fridge door and started looking for paintings in there.

She didn't find any, but she did find some cake.

The next place she looked into was the pantry, where she found an entire box of unopened Winkies. She tossed that out of the window so the her outside could enjoy it while she kept on doing important work.

Unfortunately, there weren't any paintings in the kitchen, so she didn't have a choice but to move on into the dining room. There was an image there, hanging by one wall. "Found one," she said.

"What's it a painting of?"

"Ship, with water and stuff. I think those are birds in the corner, and there's a lighthouse."

"I . . . don't think that's it. Can you move the painting aside?"

It was a pretty big painting, and she was a small girl. She tugged a chair over and winced as it squeaked against the hardwood. She climbed up, and with her arms stretched as wide as they'd go, she unhooked the painting, then let it slip down and down until the edge was against the ground.

"It's just a wall," she said.

"Not it then," Emily said. "Keep looking around."

Trinity nodded and left the living room for the dining room. She had to be careful because a window overlooked the street; she rolled behind the nearest sofa and eyed the television.

It was a big one. She bet that it was worth a thousand dollars. But it wouldn't fit in the window in the kitchen.

Too bad.

There was a small painting in the living room, some image of a forest. She didn't know much about interior decorating, but she felt like this place was pretty nice. Nice in a sort of very boring way.

She climbed up a sofa and was unhooking the frame from the wall when she heard the door rattle.

All of Trinity froze.

The door clicked, and someone stepped in, a black figure, in a long coat, with a hood on their jacket that concealed their masked face.

Trinity stared at the mask, and the mask stared at Trinity.

"Oh, shoot!" Trinity said next to Emily.

"What is it?" Emily asked.

The Trinity in the house flung the picture frame at the mask, then darted away, but to leave, she had to squeeze past the entrance and get back in the kitchen, and that meant that her head start wasn't all that great.

Still, she was fast!

She scampered past, jumped up onto the counter in the kitchen, and was shuffling through the window when the no-good mean person caught her by the ankle. "Oh no you don't!" they said. A woman's voice.

And then Trinity was jerked back into the house.

"I . . . may have made a small mistake," she admitted to Emily.

CHAPTER SEVENTY

Up and Over

Emily felt as if cold water were being pushed through her veins.

"Are you okay?" she asked.

It was strange, asking the girl right next to her—who was clearly fine if a little uncomfortable—if she was okay, while knowing full well that same girl was in trouble elsewhere. The dichotomy was a little confusing, and Emily didn't have room for any confusion.

"I'm all right," Trinity said. "This all-good Hero jerk's got me by the foot. I'm kicking them in the face, but they're using stupid powers to stop it."

Emily nodded. She needed a plan, and she needed it *now*. There was no time for hesitation or waffling. She needed to act.

"What's the Hero look like?"

"Uh, I think it's a girl. She has armor, and a big shield thing over her arm."

"Black Shield," Emily guessed. Cement had warned her as much. "Trinity—the you that's free—run around the building, and tell me what you see out front. We need to know if there are more of them."

"Got it!" Trinity said.

Emily saw a blur of motion through the slats in the fence as the Trinity still hiding out back spun around and ran.

"If they're alone . . . I think we might be able to fight them. Maybe."

"Heck yeah," Teddy said, her fist pumping. "I'll beat them down, no problem."

"I'll do what I can to help," Athena said. "I'll put the fear of Big Sister Emily in them."

Trinity nodded. "I'm at the front. There's only one car. It's blue."

Knowing the car that'd likely brought Black Shield to the safe house was blue didn't help Emily much, but she figured that didn't sound like an official sort of vehicle.

"Okay, we're moving in," she said. "The goal isn't to fight them, it's to find that painting. Trinity, one of you stays near me, another needs to look for the painting."

"And the third one fights?" Trinity asked.

"We'll see," Emily said.

They needed to get to the Hero first. Which was a thought Emily wasn't very happy she was having. She looked both ways down the fence, then nodded to herself before running up to it and grabbing the edge. Emily started to lift herself up and over it. She grunted at the effort, arms trembling even as she scrambled up the fence.

"Lemme help!" Teddy said.

"Help how— Oh," Emily said as she half turned and found a large grizzly bear behind her. Teddy reached out, paws carefully angled so her claws weren't pointing toward Emily, and grabbed Emily around the waist. She squeaked as Teddy rose to her full height, then pushed her toward the fence.

Emily swung her legs over, then sat on the edge. "Okay, okay," she said as she hung on and balanced herself. "Athena, give me your hand."

She grabbed Athena's hand and pulled her up, the girl scrambling against the fence until she was over it and crouching on the lawn.

"Teddy, you're next, then Trinity," Emily said. "Trinity, can you keep the Hero distracted?"

"Oh yeah, she's asking me questions and I'm kicking her," Trinity said. "I'm kicking her real good too."

"Uh, well done," Emily said, pulling Teddy up with a grunt when the girl returned to being a girl. "Keep it up, and don't tell her anything. We'll be there to save you soon."

"So we're going to kick her butt?" Teddy asked.

"That's . . . no, we shouldn't," Emily said. "She's more experienced, probably has better equipment, and she might be able to call in reinforcements. But I don't want to just . . . let her win either."

Athena nodded, and, out of all her sisters, Emily supposed she was the one most likely to get it. "Our win condition isn't beating the enemy, it's retrieving the stuff."

"Exactly," Emily said.

Athena's smug smile was practically radiant. Emily landed next to her with a thump of her shoes against the ground, then she pointed to the house and ran over. Her gaggle of sisters followed, surprisingly quiet.

"Oh, she's tying me up," Trinity said.

"With what?" Emily asked as they arrived next to Cement's home. She kept her voice low, a whisper she hoped wouldn't carry.

Trinity's nose scrunched. "You know those plastic things, with the knobby bits? They go *click-click-click*?"

"Zip ties," Athena said. "Did she have them on her?"

Trinity nodded. "She has a pouch."

Emily took that in, then closed her eyes. "Okay, here's the plan. Trinity, I want one of you to sneak in while the Hero's busy. Athena, I need you to find a way to see her. Make her paranoid—I want her focused on anything but us. Teddy, stay with me here."

"Yeah, I'll keep you safe," Teddy said.

"Trinity, you're looking for a painting. There should be a ship on it. A big boat."

Trinity nodded. "Got it," she said. "Do I go in as two of me?"

"Uh, no, one of you stays here," Emily said. "Everyone knows their part? Good, let's go!"

Emily grabbed Athena under the armpits and raised her so she could grab onto the banister around the balcony. She scurried up and over the edge, landing with a light thump that still sounded far too loud.

"My other me's going around," Trinity said. "And the Hero's asking questions."

Emily nodded, then paused. She could hear something from just above. She glanced up and noticed the window Trinity had snuck into, still wide open.

Barely hesitating, she grabbed one of the rails and pulled herself up so she was closer to the window.

"—won't tell me who you are?" an unfamiliar voice asked. It was muffled, a voice passing through a mask.

"I'm not telling you nothing!" was Trinity's reply.

"If you won't tell me, then perhaps you'll squeal to the authorities. You do know that breaking and entering is a crime, right?"

"I wish being ugly was a crime. That way you'd be all arrested and stuff."

"You're one of the reasons I hate children," the Hero said.

Athena leaned over next to the window, then pulled back. "I see her," she whispered. "I can start?"

Emily gave her a thumbs-up. "Distract her away from Trinity," she said.

The owl girl nodded, then frowned as she peeked back out again. Her power didn't have much flashiness to it, so it didn't surprise Emily that there wasn't much to see. The Hero did pause, her questions to Trinity stopping.

Athena pulled back, not quickly, just a slow movement that wouldn't draw attention. She gave a thumbs-up to Emily without looking back.

Footsteps in the house as the Hero moved around, slow, cautious steps.

Emily tried to think of a way to get the Hero to leave the house outright, but nothing came to mind.

"I'm almost there!" Trinity said. "Should I try to rescue the other me?"

Emily shook her head. It wouldn't do to have the Hero turn around and see a missing Trinity. They weren't exactly being subtle as it was. She was almost afraid that the Hero would hear her heart, pounding away in her chest like a war drum.

"I'm in," Trinity whispered. "She didn't see me."

"Nice work," Emily whispered back. "You, too, Athena."

There was a crash in the house, a loud bang, and the crack and clatter of glass bursting apart. "Oops," Trinity said. "I, uh, have good news and bad news," she said.

"What is it?" Emily asked.

"Found the safe thing. And, uh, I got the painting off from in front of it," Trinity said.

"Wait, how did you— Come here!" came a shout from within the house.

"Okay," Emily said. "Plan B. Athena, keep her off balance. Teddy, get in there and corner her. Trinity, one of you stay out of trouble, but try to free yourself and . . . I don't know, hit her from weird angles."

"Got it!" Trinity cheered.

There were more sounds in the house, things crashing, stuff falling down, drywall being cracked, and a few choice words from the so-called Hero that Emily really didn't approve of hearing near her sisters.

Emily jumped over the balcony fence, then reached out and tried the back door. It wasn't locked.

"Teddy, get in there," she said.

"No problem, Boss!" Teddy said before she bolted past her.

Emily only had a moment to take in the kitchen and the living room past that before she ducked back into cover.

She figured everything was about to go terribly wrong.

"Who are you? Why are there so many violent children in this stupid house?!"

"Die, capitalist scum!"

Terribly, terribly wrong.

CHAPTER SEVENTY-ONE

Getting Saucy

Isabel had been told that this was going to be a routine job.

All she had to do was drive over to some middle-class Merican dream house, slip in the front, and then poke around. The Cabal had a few guys with weird powers who let them know things they shouldn't: dealmakers, social manipulators, mind readers, and a few who could predict the future in weird ways. They were part of the organization's backbone.

They were also a pain in the rear to deal with.

Their little in-group had this self-important, elitist attitude about everything, which rubbed Isabel the wrong way. They thought they were cleverer than everyone else, and them being right about it most of the time made it worse.

So here she was, following their cryptic orders to go over to some nobody, B-list Villain's place to look for a bundle of information about the Cabal that could be troublesome if it fell into the wrong hands.

This was going to be far, far beneath her. She was Black Shield, the untouchable, unhurtable Hero, not some errand girl.

Of course, the errand she was running wasn't meant to involve little raccoon-girl thieves.

She walked into the house, expecting it to be the boring middle-class haven she'd seen in a hundred sitcoms with those cheap interior decorating magazines she was inexplicably fond of.

Catching someone in the house was unexpected; it made her heart skip a beat, and an electric surge of adrenaline jolted up her back. Training kicked in, and she slid into a fighter's stance, ready to summon her shields to stop any blow . . . Then her brain caught up, and she made out the scrambling figure who had been robbing the place.

She assumed it was a thief. The girl was literally wearing a striped shirt and a domino mask, with a bag by her hip that had a large dollar sign on it. There was little room for interpretation, except that no actual burglar would wear such a cliché outfit.

An ironic statement, maybe? Isabel didn't have time to parse it because she was running after the girl.

She made out more details as she caught up with her and grabbed the kid's ankle. She had ears, animal ears, and a large, fluffy tail, black with white rings around it. "Oh no you don't!" Isabel said as she tugged her back into the house.

This situation had just gone from routine to not. She had to call it in. The rules about it being a clandestine operation could rot.

The thief girl kicked and twisted, but Isabel interposed her shields before any blow could land, small, paper-thin panes of black nonenergy that would move in relation to her, and couldn't be broken, not by anything she'd discovered yet.

Isabel dragged the kid back into the living room. She wasn't heartless; she wasn't going to pin the girl on the floor when there was a perfectly serviceable couch right there. "Stop kicking me," Isabel ordered.

"No! You suck!"

Children. "What were you doing here?" Isabel asked.

"I heard there was someone really ugly here, then you showed up! You're so ugly I decided to run away."

Isabel glared. Sure, she had a full-face mask, and sure, it was a childish insult, but still. "Just answer my question," she said as she reached into a thigh pocket and tugged out her phone.

Then the kid whipped her tail at Isabel's face. A shield stopped it, but it blocked her vision for long enough that the kid was able to kick her phone away.

"Dammit," Isabel muttered. She summoned a few shields to pin the girl in place while she went to fetch her phone. The entire time, the girl called her a poop-head, a jerk, a stupid doo-doo eater, and a few other creative yet still somehow entirely child-friendly curses.

"This has got to be some sort of joke," Isabel muttered. She walked over to the kitchen, opened a few drawers, and grinned to herself as she found a roll of tape. "Never having kids."

The girl had powers, that much was obvious, and she was on the Villainous side of the spectrum, too, if Isabel had to guess. A Mischief Maker or a Scoundrel or something to that effect.

Maybe a potential new recruit? That would be nice. There was a bonus for that, and Isabel was saving up to buy a nice house in the suburbs. She still had her mission to carry out here, too, but she figured her priorities had just shifted.

She questioned the raccoon girl while she was squirming and jerking around, trying to force her way out of her zip tie bonds. Her answers were all very predictable and rather insulting. Isabel figured it was the kid's defense mechanism to insult her betters. Hence, the tape. If the kid wasn't going to stop, then the duct tape would stop the kid.

As soon as the kid's mouth was taped over, Isabel raised her phone and started to tap in the numbers to a contact when she paused.

Isabel had been in her share of fights and scraps. She'd tangled with Villains and Heroes both, and even if she'd only been at it for a couple of years, she felt as if she'd developed something of a sense for trouble.

That sense was going off now. A sound, maybe? A shadow that moved wrong?

She quieted down and moved toward the kitchen, her power on a hair trigger to summon her barriers. A shiver went down her spine, and she almost felt as if the shadows in the corners were lengthening.

"Oh no," she muttered.

She'd fought emotional manipulators before—she knew the first signs. This was subtle, but it wasn't so subtle she didn't feel it.

The problem with some of those powers was that even knowing you were being manipulated wasn't enough to stop them.

The girl!

Sure, she had a raccoon tail and ears, but those weren't a power. Maybe she had more than a changed physiology. "Hey, kid, what do you think you're doing?" she asked as she stomped back into the living room.

The brat looked up at her, drooling around her mouth from where she was chewing at her bonds. The tape stuck to her cheeks was already half peeled.

Then something crashed deeper in the house. Wood hitting wood, glass bursting apart.

Isabel stomped over to investigate. That feeling, the niggling doubt, was still there, but she could force past it. She stalked into a bedroom at the end of a corridor and hissed as something flew toward her face.

It bounced off a shield.

The issue with her shields—one issue, at least—was their lack of visibility. They weren't black so much as they were lightless. Spots in the world where nothing, not even ambient light, could impact with any success. It meant she had no idea what she'd just blocked until she stepped aside and lowered the shield.

She stared at the pillow on the floor.

"And if you come in here, I'll smack you with another!" came a familiar voice from within the room.

"Are you kidding me?" Isabel asked.

The familiar sound of a door sliding open came from the kitchen.

Had the girl she'd tied up escaped? She burst into the bedroom, then swore as a raccoon-tailed figure darted past her legs and back out into the corridor.

Isabel noticed an unmade bed, a broken painting frame, and some detritus strewn across the ground, but her attention was mostly on the brat scrambling away. "No! Come back here!" she yelled as she went after the girl. "Who are you? Why are there so many violent children in this stupid house?!"

"Die, capitalist scum!"

And then, out of nowhere, a bear leapt at her.

Her eyes widened, and she felt an overwhelming sense of *dread* wash over her. It was a bear. An actual, enormous bear, with claws digging into the linoleum and a large gaping maw opened wide to consume Isabel.

The bear bounced off her shield without even a thump.

Isabel lowered the shield while readying her weapons. Two laser cannons—with settings that went from stun to burn—over each arm, within shield-shaped casings.

Then two more girls stumbled into the kitchen, one looking like a mobster, the other a girl in a leather jacket like a wannabe biker.

Isabel wondered just what in the world was going on.

An incoherent scream from behind her was the only warning she received before the raccoon girl rammed her in the back of the knees. She stumbled back, but she summoned a shield right behind her, giving her something to crash into and push off of.

The bear roared, and Isabel felt the world darkening in the corners again. Her heart started to beat faster. She was outnumbered!

No. It was fear. Someone was playing with her feelings and pushing fear onto her. She couldn't give in.

With a twist, she aimed her arm at the bear and fired. A buzzing zap sounded, and a red beam lanced into the huge creature and singed its fur. It roared, but that wasn't enough to take it down.

The Hero growled and adjusted the beam upward, making it stronger.

Then the raccoon girl jumped onto her arm and pulled her off-kilter. "Let go!" Isabel shouted.

"No, you!"

"That didn't even make sense!"

She raised her free hand and fired.

The beam lanced into, then through the raccoon girl's leg.

The girl stared at the wound, then screamed.

Everyone paused.

Isabel's breath hitched. Had she . . . had she just . . .

She stood there, confused and entirely uncertain what to do, then a saucepan crashed into the side of her head.

CHAPTER SEVENTY-TWO

Reversal

Emily snuck into the house, for a certain definition of snuck. The floor creaked, loud and grinding to her ear, and she couldn't help but feel like every one of her footfalls was a heavy wallop.

Still, it wasn't that loud, and she figured she wasn't making too much noise.

Some of her sisters could certainly stand to learn a thing or two.

Teddy stomped over to the side of the corridor where the Hero had gone down, each step coming with a thud that had Emily wincing. She couldn't exactly call out to Teddy and tell her to make less noise.

Then the Hero screamed, and any noise Emily and Teddy were making was drowned out by the cacophony of two people chasing after each other down a narrow corridor. "No! Come back here!" the Hero shouted.

A grinning Trinity shot out of the hallway opening, nearly running on all fours and tail wagging through the air behind her in all its striped glory. The Hero followed right after her, arm outstretched as if to catch the girl.

Teddy roared, her scream turning from that of a child's to a full-bodied, rumbling bellow that almost made the walls shake. She swung a massive paw forward, and Emily was infinitely glad to see that she wasn't trying to hit claws first.

A black barrier snapped up in the air, thin and wide, like a glass pane but entirely dark, as if no light was allowed to enter or escape that one area.

The Hero stumbled to the side, her balance off as she moved to dodge Teddy's attack.

It meant her back was to Emily.

Emily looked around, just a quick glance, enough to notice the saucepan hanging from a hook above the kitchen island, out of her sisters' reach, but not hers.

There was a scream, loud and painful.

It sent a cold shiver down Emily's spine, and she spun around to see one of Trinity crashing to the ground, a hole in her leg.

The Hero wasn't moving.

Emily grabbed the saucepan, and, without putting much thought into it, stepped up and swung.

The edge of the pan rammed into the Hero's head with a loud clang of metal meeting hard plastic. Emily's arms shook and the pan slipped out of numbed hands.

It clattered to the ground a moment before the Hero crashed down.

The shield hovering before her winked out, and Teddy aborted a second roar, looking down, then back up at Emily, then down at Trinity.

"Trinity! Are you okay?" she asked.

"Ow!" all three of the girl said.

One of the intact Trinitys rushed toward Emily while she stared, not knowing what to do. The girl picked up the saucepan and ran back to her downed body.

"Wait—" Emily said. But it was too late.

Trinity bonked her hurt self atop the head, like someone driving a spike into the ground with a sledgehammer.

The injured Trinity burst apart.

A new Trinity popped into existence next to herself. "Oh, that's much better!"

"Uh," Emily said.

"Whoa!" A third Trinity poked out from behind the couch. "Awesome takedown, Best Sister," they said in stereo.

"We need to tie her up," Athena said as she moved in, entirely unfazed by Trinity's Trinityness. The owl girl grunted and shoved the door closed. "Before she wakes up. Quick!"

Emily jumped. Athena was right, of course—the Hero wouldn't stay down forever. Unless she was dead . . . Emily paused, then looked down and noted the slow breathing from the figure below. Not dead, then.

"I have tape!" a Trinity said as she raised a roll of duct tape clutched in both hands. The other Trinity grabbed the roll and underhanded it to Athena, who caught it out of the air and pulled a long strip loose.

"Teddy, grab her hands," Athena said.

"Yeah, I got you," Teddy said. "We should tie her hands and feet together behind her back."

"Why?" Athena asked. "I mean, sure, but you turn her around."

Teddy dropped to her knees and with a grunt, flopped the Hero onto her front. "'Cause that's how you tie up pigs, and all capitalists are pigs."

"Wow, that's dark," Athena said. "Let's start with her hands first."

Emily blinked, everything snapping back to attention. Her sisters were acting without her input, which was probably not ideal. "Trin . . ." She paused, took a deep breath to properly recenter herself, then pointed to one Trinity. "Help yourself get your hands free. And get your other you inside to follow me. Uh, after that, keep watch by the front and back of the house, in case someone shows up."

"Yes, sis!" Trinity said. One of the girls hopped over to the kitchen with both feet tied together while the other ran to the front and peeked out from behind the curtains.

"Athena, can you tell when you're using your power on someone?" Emily asked.

"Yes?"

"Then use it on her. Tell me if she's waking up. Keep her down. Teddy—bear form. Don't hurt her, but keep her on the floor." Emily took a moment to still her heart while the Trinity that had been outside slid in. "Right, you're with me," she said.

"Okay?" that Trinity replied.

Emily walked past the entire disaster and into the corridor the Hero had run out of, Trinity hot on her heels. "Tell me if things change," Emily said.

"Can do," Trinity replied. She seemed quite pleased with herself. "I'm not tied up anymore. The other me, I mean."

"Good. Keep a watch over the house and outside it. I don't want more surprises," Emily said as she walked into one of the bedrooms. There was a broken frame on the ground, glass scattered around, and a likely expensive canvas flat on the floor. The place where it'd hung was obvious—a rectangle of slightly discolored paint, with a large safe smack in the center.

Emily considered covering it up. Another frame from elsewhere in the house, some ten minutes spent cleaning things up . . . she abandoned the idea. The Hero had likely seen the safe, and it wouldn't take much searching to find it.

She stepped up to the vault and eyed the keypad, then she squeezed her phone out from her pocket. Three texts from her mom, she noted idly as she swiped over to a notepad app where she had a series of numbers jotted down from her conversation with Cement.

She tapped them into the pad with a knuckle, just in case she ended up being fingerprinted one day.

The safe clicked, and she reached for the handle, then stopped. "Trinity, when you die, you respawn, right?"

"Yup!" Trinity said. "Next to myself."

"Right, can you open this safe in . . . about thirty seconds?"

The girl shrugged. "Sure."

Emily stepped out of the room and squashed a kernel of guilt under a heavy load of simple practicality. She moved out of the corridor and found a bear sitting next to a downed Hero, one paw carefully placed on the Hero's chest.

"She's coming around," Athena said.

"Good," Emily replied.

"It's open," the nearest Trinity said.

Emily looked around to make sure things were still . . . mostly sane, then returned. The safe, as it turned out, contained a few file folders thick with loose papers, and nothing else. She tugged them out carefully and opened the one at the very top. The text within was thick and small, written in the boring no-nonsense vocabulary she'd only seen in the worst textbooks. But it was immediately clear that the file was talking about Heroes and Villains. She closed it and searched around for something to put them in.

"Trinity," she said at last. "Can you find me a bag?" Trinity gestured to the big bag with the dollar sign on it hooked to her belt. "That'll do," Emily replied.

She stuffed everything away while Trinity held the bag open. "Oh, oh," Trinity said. "The Hero lady is awake, and she's not happy about it."

"Oh," Emily said. "Well, I think I'm going to have some words with her. Just . . . don't call her a Hero. We'll pretend that she's a Villain. Can you tell that to Athena and Teddy . . . but discreetly? Without the Hero hearing it?"

"Uh? I guess I can, yeah. But aren't we the Villains?"

Emily nodded. "Yes, but we're pretending to be Heroes, so we'll have to pretend that she's the Villain, because Heroes wouldn't fight other Heroes."

"That makes sense," Trinity said with a nod.

"Thanks, I think," Emily replied. She gestured to the bag. "Make sure she doesn't see that." Emily reached back and closed the safe, being careful not to make too much noise.

"Got it," Trinity said.

Emily dithered, psyching herself up. She bounced on the spot a few times, adjusted her coat and pants, and brushed some imaginary dust off herself.

Enough stalling.

She walked back out into the corridor and instantly heard some struggling from the other end of the house. "Do you have any idea who I am?"

"No," Emily said, her voice more snappish and hard than she was used to hearing from herself. "And I'd very much like to know who you are and who you're working for . . . Villain."

CHAPTER SEVENTY-THREE

Interrogations

Emily didn't quite know how or where to stand at first. In fact, she wasn't sure she wanted to question the woman on the floor at all. It didn't help that Black Shield had her hands and legs tied behind her back and was resting on her side. It was an awkward position to be in no matter how she looked at it.

"I'm not a Villain," the woman said. She tugged at her arms, trying to free them.

Teddy growled, her large paws flexing from their position in front of the Hero's face. She stopped wiggling.

"That does sound like what a Villain would say," Emily replied. She had to reframe things. Her interrogating a Villain, for the second time, no less, was . . . too much. But her chastising an unruly child? She was growing increasingly familiar with that. "I need a chair," she said.

Athena was the first to jump up and run over to the kitchen. She came back, a chair dragging across the floor with a loud squeal.

Emily took the seat, spun it around so that it was facing the Hero on the ground, then she sat down and shifted until she was comfortable.

She folded one leg over the other and put her hands on her lap while the Hero stared up at her from the floor. Teddy edged closer, a huge, comforting presence, and Athena grinned wide and planted herself on Emily's other side. "My name is the Boss," Emily said. She was impressed that her voice didn't waver.

"That's cute, now untie me. I was here on official business."

"On whose behalf?" Emily asked.

"The police!"

"So you have a warrant to enter this property?" Emily asked.

"What? No, but I'm allowed to be here."

Emily sniffed, as if she'd heard one of Teddy's excuses. It was so easy to imagine the Hero's reply sounding like *The cookie jar fell and the cookies just happened to land in my mouth.*

"I don't believe you," Emily said.

"You were here first! That raccoon girl!"

"Are you wearing a camera? Do you have any proof of that?" The Hero squirmed. "So, you broke into this home, and seeing as how we're all Heroes, we stopped you. You . . ."

Emily glared.

"And you shot a laser into my sister."

"She . . . she doesn't look injured?"

"She got better, but that doesn't change anything! Heroes don't laser kids. Even when they deserve it!"

"That is *not* what happened!" she screamed. Teddy growled, and the Hero's attitude calmed down a notch.

Emily shook her head. "Indoor voice."

"Should I?" Athena asked.

" . . . Yes," Emily said.

"What?" the Hero asked. "You can't use mental powers on someone! That's illegal."

"You haven't been terribly forthcoming about what you're doing here, who you are, or who sent you," Emily said, signaling Athena to wait. "What am I supposed to do?"

The Hero twisted onto her back and looked up at Emily. "You let me go, because I'm a Hero," she said.

"Likely story," Emily said. "Do you know what happens to liars?"

"Oh no," Teddy growled. Emily knew she sounded concerned, but when a massive bear said "Oh no," that lent a whole new level of distress to the words.

Emily nodded. "Liars get punished. I'm not beyond putting you in time-out, and spankings are very effective." That was a twist on the truth. So far, the threat of those had been more than enough.

"What is *wrong* with you?"

Emily sighed, moved on her chair so that she was sitting wide, then leaned forward and rested her elbows on her knees. She stared into the woman's visor, and into her own tiny reflection in the blackened glass. "I don't know who you are. But I do know about this place. This is the home of a Villain, isn't it? A small-time, local Villain, one who was just taken out. Now, let's be a little more honest with each other. What were you doing here?"

"There was a noise complaint."

"Lie," Emily said. She turned to Athena. "Not too strong."

"Hey, hey, wait, what are . . ." The Hero paused and then shivered, her head turning to look this way and that. "Oh, that's not good," she muttered.

"What were you actually doing here?" Emily asked.

"I . . . I don't have to tell you anything."

"Who told you about this place?"

The woman clammed up, jaw working and mouth set in a straight line.

"Fine," Emily said. "Does anyone know you're here?" There was a slight twitch that Emily decided was a yes. "All right then. My companions and I are leaving. We will be calling the police to come and take you in. Enjoy your stay on the floor."

"You're going to leave me here?"

"I have things I need to do. And between the two of us, I think I've learned plenty." Emily gestured to the chair. "Could you put this back in its place, please?"

"Yup," Athena said. She dragged the chair back while Emily headed for the back door.

She inspected the house. It was probably full of hairs and fingerprints and all sorts of evidence, but she couldn't think of a way to wipe it clear that didn't devolve into arson. "Come on, everyone, we're heading out."

The moment she was on the back porch, Emily started to shake and shiver. That had been a lot. "You okay, Boss?" Teddy asked. She'd returned to being a plain girl and was currently fixing her mask back on.

"Yeah, yeah, I'm fine," Emily said. She began walking after taking a quick head count.

That was it. They'd gotten the files, they had the information, and, if anyone asked, she could say they'd been doing their Heroic duty. It was . . . not perfect, but it was something. She didn't know if it would hold up to inspection, but maybe it would win her some time and an excuse.

Quest Complete!
Fighting Good
Join the battle against the forces of good.
Reward: +3 Skill Upgrade points per Hero incapacitated!

Emily glared at the prompt. Typical. Though she admitted to herself that the added points might come in handy.

They reached the fence at the back, and Emily helped her sisters up and over, then she hopped up and climbed over herself with just a bit of sweating and cursing her weak arms on the way up. Once her feet hit the ground on the other side, she tugged her phone out of a pocket and texted Melaton.

Emily didn't exactly trust Melaton, but the woman was a decent contact. She gave her the address and said that she'd captured someone she thought might be a Villain and left them in that house.

Melaton's reply was fast, but Emily ignored it in favor of tucking her phone away. "Okay, now we go home," she said. "Or . . . well, I suppose we stop to get changed first."

"All right," Teddy said. "Come on, I remember where home's at. Bears have a natural sense of direction for that kind of thing."

"No, they don't," Athena said.

"How would you know? You're just an owl."

"Owls are best. They can fly."

"Yeah, but they don't migrate, do they?" Teddy asked.

Athena sniffed. "We don't need to migrate. We're too cool to be scared off by something like a bit of cold or whatever. Unlike bears that need to hide away."

"It's not hiding, it's hibernating."

"Same difference," Athena said.

"Raccoons eat trash," Trinity added to the conversation.

Her sisters both stared at her.

"What?"

Emily held back a laugh. At least she had three good distractions to keep her thoughts from straying too far into the dark and depressing. "I think we can put all that aside for now. All three of you are great . . . part-animals."

"Hell yeah," Teddy said. "Hear that? I'm the best."

"That is not what she said!" Athena shot back.

"I'm the most animal of the bunch of you."

"But there's three of me, so I'm twice and one more more animal than you."

Emily rolled her eyes. There was no avoiding dumb arguments, it seemed.

Epilogue

rriving home was meant to be relaxing; she was supposed to open the door and just . . . be free.

To some degree it was like that still. She shoved open her little dorm room's door and then stepped aside to let her sisters in. Five heads passed by, Emily counting them absently before she stumbled into the room after them and shut the door behind her.

Safe.

She was, for the most part, safe. It was a nice feeling to have.

Now she only had to deal with three brats who would be set on making her life more complicated. Also, she had homework to do. "All right, what are you girls planning on doing?" Emily asked.

"I could use a nap," Teddy said, the first to speak up.

"Can I read?" Athena asked. She gestured to some of the books on Emily's desk.

"I'm gonna make toast," Trinity said. One of her bodies ran into the bathroom and returned with Mister Toas— the toaster.

"Okay," Emily said. "Right, those all sound like great ideas. Teddy, please use the mattress. Athena, you can have the chair if you want, and remind me to go to the library with you—we can pick up books that are more fun. Trinity . . . don't make too much toast? Where did you even get the bread from?"

"Downstairs," Trinity said.

"And what are you going to put on it?" Emily asked.

"Nothing?" Trinity replied. "It's crunchy."

Emily nodded slowly. "Okay. I'm going to do my homework, and de-stress a little." The dollar-sign-covered bag, the one with all those secrets within, was right next to the door, waiting for her to pore over it. But that could wait.

The dorm room filled with chaotic noise as sisters bumped into one another, argued, then resolved those arguments in the time it took Emily to huff. Then everything just . . . settled down.

Emily sat on her bed, laptop on her lap, back against the wall. She opened the file for her homework and read the instructions without understanding any of them.

Instead, her mind wandered.

Teddy snored, a low rumble that was already growing familiar. She was the dependable one. A little strange, a little goofy at times, but Emily found the little bear girl actually cared. She wanted to be the one the oth-ers relied on, and it showed in the way she always put herself second . . . most of the time.

She couldn't exactly call Teddy lazy—the girl was merely very enthusi-astic about her sleep and her hobbies.

Teddy was nice. Emily found herself smiling as she thought of her. A brat, certainly, but a good little sister.

Athena was on Emily's chair, legs tucked under her and neck bent over one of Emily's course books. She was squinting at the text, which seemed almost comical with her large eyes.

Emily wasn't sure what to think of Athena, really. The owl girl was complex. Clever, though, in her own way. Likely the smartest of Emily's sisters, but with that came the impression Athena desperately wanted to *be* the smart one.

Emily shifted where she sat. Maybe she could spend a little more time with her middle sister. Athena had a good heart, too. She was, Emily real-ized, the sister closest to herself. Maybe not quite as anxious, but she had something similar to Emily's own approach to things.

Then there was Emily's newest sister, Trinity, currently with all three of herself huddled around Emily's desk and staring at the toaster with an intensity that was downright terrifying.

Trinity felt younger than the other two: more energetic, more inno-cent, a little more naive; but kind and lovable, eager to please and make friends. She was hard to dislike, even if she had more energy than Emily was ready to deal with.

She smiled to herself and refocused on her homework. There was still a lot to be done.

Then someone knocked at her door.

Emily's blood went cold, and she heard her chair creak as Athena looked up, and Teddy's snores cut off midrumble.

She set her laptop to the side and bounced off the bed.

The toaster went off, and Trinity gasped. "Missed it," all three of her muttered before two of her grabbed some toast.

Emily moved over to the door. Maybe it was Sam again? She desperately hoped it was Sam.

"Everyone, up," she whispered. "We might have trouble."

That got her sisters moving, with more noise than she wanted, but still, they were standing and at attention.

Emily cracked the door open and peeked out.

The person on the other side wasn't Sam. It was a woman, a few inches shorter than Emily and a couple of decades older. A woman who bore more than a passing resemblance to Emily herself.

Emily slammed the door shut.

"Emily? Sweetie?" her mom asked from the other side. "Um . . . if you're really busy, I can come back? Give you time to clean up or . . . sweetie, are you with a boy? I hope you're using protection."

"Who's that?" Teddy asked.

Athena dropped the book in her hand onto the chair she'd been sitting in. "Should I get my jacket on and look tough?"

"Is it a friend?" All three of Trinity asked.

Her mom knocked again. "Sweetie? I'm sorry, but I did call. You haven't been answering your phone."

Emily closed her eyes and, as she hadn't done in a while, wished the floor would swallow her up whole. She didn't have much of a choice. Still, that didn't mean she couldn't think things through.

Opening the door up a crack, she looked at the familiar face in the corridor. "Mom. Give me two minutes."

"Sweetie?"

"I'm naked."

Her mom looked at her very much clothed shoulder. "Okay?"

Emily nodded and closed the door. Then she turned. "All right. Teddy, keep the talk about communism to a minimum. My mom's a boomer— they don't do politics well. Athena, no scaring her. Trinity . . . Only one hug at a time, all right?"

She received five nods. That was about the best Emily could expect.

"And be polite. Mom is . . . actually, she's pretty nice, I'm sure you'll like her. But no"—she wiggled her hand—"crazy stuff."

"That's easy," Teddy said.

"I've never done a crazy thing yet," Trinity said.

Athena just shrugged. "I'm the sane one here. You probably don't need to worry about me."

"Right," Emily said. She spun around, took a deep breath, then opened the door.

Her mom was still there, standing in the corridor and looking a bit lost. Emily reached out, grabbed her hand, and pulled her in before closing the door. "Emily?"

Emily wrapped her arms around her mom and tucked her head into the nock of her shoulder. It was nice. Warm, and it smelled like her mom's shampoo. She felt the stress keeping her back tense washing off.

"It's good to see you, sweetie," her mom said as she dropped her purse and returned the hug. "But who are all these girls?"

The tension returned.

"Mom, we need to talk."

"I can imagine," her mom said as she broke up the hug. "You need to tell me how you've been? How are classes? Did you make any friends? Why do you have five children in your room? That last one especially."

"Right, right. You might want to sit down for this," Emily said.

Her mom placed a hand on her hip and raised an eyebrow. "I might not be a spring chicken, but I can still take a surprise or two."

Emily licked her lips. "Right," she repeated again. "Like ripping off a bandage then. I'm . . . a Hero. More or less."

"Pardon?"

Emily laced her fingers over her stomach and focused on the ground. They really needed to vacuum. "You remember Power Day, uh, about a week ago?"

"Yes?" She was starting to sound concerned.

"Well, I got a power. I can make, um, little sisters for myself. Sorta." Emily gestured to the girls, who were all smiling. "These are my summons? I can't unsummon them or anything. They all have their own powers too."

"Can I sit on the bed?" her mom asked. "Or would you rather I use that chair?"

Teddy raced over to Emily's chair, then rolled it over so that her mom could plop herself down on it. "There you go, uh . . ." Teddy turned to Emily. "Hey, Boss, what do we call the old lady?"

"Anything but 'old lady,' you dumb bear," Athena said. She yanked Teddy back and stepped up to Emily's mom to bow. "Hello, Grandmother."

"Emily, you know how I always wanted to have grandkids one day?" Emily's mom said. "I was expecting maybe one. Two at most. This is considerably more than that."

"It's okay," Trinity said. "You can count all three of me as one."

Emily rubbed her face. "So I should probably introduce everyone. Mom, this is Teddy. She can turn into a bear. She won't demonstrate that here because it's against the rules."

"I'm real soft," Teddy said. "Way more soft than any of the others when I'm a bear. I bet you'd like petting me just as much as the Boss does."

"The Boss?"

"That's Big Sister Emily's Hero-slash-Villain name," Athena said.

"Villain?"

"Don't worry, Best Mom," Trinity said. "We wouldn't Villain you."

"Emily?" Her mother looked at her. The smile she wore was a bit brittle at the edges, and she looked like Emily did when shoved into any sort of social situation.

Teddy, of course, noticed that too. "Hey, Boss, does your mom need to poop?"

"No, Teddy, my mom doesn't need to poop," Emily said. She patted Teddy's head absently, if only to give her hands something to do. "Okay, Mom, where do you want me to start?"

"I think that maybe you should start from the top?"

Emily nodded. She could do that.

"So, it all began on my first day here . . ."

About the Author

RavensDagger is a Canadian writer who wants to make people smile. The best way to do that, he has found, is by pecking away at the keyboard and hoping for the best.

Podium

www.ingramcontent.com/pod-product-compliance
Lightning Source LLC
Chambersburg PA
CBHW021803110726
47902CB00006B/1633